THE SONS OF ADAM

By the same author

The Money Makers
Sweet Talking Money

HARRY BINGHAM

The Sons of Adam

HarperCollins*Publishers*

This novel is a work of fiction. The names, characters and incidents portrayed in it are the work of the author's imagination, other than the names of certain historical characters from the early days of the oil industry. Any resemblance to actual persons, living or dead, events or localities, is entirely coincidental.

HarperCollins*Publishers*
77–85 Fulham Palace Road,
Hammersmith, London W6 8JB

www.harpercollins.co.uk

This paperback edition 2004

1

First published in Great Britain by
HarperCollins*Publishers* 2003

Copyright © Harry Bingham 2003

The Author asserts the moral right to
be identified as the author of this work

ISBN 0 00 715793 2

Typeset in Sabon by
Palimpsest Book Production Limited, Polmont, Stirlingshire

Printed in Great Britain by Clays Ltd, St Ives plc

To my beloved N,
My writing partner

May this marriage be laughing for ever,
Today, tomorrow and all the hours of Paradise.
Rumi (1207–1273)

PROLOGUE

A man crawls forward on his belly. He's covered with mud. It's night-time.

The man is young, a British lieutenant. Although he moves carefully, there's urgency in his movements, something breathless, something desperate. It's a dangerous attitude at the best of times. Out here in no man's land, just three dozen yards from German lines, the attitude seems almost suicidal.

For almost three minutes, the lieutenant moves in silence. Every now and then there is the crack of a rifle or the whine of bullets. He appears to ignore them. Eventually, he comes to a shallow shellhole and rolls down into it. He catches his breath a moment, then shouts.

'Tom! Tommy! Tom Creeley!'

For a moment, the night is silent. A scrappy moon plays hide-and-seek. Earth and flint scrape beneath the lieutenant's boots. In the distance, big guns thump the horizon.

Then a voice answers. It's no more than a groan, but the lieutenant is instantly alert.

'Tom? Tommy? Is that you?'

His hope is painfully evident. He climbs quickly out of the

1

shellhole in the direction of the voice. He wriggles forwards, hardly concerned to keep his head and body low.

Within forty seconds, he has covered almost thirty yards. The voice belongs to a young boy, a British infantryman, horribly wounded in legs and belly. The boy is obviously dying.

A look passes across the lieutenant's face. It's one of painful disappointment. Whoever this boy is, it isn't Tom Creeley. But the look passes.

'All right, sonny,' says the lieutenant. 'I've come to get you home.'

The boy's face is shockingly white in the moonlight. 'I'm hurt pretty bad, sir.' His voice is a whimper. He is afraid of death.

'Hurt? Nothing too bad, son. We'll get you patched up in no time and on a train back to England. How's that?'

'Oh, yes, sir! Oh, yes!'

The lieutenant nods. In one hand, he holds a canteen of water to the boy's mouth. 'Drink this.' The boy drinks. As he does so, the lieutenant's other hand snakes round in the mud, holding a revolver. The boy lowers the canteen. His eyes are grateful.

'Good lad,' says the lieutenant. He holds his gun to within an inch of the boy's head and fires. The boy drops back, dead.

The lieutenant lies low for a minute or so, then briskly searches the boy's pockets for any personal papers. He takes whatever there is, then, once again, flattens himself against the earth. He lifts his head and shouts.

'Tom? Tommy? Tom Cree-*leeeeeee*?'

And this time there's no answer. No answer at all.

PART ONE

Rise early, work hard . . . strike oil.

J. Paul Getty

1

The beginning?

To hell with beginnings. Beginnings are excuses, apologies for failure. If things turned out disastrous – and they did – then that had everything to do with the way three young men chose to behave, nothing to do with the way things started out.

On the other hand, people are only human. Once a ball starts rolling it's hard to stop it. A beginning is a beginning, and on this occasion, the beginning wasn't just bad.

It was awful.

It happened like this.

A small boy, a seven-year-old, stands in a kitchen. He's building himself a blackberry pudding as big as his head. The cook stands by, face red in the firelight, managing pots of water boiling on the stove, a newly made pot of coffee steaming to the side. The scene is domestic, quiet, happy.

Upstairs, the little boy's mother, Lady Pamela Montague, is in labour for the fourth time. Of her first three children, only one – the blackberry-pudding-guzzling Guy – survived more than a few weeks. She and her husband, Sir Adam, are understandably

5

anxious this time, but everything is proceeding normally. The doctor and midwife are in attendance.

So far, so nothing.

No births. No deaths. No hatreds. And best of all: no beginnings.

But, in a second, that changed.

All of a sudden there was a bang at the door, the jiggle of a latch, a blast of cool air. A tiny girl flitted in, as though blown by the wind. A sweep of rain washed the step behind her.

'Please miss, please sir, please help.' The tiny girl bobbed and curtsied, desperate with anxiety. 'My ma's ill. She's having a baby, only it's got stuck, and she says she can't, and she's gone as white as anything, and my dad said to run to the big house for help as fast as I could, and please miss, please miss, please miss.'

Mrs White, the cook, brought the girl further into the light.

'Are you Jack Creeley's little girl, dear?'

'Please, miss. Yes, miss. Sally Creeley, and my ma's having a baby and –'

'Well, dear, it never rains but it pours. You just pop yourself down while I go and speak to Sir Adam. If you want you can –'

Guy stopped her.

It wasn't a big interruption, but it was a decisive one. He raised his hand, like a man stopping a horse.

'No need, Cookie. I shall tell him myself.' He lifted his pudding, the coffee for his father, then turned to the little girl. 'You can go back home and when the doctor is no longer wanted here, he can come to you. For the time being, he's required here.'

He set off up the stairs. As he did so, he muttered to himself, 'Oh, and it's five guineas the visit, by the way, and someone to take care of his horse.'

Once upstairs, he set down his trophies. Coffee for his father, blackberry pud for himself. He said nothing about Sally Creeley. He said nothing about the little girl's mother.

6

In the seven years he'd been alive in the world, Guy Montague had learned that there are two sorts of people: those who can afford doctors and those who can't. It seemed like a simple lesson, the most obvious thing in the world.

He finished his pudding, concealed a belch, and went to bed.

~

That night, after a twelve-hour labour, Pamela Montague gave birth to a healthy baby boy, a bawling little bundle with lungs like steam-bellows. The birth proved to be perfectly simple. No complications. No difficulties at all.

The same night, in one of the short rows of cottages that housed the estate workers, a young man, Jack Creeley, was forced to watch as his wife screamed through the night, helped only by a couple of untrained girls from the village. In the end, Creeley himself ran up to the big house and begged to speak to Sir Adam. As soon as Sir Adam heard the man's story, he sent doctor and midwife racing across to the cottages.

Too late. A simple breech birth, which any doctor or any midwife could have simply and speedily corrected, had exhausted the mother and complicated the baby's position. The doctor, acting quickly, made the incisions that enabled him to deliver the baby by Caesarean section. The doctor was a good one, skilled and decisive. A baby boy was delivered, healthy and screaming, into the little cottage bedroom.

Healthy but motherless.

Poor Betsy Creeley, just twenty-six years old, was exhausted even before the operation began. She lost too much blood and never recovered consciousness. By the time dawn broke on 24 August, the little boy's mother was dead.

And there it was.

Two births.

One death.

One selfish act with terrible consequences.

A beginning.

2

Jack Creeley couldn't keep his son, of course.

He was a single working man with a little girl already dependent on him. In the short term, there were local women happy to help out, but in the longer term, he could see no option other than to ask his sister – now living ninety miles away in Devon – to take both the girl and the baby. His sister would certainly agree, but Devon might as well have been the other side of the world for all that Jack would ever see them. He felt like a man living with the pain of a triple bereavement.

But help was closer than he thought.

Up at the big house, Sir Adam and Lady Pamela had a worry of their own. Their new-born son, Alan, had a cough. Not a big one. In fact, it was quite definitely a minor one. The midwife said the cough was normal. The doctor agreed. Sir Adam agreed. But it was a cough. Pamela had already lost two children under the age of six weeks and she was terrified of losing a third.

Sir Adam spent a day thinking things through before making his suggestion. His wife agreed instantly and Sir Adam went to approach Jack Creeley. His proposal was this.

Jack Creeley's young boy, christened Thomas after his maternal grandfather, would be taken in by the Montagues.

He and the tiny Alan Montague would grow up as brothers. They would share rooms, toys, schooling – everything. In Sir Adam's words, the infant Tom 'would grow up as one of our own. He would in all ways be brother to our own son Alan. You, of course, will still be his father. He'll call you Father and me Uncle. You'll see Tom whenever you wish, just say the word.'

For Jack Creeley, the offer was far too good to refuse. It meant his son would grow up in sight and sound of his father. It gave the poor man some good thing to snatch from the wreckage his life had so suddenly become. He said yes.

For the Montagues, the new arrangement brought only benefits. There was guilt, of course. Guy's behaviour had been unforgivable – and he had been well beaten for it. On a more constructive side, offering a home to Tom seemed like the least they could do.

But it was more than that. Pamela loved babies, and the borrowed child went some way to make up for the two she had lost. But what was more, something about Tom's arrival seemed to work like a charm on the infant Alan. From the moment Tom's crib arrived in the big house, Alan's cough went away, never to return. All through the dangerous first years of childhood, neither Alan nor Tom was once affected by any serious illness.

Even better, and from the very first months, it became clear that the two boys were unusually close. As babies, their cribs stood in the same room. If, for any reason, one of the cribs were moved, the other baby would instantly wake up and scream. Likewise, when they were toddlers Tom began to be taken down to his father, Jack's, cottage for regular visits. At first it was thought that Tom would prefer to go by himself, but any time the experiment was tried, the little boy would turn black in the face and knot his fists until Alan was allowed to come along too.

By the end of the century, the two boys were six and a half years old. They were thriving, happy, and healthy.

Alan had grown a fraction taller, Tom a fraction broader than the other. Alan was pale-haired, with eyebrows so blond you could hardly see them. Tom was already developing dramatic good looks: glossy, dark, curly hair with eyes of a startling blue. The boys were infinitely close. They went everywhere together. Their communication was so close, they often appeared to read each other's thoughts.

Visitors to the house invariably mistook them for twins (not identical, of course), and after a while the Montagues stopped bothering to correct them. The boys *were* twins. Born the same night, reared in neighbouring cribs, suckled at the same breasts. The boys *were* twins. The only difference was that one called Sir Adam 'Father', the other referred to him as 'Uncle'. The difference is a small one, even tiny. But that wasn't the point.

Even the smallest things can grow big enough to kill.

3

New Year's Day 1901.

In the newly sanded stable yard, horses and huntsmen milled in impatient circles. Frost glittered from the clock-tower. Hounds pawed the ground, anxious to be off.

Tom Creeley, seven and a half years old, wasn't yet old enough to ride with the hunt, and he was annoyed. For the last half-hour, he'd hung around the stable yard with Alan. The two boys attempted to scrounge one of the glasses of sherry that were being passed amongst the horsemen. They'd stolen hot pastries from the kitchen to feed to the dogs. But Tom was still annoyed. He wanted to ride and wanted to hunt.

'I'm going in,' he announced.

On the way back in, he passed close by Guy's grey mare. The mare bristled at something, and stepped backwards, knocking into Tom.

Guy turned in the saddle. 'I'm so sor –' he began, before seeing who it was. 'Careful, brat,' he said, flicking his whip so Tom could feel the rush of air above his head.

Tom scowled. There was no love lost between the two boys. Guy was a bully, Tom his target. But Tom was a fighter, who gave as good as he got. On this occasion, Tom dodged away from the whip, braying as he did so. The braying sound was a carefully chosen insult. As a boy, Guy had been nervous of horses and had been taught to ride on a donkey. Tom, as fearless on horseback as he was in most other situations, was already confident on Sir Adam's sixteen-hand hunters.

'Stable boy!'

But Guy's last insult bounced off Tom's back. Tom was gone to search for new entertainment.

His first trip was down to the kitchen: usually good for warm food and interesting gossip. But today his luck was out. He'd been spotted pinching the pastries and right now he wasn't welcome. Tom thought about getting Alan and going down together to Tom's father's cottage. Jack Creeley had been teaching the two lads how to poach: how to tickle trout, how to set traps for rabbits, how to move silently in the dark. But just as Tom made up his mind to go, he heard a noise from the library. He was puzzled. Sir Adam was with the hunt. So if not him, then who was it in the library? Tom pushed the door open.

The man bending over Sir Adam's desk wasn't much to look at. He was a plump, overtailored man, with a walrus moustache and a chalky complexion. He was bent over the telephone apparatus in the corner of the room, shouting down the speaking trumpet, the earpiece jammed hard against his head.

And he was shouting – shouting about money. Business, money, the purchase of rights, company incorporation. Tom's feelings of restlessness disappeared in a flash. He was rooted to the spot, burning to hear more.

And why? Simply this. In the seven and a half years he'd been alive, he'd never heard a rich man talking about money. He'd heard his father talk about it. He'd heard servants talk about it. But to Uncle Adam and people of that class, the subject seemed to be unmentionable. It was as though, to people who were already rich, money was like air: something that surrounded you, something you didn't have to think about. And already Tom knew he wasn't like that. He knew that Guy would one day inherit Whitcombe House and all the surrounding fields and farms. He knew that Alan, somehow, was in the same position: not as lucky as Guy, but still all right. And Tom? He didn't know. He dressed the same as Alan, he ate the same meals, he studied the same books, he played the same games. But Alan's father was a gentleman. Tom's father was not. Seven and a half years old, and Tom didn't know where he stood.

Tom had seen enough. Seen but not heard. He knocked loudly at the already open door and strolled on in. The man looked up.

'Why, hello!'

'Hello.'

'You must be young Alan, I suppose.'

Tom shook his head. 'I'm Tom.'

'Oh, Tom! Well, good morning, young man.'

'Who are you?'

'My name's Knox D'Arcy. Robert Knox D'Arcy.'

Tom wrinkled his forehead: the name meant nothing. On the table in front of D'Arcy, maps were spread out, maps traced in wild contours of brown and pink, maps speckled with place names that sounded like something from *The Arabian Nights*. Tom peered at them curiously.

'Where's that?'

'Persia, Western Persia and Eastern Mesopotamia, to be exact.' The man smiled at Tom's blunt interrogation.

'Why? Are you going there?'

'No. I'm looking for something.'

'What?'

'Oil.'

There was a short silence.

'What?'

'Oil.'

Tom wrinkled his forehead again. This time his puzzlement ran deeper. 'If you need oil, we've got plenty in the kitchen.'

The Walrus laughed. 'Not that sort. The sort you put in your motor-car.'

Tom was about to point out the blindingly obvious, that the village carrier would happily deliver cans of petrol to the door, but the Walrus continued.

'Not because I need petroleum spirit, but because I want to make some money.'

'Money?'

The Walrus nodded. 'Money, young man. I hope to purchase the right to look for oil in Persia. If I find it, I'll collect it up and bring it in ships back to England. When I get it here, I'll sell it to anyone with a motor-car – anyone with an engine, in fact.'

Tom's eyes were as wide as soup bowls. He couldn't have said why, but he felt he was in the presence of some vastly important truth. He sat down, staring at the maps.

'In Persia?' he asked. 'There's oil in Persia?'

'I certainly hope so.'

'Where in Persia?'

'Under the ground. Perhaps even one mile down.'

'Like coal mines?'

'Yes. A little bit like coal mines.'

'And money? If you dig up some oil, you can make money?'

'That's my intention, young man.'

'A lot? A lot of money?'

And then the Walrus did something that – just possibly – would change the course of Tom's life for ever. He hoisted the little lad up onto the desk, then squatted down so their faces were on a level.

'Young man, do you want to know a secret?'

Tom nodded. 'Yes, please.'

The Walrus paused a moment. His face was sombre. 'Oil is the future,' he said. 'Oil is the fuel for the new century. Cars will guzzle it. Ships will swallow it. Factories run off it.

14

Whoever can find the oil will be rich. Not simply rich – they'll be kings of the world.'

~

That evening, Tom spoke to Sir Adam.

'Uncle, who is that new man? The friend of yours. Knox somebody.'

'Knox D'Arcy?' Sir Adam chuckled. 'He told me the pair of you had had a chat. Mr D'Arcy is a friend of mine, a businessman.'

'Does he know a lot about business?'

'I should say so. He was an ordinary fellow, living out in Australia, when he came across two miners who told him they thought they'd found some gold.'

'And?'

'And they had. D'Arcy helped them make a business out of it. A very, very good one. He's ended up one of the wealthiest men in England. One of the wealthiest men in the entire world.'

Tom's eyes widened. 'Uncle, he says that the best way to be rich is to look for oil. Is he right?'

Sir Adam laughed again. 'If Mr D'Arcy says so, then Mr D'Arcy is almost certainly right.'

4

Right or wrong, D'Arcy was a betting man. Having accumulated one colossal fortune in gold, he was keen to plunge a vast chunk of it into the search for Persian oil.

But things weren't that simple.

For one thing, no oil had ever been found in Persia. Or rather: there were numerous traces of it in the geology, but no one had ever sent down a drill and come up with oil. Not in Persia. Not in Mesopotamia. Nowhere in the entire peninsula of Arabia.

And there was a second problem. The kingdom of Persia itself. The country was a poor one, squashed between British India on the one hand, Mother Russia on the other. The two giants jostled for control. Obtaining the right to drill wasn't simply a matter of commerce. It was a question of politics.

Hence Sir Adam.

Before settling back in England, Sir Adam had been a diplomat, rising to become the British ambassador in Tehran. He knew the Shah. He knew the country's politics. He'd learned who mattered and who didn't.

And that was why D'Arcy had come to Sir Adam that New Year's Day. He had a proposition. The proposition was this: Sir Adam would help D'Arcy win an oil concession, giving D'Arcy the right to drill. In exchange, Sir Adam would earn a generous commission. Sir Adam, delighted with the adventure, agreed at once. He went to Tehran. He negotiated skilfully. He bribed the highest officials with gold, he bribed the lowest officials with paper. He even bribed the eunuch who brought the Shah his morning coffee.

Sir Adam did everything he needed to do.

And on 28 May 1901, he got what he wanted. He won the deal.

5

It was two months later. The family was at breakfast. Tom and Alan poked unhappily at their platefuls of porridge.

Then a footman came in with the mail. Normally, the mail would have been taken to Sir Adam's study to wait for him there, but today Sir Adam was off to town and he couldn't wait. He read a couple of letters in silence. Tom and Alan fidgeted with their porridge. Guy – who was no longer forced to eat the stuff – made a big show of filling his plate with kippers and scrambled eggs, as a way of annoying Tom. Pamela, who normally breakfasted in bed, came down to take a cup of tea and see her husband off. A little conversation moved in stops and starts. The wind outside creaked a shutter.

Then Sir Adam broke the silence.

'Hello! Fancy that!' He flung the letter down. 'Very handsome of D'Arcy! Very handsome indeed!'

He was begging to be asked the news and Pamela was first to ask it.

'D'Arcy, dear? What has he . . . ?'

'The concession. He's split off a chunk for us.' He picked up the letter again. '"Delighted with your excellent work . . . blah, blah . . . Very happy to make you a small present . . . Gift . . . Drilling rights south of a line drawn from Bandar-e Deylam across to Persepolis." Great heavens!'

18

But, surprised as Sir Adam might be, his surprise was as nothing compared to Tom's. Tom was sitting bolt upright, white-lipped, open-eyed.

'You mean to say we can drill there? By ourselves? We don't have to ask anyone?'

Sir Adam laughed. 'Yes, Tom. We have the drilling rights. We don't have to ask anyone.'

'Everywhere south of Persepolis? Anywhere we want?'

'That's right.'

'The mountains,' he said. 'We've got the mountains.'

And he was right. Since his meeting with D'Arcy – and even more so since Sir Adam's own involvement in Persian oil – Tom had become an oil obsessive and a Persia fanatic. He knew as much about the geography, climate, geology, tribes and politics of Persia as he'd been able to learn from Sir Adam's library.

'That's right. The mountains of the Zagros. The wild country around Shiraz and the Rukna valley. Heavy work to look for oil there, I should think.'

Tom shook his head with an angry little flick. 'There isn't much chance of it there. The best places are further north.'

'Well, you can't expect the fellow to hand over his crown jewels. After all –'

'But some.'

'What?'

'There is some chance. I didn't say there wasn't any chance.'

Sir Adam laughed at the youngster's intensity. 'Lord, Tommy! D'Arcy's pocket is as deep as any, I believe, and I don't think he's ready for the expense of drilling there. I shouldn't think that we –'

'Can I have it then?'

'I beg your pardon?'

The silence at the table grew suddenly cavernous. The family of five might as well have been breakfasting alone beneath the dome of St Paul's.

'Can I have it? The concession? If you don't want it.'

Sir Adam smiled. Perhaps he'd been hoping to encourage Tom to drop the directness of his demand. Perhaps he'd been hoping to soothe away the sudden sense of danger that had for some reason arisen. In any case, he smiled.

It was the wrong thing to do. Something flared in Tom's blue eyes. He pointed at Guy.

'He gets the house and all the land. Alan gets – I don't know – money? A farm or something?'

Tom was just about to turn eight and he was piecing together the facts from half-heard servants' gossip. But he was more right than wrong.

Sir Adam looked stern. 'Alan will get some money. And yes, there's a little estate for him outside Marlborough. There'll be some income from that.'

'And? What about me? What do I get?'

Sir Adam licked his lips. Tom's directness often came across as insolence. What was more, it was detestably ill-bred for anyone to talk this bluntly over breakfast – let alone a boy of eight. But, just as he was ready to speak a sharp rebuke, Pamela interrupted.

'Well?'

She barely whispered the word. She did little more than shape her lips and breathe it. But Sir Adam heard it all right. He exchanged glances with his wife. The issue that Tom had raised was one that the two of them had often enough spoken about in private. Pamela wanted Tom's share of the estate to be every bit the equal of Alan's. Sir Adam, on the other hand, knew that his assets weren't unlimited. Every penny he gave to Tom would have to be cut out of Alan's or Guy's inheritance. As he saw it, there was the issue of justice towards his sons. In his heart, he was unable to feel that his adopted son had the same rights as the children of his own flesh and blood.

'Well?' said Pamela again. 'Or are *you* intending to drill there?'

Tom stared, as though the most important thing in the

world had walked into the room and might be lost for ever if his concentration flickered even for a second.

'Tommy, you wish to be an oilman, do you?'

'Yes, Uncle.'

'It's no easy business.'

'No, Uncle.'

'It's not enough to have a patch of land to drill on, you know. You need money and men and machines and –'

'I know, Uncle. I know.'

Sir Adam gulped down his tea and stood up. He rumpled Tom's hair. 'An oilman, eh?'

'I hope so.'

'Well, good for you, Tommy. You've a fine piece of land to begin with.'

6

Tom had his concession.

Not legally, of course – the boy was only eight, after all – but his all the same. For the first time in his life, he felt he had something equivalent to what Guy had, to what Alan had, to what Sir Adam had.

And not just equivalent. Better.

Because, young as he was, Tom had understood something from the very start. He couldn't have put his understanding into words, but he understood it all the same. And he was right.

Because oil isn't just oil, the way cabbages are only cabbages, or steel is only steel. Oil is more than a liquid. It's more than another commodity. Oil isn't precious, the way gold is, because it sparkles nicely and looks pretty on a lady's neck.

Oil makes the world go round. Even in the opening decade of the twentieth century, its massive power was becoming visible. Cars ran off it. Ships burned it. Factories needed it. On land and sea, the world went oil-crazy. Navies were converted to burn oil. Armies packed their shells full of high explosive made with oil by-products. And every day chemists found new uses for it; speed records were being shattered with it; men dreamed of powered flight with it.

But even that wasn't the reason why oil mattered.

The reason was this. Man doesn't make oil; God does. If you've got a big enough field and a big enough bank account, you can build yourself an auto factory. Don't like cars? Then get a bigger field and build yourself an airplane factory. Or start an airline. Build a store. Open a bank.

Oil isn't like that. Not anyone can start up in the oil business. To start in oil, you've got to have some land that sits over an oilfield. No matter how rich you are, if you don't own the drilling rights, you don't have squat. And that's the reason.

Oil isn't just fuel, though it's the best fuel in the world.

Oil isn't just money, though it's the closest damn thing to money that exists.

Oil is power, because everyone wants it and there's only so much to go round.

'*Talibus orabat dictis arasque tenebat,*' said the schoolmaster, '*cum sic orsa loqui vates.*'

He walked around the schoolroom at Whitcombe House tapping out the rhythm of the Latin with his hands. Tom and Alan sat with their schoolbooks lying closed in front of them. They would have looked out of the windows, except that the schoolroom windows were pitched deliberately high, revealing nothing except a wide, bare square of sky. Tom yawned.

'*Sate sanguine divum, Tros Anchisiade, facilis descensus Averno,*' continued the schoolmaster. 'Creeley, translate for me, if you please.'

Tom said nothing. He didn't move to open his books.

'Creeley, if you please.'

Silence.

The schoolmaster frowned. 'Montague, then. Translate for me, if you would.'

Alan too sat like a stone, staring down at his desk. Unlike

Tom, who actually enjoyed these moments, Alan found them difficult – difficult, but in this case essential.

'Am I to understand that neither of you has prepared today's lesson? Creeley? Montague?'

Then Tom spoke. 'Please, sir, we would prefer to study Persian.'

Six minutes later, the two boys were standing in front of Sir Adam. A cane lay on the table in front of them. The cane was yellow and knobbled all the way along its length. It wasn't an implement they'd seen used very much, but that didn't mean it mightn't be now. Tom and Alan stared at it unhappily.

'You won't learn your Latin?' said Sir Adam.

Tom shook his head, slightly but definitely.

Alan echoed his twin's gesture, but added, 'We don't mind learning Latin, Father, but we think it would be better to learn something useful as well.'

'Persian? That's your idea of useful, is it?'

The two boys exchanged glances. So close was their communication, they hardly had to speak to understand each other. It was a fact of life that the adults of the family needed to get used to. Alan nodded slightly to Tom, as though to confirm some invisible agreement.

'It's for the oil, you see,' said Alan reasonably. 'We're going to need to speak the language.'

Sir Adam held his hand over his mouth. The two boys looked back at each other, then at the bamboo cane.

'If you boys want to learn Persian, I suppose that might be arranged,' said Sir Adam. 'What I don't like is the fact that you didn't prepare your Latin lesson. That's no way to win an argument.'

'Oh, but we did,' said Alan.

'You did? That's not what –'

'Of course we did, Father,' Alan interrupted, supplying a quick translation from the morning's lesson. 'We only said we didn't because we didn't think anyone would take notice of us otherwise.'

24

Sir Adam frowned. 'You could have asked. If you had –'

'I did ask,' said Tom, interrupting. 'Twice. Two weeks ago at breakfast. Again last week.' He spoke with a kind of flat stubbornness; not exactly asking for trouble, but quite ready for it if it came. 'You kept saying maybe.'

'Very well, then. Persian it is. I shall give you the first few lessons myself, until I can find a schoolmaster to take over.'

'Thank you, Father.'

It was Alan who spoke, but with the two boys it hardly mattered which of them said the words: each always spoke for them both.

'Good. Then it's back to your Latin. At least, I assume so. Unless you have any other ideas I should know about?'

His tone was sarcastic, but sarcasm has a habit of bouncing off eight-year-olds. The two boys exchanged glances again. This time, it was Tom's turn to speak.

'Thank you, Uncle, yes. We think it's high time we learned some geology.'

Tom's face looked perfectly innocent, but Sir Adam knew that the look concealed a will of steel. The older man was exasperated, but proud. Proud and fond. He rumpled the two boys' heads.

'Geology too, eh, Tommy? Very well then, geology too.'

7

For two long years, the drillers drilled.

1902 and 1903 passed away. Knox D'Arcy, by now a family friend, kept Sir Adam closely informed about his progress out in Persia. Sir Adam told Alan and Tom. Conditions were almost intolerable. Heat, dust, insects, equipment failures and disease were turning the search for oil into a nightmare. Costs spiralled wildly upwards. Even a man as rich as D'Arcy began to worry about the impact on his purse.

But that wasn't the worst of it.

The worst was simply this: so far, two years and hundreds of thousands of pounds into the search, no oil had been found.

Tom somehow managed to maintain his enthusiasm, though each new disappointment was like a personal setback. The two boys stuck to their Persian studies, but when Sir Adam suggested that their lessons be reduced from three a week to just one, neither boy objected. Their geological studies continued for a while, then lapsed when their teacher moved abroad. Sir Adam didn't seek a new teacher. The children didn't ask that he did.

And then it changed.

One marvellous day, in January 1904, when the two boys were ten years old, a telegram came from Knox D'Arcy in London. 'GLORIOUS NEWS,' he cabled, 'OIL AT LAST.'

Tom went wild.

When he saw the telegram, he let out a yelp of excitement so loud that the dogs were set barking as far away as the stable yard. Together with Alan, he set off on a dance of delight that sent him tearing right through the house, right through the grounds, down to his father's cottage and then back again. Tom's joyous energy lasted all that day.

At dinner that night, when Guy happened to admire the new gunroom that Sir Adam had installed, Tom nodded his young head and commented, 'Yes, Uncle, you've done it very well. I shall do it like that in my country house, when I get it.'

8

It was Guy who cracked first.

There was something about Tom's new-found confidence that he couldn't stand. The enmity that simmered between the two of them crackled and spat with renewed energy. Boiling point arrived one weekend in early February, when the house was full of guests – including the pretty young daughter of an earl, whom eighteen-year-old Guy was sweet on.

'Fetch my horse, stable boy!' said Guy, passing Tom in the hallway and casually reaching out to flick his ear.

Tom stopped dead.

'Your horse?'

'You heard me, stable boy. I feel like riding today.'

Tom's face whitened. The seven-year age gap between the two of them had never held Tom back from a physical confrontation when necessary. He looked Guy up and down, from boots to head and back again. His gaze seemed to assess Guy truthfully for the very first time. Then he dropped his gaze. He shrugged and said, 'If you like. I don't mind. I'm going that way anyway.' He sauntered off.

Guy couldn't quite believe that Tom was going to do as he'd asked, but didn't mind waiting to see. A group of house guests emerged from the drawing room and Guy strolled with them to the front of the house. Guy, in riding costume, stood and chatted. The earl's daughter was there and Guy (slightly plump still, but charming and handsome enough to make up) stood swishing his whip and trying to impress her. She laughed a lot and blushed slightly when she caught his eye.

Then Tom arrived.

He had complied with Guy's request to the letter – or very nearly. He had gone to the stable yard and saddled a mount. He led the animal in question by its bridle to the spot that Guy had indicated.

But it wasn't Guy's grey mare he led. It was the donkey Guy had learned to ride on, a dozen years before. Guy's saddle and stirrups drooped ridiculously low off the donkey's back. The animal was old now and nodded its head ludicrously as it walked, as though deliberately setting out to provoke laughter. Tom himself walked with the exaggerated dignity of an expensive manservant. He had even, absurdly, found a pair of white gloves from somewhere and an old footman's cap.

'Your horse, sir.'

The assembled house guests laughed and clapped at the spectacle. It seemed like a harmless comic turn, deserving its applause. But Tom hadn't finished. He brought the horse close to Guy and his girl, before addressing the girl in a confidential whisper.

'Excuse the donkey, ma'am. He learned to ride on one, you know. Poor chap's just a little bit yellow.'

Guy was white with anger, but with an audience all around him he was forced to act as though he didn't care. He laughed and clapped with the rest of them, before taking the donkey and heading back with it to the stables. After hanging around to milk the congratulations, Tom hurried off to join him.

'I'll kill you for this, you little brat,' said Guy, without turning round to look.

'Like you killed my mother, you mean?' said Tom, who

had long ago heard the story of his birth in the various versions that flew around the servants' hall.

They had arrived at the stable yard. A couple of stable lads sniggered discreetly as they watched. Guy stopped. He flicked his whip at the stables and the big house beyond.

'None of this is yours, you know. Not now. Not ever. Got that, garden boy?'

~

For a short while, that had appeared to be that, but Guy hadn't forgiven, hadn't forgotten.

Four days later, Guy was alone with Sir Adam in the billiard room. Sir Adam had just had news from Knox D'Arcy. The oil well in Persia was yielding just a hundred and twenty barrels a day, but there was great expectation of enlarging the strike to something far more lucrative. D'Arcy was already hopeful of finding City investors to share the risks and profits.

'Must have increased the value of our own little bit of concession,' remarked Guy.

'Yes, I should suppose it has. I suppose once they've discovered even a little bit of oil, it makes it all the more likely that there's more to be found.'

Guy, who was a decent billiards player, threw the three balls softly on to the table and began to knock them around with a cue. Sir Adam watched the game, but hardly played any more these days and was happy to drink his brandy and watch his son.

'What will you do with the concession?' asked Guy. 'I suppose if you were going to sell, now would be the time.'

Sir Adam looked up in surprise. 'Why, that's hardly a fair question! It's not really mine to sell. Little Tommy absolutely treasures the thing.'

Guy let out a small puff of laughter as he took his shot. The three balls, trapped on the same bit of baize, clattered round and round against each other. Guy straightened again and chalked his cue.

'Little Tommy might absolutely treasure one of your paintings, Papa, but if it made commercial sense to sell it, then I dare say you would.'

'I dare say, but the concession belongs to Tommy.'

'Legally, Father? I'm surprised.'

'No, no, no. Of course not legally. Morally. I told him he could have it.'

'Did you? Really? As I recall, you told him it was a fine patch of land. That's hardly the same thing.'

'Oh, for heaven's sake, Guy! I meant he could have it. He knew I meant it. The boy's besotted with the damn thing.' Sir Adam spoke sharply. Guy was his elder son and heir, but there were times when his behaviour wasn't all it should have been. There were times when Sir Adam didn't entirely *like* his own son.

'Yes, Father,' said Guy, 'but, with respect, you're missing the point. You gave him the land because you were certain it was worthless. If you had been sure it had been worth something, you wouldn't have dreamed of conceding it like that.'

Sir Adam frowned, waving his brandy glass as though to brush his son's point aside.

'Well? Would you?' Guy insisted.

'No, I suppose I wouldn't. But that's hardly –'

'Father, may I be blunt?'

'It would seem you're more than capable of it.'

'The concession is yours. Legally yours. You let an eight-year-old boy dream about managing it because he clearly wanted to dream and you saw no reason why not. But now, against all probability, the concession may actually have a value. Suppose, sir, a syndicate of investors in London were prepared to pay something for the blasted thing. A hundred thousand pounds, let us say. What then? That would dwarf any settlement you're able to make for Alan. I don't think of myself in this matter, but it's hard to avoid noticing that it would look like a very fine thing if your elder son and heir

31

had barely greater expectations than the boy you rescued from the kitchen garden.' Guy struck the balls savagely round the table. Again and again, the cue ball slammed the red into the pockets. The red disappeared with an abrupt clack of ivory against wood. 'I think you have been very generous to young Tommy, Father. I'm not sure you're holding Alan sufficiently in your thoughts.'

9

From that point on, events ran a hideously predictable course.

Sir Adam, unable to put Guy's comments out of mind, decided to write in confidence to his London stockbroker, asking him – discreetly – to try to gauge whether there was any value in the Persian concession. Sir Adam told Guy that he had done as much. Guy let a few days pass, then told Tom.

Angrier than he'd ever been in his life, Tom flew to Sir Adam.

'Uncle?'

'Tommy! Hello there!'

'What's this about the concession?'

Sir Adam liked and admired Tom. The boy had pluck, doggedness, flair and passion. But, in moments of fury, he could also be rude, even violently rude. Sir Adam frowned.

'What's what?' Sir Adam's voice should have sent a warning, but Tom was unstoppable.

'What are you doing with my concession?'

'It's not your concession, Tom. It's in my name as your guardian.'

'What are you doing?'

'What makes you think I'm doing anything at all?'

'Guy.'

Sir Adam answered slowly, trying to keep his calm. He nodded. 'At Guy's suggestion, which was a good one, I am taking steps to discover if the concession has marketable value. It may well do, seeing as D'Arcy seems on the verge of a major discovery in a region not so very far from our own patch.'

'*My* patch. *My* concession.'

Then Sir Adam got angry. Tom's impertinence was too much.

'It is not your concession, Tom, nor is anything else for that matter, unless and until I damned well give it to you.'

'You did give it. You said.'

'I said it was a fine patch of land and I hoped you'd have fun dreaming about it. The idea that it *might* come to be yours – might *one day* come to be yours – arose when I believed the property in question to be without value.'

Tom almost staggered backwards. He crashed back against a mahogany sideboard.

'You gave it to me because you thought it was worth nothing?' Tom half laughed to himself. 'And you've taken it back, at Guy's suggestion?' He blinked and looked down at the sideboard, where there stood a vase and, next to it, a framed photograph of the family: Sir Adam, Pamela, Guy, Tom, Alan. 'Thank you, Uncle. I understand.'

He nodded once as though confirming something to himself, then swept his hand along the sideboard, knocking the photo to the floor. Almost by accident, he also caught the vase and toppled that too. The blue and white china shattered with a hollow boom and littered the floor with its wreckage.

Tom stared briefly and unemotionally at the mess, before walking quickly out of the room.

10

Alan paused at the door to the seed shed.

The building was invisible from the big house and the nearest gardeners were over the far side of the kitchen garden. Alan watched them go about their business, until he was sure that none of them was watching. Then he quickly slipped the catch and entered.

The wooden-built shed was about twenty-five feet long by only eight wide, with a line of windows running down the south side. Now, with winter ending, the workbenches were crammed with trays of compost, ready for the March sowing. The shed had a warm smell of earth and wood and growth and sunlight. A couple of mice scuttled away as Alan closed the door. Apart from the mice, there was total silence inside the shed. Once again, Alan checked he hadn't been seen, then he raised his arms to one of the roof joists and swung himself up.

The roof space was narrow and only two and a half foot high at its highest. Boards lay loosely along the joists. Apart from some cobwebs and some rusty old garden tools, there was nothing up there. Nothing except Tom.

Alan squirmed forwards to join his twin.

'Hello,' said Tom.

Alan produced a paper packet containing bread, ham

and cheese. 'I've got apples in my pocket,' he said.

Tom took the gift in silence. His eye asked a question of Alan and, without needing any further explanation, Alan answered it.

'There's an awful fuss,' he said. 'They're looking for you everywhere. Everyone's sure you've gone to your dad's house. He's saying not, of course, but I made them think so by pretending to try to get in there when I thought no one was watching. Only they were. I made sure.'

Tom nodded. Alan had done well. It hadn't needed any secret signal to let Alan know his whereabouts. The two boys had maybe half a dozen favourite hiding places round the house and grounds. Alan had, by instinct, come first to the one where his twin lay hidden.

'I won't, you know,' said Tom. 'Not until . . .'

'Yes, but he's in an awful stew.'

The two boys' conversation was always like this: all but incomprehensible to an outsider. Tom meant that he wouldn't return to Whitcombe House until Sir Adam made the concession over to him properly and for good. Alan doubted that that would happen.

Tom looked at the other and grimaced. 'I'll be stuck here for ever then.'

They both laughed.

'And what about the Donkey?' Tom made a braying noise and pretended to jump on Alan. They laughed a second time, but Alan was uncomfortable as he answered.

'Guy got a terrific dressing-down. Father said he'd been told in confidence. Guy said he thought you already knew. I don't know if Father believed him.'

'He always does.'

'Probably.'

They slipped into silence for a while.

'What'll you do?' asked Alan eventually.

'Oh, I s'pose I'll stay here for a day or two.' Tom waved his hand airily round the tiny loft, as though it were an apartment he often rented for the summer.

'Then what?'

'It *is* my concession, you know.' Tom rolled onto his elbow and looked directly at his twin.

Alan nodded.

'But it *is*.'

'I know. I said yes, didn't I?'

'No.'

'I nodded. That's the same.'

''Tisn't.'

''Tis.'

'Then say it. Go on then. Say it's mine.'

'Look, Father probably will give it in the end. It's just Guy got him into a stew about it.'

'There! See? You said he'll give it in the end. He can't do that, he's already given it.'

'Not with the legal bit as well,' objected Alan. 'I meant with the legal bit. I mean, I know it's yours.'

Tom stared hard at the other, little spots of red appearing high on his cheeks. Then he rolled away, staring out of the tiny cobwebbed pane of glass that was his only window.

'Then I s'pose I'll have to go to Dad's place. I'm old enough now.'

Tom didn't spell out what he meant, but he didn't have to. Alan understood. Tom meant that he'd go and live permanently with his father, away from Whitcombe House, away from Alan. The only thing that would stop him would be if Sir Adam backed down and made definite and permanent his gift of the concession.

Alan swallowed. He pretended to be calm, and began poking at the cobwebs with a bit of twig, while kicking his feet against the low roof just above. But he wasn't calm. Tom was threatening to leave. Tom was implying that a quarrel over property was more important than the two boys' friendship. He scooped up a bit of cobweb that had an insect caught in it: trapped and dying.

'Look.'

'So?'

Alan shrugged and scraped the insect off.

'You know that vase?'

'Yes.'

'Apparently it was worth tons of money. About a thousand guineas, I should think. It didn't help.'

'So what? He shouldn't have –'

'You could say sorry.'

'What!?'

'Just to get him to calm down a bit. I only mean to make him calm down.'

'You think I ought to say sorry?'

'Look, he's probably not going to sell the concession. He probably knows it's yours really.'

'*Probably*? D'you think you're *probably* going to get your stupid farm or whatever? Do you think the Donkey is *probably* going to get everything else?' Tom's blood-spots had vanished now, leaving his face pale, and there was extraordinary intensity in his long-lashed blue eyes. As Tom looked at things, every time he challenged Alan to take sides, Alan tried to be nice but ended up taking his family's cause. Even now, this late in the conversation, Alan hadn't even said directly that the concession was Tom's.

'Anyway,' cried Alan, 'what does it matter? If I get the stupid old farm, then you can have half of it. You don't think I wouldn't share? Who cares about the stupid concession?'

It was a disastrous thing to say.

Tom stared for a full ten seconds at his twin, then looked away. He put the paper packet of food in his pocket, wriggled backwards to the gap in the boards, then swung the lower half of his body down. With his head still poking through into the roof space, he said, 'I've changed my mind. I'm going to my dad's now. I don't care if they see me. They can't stop me, can they? Bye.'

And he was gone.

Away from the seed shed, away from the big house, away from the family that had brought him up.

11

For twenty-four hours: stand-off.

In Tom's eyes, Alan had said the worst thing he could have possibly said. 'Who cares about the stupid concession?' As far as Tom was concerned, Alan might as well have said, 'Who cares if you're a proper part of the Montague family or not?'

At the same time, as far as Alan was concerned, Tom had also committed the worst crime imaginable. As Alan saw it, Tom had placed a trivial argument about money and land over the best thing in the entire world: their friendship, their twinhood.

And so the quarrel persisted. Tom stayed at his father's cottage. Alan stayed in the big house. For the first time since they'd been able to talk, they spent an entire day without speaking to each other. For the first time since they'd been able to walk, they spent an entire day without each other's company.

On the evening of the following day, Alan slipped away early to bed.

To bed, but not to sleep. He opened his bedroom window, climbed quickly across the kitchen roofs, slid down a drainpipe and ran across the lawns and fields to Jack Creeley's cottage. Once there, he tossed a pebble up at Tom's window, saw it open, then scrambled quickly up the branching wisteria and tumbled in over the sill.

The room was lit by a single paraffin-wax candle. Tom was sitting on the bed with a boy's magazine open in front of him. He nodded hello. Alan grinned back: the smile of a would-be peacemaker.

'Well?' said Tom.

Alan was momentarily confused. He didn't know what Tom meant by his 'Well?' and he was taken aback by the loss of their normal invisible communication.

'What do you mean?' he said stupidly. 'Well, what?'

'You know. I mean I s'pose you've come to say sorry.'

'What?!'

'You heard.'

Alan was temporarily blank with astonishment. He knew perfectly well how remorseless his twin could be: remorseless and even cruel. But he'd never expected to feel the edge of it himself. Alan's head jerked back.

'No.'

'No?'

'As a matter of fact, I came to see if *you* were sorry yet. Obviously not.'

Alan was still sitting on the ledge of the window and he swung his legs out of it again onto the wisteria branch. But he didn't drop away out of sight. He hung there, half in, half out of the room, waiting for Tom to say something that would let him come back in. But he was disappointed.

'No,' said Tom. 'Obviously not.'

Alan shrugged. The shrug was meant to be a defiant, couldn't-care-less affair, but the candle's light was enough to show that his mouth and eyes obviously cared very much indeed.

'Well then,' said Alan, still hanging in the window.

'Well then.'

41

The two boys stared at each other a few seconds longer. Eventually Tom looked away, back at his magazine. Alan found a lower hold for his feet, wriggled once, then dropped away out of sight.

Alan went straight home, but not to bed.

He climbed up onto the kitchen roof and lay there on his back, looking up at the starlight overhead. He was angry with Tom. As angry as he'd ever been. The two boys quarrelled often enough, but always made up quickly. When they fought, as they often did, their rules were simple.

Never submit.

Never give up.

While Tom was a little stronger, Alan had a longer reach. While Tom could be surprisingly fierce, Alan's pride and determination always kept him in the fight to the very end. And then, when the fight was over, it was over. The two boys were the best of friends. They could be at each other's throats one minute and walk away, calmly chatting, the next.

But this was different and Alan knew it. For two and a half hours, he lay on his back watching the stars wheel and turn. He went over everything in his mind. On the one hand, there was Tom's temper and recklessness, and his stubborn refusal to compromise. On the other hand, there was Guy's unkindness and Sir Adam's unfairness. By the end of his long vigil, he'd made up his mind. It was he, Alan, who was going to have to do the impossible. It was he who was going to have to make things right.

Having made up his mind, he went to bed.

In the morning, after breakfast he spoke to Sir Adam.

'Father, I want to ask you something.'

'Yes?'

'I think you should give Tom the concession. Properly. You did give it to him before, you know. I know you didn't exactly say so, but everyone knew what you meant.'

Sir Adam sighed and bent down so that his face was on a level with his son's.

'But see here, Alan,' Sir Adam said, 'just suppose the thing turns out to be worth a fortune. It could be worth as much as Whitcombe House and all its land. It's not that I don't think that Tommy's worth that. Of course he is. But there's you and Guy to consider. How would you feel if Tommy was as rich as Mr D'Arcy and you were stuck with your very little patch in Marlborough?'

'I shouldn't care.'

'Not now, maybe, but perhaps you would. These things do matter more as you grow, you know.'

'Then give it to us.' It was an idea of genius – the idea that had come to him last night on the tiles of the kitchen roof.

'What?'

'If that's what you're so worried about, then give the concession to me and Tom. Both of us. Only then you have to share the Marlborough place between us too. Then we'd be exactly the same, whatever happens.'

'But . . .'

Sir Adam swallowed his protests. In the much more likely event that the concession was worthless, he'd be halving the property he'd set aside for his own blood-son. But, however much he felt this, he knew better than to argue the point with a passionate Alan.

'Because we are the same, aren't we, Father? Exactly the same.'

Of course you are, only –'

'Well, there you go. Simple! Can I go and tell him now?'

'It isn't that simple. Your mother and I –'

'Oh, don't worry about her. *I'll* go and talk to her.'

Alan ran off to his mother and argued the case with her. Although she said little, Alan quite correctly sensed that she was on his side.

'I'll talk it over with your papa,' she promised.

She was as good as her word. That morning she spent an hour or two in patient argument with her husband. Sir Adam's sticking point remained the likelihood that he'd be disinheriting Alan. Sir Adam was prosperous enough, but he certainly wasn't vastly well off. Alan's portion was never going to have been large and Sir Adam was anxious not to cut it in half. But Pamela was determined. She had some money of her own that had lain dormant with a City bank for many years. When she looked again at how much she had, it was much more than she'd believed. She insisted on adding her own money to Alan's portion, but on condition that Sir Adam did as his son wanted.

And in the end he agreed.

By the end of that day, when lessons were finished, Sir Adam called Alan into his library.

'Well, my boy, I've news for you.'

'Yes?'

'I've made certain arrangements, the upshot of which is that you and Tommy can share the farm and share the concession. Because of your mother's generosity, there may even be a little money to go along with it as well.'

Alan stood open-mouthed, hardly daring to believe that he'd won. 'Really, Father?'

'Really.'

'With all the legals and everything?'

Sir Adam smiled. 'You're ten and a half, my boy. So is Tommy. There'll be time enough for the legal side when you're of age. But if you mean, is my decision final, then yes it is.'

Alan breathed out a sigh of relief. It seemed an eternity since Tom had gone.

'Thank you!'

'Now, it's up to you, young man, but there may be somebody you want to go and tell about this.'

Though it was still only spring, Sir Adam's window was set half open. Alan paused an instant longer, as though to check that what he'd heard was real, not an illusion. Then he moved. He ran across the room, jumped through the open window, and went streaking across the lawns to find his twin.

He wasn't disappointed.

Tom wasn't simply pleased, he was ecstatic. And (from Alan's point of view) what mattered most was that although Tom *was* delighted to have won his concession, his joy over the reunion with Alan was greater still. The twins were together again – stronger after the break, it appeared, than before it. With joint ownership of the concession, they became oil fanatics together. Oil was *their* obsession, the sign of what united them as twins. Whitcombe House welcomed Tom back.

Life resumed its normal course, only better.

That should have been it. Argument over. Done and dusted. Forgotten and forgiven.

And so it was. Almost. But when emotions run so high and for so long, they leave their mark.

Alan had learned a lesson – an almost unconscious one, perhaps, but one so deeply etched that he never forgot it. When Tom's passions were aroused, he could be dangerous, irresponsible, uncompromising.

And Tom too had learned his lesson. When the chips were down, Alan had proved unreliable. Given the choice between Tom and family, Alan was a compromiser, an evader, an ally of divided loyalties.

The lessons had been learned and would never be forgotten.

And the oil?

Knox D'Arcy's glorious news looked feebler and less glorious by the week. By the end of May, and despite all the efforts of the drilling team in Persia, the flow of oil dwindled and died. D'Arcy's expenses continued to mount. The chances of finding oil anywhere – let alone in the twins' stony stretch of mountains – seemed ever more remote. D'Arcy searched for new investors to share the strain.

It seemed that he had gambled vastly and lost utterly.

The two boys continued to learn their Persian and their geology. They continued to follow D'Arcy's fortunes at the new drilling site of Masjid-i-Suleiman. Their fascination with the business continued unabated. In fact, if anything, with the oil concession now fairly and squarely shared between the two of them, their determination to explore for oil together was stronger than ever before. But, aged only ten, they'd already learned the most important lesson the oil business had to teach.

You could drill hard. You could drill well. You could drill in a place where oil was literally seeping from the ground.

And you could still fail.

Lose money.

Go broke.

PART TWO

Do you know, brother, that you are a prince?
A son of Adam?

Jalal al-din Rumi (1207–1273)

12

It's late June 1914.

The summer is a warm one, golden even. The international scene is peaceful. The tensions that have bubbled away in Europe for the last dozen or more years are certainly no worse than they have been and quite probably a good deal better.

Seven British warships have joined the German Imperial High Seas fleet for the Elbe Regatta: a week of racing, dancing, music and fireworks. When finally the British fleet steams away, the British admiral signals to his hosts: 'Friends in the past and friends for ever.'

In Serbia, an archduke has been killed by an anarchist, but who cares? Serbia is Serbia, and in that part of the world, archdukes are two a penny.

Alan and Tom are grown men now, twenty-one years of age. Their future lies ahead of them, a sparkling ocean on which anything could happen.

Alan has grown into a tall man, pale blond hair, eyes of pale blue, eyebrows so fair you can hardly see them. He has his father's lean hawkishness, though softened by hints of his mother: her smile, her appearance of mild worry.

Alan is at Oxford, finishing his final examinations. The

exams have been gruelling and exhausting, but they'll soon be over. His degree will be in Natural Science, a subject he has little time for, except that it allows him to specialise in his chosen field of geology.

Because D'Arcy's adventures in oil hadn't ended. He'd found his investors, he'd continued to drill. And in 1907, six years from first beginning, he struck oil.

Oil on a huge scale. No trickle this time, but a gush so vast that one of the world's great companies was in the process of being built upon it. The company, now named Anglo-Persian, has a use for resourceful young geologists, and, as soon as September comes around, Alan will start work on the Persian-Mesopotamian border, scouting for oil. But that's September. In between now and then, he has two clear months for riding, shooting and fishing in the country, and for balls and parties in London.

~

Tom, too, is doing well.

He's shorter than Alan, but stronger, broad in the shoulder, glossy dark hair with a hint of curl. His face is almost picture-book handsome: wide, strong and with a dazzling smile that comes quickly and fades slowly. Unlike Alan, Tom is already highly experienced with the girls. It seems he's never without them. Alan laughs about it, but also finds it embarrassing. Where Tom is a veteran, Alan is wholly inexperienced.

And there's another way in which Tom is running ahead of Alan: in business.

Once his schooling was over, Tom rejected a possible schol-arship to Oxford and instead won a position with the American giant, Standard Oil, in their London office. He's doing well. Talented and energetic, he's already building a name for himself as one of the most able young men in the company. Though Tom works hard, he joins up with Alan every weekend and they spend their time together either dancing and socialising in London, or riding and shooting in the country.

And Guy?

These days, Guy seems altogether less significant. The enmities of childhood appear to have faded. If the old hatreds haven't exactly disappeared, they don't make a lot of difference now. Tom is in London. Guy seems to be anywhere but. Guy is a soldier, a major, with a particular aptitude for staff work. Tom and Guy don't see much of each other, aren't likely to see each other much in the future. When their paths do cross, they are coldly polite.

But, meantime, summer 1914 is a golden one.

It's one to be enjoyed, a time when the best thing in the world to be is a young Englishman with the future a sparkling ocean at his feet. Tom and Alan hardly feel the need to signal anything to each other, but if they did, they'd send the same signal as the British admiral in Kiel. 'Friends in the past and friends for ever.'

The trouble with archdukes is that if you have one and you lose one, you can't just say to hell with it, we'll get another. So Austria, who happened to own the archduke in question, sent an ultimatum to Serbia, who stood accused of supporting the anarchists. Roughly speaking, the ultimatum said, 'We're very upset about our archduke and we'd like you to do some *serious* grovelling.'

So Serbia grovelled.

Serbia was little and Austria-Hungary was big, not to mention the fact that the Austrians and the Germans were best of friends and the Germans were well known to fancy a spot of military adventure. So Serbia grovelled. Profusely. Unreservedly. Embarrassingly.

But, unfortunately, if you fancy a spot of military adventure

– if you're all geared up for it, looking forward to it, been promising Auntie Helga a postcard from Belgrade – then a conciliatory reply isn't necessarily enough to hold you back. So Austria declared war.

Now the trouble with starting wars is that your neighbours are apt to get a little nervous. Russia sat right next to strong Austria and mighty Germany, and it seemed that there was about to be a war on her doorstep. This made Russia a little twitchy, so she mobilised her troops, all six million of them.

Whoops! Here was Austria-Hungary hoping for a nice little war in its back garden, when all of a sudden the biggest country in Europe has mobilised its massive population and placed it on a war footing. Germany called on Russia to demobilise, but, as the Russians looked at it, that was a bit like the fox inviting the chicken to come out of the roost. Russia told the Germans to get lost, and Germany too got ready for war.

Now the trouble with Germany mobilising *its* army is that the French feel kind of twitchy. The French are a generous race with a well-deserved reputation for hospitality, but when you've had a few thousand uninvited guests marching through your capital city only a few decades before, you can be excused for getting nervous. What's more, France had an alliance with Russia, and the Germans and Russians weren't looking too friendly these days. Germany asked France to abandon her alliance with Russia, but France said no.

The way Germany saw things, if war was coming then it made a whole lot of sense to stay one step ahead of the game. And, say what you like about the Germans, when they set out to do a thing, by golly they do it thoroughly.

Looking back on it, neither Tom nor Alan nor anybody else could have explained why one more assassination in the assassination capital of the world should have triggered the largest armed conflict in world history. But, explicable or not, that's precisely what happened.

Needing a quick victory in the west to ensure decisive gains in the east, Germany sent its troops into Belgium, destination Paris. The British – deeply reluctant to go to war, but equally reluctant to hand Europe over to the Germans – asked Germany kindly to leave Belgium alone. The Germans said no, and Britain too was at war.

13

May 1915.

The night sky rumbled with a general low thunder and the horizon sparkled with the flashes of shells bursting miles away to the north. The largest French farmhouse seemed to have given up the notion of farming anything and had turned itself into a kind of hotel instead. In the spacious kitchen, three or four wooden trestle tables were crowded with soldiers, each paying half a franc for a vast plateful of fried potatoes together with a scrap of bacon and a glass of watery beer.

Alan and Tom, only just arrived in France, blinked at the light and the noise, and stretched their legs, cramped after a two-day journey by boat, train and cart. They weren't left alone for long. A pale-faced man – a corporal, from his uniform – came running up to them.

'Mr Creeley, sir? Mr Montague?'

The twins nodded. They had signed up shortly after the outbreak of war. After months of training in England, and still longer months of sitting around in a gloomy transit camp outside Manchester, they had finally arrived in France. They were second lieutenants and would each command a platoon of soldiers as new to the game as they were. The two men were uncertain of their soldiering skills, sobered by the strangeness of the fiery horizon.

'Company Commander wants to see you, sirs,' said the NCO. 'Wants to know why you didn't arrive yesterday. We move up to the line tomorrow morning.'

The NCO ushered the two men into what had obviously once been the farmhouse's creamery – idle now that there were no cows to make the milk. An oil lamp hung from a hook in the beamed ceiling and a uniformed major was bent over some papers, booted feet across a map-covered chest, drinking coffee. He looked up.

'Filthy stuff, French coffee. D'you have any? English, I mean?'

The newcomers shook their heads. 'Bacon, sir,' said Alan. 'And marmalade.'

'Uh.' The major grunted. 'Coffee. Best thing to bring.' He put down his paperwork with relief and stood up. He was surprisingly tall, and had muscular in-swinging arms that made him look a little monkey-like: strong and potentially dangerous. He stretched out a hand. 'Wallace Fletcher.' They shook hands. 'Take a pew.' The pew in question was a couple of planks over a collection of milk churns. 'Why the hell weren't you here yesterday?'

Alan began to explain, but Fletcher shut him up. 'Military organisation. Contradiction in terms. Wonder is you're here at all. We go up into the line tomorrow, relieve C Company.'

'Yes, sir.'

'Mr Creeley?'

Tom nodded. 'Sir.'

Fletcher screwed up his face, appeared to assess his new subordinate, and made a grunt of reluctant approval. Then he looked at Alan.

'Then you must be Montague, eh?'

'Yes, sir.'

'You don't have a brother do you? A major? One of our dear friends and brothers on the General Staff?'

Alan said he did.

'Hmm!' This time Fletcher's grunt was disapproving. He

picked up one of the sheets of paper from the stack in front of him and read out loud. '"It has come to our notice that in a number of companies the daily practice of rifle cleaning is not being correctly attended to . . . All company commanders . . . blah blah . . . regulation procedure . . . blah blah . . . inspections . . . blah blah. Please submit a report detailing . . . blah blah blah blah blah."' Fletcher dropped the paper with disgust. 'Signed Major Guy Montague.'

There was a long moment's silence. Alan was plainly uncomfortable. Tom, on the other hand, enjoyed the moment – or at least he did until it dawned on him that Guy was in France. He wasn't precisely in command of Tom, but he was out here, in a position of authority, obliged to interfere. Once again, Guy's shadow had come to fall over his life. Tom felt a surge of anger at the thought.

'Want to know what the bloody trouble is?' said Fletcher, at last.

'Sir?' said Alan.

'My men keep firing their bloody rifles.'

'Yes, sir.'

'Makes 'em dirty. The rifles obviously, not the men. Men couldn't get much dirtier.'

'No.'

There was a pause. Then Alan began to defend his brother. 'I believe my brother has no desire to –'

He would have continued, but Fletcher interrupted. 'Oh, doesn't matter. It's all balls. I just tell 'em what they want to hear. Shiniest rifles in France. Cleaning drills five times daily. That sort of thing.' He sat down, put his feet back on the chest, and started his second cup of the coffee that he so detested. 'You're new boys, I take it?'

'That's right, sir,' said Alan.

'You're not going to be too bloody useless, I hope?'

Alan's eyes jerked in surprise at the question and the tone, but before he could find an answer, Fletcher interrupted again.

'Don't worry. Training's a waste of time. The only soldiers

in the battalion are me, the CO, the adjutant, two young-sters from Sandhurst, and a sergeant-major who thinks the whole New Army idea's a bloody joke. Here's all the training you need. If you see Fritz, kill him. Keep your own bloody head from being shot off. Keep your men out of trouble. And let the CO go on thinking he's Lord God Almighty. Got it?'

There was a silence.

'And the coffee,' said Tom.

'Damn right. And mind the bloody coffee.'

14

Their introduction to the front line came all too soon.

'Chalk. Lucky sods. Cushy first posting.' Major Fletcher jabbed the bank at shoulder height and released a shower of white soil into the trench floor. 'Dry as a stallion's tit, even when it rains. You should see the bloody clay pits we lived in over winter. Two feet above the water line, three feet below. And Fritz taking a pop at you every time you tried to build the parapet an inch or two higher. Only buggers who enjoyed it were the rats.'

Alan kept silent. He and Tom were both shocked. They were shocked at the mud, the vermin, the maze of trenches, the danger that lurked in every gun slit, every weakness in the fortifications, every whistle of passing shells.

A little way beyond the dugout, lodged in the wire eighteen inches off the ground, there was a severed head. According to the British Tommies who had taken over this stretch of line, the head had once belonged to a French soldier killed by a shell blast. It would have been easy to release the object one night and dispose of it, but it had come to take on a kind of superstitious importance amongst the troops. The skull was known as Private Headley, and was treated as a regular member of the battalion. Food was tossed out to it, drinks thrown at it, even lighted cigarettes hurled as a kind of good luck offering.

'And here's your digs,' said Fletcher, introducing Alan and Tom to their dugout. 'You'll want to get some more earth on that bloody roof of yours. It's not going to stop a direct 'un, not built like it is at the moment. Any food, hang it up. If it's on the floor, Brother Rat will have it and that's against regulations. Corpses for them, food for us. Got that? Good men.'

Fletcher went, leaving the two young men alone in their new home. Tom looked at Alan. Alan looked at Tom.

Tom cracked a smile. 'Well, brother, here we are.'

Alan nodded. 'Yes. Here we are.'

They sat down on their beds, running their hands over the rough wooden walls, feeling the weight of earth above their heads. They remembered Fletcher's comment that a direct hit would kill them both. They thought about the summer before and how impossible it seemed that that life would ever return.

But there was something else in the atmosphere as well. Something positive. The shocking reality of their new home made them feel more strongly than ever the bond between them. They had arrived on the front line, only a few dozen yards distant from an enemy that wanted to kill them. Their task was to do the same to the enemy. But they were brothers. More than brothers, they were twins. It seemed like no power on earth could break them apart.

The two men sat on their beds, stared at each other, and began, for no reason at all, to laugh and laugh and laugh.

15

It was nine weeks later.

Tom and Alan were novices no longer. They knew how to protect their men, how to harass the enemy, how to lead a patrol out in the dangerous silence of no man's land. They had experienced rats, discomfort, shelling, gunfire, and the loss of men they knew. But one thing was still unknown to them. They hadn't faced serious action and all that does to a man. Not yet.

But that was about to change.

Tom drew back the sacking that curtained the men's dugout. The smell of unwashed bodies and burnt cork raced out, followed by the quieter odours of kerosene and tobacco smoke. Half the men already had their faces blackened, the other half were fighting over a single shaving mirror or letting their mates do it for them. One man had his face marked with love-hearts and messages to his girlfriend. Another had his face covered with obscenities.

'Widdecombe,' snapped Tom, 'get this man's face properly blacked. And you, Tinsey, get away from that chalk unless you want to make Fritz think you're a blasted ghost.'

The men fell quickly into order, under Tom's eye. He counted them. There were eight.

'Corporal, how many men d'you make it?'

'Eight, sir.'

'Where the hell is the last man?'

'Last man, sir? Eight's what Major Fletcher –'

'Private Headley? Where is he?'

The dugout filled with laughter at Tom's joke, but he wasn't done yet.

'Oh, don't worry,' he added. 'As a matter of fact, I believe I told him to go on a-*head*.'

Shrieks and howls of laughter followed this witticism, which was already being repeated to the dullards of the platoon. Tom's rapport with his men had been more or less instant from the start, and though they were thoroughly nervous now, they were high-spirited as well.

And yet, for all his joking, Tom was acutely worried, not for himself but for Alan. Earlier that day, at company mess, Fletcher had asked for volunteers.

'We need a chap to lead a recce party. Purpose of the recce is to find the gaps in the bloody wire – assuming there are any bloody gaps, that is – then come home. On the way back you'll drop a trail of lime for the other lads to follow later on. If you can avoid making a bloody hullabaloo while you're at it, we would appreciate it. The raiders will follow the trail, skip lightly through the holes in the wire, and give Fritz a faceful of bayonet before he's woken up. Got it? Who's game?'

Alan and Tom were, of course, both game.

'New boys, can't wait to get at it, eh?'

Neither man answered.

'Anything to get Colonel Jimmy his DSO, what? Jolly good. That's what we all want.' Colonel James 'Jimmy' McIntosh was the battalion commander – and a man who, according to rumour, was desperate for a medal. There were faint smiles around the table as Fletcher continued. 'Montague, you take charge of the recce. I'm in command of the raid. Creeley, you'll be my second. Any problems, you take over. All clear?'

It had been perfectly clear. Both men nodded, grave and subdued at the thought of what was coming.

Then Fletcher had paused, his expression torn between the desire to say something and the feeling that he shouldn't. The mess waited breathlessly for the outcome.

'Hmm – Montague – I don't suppose your brother Guy will be out hunting Fritz tonight – might find the shock was too much for him, eh? Face some bullets, for a change – any case, better things to do, I expect – the King's rifles to keep clean – don't mean that – does a good job, I'm sure – anyway, that's what I mean, he'll be proud of you, what? First mission and all that.'

Fletcher stumbled to a close. Everyone listened in astonishment. Fletcher had come very close to insulting Guy, almost accusing him of shirking danger. Of course, it was common enough for soldiers in the field to complain about those stuck away behind the lines, but Guy was Alan's brother and Fletcher's comments had gone beyond acceptable barrack-room humour.

Alan could see Tom's smile grow wider and wider, and it was with a frosty voice that he said, 'Thank you, sir. Yes, I hope he will be proud.'

'Yes, yes, quite, quite,' said Fletcher, quickly moving away from dangerous territory. His attention fastened with relief on a pair of rats copulating on his own private store of marmalade. 'Rat ahoy!' he cried, drawing his revolver. 'On three, please, gentlemen. One . . . two . . . three.' He led the others in a volley of gunfire, which left both rats dead in a glue of marmalade. 'No lovemaking in company mess. Leave that sort of thing to the Frenchies.'

That had been eight hours ago.

Alan, having been chosen to go out first, would be the first to know real mortal danger. Tom would follow only after Alan was home.

Tom's body hummed with a double nervousness. Once for himself and the danger he was about to face. A second time for Alan and the danger he was in right now.

Alan's job was find gaps in the wire. Would there be any? Tom doubted it. Alan had strict instructions not to spend time cutting the wire, but Tom knew Alan. His twin would never let a troop of soldiers march up to an obstacle they couldn't cross. Tom guessed that, even now, Alan would be on his belly, wirecutters raised, snip-snip-snipping at the deadly coils. A single noise or glimmer of moonlight could give away his position and his life.

Tom smoked cigarette after cigarette, extinguishing each one against the silvery sandbags in the parapet. The glowing tobacco charred its way through the sackcloth and released a tiny hiss of falling soil. 'For God's sake, look after yourself, brother. For God's sake.'

A voice behind him made him jump.

'What's that? Eh?' It was Fletcher.

'Nothing, sir. Wondering where Montague is.'

Fletcher harrumphed. 'Your men are ready?'

'Yes, sir.'

'Then we leave in fifteen minutes. Tell your men.'

'And Montague, sir?'

Fletcher shrugged, sinister in the moonlight. 'Montague, Mr Creeley, will have to take his chances.'

16

The minutes passed.

Still no sign of Alan.

The fifteen minutes were up. Fletcher signalled that it was time to go.

One by one, they ascended the stumpy little ladder into no man's land. Away from the claustrophobic tunnels and parapets of the trenches, the world seemed suddenly vast and shelterless. Ahead of him, Tom could see Fletcher's ape-like figure and the dark shapes of his men. Tom, in charge of the second detachment, counted off thirty seconds then headed off in slow pursuit. Nowhere was there any sound louder than the muffled impact of boots on earth, the scrape of rifle butts along the ground. A couple of minutes went by, each one as long as a century.

Then something peculiar.

The soil under Tom's hands began suddenly to glow white. He stopped for a second in astonishment. It was lime, shining in the moonlight. But if it was lime, then . . .

Alan bounded forwards out of the darkness, grinning. Tom suddenly realised how desperately worried he had been. It was all very well being twins – it was a friendship other people could never hope to match – but there was a downside too, which was simply this: Tom had more to lose.

He embraced Alan. 'Look after yourself, brother. Whatever happens, look after yourself.'

Alan returned the embrace then pulled away. 'I did. Now it's your turn.'

~

Tom looked up. He had already delayed longer than he should. He crept off again along the trail of lime with his men, while Alan returned to British lines and safety.

The raiding party moved slowly onward. For a minute or two things continued to go well. The raiders were silent, invisible, undetected.

Then it happened.

Somewhere ahead of Tom, in Fletcher's party, one of the Tommies slipped on the side of a shell crater and went slithering down to its muddy bottom. Though he swore, he swore quietly, but his equipment broke from his pack and rolled clanking down the short slope.

The noise rang out like a siren.

For a moment, Tom held his breath. He could feel everyone behind and ahead of him doing the same. The night air remained quiet.

Then a gun opened fire, a rifle, sounding repeatedly. Whether the rifleman was German or British was never quite clear, but it took just seconds for the German lines to light up with fire. Tom felt the sudden, shocking horror of finding himself under attack. For an instant, he felt dull, stupid, incapable of action.

He looked around. Over to his right, he saw a shellhole, deep and – for the moment – safe.

'Get into the shellhole *now*,' he screamed, using all his lung power to bend his soldiers to his will. The force of his voice shocked them into compliance.

The men piled into safety. Tom counted them in, then followed.

The German fire intensified. A rising flare lit up the night sky. With the utmost caution, Tom raised his head to look out. First he saw nothing. Then, lifting himself still further, he caught a glimpse of Fletcher's crowd, shockingly far off, in a crater much closer to German lines, and witheringly exposed. The light of the flare faltered and died. Tom lowered his head, just as bullets began to spatter into the earth above and around him.

He looked at his men, who were sitting safe but terrified in the bottom of their crater. He began to speak, but the men were still distracted and shocked. One of them – Tinsey – was nodding his head and rhythmically chanting: 'Stupid, fucking, German, bloody –'

Tom struck Tinsey hard on the arm. Tinsey stopped. The other men looked wildly at Tom.

'Now listen, all of you. You men are to get back to shelter, as quickly and safely as you can.' Another burst of fire interrupted his words. Tom was sprayed with earth and he assumed everyone else was too. 'You will leave in pairs and move when I say the word, not before. You will run like hell. If you find any man wounded or hurt, you will not stop. You will just run.' One of the men was struggling with a big clumsy satchel of hand-hurled Mills bombs. 'Denning, leave that. Leave it! Just put it down, man. All you others, are you completely clear about what to do?'

They were clear. Detaching the men in pairs, Tom sent them running for safety. The shellhole emptied. Tom was alone.

Particles of chalk moved grittily beneath his tongue: soil put there by a German bullet. Anger lit a fuse in him.

'You stupid bastards,' he screamed. He screamed it at everyone. The Germans, Wallace Fletcher, Colonel Jimmy, the good-natured riflemen of his battalion. He was screaming at High Command, whose war this was. He was screaming at Guy, who'd never been under fire and probably never would be.

The shooting was still intense, but it was concentrated on the party further ahead, pinning them down, leaving them unable to move. They'd be finished off by mortar fire, come the morning. Shifting position, Tom noticed his foot knocking against young Denning's bag of Mills bombs.

His tide of anger rose higher.

He picked up the satchel and began to run.

17

It was three weeks later. Midday. The battalion had dropped back out of the front line, for two weeks of rest in the pretty village of Le Hamel, just six miles from the front.

Alan jogged along a narrow lane that wound down to a tiny stone-built cottage. His boots scuffed up the white dust that settled gently on the roadside flowers, poppies and saffron weed. As he reached a bend in the lane, Alan's jog turned into a run. He ran up to the cottage and thumped on its crude wooden front door. From a window upstairs, he heard a voice.

'Up here, old man.'

Tom had lived, but only just.

His anger had carried him all the way to within spitting distance of German lines. Once there, he'd thrown himself flat and begun hurling Mills bombs like a bowler at some demented cricket match. His fury kept him at it, aiming and throwing with an extraordinary intensity. What he managed to hit, nobody knew, but this much was certain: the fire that had swept over Fletcher's men became scattered and confused. Fletcher seized his opportunity and raced home with his men: their lives saved.

Once Tom had finished his satchel of bombs, he'd done everything he could. His anger left him. Clarity returned.

Somewhere to the east, dawn was getting ready to light its lamps. Tom was so close to the German lines, he could hear their sentries break wind. Slowly and with infinite care, he'd backed away. As he'd crawled, he must have been hit, because he felt a sudden impact in his left arm, followed a few seconds later by the slip and slither of blood. He'd found a shellhole and tumbled into it. He'd put a dressing on the wound, closed his eyes a moment – then woke at noon with the sun high in a perfect sky and larks singing crystal in the echoing air.

He had no food or water.

The crater around him was hopelessly shallow.

So he'd lain there. All day, all through a golden evening into night. Then when darkness had fallen, he'd begun to crawl home, desperately weak. He would never have made it, except for Alan.

About three in the morning, Alan found him, stretched out unconscious, head pointing for British lines. He'd hooked a hand into his belt and dragged him home.

Alan crashed open the wooden cottage door, and leaped up the rough ladder leading into the loft. Tom lay on his bed, half-dressed, left arm in a clean white sling. He put down a book and smiled. Except for his wounded arm, he looked astonishingly fit and healthy. Soldiering had given Tom (and Alan supposed, himself as well) an extra edge to his physique: more hardness, more confidence. The two men clubbed hands together, a new gesture for them.

It was the first time they'd seen each other since the raid. They were changed men. They'd both experienced danger and death close at hand. They'd both come to understand fully what war might mean.

'By God,' said Alan, 'so now we know what it's all about.'

Tom nodded. 'Yes. It was one hell of a night. Two nights, actually. I didn't think I'd see a third.'

Alan nodded. Then his expression lightened and he released Tom's hand. 'Anything to bunk off duty, eh?'

'One of my brighter ideas, wouldn't you say?'

'Yes, well, everyone has you marked down for an MC now. And a bloody well deserved one at that.'

He *was* pleased for Tom, of course. He knew that Tom deserved a Military Cross and would almost certainly get it. And yet . . . the twins had always been competitive. They'd competed as boys, competed as young men, and now seemed destined to compete as soldiers. And just as it had been Tom who'd more often won their wrestling matches, won their riding contests, won every attractive girl in Hampshire (or so it had seemed), now, once again, it was Tom who'd won the soldiering race. The fact shouldn't have rankled, but it did, if only a little. Alan smiled carefully, anxious not to let any of this show.

But the two men were twins and they didn't only rely on words.

Tom asked gently, 'Does it bother you, brother?'

Alan shook his head. 'You're a good officer and a courageous one. It's right these things are recognised.'

Tom pursed his lips. 'Really? I don't know if I am a courageous man, let alone a good one. I fell into a bloody fury that night. I pitched bombs at Fritz because Fritz was close enough to get hurt. If it had been our own High Command beyond the wire, Haig and French and all those other bastards, then I'd have killed the lot of them instead.'

'You wouldn't.'

'*You* wouldn't, you mean. If they wanted to reward decent courageous men with these baubles, they ought to be picking chaps like you.'

Alan smiled to acknowledge the compliment, but his eyes remained serious. 'You're a better man than you give yourself credit for. But it wouldn't hurt you to fool around less. No one would like you the less for it.'

It was Tom's turn to smile. He looked at his watch. 'Talking of fooling,' he said, 'I've a little fool who's waiting for me right now. But I'll be back for supper, if you'd care to share it.'

'A fool? You mean a – a girl? Good God, you don't have a girl *here*, do you?' Alan was shocked, then embarrassed, then annoyed with himself for being either.

'A girl? Maybe.' Tom laughed. His open smile and shiny unmilitary hair seemed like reminders of an already lost age, those untroubled years before the war.

'Good God, you *do*!'

'Yes, and do you know, you ought to find someone too. I can tell you, if there's one consolation for a horrible spell in the trenches, then it's an afternoon in bed with a little French fool.'

Alan blushed slightly. He was embarrassed by this kind of conversation, and he disliked it when he heard officers talking about prostitutes as though they were horses. 'I'm not sure I could. Not with a . . .' Alan let himself tail off rather than speak the word 'prostitute'. 'I don't mean to be preachy.'

'It's true, though, all the same. There's nothing to beat the comfort of a pretty French fool. I'm being perfectly serious. If you ever wanted me to help, I'd be happy to.'

'I'm amazed you're able to –' Alan blushed. 'Sometimes I come back from our time in the front and I find myself hardly able to eat, let alone . . . let alone, do *that*.'

'I don't always. But you can lie in a girl's bed without making love and there's still a damned lot of comfort in it . . . In bed, you don't have to act the British officer. The girls here do understand, you know. It's not as though they're ignorant of what war does to a man.'

Still blushing deeply, Alan asked, 'Look, do you . . . ? God, I don't mean this badly, it's just I really don't know. When you . . . do you . . . ?'

'I don't pay, no. My pretty little fool doesn't charge me, but I imagine she sees other men and if she does, she probably charges them. It's only sex, you know. She doesn't love

71

me and I don't love her. When the war ends, I expect she'll marry a French farmer and be faithful to him all her days . . . I think she wants to help the war effort. This is her way and it's a damned good one, if you ask me.'

Alan's blush had settled down and made itself at home. Rose pink had made way for tomato, which had given up and handed over to beetroot. 'I see. Thanks. I didn't mean to . . . I wasn't trying to . . .'

'You weren't trying to admonish me, I know.' Tom got up, smiling. He squeezed the other man's shoulder with understanding. 'I'll see you later. For supper.'

Alan nodded stupidly. 'Of course. Later. For supper.'

Tom pulled a clean shirt over his damaged arm, ran his hands briefly through his curly hair, twinkled a smile – and left.

18

The trouble with fate is that it leaves no tracks. Fate never looks like fate. It doesn't come crashing into a person's life with heavy bootprints and a smell of burning.

Instead, fate lives in the little things. A child's fondness for blackberry pudding. A father's slight unfairness between two boys. The chance results of battle. A tiny scrap of purple and white medal ribbon.

And that's a pity. Because danger noticed is danger avoided. Because what is invisible can nevertheless be lethal. Because even the smallest things can grow up and destroy a life.

On 25 September 1915, the British mounted an assault at Loos. Six divisions attacked and were halted by devastating machine-gun fire. The following morning, in an effort to maintain momentum, two further divisions – fifteen thousand men, all of them volunteers – were sent forward in broad daylight, in parade-ground formation ten columns strong. The German gunners were simply astounded. Never had an easier target presented itself. They blazed away until their gun barrels were burning hot and swimming in oil. The men fell in their hundreds, but they continued to advance in good order, exactly as though all this were part of a plan, unknown

to the enemy, but certain of success. And then the survivors reached the German wire. It was uncut, unscathed, impenetrable. Then and only then did they retreat.

Tom got his medal: the Military Cross, a little strip of white and purple stitched to his uniform tunic. He was proud of it, of course, but it sank quickly into the background. It no longer seemed important. But it was.

Alan and Tom heard about the massacre at Loos from Guy, on one of his rare visits to the reserve lines. It was a chilly day at the start of October. Alan and Tom had been lying on the roof of a dugout, smoking and watching an artillery team sweat as they dug in one of their thumping 60-pounders.

'Good morning, ladies,' said Guy, sitting down beside them without invitation. 'Good to see our front-line troops straining every sinew.'

'Go to hell, Guy,' said Tom, neither looking up nor changing posture.

They chatted briefly about trivia, but it wasn't long before Guy began venting his frustrations with the assault at Loos and the conduct of the war more generally. 'Sir John French was a bloody fool – a decent chap but totally useless. Haig's not like that. On tactics, gunnery, supply lines, all that kind of muck, he's absolutely first rate, the very pattern of a modern general. But – my God! – he's obsessed with attack. He literally doesn't care about casualties. I've seen him in the bloody map room, hearing about the losses at Loos, the slaughter of the 21st and 24th, and his only reaction was to make changes to the ammunition supply arrangements. Not a hint of anything else. Nothing.'

'Poor bastards,' said Alan. 'It makes it worse somehow that they were all volunteers.'

Guy nodded. 'And damn short of officers now. Men too, of course, but the officers did the decent thing and made sure they got even more thoroughly killed than the men. They'll be scouring the other divisions now, looking for chaps. Either of you boys fancy a change?'

Alan and Tom glanced at each other, sharing the same thought, but it was Alan that spoke it.

'Neither or both, Guy, neither or both.'

The conversation ended there that day. Guy was soon off – efficient, reliable, thorough. But the issue wasn't over, not by any means.

A few weeks later, when Alan and Tom had returned to the front line and after enough rain to make everyone miserable, Major Fletcher came splashing down the trenches in search of Tom.

'Ah, there you are, Creeley. Duckboards are a bloody mess, slipping and sliding like a bloody vaudeville act. Get 'em sorted out.'

'Yes, sir.'

'On second thoughts, you may not need to bother. The company's been asked to find an officer to make good the losses for the 21st and 24th divisions. The word from on high is that you'd be just the chap. MC and all that. The men'll respect you from the off.'

'You want to transfer me?' Tom's voice was shocked, but also belligerent.

'Not want to, old boy. God knows who they'll give me in your place. Some bloody milliner from Bristol, I expect. Thinks a bayonet is a bloody crochet hook. Not forward march, forward stitch, more like. But no use in arguing. We answer to the King, the King answers to God, and God answers to Sir Douglas Haig. Yes sir, no sir, at the double sir.'

'I won't go.'

Fletcher suddenly caught the tone of Tom's voice, the glare in his eye. Fletcher's tone changed as well. 'If you're told to go, you will go, Creeley. And when you speak to me, you will address me as "sir".'

'Yes, sir, but may I say that I won't go anywhere without

Montague. I don't mind going anywhere, but I go with him or not at all.'

'You do not tell me what I may and may not do, Creeley. I'm putting your name forward to Colonel McIntosh tomorrow morning and to hell with you. And sort out those bloody duckboards.'

Tom let Fletcher go, then burst from his dugout.

'Watkins,' he yelled, 'Watkins.'

A corporal came running.

'Sir?'

'Get those bloody duckboards sorted out. They're sliding around like a vaudeville act. And if anyone asks for me, tell them I'm seeing the medics.'

He began to climb over the parapet to the rear, preferring the relatively open country between the trench systems to the muddy darkness of the trenches themselves. It was an unnecessarily dangerous route, but Tom was in no mood for caution.

'Yes, sir . . . Should I tell them what's wrong with you?'

Tom was already mostly gone from view, but he turned round to yell his answer. 'Certainly you should. You should tell them I've got a bloody arse for a cousin.'

He disappeared into the night.

And if there had been any doubt before, there was none left now. Fate had set her trap. The three men – Alan, Tom and Guy – had acted as they were bound to act. What followed, however disastrous, was certain to happen. Only a miracle could save them now.

19

At two in the morning, a motorcycle roared up outside a pleasant residential street in Arras. Late in October, the gardens were nothing more than a collection of black and dripping twigs, bounded on the street side by iron railings. Out in the street, a silvery motor-car stood in quiet splendour.

Tom stopped the motorbike, slammed the garden gate open, and struck the lion's head knocker on the front door with three or four crashing blows. A few seconds passed without response, and Tom struck again, smashing the stillness of the night.

'*C'est qui, ça? Mon Dieu, je viens, je viens.*'

From outside, Tom could hear the heavy door being unlocked, and as soon as the last lock was turned, he thrust the door open and entered. He strode past the housekeeper – sleepy, outraged, in dressing gown and curling papers – and stormed upstairs. He didn't know which room he was looking for and flung open doors and slammed them shut again, until he came to the front room of the first floor. There was Guy, in pyjamas and his uniform tunic, standing at his dressing table, checking his revolver. As the door crashed against the wall, Guy turned with his hand just inches from his gun.

'Stay right there,' cried Guy. 'Don't advance another step.'

His hand was on the gun now, altering its position on the dressing table so he could snatch it up easily.

'Leave the gun alone, you fool,' said Tom.

'Why have you come here? Who gave you permission to leave your post?' Guy was backing away from Tom, towards his bedside, where a candle flickered smokily.

'It was your idea to separate me from Alan, wasn't it? You can't bloody leave things alone, can you?'

'It wasn't my idea to slaughter the 21st and 24th. The poor bastards need officers. The idea at HQ is that we should give them chaps with a decent fighting record. Chaps like you.'

'Alan's every bit as good as me and you know it. Better. He looks after his men better than I do. He'll keep his head better if it comes to an offensive. I personally don't give a damn which division I serve in. I don't care which pointless battle I'm sent to die in. But I will not be separated from Alan. *Will not.* Not by anyone and least of all by you.'

Guy had grown calmer now that his fear of an outright assault had passed. Something like his customary smirking crept back into his manner.

'It wasn't me that made the decision, was it? And though we need to bring in new officers, we don't want to unsettle existing battalions, let alone take two officers from a single company. So it's you or Alan, but not both. And that isn't my decision, it's Haig's. You can go and argue it out with him, if you want. He's just four streets away.' He gave Tom the address.

Tom ignored the sneer. He paced around the room, which was of a pleasant size and pleasantly furnished – a far cry from the squalor of a front-line dugout. Tom fingered the silver-backed hairbrushes, which lay next to the revolver on the dressing table.

'Alan thinks you don't really hate me,' he murmured. 'He thinks it's just an act you put on. But I know you better than that, Cousin Guy, and it's because I know you that you hate me.' Tom's fingers had wandered from the hairbrushes to the gun. His thumb flicked the safety catch off, on, off, on, off, on.

'Leave that,' said Guy unsteadily.

'I know who you are, Cousin Guy,' said Tom again. He lifted the revolver, took the safety catch off and cocked it. He pointed it straight at Guy's head. Guy was on the far side of the room, but it was an unmissable distance.

'Put that down,' said Guy, dry-mouthed. 'Put it down. That's an order.'

'Down? Like this?'

Tom lowered the gun until it was pointing at Guy's groin. The barrel gleamed dully in the meagre candlelight. The aim didn't waver by even a fraction of an inch. Guy stood, mouth open, perfectly still, slightly on tiptoe, as though he could deceive the bullet into passing underneath him between his legs. Tom, meantime, looked hardly threatening; meditative, rather; calm. After a second or two, Tom dropped the gun back on the table behind him. The heavy metal clattered loudly on the waxed mahogany. Guy relaxed. His mouth closed and he came down from tiptoe.

'You think I'm asking you a favour for my benefit,' continued Tom, as though nothing had happened. 'You think I'm asking because I can't bear to be without Alan. That's not true. Of course I want to be with him. He's worth a hundred others, and he's worth ten thousand like you – but he needs me, he *needs* me if he's to survive this war. I don't know why, but that's how it is. You can do whatever the hell you want to me, Cousin Guy, but if you want to keep your brother, you'll keep us together.'

'You could be shot for this.' Guy's voice was husky, little more than a croak.

'Oh, and one other thing. It's no great odds to me, but I know Alan would prefer not to be separated from his men. He's not quick to win their liking, but now he's got it, he'd be desperately loath to start the whole business again from scratch. As they are now, his men would walk through fire for him.'

'It really isn't up to me.'

'No. I don't expect it is. But you're a highly thought-of staff officer with the ear of General Haig. You can sort this out if you want to, just as you helped create this situation in the first place.'

'I can't promise anything.'

Tom smiled. His hand was on the door. 'You don't have to. When you wake up, you'll remember that I deserted my post on the front line, stole a motorcycle, broke into your room, and pointed a loaded revolver at your head. So you'll do everything you can, won't you, cousin?' Tom didn't wait for an answer. He opened the door, and, for the second time that night, brushed aside the night-gowned housekeeper who had been listening at the door. His footsteps marched off across the landing and down the stairs. 'Don't forget, cousin, I know who you are.'

Ten seconds later, a motorcycle roared into life and shot off into the enclosing night.

~

It wasn't long before Tom was proved right.

Five days later, Major Fletcher loped his way ape-like into Tom's dugout.

'Good news for you, Creeley. Mix-up at HQ. You're sticking here instead of buggering off to the 21st. It's a bloody shame from my point of view, though.'

'I beg your pardon?!'

'Won't be able to get my millinery done for free. What? What? What?'

Fletcher roared with laughter at his joke and dug down amongst Tom's belongings to find the bottle of whisky he kept there. Shellfire, heavier than usual that night, thumped the air and sent shock waves through the ground. Particles of chalk fell from the ceiling. Fletcher poured the whisky into a couple of mugs.

The earth quaked around them. They drank.

20

Incident and consequence. Cause and effect. Each effect becoming in its turn the trigger of a whole new cycle.

A trench raid. A medal honourably won. A need for officers. Guy seeking to separate Tom from Alan. Tom breaking in on Guy. A junior officer pointing a loaded gun at a senior officer's head. The causes started out small, hardly visible even. But the effects were no longer so small.

And they were growing all the time.

Beechnuts crunched underfoot. It was the first hard frost of November and ice glittered on the empty twigs. The forest felt like a fairy-tale wood. The two men walked a good distance, chatting about a hundred things, but it was only when they were deep into the forest silence that Alan finally brought up the subject that had been plaguing him.

'I happened to see Guy in the village the other day,' he said.

'Oh?'

'He had some extraordinary story about you and that transfer to the 21st.'

'Yes?'

'That you thought he had been behind the transfer instruction in the first place, that you wanted him to reverse the decision.'

'Perfectly true.'

'And that you burst in on him waving a gun.'

Tom laughed. 'Almost. I *did* burst in on him. I didn't have a gun on me. He had one on his dressing table, which I think he'd started to load when he heard me come in downstairs. I did point that at him briefly. I don't really know why.'

He was completely without embarrassment. Alan stared at him incredulously. 'You aimed a loaded gun at him?'

'Yes – at least I assume it was loaded. I didn't really bother to check. Look at this.' Tom eased some leaves aside with his toe and revealed the gleam of copper wire by a bare root. It was a trap laid for rabbits. 'Neat job, eh? Here, what about this?' Tom pulled a salami from his pocket that the two men had been intending to eat for lunch. Tom slipped the sausage through the loop of wire and drew the wire tight. He scattered leaves back as they had been before. Tom began to shake with laughter at the thought of the trapper returning to find his catch.

'Tom! For God's sake!'

'What? I'd be damn pleased to trap a sausage.'

'Not the trap, you idiot. Guy. You aimed a gun at him?' Alan was shocked. He was also upset and torn, as he always was when Tom and Guy quarrelled.

'Yes. I don't think he enjoyed it much. But it did the trick, didn't it?'

'But for heaven's sake! You can't just go waving a gun at him. What in hell's name did you think you were playing at?'

Tom's nonchalant attitude suddenly disappeared. Alan had begun to shout and he had a tendency to sound preachy and schoolmasterly when he was angry about something. Tom never put up with that and he didn't now.

'I'll tell you what I think,' he said coldly. 'I think – no, that's not right, I *know* – that your so-called brother wanted to see us separated, and I knew that I could frighten him into undoing the damage. What's more –'

'But you *can't* just aim a gun at him.' Alan was angry and his voiced was raised. 'You have to learn some limits. Guy has his faults but he *is* my brother –'

'Oh? He's your brother, is he? So what the hell was he thinking of then, separating the two of us?'

'You've no evidence that he ever wanted to separate –'

'No, you're quite right. And after all, as you point out, he is your brother so he couldn't possibly wish to hurt you.'

'Listen, whatever else he may or may not be, Guy is family – *my* family, I mean, and –'

'Your family? *Your* family? What am I then? What am I? The fucking gardener's boy?' Tom was shouting, his breath building storm castles in the freezing air. He was extremely angry.

'For God's sake, Tom! Calm down! If you'd mentioned your suspicions to me I could have had a word. It didn't need you to aim a bloody –'

'And just possibly you're wrong. Had you thought of that? Perhaps aiming a gun at his head was just precisely what *was* needed. Or is your bloody good nature going to get in the way of seeing straight every time there's a problem?'

Up till now both men had been panting with the effort of the argument. They were shouting hard at each other and Alan had unconsciously picked up a stick as though intending to assault Tom with it.

They felt ready to murder each other.

And then, as so often in the past, the anger slid away as though it had never been. The bottom dropped out of their rage and calmness returned. Though he wouldn't admit it – not even to himself, perhaps – Alan knew that Tom was right. Alan's reliance on decency and fair play would never have had the impact on Guy that a loaded gun would have had.

'Listen, old fellow,' said Alan. 'You and I have always been close. Closer to each other than to anyone else. Guy doesn't get a look-in. But when all's said and done, and whatever Guy did or didn't do, I think –'

'He *did* do it. I *know* he did.'

'Well, even so, I could have spoken with him. It didn't –'

'And he'd have told you that the whole matter had nothing to do with him and you'd have believed him. You always do.'

They walked a few paces more in silence. Alan looked long and hard at some animal tracks. Hare. He could see fox tracks as well. If he listened carefully, he could hear the almost silent animals of the forest: the cautious footfalls of the deer, the quiet munching of the rabbits, the tapping of woodpeckers in the trees. He looked up.

'Take care, brother,' he said. 'You play a dangerous game at times.'

Tom smiled brilliantly and gave an airy wave. 'That's what comes of being a gardener's son. Nothing to lose.'

He was wrong, of course. And it wouldn't be long before he knew it.

21

It was nine months later, 10 August 1916.

Alan and Tom were both alive, both intact. That was the good news.

Meanwhile, the war was continuing. The Battle of the Somme was in progress. In the last six weeks alone, a hundred thousand British soldiers had been killed or wounded. So far, Tom and Alan's battalion had been kept out of the conflict, but that happy interval was about to end. The battalion was due to attack the very next day. The fighting would be as severe as anything the two men had ever experienced. Casualties were certain to be high. Perhaps colossal.

That was the bad news.

And, in a way, it was untrue to say that both men had survived intact. They hadn't. They couldn't. No man survives life in the combat zone for very long. Nerves shred. Humanity frays. The spirit fails.

Of the two men, Alan had been worse affected. Devoted to his men, he often pushed himself too hard. Too serious to unwind easily, he found relaxation difficult. He smoked. He rode. He wrote letters home.

And he'd found a girl.

Called Lisette, she was pretty, dark-haired, smiling and

kind. They'd met by accident one day in a village seven miles behind the lines, Ste Thérèse-sur-Tarne ('Saint Tess' to the men). He was billeted there. She was the daughter of one of the local farmers. Caught outside during a rainstorm, he helped her home. They ran into her farmhouse, shared some coffee, laughed together. She invited him back. And back. After three visits, he could take a hint. Excited and embarrassed in about equal measure, he undressed in her little bedroom. They made love. During the rest of the fortnight that Alan was in Saint Tess, they met on a further nine occasions, making love on eight of them.

The evening before the assault found the battalion sheltering in the wreck of what had once been a village. The officers' mess was a ruined cellar, whose entrance was neatly flanked by two rows of shell cases, graduated in size, ranging up to the height of a man.

Tom was still Tom. He was handsome, brilliant, unmilitary, courageous. But over time, his outlook had blackened. He lounged against the cellar wall, barely protected by the sandbag parapet in front of him. He picked up a flint and threw it out beyond the sandbags.

'A fine place to die,' he commented.

'For God's sake!'

Alan jumped to find a piece of wood to ward off Tom's unlucky words. A discarded crate lay nearby and Alan passed a chunk of it to Tom, who touched it absently. The side of the crate was marked in English: 'Shell Motor Spirit'. Tom nodded at the marking and smiled.

'Good choice.'

'Let's get out there right away, shall we?' said Alan. 'After the war, I mean. Not wait any longer.' He meant get out to Persia, of course.

Tom laughed and shook his head.

'What?' said Alan defensively. 'You can't want to go back

86

to Standard, can you? Lord knows, I couldn't stand to be cooped up in somebody else's office.'

Tom laughed again, kindly this time. 'That's not what I meant, old man. I meant . . . Look, you don't think we'll both survive this, do you?' Tom spoke quietly, talking almost to himself. 'But there are worse things, after all.'

'Tom, for God's sake!'

'If I'm to die, I've decided to fight like a maniac first. Take a few Boche with me.'

'Don't speak like that. Don't even think like that.'

Tom shrugged. 'I haven't always thought like that. This whole damned war is so stupid, I couldn't see much purpose in trying to fight it hard. I still can't, in a way, except that one has one's self-respect to think of.' He flicked his white and purple medal ribbon thoughtfully, then his tone changed again. 'If I am killed, will you promise to do what you can in Persia?'

'Of course.'

'Drill. If there's oil, you'll find it. If there isn't – well, at least you'll have tried.'

'We'll find it together.'

'You're probably right. Dead or alive, I'll be there in spirit. But promise me, brother. Your most sacred promise.'

'I promise.'

'And don't give the damn thing away to a bunch of stupid stockmarket investors. I mean, you'll have to at some point. But not straight away. Find the oil first.'

'The oil first, if humanly possible.'

Tom gravely nodded his acceptance. 'Good. Good man.'

The way he said it, it sounded like goodbye.

22

The battalion moved off at eight that evening. Its goal: a full-frontal attack on enemy positions.

It was pitch-black and raining, and the ground was evil. Three times, artillery fire forced the company to flatten itself into whatever cover was available. Each time the shelling lifted, the company moved forwards again, leaving a small handful of wounded men behind. On one occasion, Alan was struck with a shell splinter, shaped like a goose quill, in his shoulder blade. An NCO lying in the ditch next to him tweaked it out with finger and thumb and threw it away. Neither man commented on the incident, or was even thinking about it five minutes later.

They reached their designated position shortly after midnight. The men ate rations from their packs and were given permission to rest until four.

The rain settled in and grew heavier. Time moved with agonising slowness.

At four o'clock, a thunder of British artillery opened up behind them, and they could hear the torrent of shells crashing down on German positions. The men listened in silence: half pleased at the thought of what the shells were doing to the enemy, half terrified because of what this implied for the coming offensive. Alan stayed with his men. Although Tom was close by, he might as well have been on another planet for all Alan knew of him.

Four thirty approached. The rain was beginning to fall more gently and a meagre grey light began testing its options on the eastern horizon. Alan's eyes struggled to follow the luminous figures on his watch. The second hand swept remorselessly round. And finally, it was four thirty precisely. Alan raised his hand and dropped it: the signal to advance.

His men moved off. For several seconds, there was silence – beautiful silence. Then, almost simultaneously, three flares rose from the German-held salient. The flares disclosed what the German defenders already suspected. There was a trickle of rifle fire, then a din of machine guns, then the extraordinary violence of concentrated shelling. Air became metal. The noise was so indescribably loud that the sense of hearing fell away until it was almost like walking into silence.

Alan saw the men next to him hold their positions, just as they'd been drilled. No clustering together, no turning human lives into simple targets for German gunners. But the men walked as though into a gale. Bent over. Doubled up.

As he watched his men, he saw one of them struck full in the chest and sink to his knees with a soft 'Ah!' of release. Another man bent down, apparently to fiddle with his boot-laces, but he bent too far and slid to earth with dark red tongues of blood where his face should have been. All around, men were falling when they should be walking. Alan watched in mounting amazement and shock. His platoon was being destroyed, his beloved men massacred, soldierlike and courageous to the end.

Still they advanced.

Alan had no real recollection of the next few hours. Only by midday did the true situation unfold. The attack had largely failed. The attackers had bitten off a chunk of German line at huge cost. The two opposing artilleries screamed at each other. In the chaos of collapsed and broken trenches, both sides attempted to reconfigure their defences.

The day passed.

The list of known casualties was appalling. More than half of Alan's men had been killed or wounded. So had all of his NCOs. So too with Major Fletcher, whose left arm had been torn off by a shell, and who had been found sitting upright in the mud, holding his arm between his knees, repeating endlessly, 'My poor boys, my poor bloody boys . . .'

There was no word of Tom.

For two more nights and days the fighting continued. Alan was tired beyond tired, shattered beyond endurance. And then finally, he was given permission to rest.

The permission came in the form of a German *Minenwerfer*, which hurled through the air looking something like a flying dustbin, but a bin packed with enormous destructive power. The canister detonated twelve yards away on the unprotected side of the parapet. Afterwards, Alan thought he recalled seeing the flash of detonation before it reached him, but supposed he must have provided details of the explosion from his imagination.

And that was all.

The flash – then silence. No pain. No slow fade-out into unconsciousness. Simply a plunge into blackness. Total blackness.

And still no word of Tom.

23

Alan woke in a tent full of iron beds and soldiers. The atmosphere was foetid with the smell of hot air under canvas and the odours of blood, iodine and unwashed clothes. Men in the tent next to Alan and in other tents and huts beyond groaned and called out in their sleep.

Alan stretched himself gingerly. He felt indescribably sore. Although nothing felt broken or missing, Alan knew that wounded men were often unaware how badly wounded they were. He wriggled in his narrow cot, trying to get an arm down to reach his feet under their coarse army-issue blankets. He was so stiff that the effort made him pant. He finally managed it, however, and ran his hand over his toes. Nothing.

He sank back in bed, temporarily satisfied. The men in the 'moribund ward' often had red labels tied to their toes to indicate their status. There seemed nothing like that here.

He slept.

At dawn, he woke again, when a doctor, a major in the RAMC, was making his rounds.

'Am I hurt?' said Alan. His mouth worked awkwardly – even his jaw ached like hell – and the words came out as if spoken by a foreigner. The doctor reached for a pulse. The pressure of his thumb was painful and Alan felt as if he could feel the passage of blood up and down his arm.

'Hurt? Yes, that's why you're here.' The doctor kept his thumb on Alan's wrist a few moments longer. 'You were caught in a shell blast. Cuts and bruises everywhere, a few places that needed stitching. But that's on the outside. We can't always tell what's happened inside. The blast can kill without puncturing the skin. You're to stay in bed here for twenty-four hours at least. If there's no sign of any problems by then, we'll release you to one of the general hospitals. But I don't want to see you in the line again. Is that clear?'

Alan nodded. He felt a wave of relief and the urge to giggle. He shoved his head into his pillow to muffle any sound, and the doctor and nurse left in silence, too busy to pry.

24

Two men from one of the New Army battalions of the Royal Scots escorted Alan to the hospital. Alan tried to thank them, but he couldn't find the right words. He fell into bed and slept for six hours. When he woke, he ate, drank, then tried to sleep again.

He couldn't.

His emotions were blocked, like a flood that has blocked its own path with a jam of fallen trunks, boulders and landslip. He was filled with an indescribable sense of loss. He thought about his beloved platoon, about Major Fletcher, about how nothing would ever be the same again. And he kept dreaming about Tom. He asked the nurses if they knew whether Lieutenant Creeley was alive, dead or wounded. They didn't know.

For three days, he lay in hospital. As for his own well-being, it became clear that he wasn't dying, that he wasn't permanently crippled. The doctors advised plenty of rest and predicted complete recovery.

Alan wasn't so sure. He'd never known himself to feel like this – or rather *not* to feel like this. He ate what he could (not much) and drank (a huge amount). He slept, fainted or dozed through sixteen hours in twenty-four. He could think clearly, or at any rate, he was able to answer correctly the questions put to him by the RAMC doctors: name, rank, place of birth, regiment. But his feelings were gone, both physical and emotional. He lay as if doused in an anaesthetic that reached all the way to his heart.

Then one morning, he woke up. For the first time, the images that swam around his consciousness resolved themselves into just two: Tom and Lisette. He had to know if Tom was dead or alive. He had to see Lisette.

He climbed out of bed, dressed, and went outside, falling four times and clutching at the walls of the hospital like a drunk. By chance, he found a transport captain he'd once had dealings with and was able to beg himself a ride to Saint Tess.

The village had changed. Lightly wounded men were everywhere. The Lincolnshires and London Irish, who'd been billeted there a few days before, had all gone now, either fighting or dead. There were new voices now: pink-faced boys from the Ox and Bucks Light Infantry and a company of fit-looking Canadians. A group of cows had broken into an apple orchard, and some of the Canadians were throwing the hard green apples at their flanks to try to cause a stampede.

Alan sat down in the village square. His body felt as though it had been dismantled and reassembled. A man in major's uniform approached him: a good-looking officer with a drawn and tired expression. The major's face lit up as he recognised Alan.

'Alan, man! Thank God! What on earth . . . ?'

'I'm sorry, sir,' mumbled Alan. 'Do I . . . ?'

'Alan, it's me. Guy. Your brother.'

'Guy! Good God! You look . . .'

'Are you all right, old man?'

'Yes, perfectly, just a little muzzy. How do you do?'

'Alan, you've been in hospital, have you? Did you take a knock?'

'Something like that.' Alan raised his hand and fluttered it down. '*Wheeee*-BANG!'

Guy looked his brother up and down, checking for signs of obvious injury. Apart from some violently coloured bruises, there was little enough.

'Thank God you're all right! I've been worried sick. Staff haven't heard a straight word from anyone and all I knew was your crowd was in the thick of the whole bloody shemozzle. I got word that you'd been hit, but the RAMC weren't able to tell me where you were, let alone how you were.'

The two brothers embraced. Later on, looking back on it, Alan was genuinely surprised by the warmth of Guy's feeling.

'And Tom? What about Tom? Where's Tom? Don't tell me –'

'Alan, old chap, Tom's absolutely fine. He made it up to German lines – unlike most of his men – and held on to his bit of trench despite a pretty nasty counterattack by Fritz. He was relieved three days ago, completely unhurt. He's been going out of his mind trying to find out what happened to you.'

'Thank God. Thank bloody Jesus. Thank . . . Thank . . . Thank . . . and he's hurt, you say? How badly? How . . . ?'

'No. Completely unhurt, I told you.'

Alan made a face, as though ready to argue. His breath came in hard pants that hurt his lungs.

'Don't you think you should still be lying down?' said Guy. 'Why the hell did the medics let you go anyway?'

'The whole platoon went down? The poor bloody platoon!' Alan was upset now. He began reciting the names of the men who'd been under Tom's command.

'Let's get you home.'

'Not hurt? Not wounded?'

'Typical of the gardener's boy, eh? No, completely unhurt. Not a scratch. Now come on back.'

Alan giggled in relief, but his emotions were still all over the place. He was laughing but could just as easily be crying. 'Sounds like he's the hero once again. You must have been pleased to see him. *So* pleased. *Soooo* pleased.'

'Mmm,' Guy agreed, without enthusiasm. Tom's extra-ordinary record through four days of intense fighting had been somewhat muddied by a blazing row he'd had with one of the brigadier's aides on the day of his return to the rear. Tom, incensed by the massacre he'd been in the middle of, had accused High Command of butchery. He'd more or less called Haig a murderer. It had taken Guy's intervention to prevent Tom from getting into serious disciplinary trouble. 'He can be a damn fool, that man. Now look, old chap, you're looking awfully queer. Don't you think you'd better –'

But Alan's mood had become suddenly belligerent. 'You're the fool, a big bloody fool. And what's worse, much worse, you're a bloody staff officer fool.'

Guy's voice tautened. He could see Alan was hardly himself, but it was dangerous territory that he was entering. 'Alan, that's enough –'

'Bloody staff officers. Just as Tom says. Bloody, skulking, yellow, behind-the-lines, staff bloody –'

'Stop it!' Guy gripped his brother's arm, attempting to swing him back round to the village. 'I'm taking you home. You need some –'

'No, I don't.' There was a roaring in his ears and a buzzy quality to his vision. He suddenly thought of Lisette, and wanted her with a passionate longing, rejoicing in the knowledge that if Tom was alive, then everything in the whole wide world would be all right. He pushed Guy away with both hands.

'Don't touch me. There's someone I need to see . . . I have to go.'

Guy looked at his brother with sudden acuteness. 'You've got a girl, have you? *You*?'

'"I've got a little lady by the name of Sue,"' sang Alan. 'Not Sue actually, Lisette.' He was babbling. He waved at the farmhouse where she lived. 'Lisette, Lisette.'

'That farm? The one just there, with the red-painted gables?' Guy's tone was half urgent, half incredulous.

'That farm there.'

A delighted smile spread across Guy's face. He released his grip so suddenly that Alan tottered and almost fell.

'Go on then. Go.'

'I'm going.'

'Go to your precious Lisette. You'll see just how precious she is. Her and your beloved twin.'

And Guy escorted Alan the two hundred yards to the farm. Before they were even halfway, Alan lost his desire to go there. He wanted to see Tom and he wanted to sleep. 'Lisette will be there for me in the morning,' he chanted.

But Guy's determination was fixed. When Alan's feet stumbled and dragged, Guy lifted him bodily, so anxious was he to get Alan to the farmhouse door. When Guy finally had Alan propped against the doorpost, he left him there, saying, 'Go on, go in. I'm sure your arrival will be a delightful surprise. I'll catch up with you later, old man. Toodle-oo.'

The farm door was never locked and Alan let himself in. The range was warm and a couple of cakes, yellow and creamy with egg, were cooling on the sideboard, a wire net over them. Lisette wasn't there, probably out. Alan felt too happy to think. He was safe. Tom was safe. And nothing else in the whole world mattered.

There was some old coffee cooling in a pot. Alan drank it. The smell jerked at a memory. 'Mind the bloody coffee' – Major Fletcher – polished leather boots on a map-covered chest – loping monkey arms – 'Keep your own bloody head from being shot off' – then nothing: just a poor sod with his left arm loose between his knees and all his precious company lying dead about him.

Alan lifted the mesh from the cakes and stole a piece. It was good cake and he ate hungrily, before noticing that the cat was eating hungrily too. He chased the cat off and replaced the mesh. Upstairs, there was a sound: a creaking of floorboards and laughter. Of course! Idiot! Naturally, Lisette would still be upstairs. Why not? It was morning. What better place to be than bed?

Alan went upstairs, using his hands as well as his feet to avoid falling on the steep wooden staircase. The sound of laughter was louder now.

'Lisette?' Alan bounded along a corridor and burst through a door. 'Lisette!'

The word died in his throat. There in bed lay not one person but two. Lisette and, next to her, naked and at home, was Tom.

25

There was a moment's silence. All three people were shocked. In that tiny gap of time, nothing had yet been said, no damage done, no lives ruined.

The moment didn't last.

Alan's emotions looped again. An indescribable fury surged through him. 'You bastard!' he screamed. 'You thieving, sodding, bloody bastard!'

Alan flung himself at Tom, fists flailing, blind with hot tears of rage. Tom defended himself. Although Alan was hitting with all his strength, he was exhausted and weak, and his lungs were rasping for breath. Tom slid from bed, grabbed his clothes and attempted to hide from the hail of blows. He didn't fight back.

'You bastard! You steal every fucking thing that matters to me! Lisette was all I had! All I wanted was Lisette.'

'Alan, old chap – steady on – I didn't know you were coming back.'

'*Alain, tais-toi, sois sage!*' cried Lisette, frightened and appealing for calm.

'Everything that ever matters.'

'Jesus, brother. There's no need. You can have her. I didn't –'

'I don't want to have her because you say I can. I don't

want . . .' Alan's attack was hardly serious now. Tom struggled to get his trousers on, keeping Alan at a distance with his stronger right arm. Lisette helped as well as she could.

'Guy was out there, wasn't he? Why in hell didn't he keep you away? He knew I was here.'

'Guy? He knew, oh yes, he knew. He carried me here. *Carried* me. So I would know who you were. And I know now, all right. I *know*.'

Tom was dressed from the waist down now and had his hands on his boots. 'Take care, Alan, take care what you say.'

Alan steadied himself with his back against the chalky limewashed wall. Although his face was purple with bruises, adrenaline had given him more control than he'd had with Guy. His extreme shock and nervous collapse was no longer obvious. It was easy for Tom to mistake him for a man upset, but otherwise in control of his faculties.

'What I mean is,' said Alan, speaking as distinctly as he was able, 'that Guy has been right about you all along. You have some fine things about you, no doubt, but in the end you're the sodding little gardener's boy. Please get your hands off my girl and get out of here.'

'Alan, for God's sake, be careful. Some things can't be unsaid, you know.'

'Alan, *s'il te plaît*, calm down, I'll make you coffee, I'll explain.' Lisette implored Alan for calm, but the situation had travelled too far.

Alan tried to pull a revolver, but he managed to snag the barrel as he pulled it from its holster, and the gun clattered uselessly to the ground. Tom snatched the gun up and tossed it out of the window into the cattle trough below.

Alan lurched to the doorway and steadied himself on the doorpost. 'Guy is my brother. You're a gardener's boy who fucks my girl.' He shook his head. 'And by the way, I'm never going to drill in Persia with you. Why would I? As far as I know, the concession belongs to the Montague family. It doesn't belong to the fucking staff.'

He stumbled away, slipping on the fourth step of the staircase and crashing all the way to the bottom. He dragged himself back to the village, found an empty bed and fell into it. He was asleep within three seconds of his head hitting the pillow.

And here was the odd thing.

He slept well. He slept without dreams, without pain, without fogginess or delirium. It was a strange way to sleep the day the world collapsed.

26

Tom buttoned his shirt. His hands were shaking violently. His face was ash.

'I didn't know you were friends,' said Lisette, begging pardon from the world. 'I didn't know . . . he was such a nice man, I really adored him.'

'Don't worry. Not your fault,' said Tom in French, before adding in English, 'Damnation. I had no idea he . . . Dammit, *dammit.*'

Tom sat on the bed and tried to calm down. *Guy is my brother. You're a gardener's boy who fucks my girl.* He pushed the words away, but what Alan had said was too big to be so easily dismissed. *I'm never going to drill in Persia with you. Why would I? As far as I know, the concession belongs to the Montague family. It doesn't belong to the fucking staff.* Tom breathed heavily, trying to calm himself. Alan was shocked. Alan was upset. Alan was talking rot –

'Will he be all right?' said Lisette, interrupting his thoughts.

'Look, he's just come from battle. It's awful up there. He's a sensitive sod at the best of times, and as for girls, he's never . . . well, I don't think that before you, he's even –'

'No, never. I had to teach him everything.'

'*Shit!*' Tom was doubly angry because he felt guilty. He'd

known Alan was seeing Lisette and until recently he'd been careful to avoid seeing her too. But the last three days had been from hell. Tom had known that Alan had been hit, but, like Guy, he'd had no end of a time finding out where Alan was and in what condition. When he'd finally heard that Alan was essentially fine, his relief had been over-powering. In some strange way, Tom had felt drawn to seek out Lisette, the one other person who had been truly inti-mate with Alan. He'd gone in search of her and charmed his way into her kitchen. He'd had no intention of making love with her, but Tom wasn't very strong-willed in the matter of sex and, in any event, with Alan safely in hospital, it didn't seem to matter all that much. He should have known better.

They were quiet a moment. Then Lisette kissed Tom on the earlobe. He smiled and stroked her shoulder.

'Do you go with many other men?' he asked.

She thumped him gently on the bicep. '*Cochon*.' Pig.

'But really?'

'Some. A few.'

'For money, I suppose?'

'Usually. Not with him. Never with him.'

'With me?'

She shook her head.

'He had no idea, none at all . . . Look I'll give him time to get over all this. Explain it. I'd better not see you again. I won't if it means upsetting Alan.'

'What is that about brothers? You are or you aren't?'

Tom explained briefly, ending by saying 'Guy's his blood brother, I'm his real brother. He knows that. In solemn truth, he knows that.'

'And will it be all right?'

Tom nodded, kicking his bare feet out on the unvarnished floorboards. He was annoyed with himself for his stupidity, but he was furious with Guy for provoking things. Anger boiled inside him, hot and dangerous.

'Well? It will be all right?'

Tom sighed heavily. 'Yes. It'll be all right.'

And once again, he was wrong, dead wrong.

It was getting to be a habit.

27

It was the following day: 19 August.

Tom was back in the support trenches when the fighting resumed. He was making a report to brigade staff, short of sleep, and stained with sweat, blood and dirt. The sound of fighting ended the brief conference. Tom excused himself, received a brusque, 'Carry on then, Creeley,' and raced on up the line.

It was an evil day. It felt like the first cold day of autumn, with enough rain to have soaked everything and given the air a biting edge. A wicked little breeze carried the smoke of guns over the battlefield, until everything was seen through the greenish, cordite-smelling glow. The wet chalk was slippery and unreliable. The way ran uphill and the trench bottom had become a gutter for rainwater, mud, rats, and blood.

Tom made his way up the trench, fast but with care. He passed two men digging it out, trying to repair a collapsed parapet, and another man who was heaving a Lewis gun into place at the bottom end. Tom charged on past, and, going too fast round a corner, clattered into none other than Guy, who'd been running fast in the other direction.

It was an extraordinary coincidence: not that they should meet, but that they should meet in a trench. Guy, as a staff officer, hardly ever entered a front-line position, still less during a time of heavy combat. But, Tom remembered, the divisional telephone exchange had been completely smashed during earlier shelling, and he supposed the divisional staff must have been desperate to obtain a reliable picture of action on the ground.

Both Private Hemplethwaite, in charge of the Lewis gun, and Privates Jones and Carragher, who were then shovelling out the fallen trench, saw what happened next. The two officers had a blazing argument. The older officer was trying to push past and the younger man was physically restraining him, pushing and throwing him back against the wall of the trench. The noise of the shelling was too loud to catch any words, but it was clear that they were shouting at each other.

The younger man began hitting the other. Hard, forceful slaps, which the other man defended himself against by putting his arms to his face. The older man kept trying to get past. The older man didn't once offer any violence at all to the younger.

Then it happened.

All three men were absolutely unanimous on the fact. The younger man drew his revolver. He pointed it at the other man's head. The older man drew back, making a gesture of surrender. The younger man was still shouting. He seemed extraordinarily angry. The noise of battle continued to drown the sounds. Then the younger man lowered his gun until it was pointing at the other's groin, or thereabouts. There was a shot. The shot was perfectly deliberate and at close range. A bloody rosette leaped into the khaki flannels. The older man jumped backwards as the bullet tore into his thigh. The younger man, a lieutenant, holstered his revolver, took one last furious look at the other and tore onwards up the line. Dark blood began to soak down the older man's leg.

And that was it.

Tom raced away up the trench. Guy came staggering down, his face white as a sheet, incoherent with shock, anger, and fear.

28

The fighting remained fierce until nightfall.

On a few bloodstained acres, too many men lay dead or dying. The air was heavy with the weight of shells and bullets. For the first time since coming to France, Tom found himself longing for the bullet wound that would send him home to England, away from the fighting.

Night came.

Tom posted sentries, praying that the Germans were as exhausted as their opponents. He desperately wanted whisky, but was pleased not to have any. This night of all nights, he'd be too likely to get drunk, when the last thing he needed was a muzzy head.

He was furious with Guy.

Furious. Far from relieving his feelings, the incident in the trenches had simply added to his fury. He'd shot Guy and hadn't even killed him. Tom's anger remained hopelessly unsatisfied, but his action had now put him into a position where Guy could, and quite likely would, have Tom court-martialled. There was only one sentence for firing on a superior officer and that was death. Tom knew that there were witnesses and he certainly wouldn't be able to rely on their discretion. Perhaps Tom's outstanding war record would make a difference, but Guy was a major and so often these things depended on rank . . .

Again and again that night, Tom relived the incident. He never once regretted firing on Guy, but his fingers curled round the butt of his revolver and he imagined a hundred times the same incident with a different outcome: Guy struck not in the thigh, but in the chest; Guy not harmlessly wounded, but killed outright.

Tom stayed on duty for the first sentry shift. So much had happened, he needed time to think. Somewhere in the afternoon's fighting, he had crushed his pack of cigarettes, but he carefully extricated a couple of the flattened paper tubes and delicately reconstructed them into something smokable. He lit up, throat aching for the taste of warm tobacco.

'Mr Creeley?'

'Yes?'

By the brief flare of his match, Tom could see a man's face – silver-haired but young, grey moustache beneath youthful blue eyes.

'Captain Morgan. Just sent across from the Warwickshires to give you lads support.'

The two men shook hands and Tom handed over the last of his battered cigarettes, lighting it before passing it across.

'Support?' said Tom, mumbling through his cigarette. 'God knows we need it.'

'Look here. I've got some rather rotten news. I'd best spill it. The brigadier wants to sweep the Boche off the salient for good. His idea is, if we can storm their machine-gun posts, we can dare to risk a general assault.'

'The brigadier is a murderous bloody-minded lunatic.'

Captain Morgan laughed, embarrassed at Tom's bluntness, but hardly denying the charge. 'Your name came up,' he said.

'Came up to do what?'

The captain grimaced. 'The guns.'

'To storm their machine guns?'

'Yes. I think it's a damn fool idea myself, but the brigadier seems blessedly keen on it.'

'It's lunatic.'

'I'm terribly sorry, old fellow – bearer of bad tidings and all that. The brigadier wanted you to take a dozen men. Use your own initiative on how to proceed, then get started at once. I'll follow with a full company to support you the moment you've put a stop to those guns.'

Morgan handed over a packet containing written orders that confirmed his summary. Tom read the papers, then tossed them away.

'My initiative? My initiative tells me that the brigadier's lost his bloody marbles.'

The captain swallowed. Even to a newcomer, it was fairly clear that the brigadier's orders were virtually impossible to fulfil.

'I can't say I don't feel for you, old man. I'd have put my own name forward, except that I really don't know the ground here. I must say, I thought the chap who put *your* name forward was a bit of a bounder. It's not really the sort of thing that one fellow volunteers another fellow for.'

'Who put my name forward?'

Captain Morgan paused. He had said more than he should and was kicking himself for it. 'Look, I shouldn't have said anything. It's really not my –'

'But you did. Who was it?'

Captain Morgan paused again, taking a long drag on his cigarette. He burned the tobacco down half an inch, then dropped the butt fizzing into the mud. 'All right, old man. I wouldn't normally say, but given the circs and everything . . . It was a chap called Montague. Mr Montague. I didn't get the first name.'

'*Mister* Montague?' Tom was horrified. 'A subaltern, my age?'

'Yes. What? You have a lot of Montagues, do you?'

'Not a major? We have a lieutenant and a major. Which one?'

109

'Lieutenant, old man. One star on his shoulder, that's all. Positive sighting and all that. Definitely lieutenant.'

'His leg? Was he wounded in the leg at all? A bad flesh wound, very recent? This afternoon?'

'He was sitting down, old boy. I didn't see his leg. But wouldn't he be in hospital with a wound like that? He wouldn't be sitting around with the brig, I don't suppose.'

'No. I suppose he wouldn't.' Tom was more shocked than he could give words to. There were two German machine-gun posts. One of them had been dug into the site of a deep shellhole, built up with sandbags and well wired all round. The other was one of the German gun posts that had survived pretty much undisturbed all through the fighting. The post had been built of poured concrete, ten feet thick and laced through with railway ties and steel bars. Attacking the posts was a short walk to suicide, nothing less. *And Alan had wanted it.* More even than the probability of his impending death – a fact which Tom treated as certain – what shocked him was that Alan wanted it.

Captain Morgan looked at Tom with a depth of feeling in his eyes. Beyond the makeshift parapet, some two hundred yards away the white concrete gun post shone pale in the moonlight. 'I'm terribly sorry, old man. I do wish you the very best of British luck.'

'Thank you.'

'There's nothing I can do, is there? Nothing you need?'

Tom shook his head. 'Just . . . Look, for reasons I can't explain, it matters to me very much indeed – more than I can possibly say – who suggested my name this afternoon. You're perfectly sure it was a Lieutenant Montague?'

Pause.

In the distance a couple of shells boomed, and there was an answering snap of rifles.

'Look, I was at Sandhurst four years ago, made captain last year. I know when to salute the pips and when to look for a salute myself. I'm absolutely positive, old man. I'm sorry.'

Tom nodded.

Another handshake. 'I'd best leave you to it, then.' Morgan began to walk away. A Very light shot up into the sky, and hung there, slowly dropping. The gloomy trench filled with its glow.

'Excuse me, Captain,' called Tom.

'Yes?' Morgan turned.

Tom held out his crumpled cigarette packet. 'I've managed to crush these. You don't have any by chance?'

Morgan felt in his tunic pocket. He had a packet of Woodbines intact and just slightly damp from a shower of rain earlier. 'Take these, old man. You're welcome.'

29

We're the boys of the New Arm-ee.
We cannot fight,
We cannot shoot,
What bloody use are we?
But when we get to Berlin
The Kaiser he will say,
Hoch, hoch, mein Gott!
What a bloody fine lot
Are the boys from the New Arm-ee.

The song in one of its many versions drifted from the slimy dugout steps like the smell of something pleasant. The dugout was one of those captured from the Germans. It was well-built and, as far as these things ever were, comfortable. After a short pause, the song changed to something more melancholy.

Tom swallowed hard. Faced directly with the fact of his imminent death, his long-held attitude of carelessness began to desert him. He didn't want to die. He was desperately keen to live. Perhaps he'd live through the night only to find himself court-martialled in the morning. But he didn't care. He wanted to survive this night. After that, he'd take his chances.

And yet his death wasn't the worst of it. Alan was. Of all

people on earth, Alan Montague had put his name forward for the mission at hand. Tom knew he should never have slept with Lisette, yet Alan's response was so coldly murderous. It was the worst side of Alan, multiplied and exaggerated. This was Alan the nobleman's son, snobbish, self-righteous and detestable.

Tom felt like a stranger in a strange land.

He walked down the dugout steps. There were thirty men crammed down there, exhausted from the day's fighting. Of the thirty, only three or four had had the energy to sing, and then only because there wasn't enough space in the dugout for everyone to lie or even sit.

The men saw the look on Tom's face, and they fell silent, immediately apprehensive. Those who were awake shook the ones who weren't. The dugout came to life and the men stood leaning against the oozing walls or sat on rough wooden benches or on the ground. Light came from a pair of German acetylene lamps, which filled the dugout with their thick petrol fumes. The air was utterly foul, but homely. A couple of rats sat chewing something in the corner.

'Raise your right hands, boys . . . Your right hand, Thompson, not both of them.'

The men silently obeyed.

'Now lower your hands if you have nippers, any children at all.'

Sixteen hands remained aloft.

'Put them down if you have a wife . . . I said a wife, Appleby, not a girl you screw when you're in the mood.'

Ten hands plus Appleby: eleven.

Tom nodded. 'You men come here, the rest of you carry on.' There was complete silence, except for a low muttering as men clambered over each other to exchange positions. ('Sorry mate', 'Careful, that's my fucking hand you're treading on', 'I'd've married the old cow, if I'd known' . . .) Eventually the eleven men found their way to Tom – or eleven boys, to be more accurate, since their average age must have been under twenty-one. Tom's orders required him to take a dozen men, but he'd disobey. A troop of fifty men couldn't take the guns, and he'd be damned if he'd have more blood on his hands than he absolutely had to. Tom took eleven matches from the box in his breast pocket and broke the heads off two of them. He jumbled the sticks and poked the ends out between his thumb and hand.

'Each man take a match.'

The men obeyed, and two ended up with the broken-headed sticks: one sandy-haired, stout but strong, and with a confident look to him; the other was a typical inner-city recruit, poorly fed, short – hardly even five foot four – with a long, pale face. Tom didn't recognise them. Because of the casualties it had suffered so far, the company had been strengthened with other men of the battalion, men Tom didn't yet know.

'Sorry, lads, I haven't got to know your names yet.'

'Stimson, sir,' said the sandy-haired lad.

'Hardwick, sir. The boys call me Shorty,' said the other.

'And what would you like me to call you?'

'Shorty, sir, I suppose. Seems more natural now, like.'

Tom nodded. He took Morgan's cigarette pack from his pocket and offered the two lads cigarettes. They all three lit up.

'Now I've got good news for you both. I've chosen you for a mission, which is going to be difficult and dangerous, but which will mean a medal for each of you, and a thumping great amount of home leave, if I can possibly arrange it. Here's what we have to do . . .'

30

Alan woke up in pain.

Somewhere there was danger; horror even.

He grabbed his revolver and held it out into the darkness, breathing heavily. He listened for shooting. There was nothing, only the continual thunder of distant guns. Half a minute passed. Alan tried to remember where he was.

He felt around him. He was lying on a straw mattress on an iron bedstead.

He could remember Guy sitting with him for some time during the day – or had it been the day before? He was still muzzy and couldn't remember. He could hear the rustle of straw under him and the quiet sounds of the village beyond the window: a horse grazing, a mechanic trying to start a motorbike. He groped for a match, lit it, then found a candle and lit that.

He stared around the little room, looking for danger. There was nothing. He uncocked his revolver and laid it down.

But waking up had brought no peace. His heart was still beating a hundred and twenty beats to the minute and the sense of appalling tragedy was still with him. He'd have blamed his dreams, except that his sleep had been dreamless and the sense of disaster was stronger now he was awake.

Alan remembered his quarrel with Tom. Pain and anger flashed through him. Tom's conquest of Lisette had seemed like a deep and deliberate insult. Although Alan had been three-parts delirious when he'd assaulted Tom, he was still deeply angry. But the flash passed. The quarrel was just a quarrel. Tom would apologise and mean it. Alan would take back everything he'd said and he'd mean it too. The quarrel was nothing.

Alan's heart was racing with something else, something worse, something permanent. For a moment, he didn't understand. And then he did.

Tom!

Something had happened to Tom.

Alan leaped from bed, found his trousers, groped round for his boots, but couldn't find them. He remembered that Guy had taken them in an attempt to stop him from wandering, but there was a pair of hobnailed peasant's shoes lying in the stable below and they would do. He grabbed his tunic, found the shoes, and ran out into the street. His body was absurdly weak still, especially his lungs, but his co-ordination had improved. He walked carefully across to the offices of the transport captain, hoping to borrow a horse.

The captain was there, bent over paperwork, swearing softly to himself. He looked up and broke into a smile. He liked Alan.

'Well, well. Good evening to you, sir,' he said, with a smart salute.

'What?' said Alan, returning the salute automatically.

'I see you've got your just rewards at last,' said the captain. 'Thoroughly well deserved too, I might add.'

Alan looked down at his shoulder. He'd become a major while he'd slept. He shook his head, puzzled. 'I've got my brother's tunic, I don't know how. I suppose he must have taken mine by mistake. Look here, can I borrow a horse? I'll give it back in the morning.'

The captain whistled, sighed, looked at his infinite requisition dockets – but within ten minutes Alan had saddled up and was trotting his way through the darkness, heading for the front line, heading for Tom.

31

The shooting, when it came, was sudden and clamorous. The guns were barely thirty feet away. By the light of the dim moon, Tom saw the courageous Stimson almost literally disappear as his body was shredded by the hail of bullets. A flare, which followed a second later, was enough to reveal Shorty Hardwick dropping to the ground, as his legs were bloodily cut away from beneath him. The firing continued. Tom reached for a Mills bomb and threw it.

That was the last thing he remembered.

32

Alan heard the shooting. It lasted for just a minute or two, then died. His horse began stumbling on the churned soil, rearing its head and sidling. He tethered the frightened horse to a shattered tree stump and continued by foot. The days of fighting had left the trenches in hopeless confusion. The ground was bare and shattered. The battlefield stunk of corpses and explosive.

He hurried, slithering down the poorly built trenches, bending double because of the weakness of the parapet. He hadn't wound puttees over his borrowed shoes and they soon filled with stony mud. His co-ordination and strength were better; only his lungs remained atrocious.

He reached Tom's section, and there he learned the dreadful worst. He heard of the brigadier's murderous instructions. He heard that Tom had crept out into no man's land with his two boys. That after half an hour of silence, the German lines had lit up with fire. That the nearer concrete gun post had opened up with its machine gun. That all three men were missing, presumed dead.

PART THREE

But these still have my garment
   By the hem
Earth of Shiraz, and Rukna's
   Silver stream

S'adi (Sheik Moslih Addin, 1184–1291)

33

Alan stumbled from the dugout into the first chilly signs of dawn. *Missing, presumed dead.* The world was colossally altered. Alan could have lost both legs with infinitely more calmness than he could bear this hideous truth. *Tom was missing, presumed dead.*

A sentry was standing on the makeshift fire-step, his face blank with tiredness. 'Any sign of life out there?' Alan asked him. His voice was harsh and the pain in his lungs still seemed to be as bad as ever.

'No, sir, nuffin'.'

'Any wounded at all? Any cries for help?'

'Well, sir . . .' The sentry shrugged, as though the request was incomprehensible. 'You're always going to get wounded, like, I s'pose. Can't say as how I listens to 'em overmuch.'

Alan wanted to strike the man hard in the face. His right arm actually ached to do it.

'I'm going out,' he said. 'Please try not to shoot me when I return.'

'Yes, sir.'

The sentry had wanted to add something about the folly of leaving the trench as dawn approached, but there was an aggression in Alan's manner that stopped him. Alan scrambled over the parapet and wormed his way incautiously

123

forwards, right out to the heart of the battlefield's horrors. The ground was littered with fragments of wire, shell canisters, human beings. A human face, detached from its skull, had floated to the surface of a puddle, and lay face up, leering at the sky. Alan noticed nothing; cared for nothing. He reached the spot where he thought Tom's raid had come to grief and began to call out.

'Tom? Tommy? Tom Creeley?'

He was being desperately foolish. He was within simple sniping distance of the German lines.

'Tom? Tommy? Tom Creeley?'

There was no sound at all, no human voice, no groan. The German rifles, which could have blotted him from existence in a second, held their fire.

'Tom? Tommy? Tom!'

There was no answer. How could there have been? Tom had assaulted the German guns. The guns had spoken. Their word was final. Tom was missing, presumed dead.

34

Headache.

A crashing, pounding tyrant of a headache that swallowed all other sensation, all other feeling. For a long time, Tom lay with his eyes closed, aware of nothing but the monster raging in his head. But slowly, inevitably, life came back. Life and, with it, awareness.

Awareness of being alive. Awareness of pain mixed with numbness all the way up and down his left leg. Awareness of finding himself safe when everything in logic said he should have been dead.

He squeezed his eyes open. Above him there was a plank ceiling, sturdily and neatly constructed. Candlelight flickered on the boards. French mud poked between the cracks. The ceiling was a pleasure to look at. Tom let his mind wander among the only objects in his little universe: his headache, the pain in his leg, the planks overhead.

But life and understanding continued to return, bringing horror in their wake.

There was light coming from somewhere: a candle. Tom rolled over to look at it. It was stuck to the top of a British helmet, beaten crazily out of shape. Tom stared. The helmet was his, but why was it so badly misshapen . . . ? He felt his leg: it was badly wounded. The pain grew stronger.

He remembered more.

He remembered Stimson being blown away and Shorty Hardwick bloodily scythed to the ground. Stimson's body had been between him and the shooting. Quite likely, Stimson's death had been what allowed Tom to survive the onslaught almost unscathed. Poor bloody Stimson . . .

He closed his eyes again, possibly slept some more. When he woke up, his headache was still bad, but his mind was clearer. Clear enough to understand that the plank ceiling above his head was too neatly built to have been made by British hands. Clear enough to understand he was a prisoner of the Germans. Clear enough to remember that it was his twin, his brother, Alan Montague, who had wanted all this, who had sent him out to die, who had wanted him dead.

The friendship that had been the best thing in his life had turned to ash.

35

Every night, for four nights, Alan searched for Tom.

He came to know no man's land as no one was ever meant to know it. He found corpses, he found dying men, he found the wounded of both sides. The dying men he shot or drugged into insensibility with morphine. The wounded he dragged laboriously back to the trenches, before squirming out once again. He called a thousand times for Tom. He abandoned caution. He stood up on moonlit nights. He used the light of flares to survey the shell-ruined landscape. He shouted for his lost brother at the top of his voice.

The Germans heard and saw him, of course. Alan could hear the German sentries echoing his call – 'Tom! Tom Creeley!' – followed by bursts of laughter and the muttered sing-song voices of the Bavarian regiments. By removing cartridges from the ammunition belts of the machine guns, they could even get their guns to rap out the same rhythm. 'TOM, Tom-MEE, Tom CREEEE-LEEE!' But there was no rifle fire, and even the machine guns didn't seem to be directed at him. From kindness, compassion, or perhaps just indifference, the Germans let the lunatic Englishman roam up and down the devastated land.

36

'Komm, Tommy, komm!'

Tom had hardly regained full consciousness before he was plunged further into nightmare.

With his good leg on one side and a burly German arm helping him on the other, Tom was escorted down a maze of trenches to a field hospital. He was given a brusque examination and a tetanus injection. Then he was marched off to a farmyard where four other British prisoners were being held under guard, before all five of them were marched further into German-held France.

By the time they reached the prisoner-of-war holding camp, Tom was on the point of collapse. His wounded left leg felt as though it were on fire, and big surges of pain washed up and down his body, like an ocean tide trapped in a goldfish pond. The camp consisted of a group of gloomy tin huts encircled by barbed wire. There was a brief search at the gate – Tom's cigarettes were removed, over his objections – and he was sent to a hut marked with the Red Cross. A nurse took a quick look at him, decided he wasn't going to die in the night, and let him collapse exhausted onto a straw pallet. He closed his eyes but couldn't sleep. Depression assailed him.

He was a prisoner of war.
Alan had tried to kill him.
On either count, he'd have preferred to die.

37

Alan abandoned the search, which had become increasingly dangerous, increasingly pointless. Furthermore, he was exhausted beyond description. He didn't in all honesty know if his body and lungs could bear another night of it. And then there was Guy. Alan got word of Guy's wound and the hospital where he was being treated.

Alan faced facts. It was time to leave the front, to leave the battle, to give up on Tom for ever.

Two days later, Alan arrived in Rouen, at the school-turned-hospital where Guy was being treated. He made his way stiffly to the correct ward. Guy's bed was empty: tumbled white sheets and nothing else. Alan stepped across to the booth where the ward sister sat.

'Bonjour, madam. Je cherche Major Montague –'

Alan was about to continue, but the sister half turned to point, saw the empty bed, then interrupted.

'Oh, là là! Comme il fume!'

She indicated a door out into what had once been the schoolyard. Alan walked out and found Guy sitting at ease in a cane chair, his bandaged leg covered with a thin green blanket and resting on a couple of packing cases marked

'War Materials – Urgent'. He was wrapped in a cloud of cigar smoke and a three-day-old *Times* lay half read on his lap.

'Guy!' he said, feeling somehow anaesthetised and shell-shocked all at once. 'How are you?'

The brothers embraced, as well as they were able, given Guy's awkward sitting position.

'Not bad, old boy, considering. Damn thing aches like the devil, that's all.'

Although he had come to Rouen specifically to see Guy, now that he was here Alan could only think of Tom and Tom's death, and the urgency of letting everyone in the world know, including Guy. But etiquette forbade him from raising the topic just yet. Guy was unwrapping some dressings and pointing out where the bullet had entered and where it had left, and exactly what damage it had done along the way. Alan found himself unable to understand anything his brother was saying. He didn't even care particularly. The wound was minor and Alan had seen too many serious ones to be much perturbed.

'How did it happen?' he asked, when it was his turn to say something.

Guy shrugged the question away. 'One of these things,' he said. 'Came clattering round the corner on my way back to the dressing station and ran right into the damned brigadier. He wasn't best pleased with me, spattering his nice clean khakis with blood. Wanted a great big council of war that afternoon, and ordered me – *ordered* me, mark you – to get the wound cleaned and dressed, then report back to him for his precious get-together. I can tell you the doctors were a bit narked. They wanted to send me straight here; thought the brig's attitude was a bit rich, frankly.'

'Yes, I suppose.'

'Not to mention that I was wearing *your* dratted tunic. I've had the thing cleaned, of course: you don't want my blood all over it.'

'Yes.'

'Yes? You *do* want my blood on it?' Guy raised his eyebrows.

'I mean no.'

'Are you all right, old fellow?'

'Guy, look, I need to tell you right away. You may not know. It's Tom. He's dead.'

Guy's face was initially impassive, before changing to something a little more sombre and concerned. He laid his cigar aside. 'Killed? Alan, I'm so sorry. It's a tragic loss.'

Guy's words were so blank, so vague, that Alan felt a sharp jab of anger. 'Tragic loss? For God's sake, it's beyond tragic. It's a bloody disgrace. It's a shame. It's a damned bloody crime, that's what it is.'

'A crime? Alan, I did what I could. The brigadier was absolutely intent . . .' Guy's words faded out. He realised he had boobed and Alan was suddenly on the alert.

'You were there? By God, of course you were. The brigadier's council of war. You were there! When it was decided. You were there and you didn't stop it.'

Guy drew heavily on his cigar and sank back in his chair, as though to invoke the protection accorded to invalids. 'I couldn't stop it, could I? I'm a major. The brigadier's a brigadier. It was him that gave the order.'

'But you knew the position. You knew that those gun posts were impregnable.'

'And so did the brigadier. He knew it every bit as well as I did. Better.' Guy had sat up again and his cigar was idle in his hand.

'But you're on the staff. You could have spoken out. You could have leaned on him or had somebody from HQ lean on him.'

Guy plucked at his collar, as though checking that it was straight. He was one hundred per cent engaged on the conversation. His normal languid confidence was nowhere to be seen. 'The brig's mind was made up. You know these types.

Field Marshal Haig could have yelled at him and it'd have made no difference.'

'But you didn't try. Because it was Tom, you didn't try.'

Guy's voice rose in answer. 'The fact was that Tom was the very best officer for the job. If anyone could have pulled it off, he could have. I thought it was a stupid mission and said so – not in so many words, of course – but if it was going to go ahead, then we chose the right man.'

Guy finished his sentence too quickly, as though with a consciousness that he'd boobed again. He plucked at his collar a second time. Alan noticed his brother's discomfort and fastened on to it.

'*We* chose? *We*? Who's we? You and the brigadier . . .' Alan paused only for a moment. Now, all of a sudden, with Tom not here, Alan was seeing something in Guy that Tom had always seen. It was as if that old intuitive communication was working one final time. 'You suggested his name,' he said in a whisper. 'The brigadier announced his bloody stupid plan. You probably argued against it. But when the brigadier insisted, you suggested Tom. Don't deny it, Guy. I know. I *know*.'

'He *was* the best officer for the job. He was the outstanding choice.'

'Oh, that's true, I don't doubt that's true.'

'It needed dash and pluck and sheer bloody-minded aggression. That was Tom.'

'You hated him, Guy. He always said you did. And I never . . . I never . . . By God, you killed him. I'll never –'

Alan shrank back, as if from a carcass. His mouth puckered in disgust. A couple of nurses were walking across the bottom of the schoolyard, their uniforms brilliant white in the afternoon sun. A doctor came running to catch up with them. His coat was white, but it was stained with blood, and didn't catch the sun in the same way.

Alan was about to walk away, but Guy leaned out of his chair to grab his brother's arm.

'Wait! There's something you don't know.'

Alan wavered a moment, as Guy hesitated. 'What? What don't I know?'

'My wound. I didn't tell you how it happened.'

'Oh, for God's sake, Guy! One little flesh wound and you think you're a bloody martyr! Grow up!'

Alan began to leave and this time Guy didn't attempt to stop him. 'Just remember, you don't know everything,' he shouted. 'If you knew, you wouldn't blame me. I did what I could.'

He shouted, but Alan didn't respond.

At the bottom of the schoolyard, the same two nurses were walking back the way they'd come, slowly. The hospital was full of the stink of death.

38

The cardboard scale wavered and sank.

Tom stared at it with hungry eyes. His fellow prisoner of war, a Canadian from his uniform, cut a crumb off the left-hand slice of bread and transferred it to the other pan. The scale levelled out. The Canadian removed both slices and laid them on a cloth. There were five slices, all precisely equal. The Canadian withdrew his hands.

Tom reached for the slice nearest him, no matter that there was a woodchip clearly lurking in the black dough. The Canadian waited till everyone had chosen, then took the one piece remaining. The other men moved away. Tom didn't.

'Got the sawdust, huh?'

Tom shrugged.

'New?'

Tom nodded.

This was his fourth day in Hetterscheidt, a prisoner-of-war camp a little way outside Düsseldorf. The camp was a bleak place of tin huts, bare earth, barbed wire, and guard posts. A thousand men lived there, sixty men to a bunkhouse. A stand of a dozen cold taps constituted the washing facilities for the entire camp. All men were made to work long hours and under constant supervision from the German guards, known as *Wachposten*. Tom himself had to smash rocks as raw material for a nearby soda factory.

But the accommodation wasn't the problem. Nor were the taps. Nor was the work.

The food was.

One loaf of bread each day between five men and that was it. Nothing else. Tom was hungry already. For the first time in his life he'd encountered men close to starvation and he had just joined their ranks.

'You can get to like the sawdust too,' said the Canadian, folding his cardboard scale away into his bedding. 'It's something to chew on.'

There was something about the man that Tom instantly liked and trusted. 'Tom Creeley,' he said, holding his hand out and introducing himself properly.

The Canadian looked round with a smile. 'Mitch Norgaard,' he said. 'Hi.'

They exchanged the information that prisoners always exchanged. Norgaard had been in Hetterscheidt since December 1915. Although in a Canadian regiment, Norgaard was actually an American citizen. He'd signed up because his mother was Belgian and he'd been appalled by the outrages committed by some German soldiers in Belgium during the first few days of the war.

'So I figured I ought to sign up and let them commit outrages against me as well. I guess my plan worked even better than I hoped.'

'You're a Yank? I thought –'

'Yeah, yeah. The Canadian regiments weren't allowed to admit us. Well, they weren't. But they did.'

'Lucky you.'

'Yeah, right.'

Tom filled Norgaard in on his own story: regiment, date of capture, work detail.

Norgaard nodded. 'Red Cross?' he asked.

Tom shook his head. 'Missing, presumed dead,' he said.

'You're kidding.' Norgaard's expression became deeply serious, as though Tom had just admitted to a terminal illness, which in a way he had. Most prisoners survived by supplementing their prison rations with parcels sent by the Red Cross from Geneva, but if you were recorded as 'missing, presumed dead' then the humanitarian bureaucracy had nothing to offer. 'Thanks to your Royal Navy, Fritz can't feed himself properly, let alone look after his prisoners. You won't survive without food parcels.'

Tom shrugged and yanked at his waist. His belt was already fastened one notch tighter than normal and his trousers already beginning to balloon.

'Friends and family?' pursued Norgaard. 'You should write. Get that "presumed dead" horseshit sorted out.'

Tom shook his head. 'No.'

'What the hell do you mean, no? You must have someone.'

Tom swallowed. He knew how serious his situation was, of course. But Alan had tried to kill him and he would be damned if he'd beg for help from the Montague family now. There was still his father, of course, but Tom knew how close Jack Creeley was to the Montagues, and writing to Jack was hardly different from writing direct to Sir Adam. He shook his head.

'I won't do it,' he said. 'I'd sooner die.'

39

It was the first cold day of autumn. There was only one fire in the room and Alan was cut off from its warmth by a long wooden table and the three well-padded bottoms that sat behind it.

The middle bottom belonged to a colonel in the RAMC. The two outer bottoms belonged to a pair of RAMC captains, ordinary family doctors who had joined up for the duration of the war. Between them, the three bottoms and their owners constituted a Medical Board, gathered to review Alan's case, among many others.

'Anderson?' said the colonel.

'No, sir. Montague.'

'Not Mr Anderson?' The colonel's tone of voice implied Alan's response was verging on insubordination.

'I'm afraid not, sir, no. My name's Montague. Captain Montague.'

And it was true. In acknowledgement of his services during the battalion's tragic assault on German lines, Alan had been promoted to captain and recommended for the Military Cross.

'Hmm . . . Ah! Montague.' The colonel found the right papers. 'Knocked about a bit by a shell. Nothing broken. Nothing hurt. Takes more than a Jerry shell to stop you, eh?'

Alan didn't answer. It was now more than a month since Tom's death and Alan was still in shock. It was as though the shell blast had never stopped ringing in his ears and heart. Worse than that, despite remaining under medical supervision away from the front line, his lungs seemed to grow worse by the day. But he hadn't cared. In a self-destructive mood, he had asked the Medical Board to rate him A1, 'fit for active service at the front'.

The colonel said, 'You feel ready to go into the line once again?'

'Yes, sir,' said Alan, conscious that he was lying.

'And, of course, you're desperate to take another crack at Jerry?'

Alan ignored the question, but the colonel didn't need an answer. 'Good man,' he said, looking sideways at the two captains for their approval. But the captains were dubious.

'Can you run without difficulty?'

'Have you attempted to carry a heavy load?'

'How well do you think you would tolerate the sound and concussion of shelling?'

'Do you think you are capable of commanding men under severe conditions? Bear in mind that the safety of your men will depend upon you.'

Alan didn't like to lie outright and his answers were visibly hesitant. The short interrogation ended.

'Excuse us a second, would you, Montague?' said the colonel, and proceeded to talk with his two colleagues in a low tone. Alan could hear the colonel saying, 'What the devil are we here for, if not to get men back into active service?' The two captains on either side were obviously disagreeing strongly, pointing at Alan's recent medical records for evidence. Alan sat in the cold room, waiting for their verdict. He chafed his hands together for warmth.

Then the doctors stopped their muttering and the colonel spoke again.

'Look here, Montague, we can't quite agree. These chaps

worry you may not be ready to face Fritz again just yet. Do you –'

But he was interrupted. Unseen by both the colonel and Alan, one of the captains lifted a file of paper and brought it slamming down onto the desk. The noise was like a pistol shot.

Although not consciously scared, Alan's body was no longer under his control. He jumped about a yard into the air and when he came down he was white as chalk, shaking, wide-eyed. His breathing had the liquid gurgle of a gas victim.

There was a moment's silence.

The only sound in the room was the crackle of the fire and the tortured sound of Alan's lungs fighting for air.

The colonel nodded sadly. 'Thank you, Montague. That will be all.'

40

It was a week later.

Tom's body grew thinner, his clothes grew baggier. His work at the soda factory grew ever more punishing as his body weakened. Every day, morning and evening, Mitch Norgaard told him to pick up a pen and write home asking for help. Every day, morning and evening, Tom said no. But on the seventh day, Tom caved in. Since there was nothing else to swallow, he swallowed his pride. He wrote home. He wrote to his father, Jack, and to Sir Adam and Lady Pamela.

He got no answer.

He wrote again.

Still no answer.

'So what?' said Norgaard. 'Write again. Write to everyone you know. Write to everyone you've ever heard of. Go on writing till you get an answer.'

But Tom shook his head. War turns a man half crazy and prison camp is there to finish the process. Tom laid down his pen and never wrote again.

It was an error, understandable perhaps, but still horribly mistaken.

What Tom didn't know was this. His first pair of letters was on a hospital ship bound for Dover when the ship was torpedoed and sunk. The second pair of letters was on a Red

Cross lorry heading through the Black Forest to Switzerland. The lorry was set upon by hungry men hoping for food. The contents were ransacked. The letters were lost.

Tom would be 'missing, presumed dead' until the war ended or he died.

41

'Darling, boy!' It was Pamela who met Alan off the train at Winchester. She hugged him tight, burying her face in his neck. When she at last released him, her face was wet. 'My poor loves, my poor loves.' She was crying for Tom, whom she'd loved as a mother, and crying for Alan, who'd lost a brother. Alan was unable to speak in reply.

At home, it was the same with his father, and with Tom's father, Jack. They were pleased to see Alan, of course, but his presence only made Tom's death more real.

'He was the very best of officers and the very best of men,' said Alan to Jack Creeley, when their voices had steadied.

'Of course, he was – you and him both . . . And I say this war's a dirty rotten stinking shame, lad, pardon me. You'll have to pardon me for saying so, but anything that could take a man like him . . .' Creeley's voice crept out into silence.

Alan spent three weeks at home. Glorious autumn weeks, with the great elms blazing yellow and gold along their boughs.

It had turned out that the shell blast had done more damage than first realised. A needle-sharp splinter had burrowed through Alan's chest, piercing both lungs. Almost invisible from the outside, the splinter had remained undetected by the original doctors. The longer the splinter had remained in

143

place, the more damage it had done. An operation to remove it had been successful, but further surgery would be needed once he was strong enough. A couple of house guests, a pair of London debutantes, now working as nurses down in Southampton, silently left before his arrival, to give the patient all the rest and quiet he could get.

Alan arrived home so weak he had to be carried to bed. But in the glow of love and warmth, he began to heal. His lungs remained poor, but his body began to grow stronger again. Apart from his lungs, he felt almost whole.

But more painful than any physical damage was the mental scarring. Alan found it almost impossible to sleep in his first-floor bedroom. The wide windows and exposed position made him feel vulnerable to the shell and rifle fire that he continually expected. After three nights of struggling with his fears, he gave in, and took over a boxroom on the ground floor, built like a bunker and with a four-foot stone wall between him and the outside. He slept with a candle burning all night.

Across the hall, in the nursery, there was a large-scale map of the Zagros mountains: a map that Tom had put there fourteen years before. A blue pencil line in Tom's wobbly nine-year-old hand marked out the family oil concession. Some nights when sleep was hard to come by, and the air laboured in and out of his struggling lungs, Alan took his candle and went into the nursery, staring at the rough contours of the map, in the mountains north of Shiraz. He had promised Tom he'd go there and find whatever there was to be found. Would it be oil or just dry earth? There was no way to find out, except the good old-fashioned way: with a drill.

Some mornings, when dawn had broken over the winter sky, he was still there in his nightshirt, with his candle, looking at the map and wondering, wondering . . .

It sometimes felt as though finding oil was the most important thing in the entire world.

42

Norgaard rolled over on his bunk and handed Tom a handful of acorns.

'Pissed up against an oak tree on my way back from the factory today. I found these.'

Norgaard had a handful himself and he began cracking the shells and crunching up the nut inside. Tom did the same, chewing carefully. His stomach was beginning to balloon outwards, but all it held was painful wind. He tried vomiting sometimes, but all he had to vomit was stale air, and the retching brought no relief. Each time that happened, he thought of Alan Montague. Anger, bitterness and self-pity jammed together in a ball that hurt every bit as much as the wind in his belly.

'What were you up to before the war?' asked Norgaard, 'and I'm not asking you to list your ten biggest ever meals.'

Tom grinned. Most conversations in the camp these days were about food, or soap, or beer, or the countless other tiny things of life. 'Oil,' he said. 'I was in the oil business.'

'You don't say?' Norgaard sat up, dropping his acorns into the blanket. 'On the drilling side or . . . ? Hey, d'you even have oil fields in England?'

Tom shook his head. 'Marketing. And no, the country's as dry as a bone.'

'Bet the King's mad as all hell about that . . . Which company?'

'Standard, actually. Standard of New Jersey.'

Tom expected the patriotic Norgaard to be pleased with his reply, but instead Norgaard pursed his lips and spat. 'Goddamn Rockefeller. Ruined the industry for all of us. And dissolution was a bust. Standard of New Jersey, my ass.'

They continued to talk. Before the war, Norgaard had been an independent oilman, a driller with his own crew.

'And every time we sent the drill bit down, we more than half expected to hit the smell of oil. Boy, I never sharpened the drill so carefully as when I was on my own thirty acres. Every single time you do it, you could find oil sands glistening on the end of the bit.'

'Did you ever make a strike? For yourself, I mean.'

'Twice, just twice.'

'Yes?'

Tom's hunger vanished, his thoughts of home, his anger with Alan. He was transfixed, the old addiction biting harder than hunger.

'First time was a little well up near Bradford, Pennsylvania. First day, I pumped thirty barrels. Two weeks later, eighty-five. Four weeks later, no matter what I did, the well gave me ten barrels of oil, if I was lucky. I ended up selling that well for the price of a new pair of pants. Two miles down the road, on land I'd offered on but never clinched, a friend of mine made a strike. Three thousand barrels a week that son-of-a-bitch got out of there.'

Tom breathed out in awe. This was the sharp end of the oil industry, where luck, adventure and geology all met in one glorious mix. 'And the second strike?'

'Second strike was sweet as a dream. I called the well Old Glory right from the start. Drilling was as easy as slicing butter. Hit gas after two thousand feet. Three hundred feet later and we were bathing our feet with oil. Six hundred barrels a day, Old Glory produced at her best, God bless her.'

'*And?*' Tom knew that Norgaard was playing with him, but he couldn't help but fall for the man's game. '*And?*'

'And John D. Rockefeller stole every last drop . . . He owned all the refineries in the area. The price he paid for oil wasn't hardly worth the cost of hauling it. He sweated me out of what was mine, then bought the well off me when I came begging at his door. It ain't enough to find the oil, Tom, it's turning it into dollars that counts.'

Over the weeks and months that followed, Norgaard continued to tell Tom of his days as an oilman in Pennsylvania and Oklahoma, and 'never did get out west to California, but if all your kings and kaisers ever get tired of fighting each other, then that's where you'll find me, drilling for oil in my own back yard.'

Tom's old addiction grew again. If he ever got out of prison camp, then he knew what he would do. He'd get into the oil business: not with Alan, but by himself. Not in Persia, but in America. And not relying on anybody else's money or goodwill, but relying only on his brains, his guts, his determination to succeed.

Stuck away in prison though he was, it sometimes felt as though finding oil was the most important thing in the entire world.

43

Alan grew stronger: strong enough for his second and final operation.

In February 1917, he was sent to a specialist hospital in Southampton. He was readied for surgery and given an anaesthetic. A nurse said, 'Count to ten for me, please. One, two, three . . .'

He woke up dazzled by light.

There was a screen around his bed, a couple of doctors, a stout ward sister, and a pretty nurse in the background. The doctors were arguing over treatment and criticising the way the sutures had been applied. When they noticed that Alan was awake, they began asking him questions to test out the extent of his recovery.

What year was it?

'Nineteen thirteen.'

What month?

'No idea.' Alan laughed at the idiocy of the question, hoping that the doctors would be able to see the funny side. They couldn't.

What was his name?

'Alan.'

Alan who?

'Creeley. Alan Creeley.'

The doctors tutted to themselves, then vanished. The ward sister looked at Alan's bedclothes with disapproval and tucked them in so tightly that she might have been packaging her patient for shipment overseas. Then she left too.

The pretty nurse, auburn-haired, freckled, and with lovely dancing blue eyes, drew closer to the bed. She loosened the bedclothes.

'It's not so tidy,' she said, 'but at least you can breathe.'

He smiled at her. 'I don't think the doctors liked me much.'

'They don't like *any*one, not unless your injury is particularly interesting.'

'I didn't come up to snuff, then? I feel rather as though I've been run over by an omnibus.'

'Well, the operation proved rather lengthy, I'm afraid. More than expected, but nothing that won't heal. I've seen worse cases do well.'

Alan realised that it must have been her who had changed his dressings and bathed him. He reddened with an old-fashioned embarrassment.

'Don't worry, I've been here two years now and I've seen everything.'

'Still . . .'

'Still, nothing.' She slipped a thermometer into his mouth, forcing him to cut his protest short. 'Mutton stew or Scotch broth for lunch?' she said. 'Nod if you want mutton, shake if you want the soup. The mutton's an absolute fright, by the way.'

He shook his head.

'Good choice. I've telephoned your mother and father. They'll be here this evening. I've told them you'll be a bit muzzy, but you'd love to see them. I'll find you some vases and sneak them away for you. Pamela's bound to bring flowers, even if she has to strip the hothouse bare.'

'Thank –'

'Ah! Thermometer! Don't talk!'

'Oree. Unk-oo.'

149

She took his pulse. Her fingers felt delicious on his wrist, making the rest of his battered body feel like a truck was rolling over it. The white of her uniform seemed dazzling. He watched it rise and fall as she breathed. It was the most beautiful thing . . . he drifted off.

When his parents did arrive that evening, they were laden with armfuls of flowers, jars of honey, bottles of barley water, and (from his father, when his mother was busy with the flowers) a flask of whisky and a handful of cigars.

'Who was that nurse?' he asked. 'She spoke about you as though she knew you both.'

'The nurse? Lottie, you mean? Reddish hair, blue eyes? But Alan, darling, I've told you ten times already. That's Lottie Dunlop, one of the girls who's been staying with us this year. A lovely girl. I've been longing for you to meet . . .'

44

'*Hier! Komm! Bitte schnell!*'

The guard was elderly, silver-haired, Jewish. He was standing thirty yards away across the prison yard, beckoning at Tom.

Tom pointed to himself. '*Ich?* Me?'

The guard nodded.

Tom dragged himself over. A bitterly cold winter had passed into spring. Tom was still losing weight, certain now that he was dying of hunger. He was listless and apathetic. His belly stuck out, jammed tight with wind and emptiness. He caught up with the guard.

'*Ja?*'

'*Hier. Ein Geschenk. Für dich.*' A present. For you.

Tom woodenly put out his hands. The guard gave him a bag of sugar, a couple of tins of goose fat, a jar of raspberry jam. Tom stared down at his treasures, hardly able to understand. The guard tried to explain further. Tom couldn't properly follow the Jew's accented German, but it was something to do with a Red Cross parcel that had arrived for a man recently dead. The guard had seen Tom's state and wanted to help. Tom was so grateful – so shocked – he began to sob out thanks, like a child at Christmas. The guard waved away the thanks, told Tom to eat slowly, and left.

The gift was like a second chance at life.

Tom was tempted to wolf the lot, but knew his stomach would quickly revenge itself on him if he did. He ate the goose fat and the jam over five days and took a spoonful of sugar with a mug of cold water morning and evening. His stomach complained, but his painful wind reduced. For the first time in months, Tom felt nearly human. And, as a human, he felt ready for action.

Speaking to Norgaard in the quiet of the camp that evening, he made a proposal.

'Let's escape,' he said.

45

Alan recovered and Lottie Dunlop nursed him. One morning, as his brain fought its way out of its post-operation fog, he sat up in bed and tried to thank her.

'Thank you so much for everything,' he said. 'I do apologise for not saying so earlier. I must have seemed very brutish. It was the anaesthetic, I suppose.'

'Of course it was.'

'Well, sorry anyway. It was ungentlemanly.'

She snorted out through her nose and began to clear away his tray of food.

'You must think me very stupid,' he said.

She stood upright, leaving his tray where it was. 'Yes. Yes, I do. So far in this conversation you've called yourself a brute, ungentlemanly and now stupid. In the past couple of days, you've said sorry because you had dressings that needed changing. You've apologised for causing trouble – by which I assume you meant being honourably wounded in the service of your country. And when I tried to pay you the compliment of noticing your Military Cross you told me that you hadn't earned it. So far, Captain Montague, I'm beginning to conclude that you're a great nincompoop.'

He smiled. 'Sorry.'

'Sorry again? What is it this time?'

'Very well then, not sorry . . . Miss Dunlop, may we start again? I'm Captain Alan Montague and I'm perfectly delighted to make your acquaintance.'

She bobbed in an exquisite curtsy and offered him her hand. 'Charlotte Dunlop,' she said. 'Do call me Lottie.'

For six weeks, Alan recovered. At first he was embarrassed that he should be cared for so intimately by a friend and guest of his parents. Then, later, as he became well enough to be pushed round the hospital in a wheelchair, he began to understand what Lottie's day-to-day job involved. The wing of the hospital in which she worked dealt with some of the worst cases coming over from France. She handled men who had lost both legs, who had been blinded or deafened, men whose lungs had been three-quarters destroyed by gas, who coughed black blood each time they tried to breathe too deeply. Compared with the things Lottie saw each and every day, Alan's personal embarrassment at being bathed seemed so trivial.

They became friends.

At the end of her daily duties, Lottie came to find Alan, bringing two steaming great mugs of tea and a slice of cake from home. He learned how she had been on holiday in France when the war broke out. She'd extended her stay, 'not wanting to travel back while the fighting was still going on – my goodness, how strange it feels to remember that now'. Staying in a hotel at Boulogne, she'd encountered some of the wounded men of the original Expeditionary Force and stayed to help. She'd been appalled by what she'd seen to begin with – 'I must have been a very sheltered little girl, I'm afraid. I hadn't imagined . . . I hadn't even imagined what it could have been like' – but came to find something like a vocation in her bloodstained trade. 'I came back from France for Mummy and Daddy's sake, but I insisted on at least coming here –' she meant the Centre for the Very Seriously

Wounded – 'as I couldn't stand to have become one of those ghastly debs who take a few temperatures and change a few dressings, then think they've earned themselves a letter of thanks from the King.'

And he, in return, told her all about himself. He found he was able to speak to her about the fighting with something approaching candour. After all, for every horror he had seen, she had heard of things every bit as bad. She had even, he reflected, witnessed more deaths at close quarters, since perhaps one-third of the men who passed through her hands were too badly injured to survive and her job kept her by their sides until the bitter end.

'When you were concussed, you used to moan a lot in your sleep,' she said. 'You called out for mother – everyone does,' she added quickly, 'everyone – but also for Tom. That would be Tom Creeley, I suppose? The boy you grew up with.'

'Yes, though that doesn't quite say it. Tom was my twin. I couldn't have been closer to him if he'd been my flesh and blood. For a few days after his death, I quite lost my head. I almost willed myself to die.'

She nodded. 'That's quite common, actually. It *is* a phase. It does pass.'

'It has passed, I think. I miss Tom every moment – does that sound absurd? It's true, though – but I don't feel that my life has to end because of it. Actually, I'm getting rather keen on life.'

She smiled at him. Her smile seemed like the most beautiful thing in the world.

'Me too, my dear captain. Me too.'

46

The escape attempt was a complete success and a total failure.

One morning in May 1917, Tom found an opportunity to throw a handful of grit into the engine that drove the soda factory's principal conveyor belt. The machinery choked and died. Sabotage was instantly suspected, and prisoners were informed that working hours would be extended until dusk that night. It was what Tom had wanted.

That evening, as he and Mitch Norgaard passed a wood on their way home, they broke from the column of prisoners and ran for their lives into the sheltering trees. Some shots rang out. Still they ran.

Norgaard was hit once in the leg. He could have stopped. Tom would have stopped there with him. But the thought of further captivity was too much for the noble-hearted American. 'Freedom!' he shouted. 'Freedom!' He ran on and Tom ran with him.

Into disaster.

As appalling luck would have it, a group of German guards on their way home from camp was passing through the woods. Tom and Norgaard ran almost into them. A shot cracked out. Norgaard was hit again and fell dead. The rifles swung around to Tom.

He thought seriously about running on. He thought about

choosing death by gunfire over death by starvation. He thought about it, but decided against. He raised his hands, and – wearily, wearily – plodded towards the guns.

This was the success: that Mitch Norgaard would never know captivity again.

Here was the failure: that Tom would, as likely as not, never know anything else.

Tom's punishment was lenient: one month in solitary confinement on half-rations. When, at the end of the month, he was brought before the camp commandant, his legs were thin, his arms scrawny, his belly jammed tight with hunger. He had lived almost a year in prison. He supposed he would die there.

The commandant frowned.

'No punishments. Satisfactory work record. Not so sick as many. Why try to escape? You were lucky not to be shot.' The commandant spoke German, a little quicker than Tom could easily understand.

'Lucky? Why lucky?' said Tom. He was dizzy from long confinement, lack of daylight, and the delirium of near-starvation. The German word for stomach shoved its way into his mind. *'Magen. Mein Magen.'*

The commandant snorted, then turned to one of the *Wachposten* at his side in order to issue a series of rapid instructions. Then, using French, he spoke to Tom. 'I have changed your work detail. We need more help on the farms. You will be ready at five o'clock, to be on the farm by six thirty. You will give me your word of honour that you will not attempt to escape again. Understand?'

Tom understood – and on that day Tom's war ended, or at least the brutal uncertainty over living or dying.

As the commandant had known, it was easy for any man working on a farm to keep himself alive. If Tom sowed barley, he ate a handful of the grain. When he split turnips for the sheep, he kept a moon-shaped slice for himself. When he

157

carried the tubs of porridge to the pigs and calves, he slurped up some of the mixture from the bottom, where the oats were thickest. In autumn, at harvest time, he chomped on fresh apples, concealed some of the waxy potatoes in his tunic, had a pocket of wheat bulging in his trousers.

For the first time since being taken prisoner, Tom remembered what it was like to be happy.

To be happy and to survive.

47

Alan too survived the war.

When his health returned, he went back to France. But not to the front line. Not to the fighting. With a rare flickering of intelligence, the War Office had the sense to transfer Alan to an outfit known as the Military Fuels Procurement Office in Paris.

Alan had had very little idea of what was involved until he got there and met his superior, a cheerful lieutenant colonel with a quick smile and a booming laugh.

'Secret of success,' said the lieutenant colonel. 'Fritz thought he was going to win this war because his railways were better. We know we're going to win, because our motor transport is better. Our lads came to France with just eighty vehicles to call their own. By the end of next year, we'll have two hundred thousand, between us and the Frogs. That's not to mention hundreds of tanks, thousands of aircraft, plus whatever the Yanks bring with 'em. But you know the best part about it all? It's this. There's no point Fritz trying to build lorries to keep up with us, because he's got no oil to put in 'em. That's our job here. Getting the fuel to the boys who need it. If we get it right, we'll win the war.'

The lieutenant colonel was right. The work was important,

even critical. And as every month went by, he was proved ever more correct. Increasingly, the Allies had a mobility that their enemy couldn't match. Mobility and, with new American troops arriving by the week, manpower. And so Alan passed the rest of the war. He was harassed, over-worked, hopelessly busy – but safe. Blissfully, gloriously, wonderfully safe.

As far as he could be without either Tom or Lottie, he was happy.

For weeks before the longed-for peace had finally arrived, Tom's prison camp swirled with rumour and counterrumour. Down on the farm where he worked, only the essential jobs were done, everything else neglected. For the first time, Tom learned about the defeat of Austria-Hungary, the surrender of the Turks, the mutinies at Kiel dockyard.

At the end of that day, when it was time to return to camp, Tom remained seated. 'I'll stay here,' he said. 'Why not?'

It was strictly against regulations. The *Wachposten* – whose rifles were leaning placidly in the corner of the room, with ammunition clips hung on a peg to stop the cats from getting at them – looked at the farmer, who looked back at them and shrugged. If the war was ending, what did they care? What did anyone care?

And one wonderful day, 11 November 1918, peace was declared.

Up and down the Western Front, men dropped their guns and stared at each other with something like bliss. A corporal from Alan's former platoon, who'd survived four years of war without a scratch, dropped all his equipment on the ground and climbed out of the trench. He stood up. The chilly November air snaked around him, but no bullets, no shells. He removed his helmet and threw it high into the air. 'You can push off now, *Kameraden*,' he shouted across to the German lines. 'We can all bugger off home.'

Down in the trench, his astonished comrades cheered.

PART FOUR

'Tis very strange but I declare
The world seems half insane,
The new disease as all will swear
Is Oil upon the Brain.
I saw a man whose garments bore
The marks of much free soil
And yet he cared not what he wore:
Beneath the stains was OIL.

from 'Petroleum, Petroleum'
by O.I.L. Wells

48

Four miles from Whitcombe. Candles glimmered from cottage windows. There was a smell of wet leaves, woodsmoke, the sweet strong odour of cattle.

The date was 14 December 1918, thirty-three days after Armistice Day. Tom had walked and hitchhiked to the Dutch port of Rotterdam. He'd caught a lift on a steamer and stepped off the dock in Southampton, a free man with nowhere to go but home.

His pace quickened. He felt a sudden overpowering urge to see his father again; to hear his voice, slow in speech, but full of warmth. Whatever lies were told up at the big house, Jack Creeley would never turn away his one and only son.

Tom walked faster, till he was almost running. Arriving undetected at his father's cottage, Tom tapped on the door and swung it open. But there, instead of Jack's sturdy figure, a stranger was seated at the fire: an old man, white-haired. The stranger turned in his chair and stared.

'Who's that? Who's that there? Come in, lad, I can't see your face.'

'My father? Is he . . . ? Where's my father?'

'Creeley, by God! Tom Creeley! And we thought you dead!' Now Tom recognised the stranger. It was old Bertie

Johnson, owner of a covered wagon, and the village carrier back when Tom was a youngster.

'No, Bertie, I'm alive all right. Where's my pa? He's moved house, has he? Not head gardener, is he?'

The head gardener had the grandest cottage of the little row of four. It had long been Jack's aspiration to possess it one day.

'Moved house, Tom, in a manner of speaking. He's with Our Lord now, God rest his soul.'

'Dead? My father's dead?' The news was unbelievable. Tom crashed down on the rush-bottomed seat by the table. In all his time as a prisoner, he had been through seemingly every possible permutation of how matters might stand at home. He had imagined anger, love, forgiveness, hostility, even that long-postponed court martial. But he had never once imagined this.

For a few minutes he sat in devastated silence, too shocked even to cry. Old man Johnson poked around in a cupboard and brought out bread, a dish of pork dripping, a bowl of apples and nuts. His movements were silent and respectful.

'How?' said Tom at last. 'What happened? I can't believe . . .'

Johnson sat down beside Tom, his hands on the table. At rest, they still held the shape of invisible reins, as though he were guiding his horses through the night.

'It was the flu, lad. As if the war wasn't bad enough, God had to send the flu as well. It took your pa, Jonah Hinton from the Tirrold Farm cottages, that pretty Jenny Manders, old Maggie Manders' girl, not to mention . . .'

Johnson recited the names of the dead. Tom knew that the flu epidemic had been terrible, but the list of names beggared belief.

'I can't believe it. My father! Of all people!'

'He didn't suffer,' said the old man gently. 'One week, he was digging over the kitchen garden. The next week he was

166

up at the churchyard beneath the ground . . . But you're right, lad. It wasn't the flu that did for him, it was the grieving.'

'He believed me dead?'

'So did we all, so did we all.'

'I wrote to him.'

'You were captured?'

'Yes.'

'In prison?'

'Yes.'

'These things go astray, I suppose.'

'I wrote not once, but twice. The other men got answers.'

And food, Tom might have added. And a chance of survival.

'He was no great hand at letters, your pa, but he'd never have just left you there, not knowing. He believed you dead, lad, I swear it.'

Bertie Johnson fell silent. With a flash of insight, Tom remembered that the village postman usually left letters for the estate workers at the lodge at the park gates. If the Montagues had decided Tom was better off dead, then nothing could have been simpler than to intercept the letters and destroy them. No wonder Jack Creeley believed he'd lost his only son.

For a long time, Tom stared into the fire, trying to make sense of things. But his loss was too great. He felt nothing but shock. He staggered heavily to his feet.

'Bertie, I'm off. And look, just one thing. Promise me that you'll tell no one, all right? Nobody. I don't want anyone to know I've been. Let them think I'm dead. There's no one here any more. No one for me. Promise me, Bertie.'

Bertie was speaking again, but Tom couldn't even face the effort of making sense of his words. There was bread and dripping still on the table. Tom tore the bread in two and dunked his half into the bowl of dripping. It would be his supper tonight. He put an apple in his pocket. 'Tell nobody. Promise me.'

The old man nodded. If he had an expression on his face, Tom didn't know what it said.

'Promise me, Bertie.'

'I promise.'

Tom left. He set out on the open road, heading north.

49

The village green was sown with crosses: low oak crosses, each one decked with flowers from Pamela's hothouse. In time, of course, there would be a memorial in stone. A memorial to the bright-faced Whitcombe lads who had never come home. But every village in England wanted such a memorial now and the stone-cutters had more work than they could handle.

The church service concluded. The mourners mingled and dispersed. The crosses sat out in a light December rain. Thirteen crosses. And one of them – the one with more flowers than any other – was marked 'Lieut. Thomas Creeley, MC, 1893–1916'.

After a sombre lunch had passed in quiet remembrance, Sir Adam called Alan to his study.

'Listen, my boy, I have some good news for you.' Sir Adam drew some papers from a desk drawer and pushed them across to his son. 'The good news is that I've arranged for the oil concession to be put into your name. Just sign here and the thing's done. And, by golly, how you've earned it.'

Alan signed, with a feeling of quiet joy. *The concession.* More than any wooden cross or any carving in stone, the concession would be Tom's best memorial. Of course, the odds were heavily stacked against success. But Tom's spirit in heaven wouldn't mind failure. What mattered would be that Alan gave it his best go, that he did the very best he could. And Alan would need to call upon everything he'd ever learned from Tom. Daring, passion, stubbornness, charm, brilliance.

'Thank you, Father. I can't tell you how much this means.'

'Then it's lucky you don't have to, my boy. I'd have liked to give you a little money as well. But to be perfectly blunt, I can't do it. The war's done my finances no good – no good at all. You'll have your allowance, of course, but I've nothing else to give you. Not without digging into Guy's share of the estate, anyway. I've spoken to him about it and he's declined. I'm not sure he's been exactly generous, but I'm afraid he's within his rights.'

'Of course. I understand.'

'So I can give you the concession, but as for money to drill there . . . I'm afraid I can offer you nothing.'

'That's perfectly all right. It's the concession I want, not money.'

'But you'll find it a damned awkward thing to make a go of the concession without some money in your pocket.'

'I dare say.'

'And Lottie, dear boy – she may not care to marry a pauper. Have you thought how this arrangement will affect her?'

Alan shrugged. He thought of the village green: the oak crosses covered with flowers, the names of the dead, the sad December rain. 'I have to have the concession, Father. Have to.'

'For Tom?'

'Yes, for Tom.'

'You made him a promise?'

'I *did* make him a promise. My most solemn promise, not long before he died. But even if I hadn't, the agreement had been made between us years before. I couldn't break it.'

'You know how the odds lie against you?'

'Yes.'

'Old D'Arcy almost failed and we thought his purse was bottomless.'

'I know.'

'Your mind's made up?'

'Absolutely.'

'You're a stubborn fool.'

Alan smiled. Coming from Sir Adam, that was a compliment.

50

Liverpool.

One of the greatest ports in Europe, and all Tom encountered was ragged kids, the smell of urine, the sharp stink of poverty that four years of war had done nothing to purge.

Tom walked quickly through the streets, down to the docks. He soon found what he was looking for. An American cargo ship, the SS *Calloway*, had just arrived, with seven hundred and fifty head of cattle mooing in the hold, and two thousand sheep bleating hopelessly on the hurricane deck. Tom ran up the gangplank and offered his services to the captain. The broad American face looked him up and down, noting the officer's tunic, the medal ribbon, and its state of age and decay.

'You want to rope cattle?' The American's voice was disbelieving.

'Yes – yes, sir.'

'You ever worked on ship before?'

'No, but I've worked with animals.'

The American wiped his chin with the back of his hand and spat over the side of the boat into the turbid water. He laughed. 'Is that what the King gave you a medal for? . . . Hell no, sorry, I didn't mean anything. Sure. We need hands.

172

A couple of the steers got loose last night and we've got four men bleeding all over the sickbay.'

'Thank you.'

There was a pause. The American seemed transfixed by the uniform and its medal ribbon.

'Listen, bud, you might want to change your coat. These here cattle are true-born Yankees. They might not know how to respect the King's uniform and all, on top of which, some of them ain't too good as sailors and the cattle deck ain't too wholesome right now.' The smell coming up from the ship's well suggested that the American was, if anything, under-stating matters.

Tom gritted his teeth and shook his head.

'No other coat, eh?'

Tom shook his head again, feeling a flash of inappropriate temper mixed with shame at his poverty.

'Hell . . . Goddamn.'

The American thought for a moment, then stuck his hand in his pocket and brought out some money: a mixture of paper and coin, dollars and pounds. He sorted through his change and gave Tom some English money. 'Go get yourself a coat, then get back here quick as you can. We lost two days on the crossing, so we need to get these cows out at the double.'

Tom took the money and bought himself a thick tweed jacket. He sold his uniform tunic for a shilling, but took the purple and white ribbon off before handing it over.

'Down on yer luck, sir?' said the shopkeeper. 'Never mind. Things are bound to look up.'

The man's face was begging to be asked a question and Tom knew what question to ask.

'Do you have children?' he asked. 'Any sons . . . ?'

'Two, sir. Both good lads. One took a bullet at Mons, but not hurt too bad, sir, thank God. The other one's a miner, sir. Couldn't be spared, though he begged to go . . .'

Tom fled the shop. He wanted never to hear the word 'war' spoken again, and the country was littered with it. The smell of war hung over England like a cloud. It clung to things like the smell of coal-smoke. He put on his new jacket and hurried back to the ship.

Unloading the cattle was unbelievable. The cattle deck was awash with the solid and liquid deposits of four hundred seasick cows. Roping them, getting a belt under their bellies, swaying them up through the hatchways and setting them safely down in pens on the dock was a violent and dangerous business.

Tom worked with eight tough and strong Americans, all of whom had done this kind of thing before. It took him a while to catch up with their skill, but he soon learned and quickly became a crucial member of the team. When the deck was emptied of cattle, it was another day's work to clear out the stalls, hose down the decks and swab the walls. By the end of the day, the deck smelled of brisk saltwater and sounds went ringing round the steel hall like the inside of a bell.

The American mate approached Tom with a roll of dollars.

'We normally pay people by the trip, but I've put you on a daily rate as a cattle hand, second class.' He held out some money.

'I don't want pay, sir. I'd like passage.'

'Passage? Hell.' The American spat. 'We're not that type of ship. We bring cattle in. We don't take nothing out. We don't need hands on this leg.'

Tom said nothing, but held the other man's gaze. The American spat again.

'Aw, hell, OK. I can't pay you, but you can berth with us if you want. But New York immigration won't let you into the country with an empty wallet. You'll need to show 'em you can pay your way.'

Tom continued silent.

'Goddamn, pal, you ask a lot. OK. You can make a few round trips with us, get yourself set up. My father left this damn port when he was eighteen. Never came back. You can see why.'

He spat.

When the ship sailed away on the evening tide, Tom watched England sinking grey and smoky below the horizon. Except a few times to unload cattle, Tom wanted never to set foot there again.

51

Alan and Lottie were alone in the drawing room of her father's huge Berkeley Square house. The room was furnished in the old-fashioned style: heavy oppressive colours and too much of everything – too much furniture, too much ornament, too much fabric. Lottie herself hardly seemed to fit. She was slim, not heavy. Her auburn hair was pinned up behind her head. Her dress was a simple modern outfit, dropping in a straight, almost boyish cut from her shoulders to six inches below the knee. Apart from a gold wristwatch and a string of pearls around her neck, she wore no jewellery. Although usually so bright, so unfazed and vivacious, today she was quiet and anxious.

'My father can be a horrible old beast,' she said.

Alan was a mass of nerves. He stood up, sat down, caught Lottie's hand and stroked it, then let it fall and lit a cigarette. 'But he must care for you. He must. He couldn't not.'

She took the cigarette from his hand and stole a puff. 'My goodness, the things you men will smoke.' She took a cigarette from her own case, waited for Alan to light it, then inhaled deeply. 'Well, if he can't not, I don't know why your hands are shaking.'

'They are not.'

'They were.'

Alan leaped up again and paced the room. 'I won't plead with him.'

'My darling, his mind is probably made up one way or another by now anyway. I don't think anything you say will make the smallest amount of difference.'

'I don't know how you can be so calm.'

'Oh, Alan, you silly.'

Her voice was small and Alan realised that she was, like himself, desperately worried. 'Sorry, my love, it's just –'

Just what, Lottie would never find out. A pair of double doors opened, and a manservant indicated to Alan that Lottie's father, Egham Dunlop, was ready to see him.

Alan squeezed Lottie's hand, got a squeeze in return, and was gone.

'A most damn bloody awful affair, this war.'

The banker was silver-haired, but powerfully muscled and absolutely certain of his own authority. A large map on his study wall was studded with pins wherever Dunlop and Partners were engaged in business. There were six pins in Australia, fourteen in Latin America, eight in Africa, and so many in Europe and North America that Alan couldn't count them.

'Yes,' said Alan. 'Lottie worked as hard as any woman could, yet even so, sir, you must have been pleased not to have any sons in France.'

'Hmm? What d'you say?' Dunlop looked puzzled.

'You were talking about the war, sir, the butchery of it all.'

'Eh? No. I mean the killing was bad enough, but our countrymen seem to breed new 'uns all the time. I meant money, damned hard stuff to replace.'

'I'm sorry, I don't . . .'

'Nineteen fourteen. British investment overseas was pretty much the equal of America, France, Germany, Italy, Russia all heaped together. We didn't just rule the world, we pretty much owned the place. Now? Gone. All gone. All sold off to pay for a few damned guns. And the British government in debt to the Americans. *Debt*, you understand! *Debt!*'

Alan took a deep breath. This wasn't the best possible start to what he had to say, though it seemed inconceivable to him that Dunlop should not have guessed why Alan had asked to see him in private.

'If I may, sir, there's a matter I wanted to discuss.'

'Yes, yes, of course.'

'You will know, I believe, that Lottie and I have grown very fond of one another, very fond indeed.'

'Hmm.' Dunlop's grunt could have meant anything or nothing. Alan was unable to pick up any clues from his demeanour about how best to proceed. He ploughed on.

'I think you should understand my financial position, sir, as I wouldn't wish to . . . to extract a promise from Lottie that I should be forced to ask her to withdraw.'

'Hmm. Yes. Financial position. You're the eldest son, no?'

'No, sir. I have an elder brother, Guy.'

'Ah!'

This was definitely a bad *Ah*, and Alan winced internally. But he drove forward.

'My father has been reviewing his affairs and has generously made arrangements to settle certain . . . certain assets on me.'

'Hmm.'

'The principal asset – the only real asset, in fact – is an intangible one, but no less valuable for that. Potentially valuable, that is.'

'Yes?'

'I own a concession to drill for oil in Persia. The concession covers the south-west corner, starting not more than a hundred miles or so from the site where Anglo-Persian has already struck oil in abundance. I can't boast of the most oil-rich lands myself, but the geologists tell me that my prospects are not entirely without hope.'

'Have you started to drill?'

'No, sir. I shall need to raise capital.'

'Your own funds are not sufficient?'

'Not at all, sir. No.'

'Have you started to raise capital?'

'No, sir.'

'Have you ever found so much as a soup dish of oil anywhere in your so-called concession?'

'No, sir.'

'And in plain English, you are asking me if I will consent to your marrying my only daughter?'

'Yes, sir. We happen to love each other very much and I can promise to do everything in my power to make her happy.'

'Everything in your power? If I understand you right, you have no income nor any real prospect of one. What exactly do you think will be in your power? Will it be in your power to place a roof over her head? Will it be in your power to put food on the table?'

Alan's face whitened. 'I have a small allowance from my father, sir. It isn't much, but we wouldn't starve. I believe –'

'Starve? Starve? You propose to take my only daughter and you promise me that she won't starve! The answer's no. Unconditionally no. You will not marry her. You will break off relations with her. You will leave this house immediately, I tell you.'

Alan's ejection from the house was delayed by one minute as a manservant ran to find his hat. Alan felt humiliated and furious, but worse than that, he felt shell-shocked by the idea of having to live without Lottie.

Lottie, of course, read his expression instantly.

'Oh, darling, it's bad news, isn't it?'

'He flew into a rage. He was only interested in money.'

'Alan, my sweet, it must have been horrible.'

He put his hand to her chin and raised her head until they were looking into each other's eyes.

179

'Lottie, darling, you do understand what this means?'

'It means we shall have to elope and live in a garret,' she whispered. 'I've always wanted to live in a garret.'

Alan shook his head. 'You know I can't let you do that.'

'I wouldn't mind.'

'My love, there are women in the world who know how to survive on five pounds a week, but you're not one of them.'

'I could learn. No one ever thought I could be a nurse, but I turned out rather well, actually.'

'You're a perfect nurse, the best nurse that ever was, but to live on nothing, week in, week out, buying cheap cuts of meat, doing your own washing, darning your own stockings, cleaning the house like any old parlourmaid . . . I won't see you come to that. I won't think of it.'

'I have jewels. We could sell them.'

'And what then?'

Alan's voice was harsh, but determined. He had seen enough during the war to know what poverty was like. It was a hard life, relentless and difficult. Alan would never allow himself to bring Lottie so low.

'Oh, dearest!' Her voice was a whisper. She was begging him to change his mind, but knew he wouldn't.

Alan stood up. 'I should go.'

'Oh, stay, for God's sake! Don't just march out on me.'

'Your father's throwing me out.'

'Oh, darling!' They could hear him stomping around in his study and it was clear that Alan's time was limited. Already the butler was standing in the door, twiddling Alan's hat, while the under-butler and first footman stood just behind, like a pair of beautifully tailored heavies.

Alan and Lottie hugged and kissed passionately.

'I'll wait for you, my darling. You go and dig for oil until you're as rich as Croesus. I'll still be here.'

'Don't say that.' Alan's voice went suddenly hard. 'Don't ruin your life to make a point against your father. You're a free woman. There's no point in me going if you don't understand that. You must seek your own happiness. You must find love, marry, be happy.'

'I believe in you. If ever a man stood a chance of succeeding, then it was you.'

Alan smiled. He adored this woman. He longed to make love with her; to spend hours learning every contour of her body beneath his hands. When he spoke again, his voice was thick and harsh.

'That's a sweet thing to say, but remember what we're talking about. This is oil, a business equally divided between man and God. If I sink a well in the right place, I've made it. If I deviate by a hundred feet, I may miss it altogether. I'm afraid your father's perfectly correct about my financial prospects at least. I'm unbankable now and I probably always will be. Goodbye, my beloved. Goodbye.'

52

'Shirt off, please.'

'I'm sorry?'

'Please take your shirt off, then climb those stairs.'

The official's voice slurred all the words into one long groan of tedium, 'Pleasetakeyourshirtoffthenclimbthose-stairs.' He pointed at a flight of fifteen wooden stairs that led nowhere. A bored doctor in a blue uniform looked dully at Tom, before his glance drifted back to the newspaper sports report. Tom removed his jacket, shirt and tie, then ran up the stairs and down. His pulse hardly accelerated. After five months of cattle wrestling on board heaving Atlantic cattle ships, his physique had regained nearly everything it had lost in the prison camp. The doctor looked curiously at the purple stains round Tom's shoulder where he'd taken his first bullet wound, and the other light scars that Tom had collected either from shrapnel scratches on the front line or from injuries received in prison.

'You've taken some knocks, huh?'

'A few.'

'Brawling?'

'War. No problems now.' He wriggled his shoulder to show off its mobility. In truth, although his shoulder was fine now, his wounded leg had never quite felt right since. Although he could walk on it all day, the wound fell into a dull red ache at times, especially if he twisted his leg at all or put his weight on it awkwardly.

'Epilepsy? Any diagnosis of tuberculosis?'

'No.'

The doctor nodded. 'OK. Shirt on.'

The immigration official stamped Tom's card. 'Move on to the Public Examination hall. Out here, right, right again, get in line. *Next!*'

Tom moved off. Behind him a Polish immigrant with a terrible limp was trying to conceal the fact as he puffed his way up the stairs. 'OK. Geddown. Gimme your card. *Next!*' The official sent the Pole in a different direction from Tom and the Pole wept bitterly with disappointment.

The Public Examination hall was packed. A long line of humanity snaked its way up and down the long bare room. Notices on the wall explained who was prohibited entry: '*All idiots, imbeciles, feeble-minded persons –*' Tom half read the notices as he walked past. The would-be immigrants were mostly badly dressed and poor. There was a preponderance of men, and a mixture of voices and accents that reminded Tom of nothing so much as prison camp. '*Persons of constitutional psychopathic inferiority; persons with chronic alcoholism –*' A few of the men were sneaking bites of food from parcels carried in their pockets: hard biscuit and fried pork, with the occasional strong smell of cheese or sausage. The air was cloudy with tobacco smoke. '*Paupers; professional beggars; vagrants –*' Tom was better dressed than average, though nobody would have guessed that he'd grown up in the twelve-bedroomed Whitcombe House, with an English aristocrat for foster uncle. He shuffled his way along, feeling the mixture of hope and fear common to everyone else in the room.

After queuing for three hours, he arrived at the head of the line. A door banged open in front of him and an official gestured him forwards. He entered a small room, decorated with an American flag and a poster advertising the Keystone Kops. Two uniformed men sat behind a simple wooden desk, with a mound of forms in front of them, half blank, half already filled.

'Card, please.'

Tom presented his card.

'D'you speak English?'

'Yes, sir. I am English.'

'Huh.' One of the officials grunted, as though Tom had been impertinent, but pens marked boxes on the relevant forms. A tattered leather Bible sat like a paperweight on a stack of blank forms. The official who'd opened the door to Tom, and who seemed to be acting like the master of ceremonies, shoved the book into his hand.

'Can you tell me what this is?'

'It's the Holy Bible, sir.'

'Please take the Bible in your left hand, raise your right hand, and do you swear to answer all questions truthfully?'

Tom did as he was told. 'I swear to tell the truth.'

Then the interview began, questions like rifle-fire, pens scratching down answers like some mad dance of the bureaucrats. Tom resented the brusqueness of his interviewers – he disliked any situation where he was in another man's power – but he kept his face and voice calm as he replied.

'Nationality?'

'Date of birth?'

'Country and town of birth?'

'Vessel of disembarkation?'

'Do you have any money in your possession?'

'Any gold, jewellery or other valuables?'

'Please lay your money on the table.'

'Please count it for us.'

'Forty-eight dollars. That's fine, you may pick it up.'

'Can you read English or any other language or dialect?'

'You can? Then please read the text set down on the printed card.' The card contained the first few lines of the American

Declaration of Independence and Tom spoke the lines with a ringing forcefulness, giving particular emphasis to the line saying 'that all men were created equal'.

'Do you have an address to go to in New York or elsewhere in the United States?'

'Please state the address and your relationship to the resident.'

Luckily Tom was prepared for this question, and was able to give the name and address of a former shipmate whose wife ran a boarding house up in Connecticut.

'Do you have a promise of employment in the United States?'

Tom hesitated.

'I asked if you had a promise of employment? A job?'

Tom continued to hesitate.

'You have any way of making money or you gonna live on the bum?'

Finally, Tom shook his head. 'No, sir. I'm going to pay my way all right.'

'Uh-huh. And how d'you plan to do that?' The official spoke to Tom as though he was dangerously close to becoming an idiot, imbecile or feeble-minded person.

A smile ghosted over Tom's face. 'I'm an oilman,' he said firmly. 'I've come here to drill for oil.'

The officials smirked at each other. 'Right. You got forty-eight bucks in your pocket. I reckon you should get an oil well for that. Maybe something nice down in Texas.'

The other official grinned and nodded and nodded and grinned like it was the best joke he'd heard since President McKinley's assassination. 'Or Pennsylvania,' he said. 'Think about it. Should get plenty of oil well up in Pennsylvania. Ha! Forty-eight bucks!'

Tom became instantly angry at their jocularity.

'I'll earn what I need, then drill,' he said.

'Right. Which was what I was asking. D'you have a promise of employment?'

Tom gritted his teeth. He did have a promise of employment,

185

as it happened. He had done well on his cattle ships, had been promoted once already and had been invited to continue with the trade as soon as he'd obtained his papers. He gave the bureaucrats the information they needed, which they wrote down with plenty of little nudges, winks, exclamations and puffs of laughter – 'An oilman!', 'Hoo!', 'Forty-eight bucks!' – that infuriated Tom. Then the interrogation continued.

'Are you willing to abide by the laws and Constitution of the United States?'

'Yes, sir.'

'Have you ever been convicted of any crime involving moral turpitude?'

'Are you a polygamist or do you believe in or advocate the practice of polygamy?'

'Are you an anarchist, a bolshevist, or a member of any organisation advocating the overthrow of the US government?'

'Yes, sir, I'm a Red Army colonel with three wives and a taste for choirboys' – or so Tom almost said. In fact, he bit his tongue and answered, 'No.'

'Have you ever been arrested?'

Tom paused. The two pens quivered and halted. Two pairs of eyes settled on his face. Tom felt a flash of annoyance. Why in hell should he reveal anything to anyone about the time he'd slipped from his column of fellow prisoners on the way back to prison camp? What the hell would this brace of pale-faced paper-pushers understand about months of starvation, the crushing load of captivity? About the good-hearted American whose last words were 'Freedom! Freedom!' before the German bullets dragged him down, or about Tom's leaden-footed surrender and rearrest?

'No, sir,' he said. 'I was taken prisoner in the war in Europe, that's all.'

The two pens hesitated another moment. It wasn't quite a clean answer. The pile of nice blank forms preferred nice clean answers.

'You fighting with the Brits?'

'Yes, sir. Right alongside some very fine American units, if I may say so. Very fine indeed.'

It was a good answer, no matter that Tom had been taken prisoner a full seven months before the Americans had entered the war. 'Wait for Uncle Sam to bail you out, huh?' The senior of the two officials shook his head, and checked the 'No arrest' box on his form. His junior twin did likewise.

There then followed a handful of questions presumably intended to check whether Tom was an idiot, imbecile or a feeble-minded person. 'You have fifteen oranges. You give five of them away. How many d'you have left? You give away another five. How many then? Apples cost ten cents, oranges cost twenty-five. Which is worth more, six apples or six oranges?'

Tom passed the exam with flying colours.

The master of ceremonies took a nod from the senior desk official and handed Tom a card, marked 'Admitted'. In a slurred impatient voice, he said 'WelcometotheUnitedStates-nextinlinetheremoveitonplease!'

Tom took the card with a surge of relief so strong, he hadn't realised how nervous he must have been. The past began to slip from his shoulders. In America, if he committed no crime for five years, he could and would become an American citizen. He was dazed. How simple it had become. The whole tangled confusion of names, birth, breeding, inheritance, and all that Alan-and-Guy versus Alan-and-Tom competition had just dropped away. Tom had just emigrated to a country where no one even gave a damn. It was so simple, it seemed impossible.

He took his precious card – 'Admitted' – to a final line leading to the immigration booth. The immigration officer took the card, then a long drag on his cigarette.

'Eight bucks, please. Head tax.'

Tom handed over eight dollars.

'Full name?'

'Thomas Albert Cree –' Tom halted.

'Just plain Thomas Albert? Or Thomas Albert Somebody? Which? *Jeez!*' Another drag on the cigarette. The ash scattered on to the papers lying beneath. The man's shirt cuff was grey from wiping over tobacco ash all day long.

This was it. The moment to drop the last unwanted stone in the cleansing ocean. The name Creeley was inextricably tied up with the name Montague. Right now, Tom wanted nothing of either. The cattle ship he'd worked on for six months, the SS *Calloway*, was a name he liked as well as any other – and one close enough to Creeley that he wouldn't be dishonouring either his father or himself. With a firm voice, Tom spoke his decision. 'My name is Thomas Albert Calloway, sir.'

'Tom Calloway, welcome to the United States.'

53

'Tie up the horses and pack the bags. No, not the tents, the rock-tools. Do it now!'

Alan's tone of command was as unmistakable in Persian as it had been in English. His experience of war had given him a cool-headedness, a speed of resolve that nothing else could have taught him. He was just twenty-six years old, but spoke with the confidence of a field marshal. His team of horse-drivers responded instantly.

'Tether the horses. Make them fast. There. That bush will do.'

As he spoke, Alan took care to remain visibly calm and unflustered. He knew perfectly well that nothing panicked men like any sign of panic in their commander. He walked among his men, giving brief orders, supervising the packing of his geology equipment ('rock-tools' as he'd dubbed them in Persian). When the packing was underway to his satisfaction, he strolled casually to his saddlebags, drew out his army-issue revolver and buckled the holster to his belt.

They had been camped up on a scrubby little plateau overlooking a shallow lake. The lake provided water and enough thorn-bushes for cooking and a fire in the evening. They had been there two days and had met nobody. Even the shepherds who came up there in summer had driven their flocks down to lower ground for the winter. But then one of the men had come hurtling into camp, terrified. 'The Qashqai are coming. Forty men. A war party.'

The other drivers had begun to saddle the horses ready for immediate flight, but Alan had roared them into silence. A raiding party of forty men could easily ride down a procession of eight tired baggage-ponies. Running away would only induce a chase that could easily lead to tragedy.

'Coffee, Ahmed. Put the water on.'

'Coffee, *aqa*?' '*Aqa*' was Persian for 'sir', and was how Alan was invariably addressed by his men. The poor boy was obviously bewildered by Alan's sudden need for hot refreshment.

'Coffee, Ahmed, coffee, coffee, coffee. Husain, why are you standing there? The fire is going out. Lend a hand.'

Baffled but obedient, the men began to boil water and the Persian adoration of coffee quickly overcame any remaining terror. By the time the hoofbeats of the approaching party were audible, the water had boiled and the coffee was brewing. Husain, the most intelligent and courageous of the horse-drivers, drew close to Alan.

'I am ready, *aqa*,' he said in a whisper.

Alan glanced down and noticed that Husain had brought the tin ammunition box out of its wrappings in one of the saddlebags. Husain had taken the party's second revolver out and was proposing to lie next to Alan and fight it out.

'Give me that bloody gun,' snapped Alan in English, adding the same thing a little more gently in Persian. 'We're not going to fight.'

Husain looked crestfallen, but there was no time to debate. The mounted tribesmen broke like a tide over the brow of the hill and swept into and round Alan's encampment in an instant. There weren't anything like forty of them – fifteen would have been nearer the mark – but every one was armed with a rifle, and their horses were of a different class to Alan's little team.

'*Salaam,*' said Alan, greeting the new arrivals with a polite but measured bow. 'You see I have your coffee already prepared.'

The tribesmen milled around. They circled the little camp, laughing amongst themselves and talking. They spoke in a thick tribal dialect that Alan was unable to understand. Most of the men carried knives, either in their belts or their headgear, and none of them looked shy about using them. For all his exterior calmness, Alan realised that his life lay in the hands of these men, who knew no law beyond raiding, theft and blood-feud.

Alan spoke to Husain in an undertone. 'Pour them some coffee. Act as if we've invited them.' Husain began to pour the coffee, swearing and punching Ali, the youngest in their team, for not having wiped the cups properly.

'I have eight cups only. But I invite seven of you to drink with me.'

Alan sat down. He allowed his revolver to be completely visible to the tribesmen, but Alan himself ignored it completely. There was more movement, more laughter among the horseback men. Then at last, one of them trotted forwards, leaped off his horse – a magnificent beast – and tossed his reins to one of the others to look after. He was very tall and erect, with an untrimmed beard and the hooded eyes of a man who spent most of his time on saddleback in the high altitude sun.

'I am Muhammad Ameri,' he said with a bow. 'These are my men.'

Ameri and a couple of his lieutenants sat and drank coffee. Alan called for *noql* – the sugar-coated almond sweets that the local Persians couldn't get enough of – and the mood began to improve. Even so, all the time the other men remained on horseback, fingering their weapons, except for a half-dozen or so, who dismounted and began going systematically through Alan's belongings. Alan's men sat together and shot dirty looks at the newcomers. Once, when one of the tribesmen began going through the saddlebag containing Alan's bedroll, shaving tackle and personal papers, the fourteen-year-old Ali leaped up and with a shrill yell began to attack the man, jumping on his back and beating him with his fists. The tribesman shook the boy to the ground and scuffed him away with a boot. There was a moment's dangerous tension, then the tribesman laughed and moved on to a different bag.

The coffee was finished and Alan called for food. Usually, his little team led a fairly spartan life: living off rice and bread, varied by eggs, tomatoes, melons, goat's cheese and almonds purchased from villagers that they passed. Luckily, though, this day they happened to have with them a couple of plump young chickens, ready for eating. Grumpily, because he'd been spoiling to play the hero, Husain ordered the others around and took charge of producing the best meal that their little camp could supply.

To begin with, Muhammad Ameri's conversation was completely centred on a few things: rifles, horses, war, blood-feuds, the superiority of the Qashqai to anyone and everyone else. Alan nodded, agreed, and played his part of polite host to perfection. He still had no idea what Ameri intended, but he assumed that the major options under review were armed robbery on the one hand, and armed robbery with violence on the other.

The chicken and rice arrived, seasoned with whatever sultanas, yoghurt, and saffron was available. The tribesmen ate greedily, leaving a ring of rice around their plates, in the true polite Persian fashion. Eventually Ameri's curiosity grew too great.

'*Farangi?*' he asked.

Strictly speaking, the word meant French, but to Persians it had come to mean anyone from Europe. Alan nodded. 'I'm English,' he explained.

'Ah yes . . .' Ameri's attention had been caught by Alan's surveying equipment, which hadn't been fully packed away. 'English . . . You are building a railway?'

Alan laughed. It was strange the associations that his nationality brought up. 'No.'

'A road?'

'No.'

Ameri paused, curiosity and suspicion competing in his face. 'You are making maps? You are a tax collector?'

'No, no, no. None of those things.'

Ameri paused, picking bits of chicken from his teeth and spitting them onto the embers of the fire. 'You have come to buy carpets,' he pronounced finally, sure of having found the right answer at last.

'No. Oil. I'm looking for oil.'

Ameri nodded gravely, then turned to his lieutenants and the three of them began speaking very rapidly amongst themselves, apparently trying to work out what Alan meant and whether he was telling the truth. Eventually, Ameri called over to one of his men to bring something. The man dug round in a saddlebag and came over with a very old kerosene lamp (stamped 'Armitage & Co Ltd, Leeds' on its rusted side). The fuel vase was empty, but the smell remained.

'Oil?' Ameri said. 'Oil for lamps?'

'Yes. You've heard of the Anglo-Persian Oil Company, working up at Masjid-i-Suleiman and Abadan?'

Ameri nodded, but Alan suspected that the nod concealed almost total ignorance.

'I think there may be oil in the Zagros and I'm here to look for it. If I find it, it will make everyone here rich, very rich indeed.'

'You have found it yet?'

'No.'

'But you have found some . . . some signs of oil, no?'

'No.'

'Nothing?'

Alan opened his hands in the expressive Persian gesture that signified nothing. 'Nothing at all.'

And he spoke the truth. Since leaving England and Lottie, Alan had spent months in the Zagros, traversing the high mountains and deep valleys, building an unrivalled picture of the geology of the area. It was a monumental work that had many months yet to run. But so far, for all his labour, he'd found nothing – not even a clue that there might be something. So far, all his work had simply proved that he was wasting his time.

Another long conversation followed amongst the tribesmen.

Alan was growing used enough to their thick dialect to understand a little even when they spoke fast. It was clear that they had heard rumours of the great industrial enterprise taking shape to the north, but that all of them had tended to dismiss the rumour as fantasy. Then the voices sank. The three Qashqai leaders were discussing something and were careful to exclude Alan from their deliberations. Bizarrely, Alan was suddenly reminded of Egham Dunlop, and the way he too had sized up Alan's money, power and prospects. He felt a desperate longing to be with Lottie again, and a moment of violent loneliness. First Tom, then Lottie . . .

At last, the tribesmen came to a conclusion. Ameri rose. He was tall and held himself very upright. 'Come.'

It wasn't an invitation. It was an order.

54

When God built America, He took special care of her. He threaded her with veins of coal. He seeded her with iron. He gave her deepwater ports and navigable rivers and fertile farmland and forests for lumber. He even showered nuggets of gold into her streams and brooks.

But best of all, He gave her oil.

Sometimes He let the oil seep right out, as though the earth was so full that something had to give. Other times He played coy. He hid the oil in places that no one would think to look for it, except that this was America, and, when there was a chance of making money, people would look pretty much anywhere and look pretty hard, at that.

He buried oil in California, oil in Texas, oil in Pennsylvania. He buried the stuff – huge great lakes of it – beneath the icy wastes of frozen Alaska.

But this is America. And when God sets out to bless a country, His gifts are prodigal. So even less well-favoured states got the treatment. He put oil in Oklahoma. Oil in Louisiana. Oil in Kansas. Oil in Arkansas. Oil in Indiana. Oil in Kentucky.

And oil in Wyoming.

Oil aplenty in Wyoming.

❧

Somewhere up the line, a long whistle moaned through the empty landscape. The line of freight cars juddered and clattered to a halt. Metal clacked against metal. In an empty boxcar at the rear of the train, a badly stowed cotton bale slid from its stack and thumped down on a crumpled-looking shape beneath.

The shape swore and rubbed its head.

Since jumping on his first freight train in New York, Tom had been jolted, thumped, bumped and tossed across no fewer than nine American states, until he felt as if the map of continental America was printed in bruises across his body. On top of the physical battering, the heat of an American summer had turned the steel boxcar into a roasting oven, Tom had run out of water in Iowa and, worse still, he'd run out of cigarettes on the wrong side of Nebraska.

He rubbed a dry tongue over a dry mouth and massaged his scalp with dusty fingers. Then, with his morning cleaning rituals as complete as possible given the circumstances, he went to the side of the gloomy car and swung open the heavy door. Brilliant Wyoming light flooded in. Tom sat on the side of the truck, legs swinging down over the gleaming wheels. He wanted to jump down and stretch his legs before the train restarted, but he hadn't had any trouble from the train's brakeman so far and he didn't want any now.

Up at the top of the train, the mournful whistle called a second time. A series of jolts ran through the train as it began to move forwards once again. The steel boxcar floor came back to life, turning into a giant skillet upon which Tom was to be shaken, fried and tossed all at the same time.

To hell with it.

Tom was – he guessed – still short of his destination, but he could see a road in the distance and he'd enjoyed as much free rail travel as he could take. He tossed his only luggage, a soft green canvas bag, onto the ground, then braced himself for the jump. For a second or two, he wondered if he'd misjudged things. The train was moving faster all the time and the railroad grade fell sharply away down a bank only a couple of feet from the speeding wheels. Tom glanced back. His entire worldly goods were in the bag he'd just tossed away.

He jumped.

He hit the ground hard, rolled with the impact, then stopped. He swore again, and sat for a minute or two, rubbing his ankle and listening to the train's thunder rolling away behind him.

Tom had arrived in America as a cattle hand, second class. He'd arrived in Wyoming as a bum. But his method of arrival didn't matter. Nothing about the past mattered any more, not even the pathetic thirty-eight dollars that he still had in his pocket.

Because Tom hadn't been quite candid with the bureaucrats of Ellis Island. He'd told them he'd come to America to drill for oil. That was the truth, but it wasn't the whole truth. Tom hadn't come simply to drill, he'd come to build himself an oil fortune on an extraordinary scale. He'd come to build an empire in oil that would rival and exceed anything that Alan might find for himself in Persia. He intended to try and he intended to succeed.

Starting today.

55

The path was too difficult for horses, so Ameri and Alan had been forced to come up on foot. The sunlight was brilliant but cold, the skies blue but wintry. In the valley two and a half thousand feet below, the camp looked like a tiny collection of dots, the horses as small as fleas and the people barely visible at all. Alan hoped they would get some rest. For the last five days, his team had been travelling hard alongside Ameri's men. In that time, the tribesmen had eaten their way through every last part of Alan's stores. For two days now, they'd mostly lived off what they'd been able to hunt: a few rabbits, a pigeon of some sort, yesterday a goat who'd injured its leg and had been left to die by its shepherd.

Ameri was scrupulously polite towards Alan, but it was the politeness of the captor to the captive. By night, Ameri posted four armed guards around the camp and tied metal bells to the necks of Alan's pack-animals. The guards weren't there to protect them from dangers outside. They were there to be certain no one escaped.

And not once had Ameri revealed where they were going. Or why.

~

Ameri climbed with an athletic intensity, breathing out in short sharp puffs. Alan too laboured in the thin air. His weaker lung ached and his heart raced. With his pale blond hair and ultra-fair skin he suffered easily in sunshine, even the weak rays of this altitude, and he wore a wide-brimmed sunhat, which had once been white and was now stained a deep dust-coloured grey.

Even as they climbed, Alan was studying the ground hard. Whether or not Ameri knew anything of value, what was certain was that the valley he'd chosen was a geologist's daydream.

For one thing, it was virtually bare. In the valley bottom, there was a little brown grass and, higher up, some tough and wizened shrubs. But mostly there was nothing to see except rocks. Rocks, dirt, sand, cliff, scree – Mother Earth without her clothes on.

For another thing, the valley wall was like a sandwich built of many layers of rock, all ripped from deep inside the earth and now exposed to view. It was like a duffer's guide to geology in one panoramic lesson. Even as he climbed, Alan's quick mind tried to puzzle out the secrets of the surrounding strata. Oil or no oil? A gold mine or a failed dead end?

On and on they climbed.

To begin with, they'd followed goat trails, but when the goat trails had finished, they'd continued both upwards and onwards, following the valley wall round as it steepened and curved. After another hour, Ameri halted. He sat on a flake of rock protruding out over the valley. Each man had a flask of water, which he quickly finished. It wasn't enough and Alan could easily have drunk another couple of pints on the spot.

'Nearly there,' said Ameri, panting. Up here on the mountainside, without his followers, he'd lost some of his chieftain's mannerisms, and found it less necessary to impress Alan with his importance the whole time.

'How do you know this spot?' asked Alan, who was well

aware by now of the Qashqai's fondness for horses above all other modes of transport.

Ameri laughed. 'Two years ago, the Shah was angry because his tax collectors came back to Tehran with their pockets empty. He sent out an army of two thousand men and sixteen field guns to make us pay. We ambushed them there –' he pointed down to the valley floor – 'and made them run home to Tehran. We captured fifteen hundred rifles and all the big guns. The rifles we kept, the guns we handed back because we have no use for them. That is how I know this path.'

They regained their breath and went on, picking their way slowly now and with care. One slip could easily result in a fall of a hundred feet or more, and they used hands as well as feet to move forwards. Alan's geology bag thumped against his thighs and he wished he'd packed the tools in a knap-sack instead.

And then, all of a sudden, they were done. Ameri threw his own small bag to the ground.

'Here.'

He took his long-bladed knife from his belt and began to hack into the hillside, where a band of sand separated two differently coloured streaks of rock. He cut away the dried-out crust, releasing a shower of fine debris to whisper its way down the side of the mountain. Then, when the whiter outside layer had been cut back, Ameri jabbed the knife into the soft interior and brought out a small pile of sand on the tip of the blade. Ameri held his nose against it, sniffed, then passed it across to Alan.

Alan smelled it. It smelled of victory. It smelled of oil.

56

'Drilling experience?'

'None.'

'Rigging?'

'None.'

'Then you'd better tell me you're a blacksmith, pal, because I seen eight-year-olds with more experience than you.'

Tom scowled. This was the sixth oil exploration outfit he'd approached since arriving in Wyoming and so far his luck was no better than it had been with the first five. His forty-dollar fortune was down to just eight bucks and his patience was running out as fast as his money.

'I can mend things,' said Tom. 'If your machines break down, I can mend them.'

'That a fancy way of telling me you ain't a blacksmith?'

Lying in the long grass, there was an old pump. It was beginning to rust and had weeds growing through it. 'I could mend that,' said Tom.

The driller kicked the pump. 'If you can fix this, then you know what I'll do? I'll throw the damn thing right back down there. It's a pile of junk, son, and we ain't got a use for it.'

A kid came scrambling across a rocky slope towards them. Tall prairie grasses waved in the valley, thinning out as they reached the higher slopes above. The kid was wearing a pair of old khaki shorts and his shins and knees were grazed and dirty.

'Please, Mr Bard, I'm to tell you that Jonah Matthews is a blockhead, an' he's gone an' drunk about half a pint of kerosene thinking it was whiskey. He's getting mighty sick right now and he ain't fit to work any.' His message delivered, the boy added conversationally, 'He's puking so bad, I even saw it coming out of his nose.'

Tom looked at Bard.

Bard looked at Tom.

Tom raised his eyebrows. Bard made a hacking noise in his throat and spat out a pellet of phlegm, which he stared at as though annoyed with it.

'The hell with it,' said the oilman. 'OK, you can cover for Matthews while he's sick. Two bucks fifty a day. Starting this minute.'

'Certainly,' said Tom. 'Sure thing.'

Bard jerked his head at the tall steel derrick ahead of them. A boiler thumped away. Thirty-foot lengths of drill pipe swung softly in the derrick. Tom gazed on the scene, his pulse quickening. Entranced for a moment, he shook himself out of it to find Bard addressing him again.

'Your name? What the hell did you say your name was?'

'Calloway,' said Tom. 'Tom Calloway.'

Bard grunted, as though Calloway was the name he most disliked in the entire world. He said nothing else, but began to walk on towards the rig. Tom picked up his bag and followed. He had eight bucks in his pocket and a job that might last no more than a day.

But he didn't care. Why should he?

His luck had turned.

57

The oil business is full of stories.

Sad ones, glorious ones, ones about the half-chances that dwindled out into no-chances, or ones about half-chances that exploded upwards in a gush of oil reaching eighty feet up to the crown of the derrick.

Here was one story that Alan particularly liked.

In California, there are places where oil literally seeps out of the ground, staining the rivers and creeks with tar. In 1864, a geologist named Professor Silliman wrote a report on the geological conditions. The report was so enthusiastic that an oil boom was sparked. Without delay, the California Petroleum Company was established with a capital of ten million dollars and drilling rights to more than a quarter of a million prime acreage. Over the next two years California Petroleum, along with some seventy other smaller companies, drilled upwards of sixty holes in search of oil. The geologists were right. Oil was present. The intensive two-year search yielded well over five thousand barrels of the precious fluid.

But here was the punchline.

The value of the oil was about ten thousand dollars. The cost of getting it had been well over a million. Although Alan was pleased to have discovered a trace of oil in the Zagros, he knew that a trace was meaningless. If he didn't strike big, there was no point in striking at all.

For thirty-five days, Alan stayed in that valley and its immediate neighbours. Ameri and his men stuck around for a day or so, but grew quickly bored and made ready to leave. Before he left, Ameri took Alan aside.

'Will you come back to dig here?'

'To drill? Perhaps. I hope so.'

'This oil. It is very precious in England?'

'It is.'

'And there will be great labour to dig – to drill – it out?'

'Immense labour. Vast labour. Drilling it, collecting it, piping it, shipping it.'

'And riches too?'

'I hope so. I certainly hope so.'

Ameri nodded solemnly. 'You will not forget?' He meant, not forget the person who had 'found' it.

'No, Muhammad, I will not forget.'

Ameri looked intently at his *Farangi* companion and his hand strayed absent-mindedly to the strap of his rifle. It was probably an unconscious gesture, but Alan understood the implication very well. It didn't matter too much whether Alan forgot or didn't forget. Muhammad Ameri would be back to remind him of his debt with fifty armed and battle-ready horsemen.

The two men embraced in Persian fashion, then Ameri leaped lightly onto his horse and led his men cantering away in a cloud of dust, heading down the valley. During their time together with Alan's party, they had eaten every last mouthful of food and stolen anything that had caught their fancy. The evening before, Alan had been forced to spend three hours making a full inventory of his surveying and geological equipment to check how much had been pilfered. Once he had a list of the essential items, he had taken Ameri aside and told him how much had gone.

'My men would never steal from their brother,' said Ameri. 'I am sure you are mistaken.' He had dismissed the matter and changed the subject.

The next morning, all the missing items that Alan had requested back were laid out, sparkling clean, on a white headcloth in the sun. Ameri said nothing about the mysterious reappearance and Alan knew better than to ask. He sent his men down the valley to buy food and to buy extra blankets for the onset of the cold season. It was already chilly at nights and true winter would be freezing and bitter.

Then the real geological work began: mapping the extent and depth of the oil seam, taking cores and samples, mapping the curve of the valley, the structure of the exposed strata, exploring the valleys to either side. It was long, exhausting work, carried out alone under difficult and worsening conditions. An early fall of snow caused the men to grow sullen and resentful. A bad fall down a mountainside left Alan completely unhurt, but caused one of his precious brass theodolites to be smashed to pieces. One of the horses slipped during a river crossing, dunking one of Alan's cameras in the freezing water and ruining it.

By night, Alan worked on his maps and geological studies by the light of coarse cotton wicks burning dingily in mutton fat. When he was done on his maps, he wrote long letters to Lottie, telling her everything about his explorations, confiding his uncertainties and doubts, speaking of his loneliness and longing. She was like a physical presence in the tent. Sometimes, he could almost swear he could smell her scent: floral, modern, unutterably feminine. When morning came, he filed his maps and studies in watertight canisters and put his letters in an inner pocket of his own personal saddlebag. When he got back to Tehran, he would take out all the letters – hundreds of pages of them in total – and burn them.

Lottie was a free woman now. He would not allow his love for her to ruin her life. It might very easily ruin his, but that was a different matter.

It was his life to ruin.

58

Jonah 'Kerosene' Matthews was back to work within three days, but Tom's luck stayed with him and the same day that Matthews came back, a second rigger fell sick with a poisoned abscess in his groin. Tom was moved up to the regular rigger's wage of three bucks fifty the day, and he quickly settled into an important part of Bard's little team.

Tom learned quickly. He learned how the boiler drove the 'kelly', the rotating square shaft that was screwed to the top of the drill pipe and was responsible for making the drill bit turn four hundred feet. Tom learned how to add new sections of drill pipe to the pipe already underground, and how to work the massive lifting blocks that raised and lowered the pipe. He learned how to fish up the bit and replace it, stacking all fourteen lengths of thirty-foot pipe upright in the derrick as they emerged from the hole. He learned the system for pumping liquid mud down into the drill hole to bring up the stone chippings as the drill worked away. In short, he learned to 'make hole', to drill, to search for oil.

For the first time in many years, Tom was happy.

Happy, but not content.

Admittedly, his fortune was now increasing by the day, instead of shrinking. He was living in a shanty-built boarding house for seventy cents a night, evening meal included. He was learning the trade at the hands of men who really knew it. And yet . . .

Lyman Bard, the team leader, was a drill-for-hire, working for a bunch of Ohio-based investors. Nine miles and two valleys away, in Nine Snake Creek, an oil strike had been made earlier in the year. The land around that strike was now producing nearly fifteen hundred barrels a day and the whole area was in a frenzy of exploration. It was an exciting place to be, but, as far as Tom was concerned, the main point was this. He was a lowly rigger working for a man who worked for some guys who owned some drilling rights which might – just might – turn out to be worth something.

It wasn't enough.

One Friday evening, Tom trudged back to the boarding house alongside Lyman Bard, the rest of the team lagging a couple of hundred yards behind.

'Are we going to make a strike, you reckon?' asked Tom, whose language was already fast Americanising.

'Couldn't say.'

'But you must have a gut feel for it. You've been in the game for long enough.'

Bard wrinkled his nose and spat. 'There's oil around here, I'd say. Nine Snake Creek ain't gonna be the only place with oil. I'd say our chances were as good as anyone's.'

'And what happens if you strike?'

Bard shrugged. 'We strike.'

'But what do you get out of it? What difference does it make to you?'

'I get two per cent of anything we bring out the ground.'

'Two per cent?'

'There are plenty of guys offer nothing.'

'Say you make a strike of two hundred barrels a day. That's around four bucks in your pocket if prices are strong. Two bucks if they're not.'

'That's why I get paid by the day, strike or no strike.'

'You never wanted to drill for yourself?'

As they were speaking, a swollen orange sun crept down behind the hump-backed mountains. The grassy hills faded from green to blue to purple as the light left them. Down in the boarding house, kerosene lamps began to sparkle – the valley was far too remote for electricity.

'Who said I haven't?'

'You did?'

Bard nodded and told Tom the story that, novice as he was, he'd already heard a dozen different times from a dozen different oilmen. Bard had finished a job, borrowed a rig, spent money to buy drilling rights, hired crewmen with beer money and promises. He'd drilled. Ran down three thousand feet through difficult ground. His money gave out. His derrick was needed elsewhere. He sold up, moved out, moved on. Eighteen months later, a team from one of the big oil companies reopened his well, went down another nine hundred feet, and struck oil.

'There's no money in drilling, I figure,' said Bard. 'Too many folks chasing too little oil. Be lucky if the oil don't give out on us sometime soon. Youngster like you oughta be in autos or radio. Something with a future.'

Tom shook his head. He didn't bother saying it, but he didn't take Bard's advice seriously. Bard didn't take his own advice seriously. The man was an oil addict. Even though he was working for someone else, he drilled like he had till the end of the week to strike oil or else lose his life. While on the job, he was never still. The only time he slowed down was when the rotating table was turning properly, the drill bit was sounding right, the boiler was giving enough pressure, and the derrick contained a section of thirty-foot pipe in place and ready to screw on to the drill as it descended.

'No oil. No hooch,' said Bard. 'That'll be one hell of a dry country.'

Tom glanced sideways. Bard was referring to the Eighteenth Amendment – the prohibition of alcohol – which had sailed through Congress and Senate almost undebated, and was on its way to being ratified by virtually every single state in the union. By January of next year, 1920, the manufacture and sale of alcohol would become an offence against not merely the law of the land, but the very constitution itself.

They were close to the boarding house now. The food that was served was plentiful but atrocious. The only thing that saved the place from being torn down in a riot was the huge quantities of beer available at absurdly low prices. The loud voices of men and beer were already mixing with the wind off the plains. Tom indicated the shapes of men moving in the twilight ahead of them.

'You reckon they'll stop drinking just because Uncle Sam tells 'em to?'

Bard shrugged. His interest in any question not directly related to oil was fairly limited. 'S'pose they'll have to go thirsty.'

'That's a lot of thirst,' said Tom.

Bard made some kind of answer and moved on into the boarding house, aiming to get cleaned up before the dinner bell rang. Tom was normally quick to the washtap himself, but on this occasion he stood back, feeling the movement of the night air on his face, looking at the stars beginning to speckle the violet sky.

Buying, crewing and running an oil rig cost around twenty-five thousand dollars. Men like Bard, who drilled on the cheap, were like poor men trying to stay in a poker game with a ten-dollar ante. Tom wouldn't make that mistake. He wouldn't drill until he was ready. He wouldn't drill until he had enough cash. He'd always assumed that he'd make his money – somehow or other – from oil, but maybe it didn't have to be like that. Maybe there were other ways. Not safe ones necessarily, but fast ones, good ones.

Tom nodded to himself. He wanted fast, he didn't need safe. His pulse quickened. He began to run.

59

Sir Adam looked at his son.

All across England, a generation of men looked older than they were. War had driven lines deep into youthful faces. The eyes of twenty-year-olds held expressions that would have been disturbing in men twice their age. And Alan? He was twenty-six years old. What with war and his hardships in Persia, Alan could easily have passed for thirty-five or even more. His face was so deeply bronzed from Persian sun and high altitudes that it seemed hard to believe he had ever been fair-skinned as a boy. His hair, meantime, had become so deeply bleached that it seemed almost white, his eyebrows all but invisible.

But there was something else in his face too. Something that Sir Adam understood but couldn't very well mention. Alan was still painfully in love with Lottie. Sir Adam gazed a little too long and hurriedly turned back to the papers. The maps were spread out on the full-size billiard table in the billiard room at Whitcombe House. Although it was broad daylight outside and the heavy brocade curtains were thrust back away from the windows, the electric lights above the table glowed at full strength to give the maps as much illumination as possible.

'These are quite astonishing. Extraordinary.'

Alan nodded. He'd stayed in the Zagros – measuring, surveying, photographing, examining – until the job was done. Valley after valley had fallen beneath Alan's rock-hammer and sample bag. He knew the geology of the northern Zagros better than any man in history. The table was littered with fossil, rock and soil samples.

Sir Adam riffled through the maps, using lumps of rock to keep them flat. His own command of geology was much less good than Alan's, but he still knew enough to identify the sites of greatest interest – and enough to know when there was virtually no hope of oil at all. Most of the maps fell into the latter category and Sir Adam's anxiety increased with each new sheet he examined. His expression must have revealed his concern.

'We always knew it was going to be difficult,' said Alan. 'I never thought we'd find oceans of the stuff.'

'Mmm,' Sir Adam agreed. He pulled one of the maps to the surface. There were some geological formations of the right kind of age, and some structures that could possibly indicate an oil reservoir underneath. 'This dome shape here. An anticline, possibly?'

An anticline is an arch-shaped structure buried deep beneath the ground. If the curve of the arch is made of a good impermeable rock and if the strata beneath contain oil, then an anticline is the perfect place for oil to collect – and the dream of every oilman.

'Possibly, Father. Most likely not.' Alan pointed out a few indications on the map that suggested the anticline was empty of oil now, even if it had ever held any.

'But worth a try, perhaps.'

'Perhaps. But look at this.'

Alan brought out the one map he'd held back. This was a map of Ameri's valley, and the neighbouring valleys to east and west. A thin red cross – the only red mark on any of the maps – was labelled in Alan's neat handwriting: 'Oil seepage!' Sir Adam studied the map with mounting interest.

'You actually found oil?'

'I found enough to light a kerosene lamp for about twenty-five seconds. Not even a teaspoonful.'

'But still . . . oil.'

'Yes, oil. It smelled good. Not too much sulphur. Not much tar. If there is oil there, it'll be a beautiful one. Light, sweet-smelling, easy to refine.'

Sir Adam stared back at the map. He was looking for the structures that might indicate some hope: an anticline, a salt dome, a 'nose' or monocline. There was nothing there. 'In America, I understand, they have places where they mine oil. They literally dig shafts into the hillside and let the oil drain out. Even if there's no chance of conventional drilling, you've found your hillside here. Perhaps a different approach . . .'

'Father, they get twenty barrels a day from those mines. Thirty if they're lucky. That's all very well when the market's on your doorstep, but this oil's got to be carried all the way to England. If we don't strike it big, there's no point in striking it at all. But look at the map. Look back at the map. You're missing something.'

Sir Adam studied the map. He couldn't for the life of him see what his son was referring to.

'Don't you see it, Father? The fault line?'

A fault was another classic way in which oil could be trapped underground. If two strata are broken and overlap one another, forming a kind of roof, then oil could some-times be found in the break.

'A fault line? There's obviously some change in geological contour east and west, but I don't see –'

'Here, Father, here.' Alan snatched a billiard chalk from the cue rack, and slashed a thick blue line right through the map from top to bottom. The line stretched for twenty-two miles unbroken. 'I didn't see it either at first. Not for two months. Like you, I was looking for something narrow. Something a mile or two in extent, even five or ten. But the fault is as classic as you can get. Every now and then you can't see it. It's hidden by snow or rockfall or subsequent geological accidents. But when you get far enough back from it – join up the clues – let yourself see the obvious – then what you have is one of the biggest natural pools ever discovered.'

Sir Adam stared at the thick blue line. His son was right. The fault was on such a vast scale, it was easier to miss it than to see it. But there it was: as perfectly mapped as you could hope to see.

'By God, Alan, that's a fault indeed.'

'Yes.'

'And once upon a time there was some oil there.'

'Yes.'

The two men looked at each other: father, son; old man and oilman. Alan had done all the research he could, but the question remained: did the fault contain oil, or was it as dry as a bone? There are infinitely more faults than there are productive oilfields, and infinitely more bankrupt dreamers than there are wealthy oilmen.

'You'll drill there?'

'If I can.'

'Do you have any money?'

'No, not a penny.'

For all Alan knew, the fault concealed an ocean of oil. Unless he could find some money to drill for it, it might stay there for the rest of time.

'Will you borrow it?'

'Against what? No one will lend it.'

'So there's nothing else for it, I suppose. Set up an exploration company and sell shares in the enterprise. It's a shame to give away control, but inevitable, I can see that.'

'I'm not selling.'

'Not selling? But surely –'

'I'm not selling.'

The years of war and hardship had hardened Alan. His voice was a man's voice: strong and decided. His father opened his mouth – then closed it. If Alan wanted to be pig-headed about selling shares, that was up to him. In time, he'd understand that there was no other way to raise capital. No other way on earth.

60

The oil was there all right.

Four miles away from the rig where Tom and the others drilled, six miles from the boarding house and a full sixteen miles from the nearest railroad, a gimcrack exploration outfit struck oil at five and a half thousand feet. The well produced just eighty barrels a day: a good strike, but hardly colossal. All the same, the excitement produced was extraordinary. If there was oil in one place, there might be oil right next door. The remote little bit of rolling country, situated where the open plains meet the mountains, began to jostle with new arrivals.

Drilling crews arrived by the day. The boarding house overflowed. The road down to town became waterlogged and near impassable. The first frosts sharpened their knives on a northerly wind. When Tom and the others went out to drill they wore woollen gloves and long undershorts beneath their trousers.

The lights in the bar were red-shaded and, in any case, were turned down low. The place was crowded with oilmen: junior roustabouts and senior drillers. An evil-looking pianist knocked out depressive tunes on the piano, while the usual half-dozen prostitutes sat in a huddle at the end of the bar and shared a drink together before the night's work started.

Tom sat apart at a table by himself. He was in town for the night only, to pick up some drilling goods from the railhead before returning next day to the well.

As he looked round the room, there was a sudden yell of laughter from the prostitutes in the corner. Tom grinned at them. And as he grinned, one of the girls caught his attention in a way that the others didn't. She was dark-skinned and dark-haired. Her face was too sharp to be pretty in a normal way: her chin was too pointed, her nose was angular and her forehead too high. But there was something unusually alive about her face. Her deeply set eyes were intelligent, alert but anxious. It was as though someone sensitive and gifted had been forced to live through a period of suffering or danger. Tom recognised the look. His years in prison had attuned him. The girl attracted him and troubled him in about equal amounts.

Tom grabbed a passing waiter and indicated the girl. 'D'you have any wine in this joint?'

'Wine?'

'Yes, wine. They grow grapes. They squeeze 'em. They bottle 'em. Wine.'

'Sure, downstairs someplace.'

'Can you bring me a bottle of wine, two glasses and invite that girl to join me?'

'That girl? The –' The waiter had been about to say 'whore' or something similar, but he checked himself in time. 'The dark-haired one. Sure, right away.'

After what had obviously been a long search, the wine arrived, followed by the girl. As she slid off her stool at the bar, she exchanged a laugh with the other girls, then tugged at her blouse to make sure her cleavage was sufficiently visible. To make doubly sure, she unfastened a button and did what she could to make her narrow chest look full and buxom.

By the time she arrived, Tom was (to his own surprise) burning with a sudden anger.

'I only asked you to share a drink. I didn't expect you to start undressing.'

The girl didn't sit, she remained standing. 'That's a pleasant way. to greet somebody.' The words could have come out tough, but actually they didn't. Her tone was cool and the rebuke was deliberate, but not at all coarse. Partly it was her accent, which was mid-European and husky.

'I only want to offer you a drink. I'm not expecting to . . . to . . . for God's sake, I'm not going to pay you.' Tom's voice hovered between conciliatory and aggressive. His mood was similarly uncertain.

The girl did up her button, and arranged her clothes more decorously. She took a longer look at Tom – again, he noticed her gaze, which almost seemed to expect the presence of danger – then a glance back at her girlfriends. She sat down, placing her bottom down on the seat first, then sliding her legs round to follow. It was the delicate way for a lady to sit, the way a London debutante might sit, not a cheap whore in a two-bit Yankee oil town. She sniffed the wine, then sipped.

'In that case you ought to have bought a better wine.'

Tom laughed defensively. 'It's all they have. I was sick of drinking beer. If you want, I can –'

She smiled. 'It's OK. I was joking. I'm sick of beer too.'

'Tom Calloway,' said Tom extending his hand.

'Rebecca Lewi,' she said. 'Delighted to make your acquaintance.'

Rebecca Lewi turned out to be solid gold. She was a Polish-speaking Jew from Vilnius in Lithuania. During the war, her family had been displaced, robbed, ill-treated and imprisoned. Somehow, they had found the means to pay for her and her twelve-year-old brother to travel first to Sweden, then on to America. They had arrived in 1916 and had been forced to wait more than three years before obtaining reliable news of the rest of the family. Her other brothers were either dead or in prison somewhere in Russia. Her parents were both alive and had hopes of resettling safely in Germany. She wanted them to come out to America, but they felt too old and too uncertain to make the move.

'It will be good for them there, as long as the socialists don't seize control.'

'And your brother? The one you travelled out with?'

Rebecca's face stiffened. 'He came out here with tuberculosis. It was the main reason we came. I was terrified that they wouldn't let him in, but even though the doctor on Ellis Island found the problem, he took pity on us.'

'And your brother, he . . . ?'

'He died. I did all I could, but . . .' She shrugged. 'The illness took him. Two years ago.'

'I'm sorry . . .' Tom tailed off, but a thought had struck him and must have been visible in his expression.

Rebecca answered his unspoken question. 'Yes. The hospitals were expensive. I got into debt. Now I'm paying it off. I thought I would hate selling myself, but apparently one gets used to anything. I don't want sympathy.'

Tom nodded. 'All right. No sympathy.'

'Good, and you?' Rebecca changed the subject brusquely and decisively. 'You're English?'

'Yes – or rather, no. I was. I'm –'

'Right, you're American now. Aren't we all? We just jump off the boat, and presto! Two thousand years of history just goes up in smoke.' She laughed. 'Go on then. You were English. Not poor either, from the sound of you. But you came over here. No family. No cash. You're working in a manual job. Why? Must be either prison, or debt, or –'

'I was a prisoner of war for two and a half years. I almost died. There was nothing left for me in England when I returned. I'd sooner be poor here than the King's Own Bootlicker back in England. And for your information, I enjoy what I do.'

'You were a prisoner of war? I'm sorry. I was too hard on you. I apologise.'

'That's all right. It's OK.'

'No it isn't. I hate it when I do that. I'm sorry.'

They finished the bottle of wine. Rebecca wiped her mouth and made a face. 'That was horrible, but thank you.'

Tom laughed. The wine had indeed been awful, but it had been a pleasure to share it with someone who knew it. But Rebecca's manner had changed once again. She wasn't exactly looking at her watch or getting up to go, but she was clearly signalling that it was time for her to get back to work. Tom even realised that she was letting him know that if he changed his mind and wanted to pay her for sex, then she was available then and there.

Tom had no problem with prostitution. Back in France, he'd usually been able to find girls who'd have sex without presenting him with a bill, but when he hadn't been able to, he'd paid for his pleasure without thinking twice about it. But Rebecca, from the very start, was different. He didn't know why and didn't really bother to ask himself the question. She unsettled him. Her businesslike approach bothered him and made him angry.

'Back to work now?' he said, with needless brutality. 'Should be a profitable night, huh?' He gestured at some young roustabouts who were already far gone in drink and were making leering faces at the prostitutes by the bar.

'You promised no sympathy. This is what I get instead, is it?'

'Hell, it's just a business, isn't it? What's wrong with that? That guy there looks flush. Have a quick screw with him, you should be able to find another couple of clients before the place closes.'

Rebecca stared coldly back at Tom, then quite deliberately undid a couple of buttons on her blouse. She stood up and walked, hips swaying, over to the man he'd pointed out. She stood there for a moment, hand on hip, deliberately provocative, and was then clearly urged to sit down amidst a torrent of drunken lecherous laughter from the nearby roustabouts.

Tom looked on with a strange mixture of jealousy, fury and confusion. He slammed some money down on the table for the wine and stomped out of the bar.

And as he left, he emerged into a town transformed. The air had been cold but now it was snowing thickly enough for the street to be carpeted in white. A team of horses that had been caught out on the wagon trail emerged from the newly frozen mire on to the main street, amidst a stream of curses and blue language. Tom stood transfixed by the sight.

He wanted money and he wanted it soon. Now, for the first time, he knew how to get it.

61

From tiny beginnings, the Anglo-Persian Oil Company was becoming one of the world's leading oil companies. This year it would drill and ship one and a half million tons of the precious liquid. Its refinery at Abadan was on the way to becoming the biggest in the world.

The Finance Director extended his hand. It was a small, dry hand without power in the grip. Alan shook it too hard and took his seat. Tea arrived in delicate porcelain, and the Finance Director fussed over cups and saucers like a maiden aunt taking tea with a bishop. Alan felt like a sunburned Persian bear, his hands still rough from his long stay in the Zagros.

'The concession, yes, the concession,' said the director, in his high-pitched voice. 'We'd like all of it, of course. The split concession . . . well, it's an *irritation* to us. I can't put it more strongly than that – but, yes, an irritation certainly.'

Alan nodded. 'It's an irritation I can let you dispose of.'

'But, you see, on the other hand, our geology people say there's really *nothing* to be had in the south and from my own point of view, paying out money to the Shah for the right to drill for nothing doesn't exactly make financial sense.'

'I can see that. I just wanted to give you the opportunity to bid.'

'To *bid*? To *bid*? You mean to imply there are *bidders*?'

The Finance Director's voice had risen to a squeak. In his excitement, he'd let some watery tea slop into his saucer. It formed a little circular lake, like a pool of oil.

Sometimes success comes from luck, sometimes from circumstance, sometimes by accident. In the case of Royal Dutch Shell, one of the two big gorillas of the international oil world, success was born of an individual: a Dutchman named Henri Deterding.

Right now, Deterding was glaring incredulously at Alan.

'*South* Persia? *South* Persia? The *south* of the country?'

'That's correct. Bandar-e Deylam to Persepolis and everything south.'

'And this is your survey, eh?'

Deterding had acquired the manners of an English country squire. His behaviour during the war had been emphatically pro-British. All the same, where business was concerned his manners became brusque, almost rude.

'Yes.'

'Of course, you can't expect us to rely on your own survey. You might tell us anything.'

'I have set down only what is true.' Alan spoke coldly. He was an English gentleman, and was not used to people suggesting he might lie. His coldness was for another reason as well: a guilty conscience. His maps contained nothing that was false, but they did not contain everything that was true. In particular, a certain red cross with its handwritten comment, 'Oil seepage!', had been left off the copies that Alan now handed round.

'Yes, yes, yes.'

'You'll find that, except for a few details where I've corrected previous work, my report is exactly in line with previous investigations – although more detailed. I would naturally invite you to send your own experts, only . . .'

223

'Yes? What? Only what?'

'Sorry. I spoke hastily. If you want to cover the ground again with your own geologists, then you must do as you see fit.'

'But you were saying something. *Only.* Only what?'

'I was starting to say that there are a couple of other companies with some interest in the possibility. They may be willing to act more quickly.'

'Other companies?' Deterding's small face with its trim moustache was suddenly alive. 'Who? Ha! Anglo-Persian. By God, I can believe they'd be keen to keep us away. God, yes, that'd be a smack in the face for them, what? Shell getting all friendly with the Shah, and who knows what might happen to the concession in the north . . . But you said two companies. *Two.* Who's the other?' His brow furrowed. 'Not the Americans, surely? Not –'

Standard Oil was the biggest, the strongest, the richest, the toughest.

Their man in London was a big-jawed American, Huckleberry Grant, who'd started out with his own independent refining outfit, before being 'sweated' to death by Rockefeller's operation. Grant had joined his enemy and risen far and fast.

'This is a helluva good job on the geology. Your own work?'

Alan nodded.

'Nice. We've had some of our own guys take a look at it. We can't confirm everything, but this squares with anything that we know.'

Alan nodded.

'And what we know is there's not much there. Maybe a little. Not a lot.'

Alan nodded. 'You may be right.'

'You're not exactly selling yourself here, feller. You don't think your concession is up to much?'

224

'It's not what I think it's worth, it's what others think it's worth.'

'But we've got the first look over this, right? You came here first?'

'I'm sorry, Mr Grant, perhaps I should have done. Unfortunately there are a couple of companies closer to home with an interest in the property.'

'Anglo-Persian, I can see – but, goddamn, you mean Shell, don't you?'

'I was with Henri Deterding this time yesterday.'

'Deterding, Jesus.' The big American crashed his big fist against the desk. Among the ornaments sitting there was an eight-inch fishtailed drill bit, well worn and still dirty in the pockmarks. Grant's fist shook the desk and the drill bit began to roll to the edge. Alan caught it and returned it.

'Thanks. Hit a gusher with this back in 'eighty-five. Molly Moran 2, name of that well. Three hundred fifty barrels a day it did at its best. Sweet old Molly Moran.' Grant weighed the bit in his hand, deep in thought. 'Deterding, huh?'

62

Christmas Eve.

Up on the hills, a second oil strike had been made, one-eighty barrels a day, and the lucky well this time no more than a mile and a half from one of Lyman Bard's. The excitement was formidable, but drilling conditions had turned from difficult to near impossible. The snow was thick, the cold savage. On days when the wind blew and snow fell, nobody left his lodgings. On clear days, the drilling crew set out at dawn, and did what they could in the short days and the bitter cold.

Tom quit.

'You what?' said Bard, when Tom told him.

'I'm taking off. It's not like you need a full crew, not with this weather.'

Bard shook his head. In theory, Tom was the most junior of his crew, but in practice Tom was faster, keener, smarter than the rest. 'The cold getting to you? I guess it don't snow in England, maybe . . .' Bard's voice trailed off as he tried to remember if England was a snowy country or not. 'Not like here, anyways,' he added to be on the safe side.

'I don't mind it cold, Lyman. But I guess you've taught me enough about drilling for now. I reckon it's about time I made a little money.'

'You want a raise? I could find four bucks a day, I guess. Matter of fact, I reckon we could say four bucks fifty.'

But Tom didn't want a raise. He didn't want employment. He'd come to America to make his fortune and he'd waited long enough. He drank a last beer with his mentor, shook hands warmly and headed off at a brisk pace down the valley to the railhead.

It was there he found who he was looking for. The pre-Christmas bar was rowdy and loud, the holiday mood only increased by the men's knowledge that in just four weeks, Uncle Sam was locking up the beer kegs and the whiskey bottles for the rest of time. Tom got to the bar early enough that Rebecca Lewi hadn't yet started her nightly trade. Tom bought a bottle of wine at the bar, then caught her eyes and held the bottle aloft. She smiled and came over. It was the sixth time they'd shared a drink together. Not once had Tom offered to pay for sex. Not once, after the first time, had she offered it.

'Merry Christmas,' he said as she sat.

'And merry Christmas to you.' She pronounced the word with a kind of grave care, reminding Tom that the festival belonged to him but not to her. He suddenly wondered if it had been her intention to remind him. He felt a brief flash of annoyance, which he quickly damped.

'I quit today.'

'I'm sorry? You left? Left work?' She bent across the table to hear him better. Her hair smelled warm and soft, but along-side that good smell there lurked the one of cheap scent that was as much a part of her profession as the low-cut blouse and dark stockings.

Tom nodded.

'Why? I thought you loved your job. Oil: isn't that why you came here?'

Tom gestured outside. 'We can't drill in this. Not really. We lose two days for every one we drill.'

'And instead what will you do?'

Tom grinned. 'I expect I'll think of something.' He refilled her glass and changed the subject. 'Listen, you were planning to work tonight?'

She nodded.

'Well, don't. There's a restaurant down the road which isn't terrible. Let me take you there. You shouldn't be working on Christmas Eve.'

She hesitated a moment. Tom could see that she was calculating whether a dinner with him was worth the sacrifice of an evening's income. She glanced towards the group of her friends – the other prostitutes who worked the town. Then she turned back and smiled. 'Thank you. I'd like that.'

Without finishing their wine, they left the bar. A rigger, who knew Tom and recognised his companion, made an obscene whistle as they left. Tom instantly stiffened and was about to turn back into the bar, fists balled, when he felt Rebecca's hand on his arm, pulling him back.

'No fighting!' she said sharply. 'I can't stand it.'

Tom turned away and went outside with her. 'Don't you mind? That idiot whistling? The picture he had in his mind?'

'Thomas,' she said, turning the pronunciation of his name into something dark and soft and East European, 'Thomas, I sell myself. It is how I live. This way, people whistle at me but I pay what I owe. It isn't for ever.'

Snow was still gently falling and her long hair began to be speckled with white. Her deep-set eyes looked unwaveringly into his. He held her gaze a moment or two, then looked away.

'OK. My Christmas gift to you, then. I won't punch idiots who whistle.'

It was cold outside and they hurried on to the restaurant. The food wasn't special, but it was OK. They talked non-stop. Rebecca's father had once been a pharmacist with a substantial shop in one of the better districts in Vilnius. In talking about their life there, she happened to mention that they had employed two maids to help them. Tom was struck by the similarity in their stories. She: robbed by war, exiled from a prosperous home, was now in effect without family. He – for all that he was an English gentleman, not a Lithuanian Jew – his story was the same. They ate steak and fried potatoes, chopped cabbage, a sticky date Christmas cake washed down with wine and coffee.

'Thank you, Thomas. It is a pleasure to feel like a lady for a change.'

Tom flung some money on the table. 'Here. I've got something to show you.'

Out on the snowy street, by the light of the moon and a flashlight that Tom carried with him, they walked together to the yard behind the railway depot. Tom led them down a side alley, to a small wooden shed, padlocked shut. He produced a key, unlocked it and swung open a door. He shone the flashlight inside.

The shed was full with cases of whiskey, four complete barrels of beer, all of it bedded under straw to keep the frost away.

'It's why I quit my job,' he said. 'The way I see it, Prohibition is a goldmine. A fellow only needs to be willing to dig.'

Rebecca's face looked gravely disappointed; upset even. 'You quit your job for this?'

'Yeah, and I know how I can get more. But listen, I've got a proposition. It's one thing to have the hooch, it's quite another to sell it. What with your job and all, I figure you're the perfect person to sell the stuff.'

Rebecca backed away. In the darkness, Tom couldn't see her face. Her shoes slipped a couple of times on an icy wagon-rut. Tom put out an arm but she waved it away. When she spoke, her voice was close to tears.

'Why? Why do you have to do this? Why can't you just leave me alone?'

'What? What d'you mean? I'll give you your share, of course. Don't you want to pay off your debts? I can't believe you'd rather . . . do what you do than sell a little liquor.'

Rebecca had begun walking as fast as she could back up the little alley. In the darkness, she was unable to see where she was going and she came close to falling. Tom slammed the door of his shed closed and locked it again before racing to join her. His head was full of arguments, but she spoke before he could get to them.

'Thomas, Thomas, why can't you leave my job out of things? Most of the time you hate what I do. You want to fight people, you are angry at me for working. Now . . . now you want to use me. You want to use my body to sell your alcohol. You are no better than . . . No, that isn't true. You *are* better. But . . . Sorry, Thomas. Sorry. It is time for me to go home.'

Pushing aside his torch, his arm, his words of apology, she hastened away from him into the night. She didn't once look back.

63

It was late at night and raining. Gaslight shone down on the puddled streets. Any motor-taxis that were still cruising for business seemed to move slowly, with a watery hiss of their wheels.

Alan walked slowly. The New Year celebrations that had ushered in the 1920s had just faded into a cold and wet January. Alan had been staying with Guy, whose hospitality he never quite enjoyed but which he was too poor to be able to turn down. Guy lived in a buzz of fast women, rich men, and much more expense and wildness than Alan was happy with.

He longed to escape. He had loved the wild Zagros. The hardships he'd endured there had been trivial compared with anything he'd been through in the war, and the loneliness had suited his mood. With Tom dead and Lottie out of reach, London felt like a wasteland – and Guy's home felt like its flashy, dead heart. He fled to Hampshire and Whitcombe House whenever he could get away.

Meantime, he trudged on west down Piccadilly, head down, hat tilted to keep the rain off his neck. Ahead of him, a hotel porter held open a door, spilling bright electric light out onto the wet pavement. A flock of young people, Alan's age, tumbled out, laughing, joking, and singing the dance tunes that reverberated dimly from inside. Alan stepped aside, when one of the women, not seeing him, stumbled into him and almost fell.

He caught her and held her upright, until she'd recovered her footing. She had a slender figure, and her hair was cut very short in the ultrafashionable 'bob' that Alan so disliked.

'How silly of me. Thank you, whoever you –'

The woman turned. The light fell on her face. It was Lottie.

Alan didn't know what his face must have looked like, but Lottie's face registered something like shock, perhaps longing, perhaps even love. He stepped towards her.

But then her expression changed. Alan stopped in his tracks. He must have been mistaken. Lottie's face wore nothing but the bright, sociable smile she usually wore. He stood in the street, his mouth hanging slightly open.

'Oh Lord, it's Alan Montague! Alan *dar*-ling, how are you? Look, everybody, this is my favourite oilman, Alan Montague. Going to be *fright*-fully rich, digging for oil in the middle of the Persian deserts. Darling, I hope you've found absolutely buckets of the stuff.'

There was nothing, absolutely nothing, in Lottie's voice to make Alan think that she held any tenderness for him any more. Worse than that, it was as though she'd almost forgotten that they had ever been deeply in love. *'Oh Lord, it's Alan Montague!'* What on earth was that by way of greeting? She had called him darling, admittedly, but she called everybody darling. There was nothing at all in her words or her voice to justify all that he had felt for her.

Alan recoiled, shocked.

This wasn't the Lottie he'd written all those letters to from his tent in Persia. His Lottie was the grave, committed, inspiring nurse of the Very Seriously Wounded. His Lottie was the one who'd preferred the long, green Hampshire walks to any amount of dances and parties. There was something else to disturb him as well. There was a man by her side, not touching her exactly, but proprietorial none the less. He looked intelligent, superficial and rich.

232

'Do join us, darling Alan, won't you? We're going on to the Medusa Club for a last drink and dance. The Blaine-Raffertys are going to be there. You remember them, surely? Ned's become awfully big in mining and I'm sure you'll have heaps to talk about. Do come!'

Alan shook his head and began muttering excuses – up early tomorrow, feeling tired, spot of flu. The man at Lottie's side moved slightly away from her, as though sensing that Alan wasn't a potential threat.

Alan apologised again, promised to get in touch, and ran away.

64

On 20 January 1920, the United States of America, in accordance with its Constitution and the duly expressed wishes of its people, embarked upon the noblest experiment in the history of the world. Up and down the land, from the snows of Montana to the dusts of Texas, from the blue Pacific to the grey Atlantic, bars closed their doors, liquor sellers ceased their trade, the old devil-in-a-bottle, John Barleycorn, breathed his last.

In theory.

The only itsy-bitsy problem with the theory was that up and down the land, from dusty Texas to snowy Montana and from one bluish-grey ocean to the next, there were folk like Tom keen to sell alcohol and other folk equally anxious to buy it.

Having sold his hooch at two hundred and ninety dollars, a fifty per cent mark-up over the price he'd paid, Tom paused to restock. He jumped freight trains and rode north of the border, where an astonished Canadian economy found that whisky selling had just become the fastest growing, most profitable business in existence. Tom called around and found a wholesaler who understood his new market.

'How d'you want it packed?'

'Huh? You'll box it, I guess,' said Tom.

'Yeah,' said the wholesaler, as if he was talking to an imbecile. 'I could leave it in the original Haig & Haig boxes, if you like. Show folks your stuff is for real.'

Tom saw the problem. The alcohol would have to ride straight back through customs, and nowadays there were times when it certainly *didn't* pay to advertise.

'I got boot polish,' said the wholesaler. 'Or ham. I'm getting in a load of condensed milk tomorrow.'

He kicked a stack of empty wooden boxes. Each box had neatly stencilled on the side 'Jo Brearley's Finest – the Boot Black's Secret!'. Next to these, there was a stack marked 'Alberta Hams & Meats, Inc. Our Taste is Our Advertisement'.

Tom grinned. 'I fancy the hams,' he said.

'Hams it is.'

The choice was almost fatal.

Thirty-six hours later, a goods train steamed slowly to a halt in a forested valley, where soot and snowflakes petalled the air. Outside a wooden cabin, the Stars and Stripes hung unmoving from a flagpole. Painted across the front of the cabin was a sign: 'UNITED STATES CUSTOMS'. Beyond the customs post, a small settlement clustered round the railroad stop, like chickens frightened of the night.

Riding legitimately this time, Tom got out to stretch his legs and watch his boxes clear the border. When the United States Congress had decided to prohibit alcohol, it had been so confident of the law-abiding nature of its citizens that it hadn't bothered to take any serious action on enforcement. Customs posts had hardly been strengthened. Federal agents were scarcely thought necessary.

Tom wasn't worried.

He stamped up and down the platform to bring warmth into his feet. He thought of Rebecca. The two of them had patched up their quarrel and were friends again.

She *bothered* him, though. He didn't find her attractive –

at least he thought he didn't – and half the time he found her conversation maddening. All the same, no sooner was he gone from her, than he began to think about her again. He couldn't explain his fascination with her and was annoyed at himself for it.

He headed out of the station, and bought himself a candy bar and some coffee from the 'Missionary Milk Bar'. The man serving the drink said, 'Praise the Lord, sir. Ten cents, please.'

Tom handed over his dime but didn't bother to praise the Lord.

'Leaflet?' said the man, shoving a leaflet over the counter. 'The One True Path to Salvation. There's no charge.'

Tom leaned over the counter. 'You want to know the one true path to salvation?'

'Huh?'

'Oil,' said Tom. 'Oil and alcohol.'

The man snatched his leaflets back in annoyance. 'The Lord loveth the sinner who repenteth. The Lord –'

'Good for the Lord. Only the sinner prefereth the hooch.' Tom tossed back his coffee, took his candy and left.

Inside the train, the customs men were still busy with their paperwork. So far as Tom had been able to see, they hadn't once bothered to open any of the crates or boxes on the train.

A scrawny dog loped up and down, cocking his leg over a pile of wooden crates marked 'Saskatchewan Furs and Hides, Inc.' The urine steamed yellow and began to freeze. Tom paced the platform, fast enough to keep warm. The customs men didn't hurry. The dog snuffled a pile of boxes containing smoked fish from Vancouver. The fish sat right next to Tom's boxes full of whisky.

Further up the platform, a customs man looked curiously at the dog. Tom looked at the customs man. The dog didn't look at anything except its fish. The customs man looked on a while longer, then strolled over to his fur-coated boss and muttered something in a low voice.

Tom turned away for another fast walk up and down the platform, when his stomach suddenly took a dive.

The dog!

The dog was theoretically standing right next to a dozen boxes of prime Canadian ham, but it hadn't once bothered to sniff them. The dog was a four-legged, flea-ridden lie-detector test, and Tom had already all but failed.

For a moment, fear left him senseless. If he was caught, his booze would be confiscated, of course, but that hardly mattered. What mattered was this. Tom's American citizenship depended upon him living in the United States for five years *without committing a felony*. If Tom's whisky-smuggling was discovered, he'd be prosecuted and deported home to England. It would be the worst fate in the world and it was now only minutes away.

The two customs men spoke together, then began to walk over to the dog and the boxes of so-called ham.

For one second more, Tom was frozen. Then he moved. He hurtled out of the station, back to the Missionary Milk Bar.

'Bless you, bro –' began the man, before noticing who his customer was. 'Oh. It's you.'

'I have seen the light, brother,' said Tom. 'Praise the Lord.'

The man looked stunned. 'Why, truly? Praise the Lord, indeed, brother. Yea, I say unto you, the Lord hath more joy over one sinner who –'

'Damn right. Any chance of some of those pamphlets of yours?'

'You want one? Really?'

'Praise the Lord!' said Tom again.

'Praise the Lord!'

The man shoved the stack of leaflets over the counter. Tom snatched up the whole bundle and dropped a dollar bill in exchange. 'I go to spread the good news. Truly is there joy in heaven this day.'

'Why, joy indeed, brother. Won't you –'

237

But Tom was gone. Back at the station, the customs men had reached the boxes. The dog had done its job and been tugged aside. A third customs man was walking across the platform with a crowbar and jemmy.

Tom skidded up to them, breath freezing in the pale air.

'Bless you, brothers,' he panted. 'All praise to them that laboureth in the sight of the Lord.'

The customs men grinned at each other. One of them cracked a joke in an undertone and provoked a burst of muffled laughter. The more senior of the officers said, 'Thank you, son. We need all the praise we can get on a day like this.'

'May I help you, officers?' said Tom, in a more normal voice.

'Help us?' The customs man used his gloved hand to flick through the freight manifest and customs forms. 'You're Calloway?'

'Thomas Calloway,' said Tom, hand over his heart. 'My earthly business is the importation of premium Canadian meat products. My spiritual business is the salvation of human souls. I am at your service in either capacity.'

The grins on the faces of the customs men grew wider. The man arriving with the crowbar let it drop to his side, saying, 'How about the importation of prohibited liquor? You able to help a soul out in that capacity?'

'Truly, is Liquor not a devil that it tempts the working man from his fireside? That it brings a man into dens of vice and gambling? That it breaks a family asunder and strikes down the wife and mother?'

For the first time, doubt appeared on the faces of the customs men. Tom produced his leaflets and handed them out.

'The One True Path,' intoned Tom, scanning the leaflet as fast as he could, while trying to look as though he'd read it a thousand times before. 'Which will you choose, brothers: the Angel of Temperance or the Demon of Drink? The Holy

Seraphim about your Fireside or the Hosts of Satan at the Gambling Table?'

The customs men smothered grins, holding hands up to their mouths and looking away. The man with the crowbar looked questioningly at his superior, who shook his head. The man let his crowbar slide to rest against the stack of boxes.

With as straight a face as he could manage, the senior customs man said, 'Real nice leaflet. We'll be sure to study it good.' He turned away.

Tom let out a long sigh of relief. 'Be sure you do that, brother. Praise the Lord.'

65

On their sixth birthday, Jack Creeley had given Alan and Tom a litter of three brown and white spaniel puppies. The young pups were healthy, playful and rumbustious. They were also competitive. If you dropped a rag in amongst the three dogs, they would fight over it for hours. They growled. They tugged. They tried winning the rag by guile and they tried with brute force. Then, with victory decided, the winner would drag the rag off to a private corner, sniff it briefly – then ignore it completely.

It wasn't the prize that mattered, it was not being beaten.

It was like that now.

None of the three big oil majors actually liked the geology of southern Persia. The world was huge and unexplored. Nobody had drilled a well anywhere in the Arabian peninsula. Vast tracts of America were still virgin territory. The riches of Mexico and Venezuela still lay largely beneath the ground. Compared with all of that, Southern Persia would have come low on anyone's list.

And yet.

Anglo-Persian felt threatened. At Shell, Henri Deterding was obsessed by his rivalry with Standard. And at Standard, the idea of stirring things up with Shell was far too tempting to resist.

They each put in an offer.

Three dogs. One rag.

Alan listened to their offers and politely refused them all.

And went on refusing until the offers had climbed as high as they'd go.

Shell and Standard made offers so similar that Alan wondered if they each had spies in the other's inner sanctums. But neither Shell nor Standard was coming out on top. The company with the most to gain – and the most to lose – was Anglo-Persian, a fact that Sir Charles Greenaway, the company's chairman, knew full well.

Greenaway reached for some cigarettes, and offered them to Alan. It was their final meeting. Alan knew he had to make a deal and live with the consequences. If Greenaway didn't offer enough, that would be Alan's tough luck. There would be no better deal available elsewhere.

'Filthy habit,' said the oilman. 'Can't stop it. Don't want to. Will you? No. Very well. Now, look here. We have to have your part of the concession. You know it and I know it. Should never have been split up. Damn bad move by D'Arcy. Hand half the country over to another crowd and the Shah won't stay quiet. There'd be trouble for us. Trouble for everyone. Trouble and expense.'

Alan nodded. He wasn't being asked for a reply just yet.

'And then there's the question of patriotism. Shell Oil, jolly good company, decent bunch, did well for us in the war, but we have to face the fact that they're sixty per cent Dutch. It's no good bringing that sort of mix into our part of the world. It'll only mess things up. And I need hardly tell you what the chaps at the Foreign Office – let alone the India Office – would say if the Yanks got in there. There'd be hell to pay, I'm afraid. Perfect hell.'

'I do see.'

'And we know they're interested, of course. Had word of

it from . . . well, wholly reliable sources, if I may put it like that.'

Alan nodded, amused to have guessed right about the amount of spying that went on. 'Yes. I must say I've been pleasantly surprised,' he murmured.

'Now what I thought was that a young chap like you really needs some adventure. Responsibility. You remind me of myself at your age, as a matter of fact. I'd like to buy the concession off you, naturally, but we should talk about where you'd fit in here, at Anglo-Persian. Maybe with our geology boys, maybe our production team. You'll do well. Your war record, your geology, terrific stuff. Just the sort of thing we need. Put you in charge of a couple of rigs. See what you could do.'

'That's a very kind offer.'

'Not a bit, not a bit.' Greenaway's cigarette was smoked down to his fingers and he stubbed it out carelessly, getting a bit of still-smoking ash on his fingers. 'So what do you say? We'll offer seventy thousand pounds for your concession – sixty-eight thousand more than it's worth, I might add – and sign you up for our production side right away. The government will be extremely pleased with your decision. Extremely.'

Alan controlled his expression with care. His next best offer had been sixty thousand from Deterding at Shell and he was quite sure he wouldn't get them to go higher. His three-dogs-one-rag game was reaching its limit, and it was time to bring it to an end. Alan frowned and asked for a cigarette. Greenaway handed him one with barely suppressed impatience. He lit it and drew on it thoughtfully.

'I understand your concern for British interests,' he said, 'but I'd sooner not be too far out of pocket. Perhaps if you said seventy-five thousand . . . ?'

Greenaway drummed on the table. 'Very well, very well, seventy-five.'

'And I'm grateful for your offer of employment, but before I take it up, there's something I want to try to do.'

'Yes?'

'It relates to the concession I'm selling.'

'Yes?'

'There's an area twenty miles long by ten wide that I'm interested in. I'd like to sublease the area from you. Any oil I find there is mine. If I don't find any, then in ten years' time the land reverts to you.'

'*Damnation!*' Greenaway was shocked by Alan's gall. 'By God, Montague, you push hard. Where's the strip? The map, the map, where in hell's name is the map?' He punched a button on his desk and a secretary came running in. 'Mrs Parker, get me some geologists, will you? Reynolds, Camberley, Keegan, Lewis, any of those chaps. Right now, please, right now.'

The secretary ran off and Greenaway found the relevant map and unrolled it.

'Here,' said Alan. Taking a pencil from Greenaway's desk he drew a mark at the four corners of his precious strip – the Ameri fault, as he thought of it. Greenaway frowned over the map, muttering 'Damnation, damnation,' under his breath. In a few moments, three geologists knocked and entered, their skin all bearing the deep tan of their trade.

'Wait outside, would you, Montague?'

Alan had to wait an hour for his answer. He tried lighting up, but his painful lung (worse always in London smoke) rebelled against the tobacco. Eventually, the door burst open. It was Greenaway.

'Five years. You have five years to find oil. If you fail, the land reverts to us.'

'Very well.'

'And you'll sign a contract as soon as we can have it drawn up. Later today or first thing tomorrow. No further communication with those dogs at Shell or Standard.'

'Very well.'

'And seventy thousand pounds sterling for the concession. Not a penny more. Not if you slice pieces off my territory.'

'I understand. Seventy thousand it is.'

'And even seventy thousand is extortionate, mark you.'

'It's a generous price, sir. Thank you.'

'And, if you don't hit oil, I want you working for us, d'you hear? Five years, that's all. By heaven, you're plucking us.'

Alan left the building, and stepped blinking out into the sun. He had five years and seventy thousand pounds to fulfil his promise to Tom. It was too little money and too little time. Alan thought of Tom that day above the ruined cellar, just before their first assault in the Battle of the Somme. Tom had promised to be careful, but what were promises amidst the lunacy of war? Alan had promised to drill for oil, but he wasn't even sure if he'd have the cash to sink a well before his money ran out. His prospects seemed hopeless . . .

Alan's daydreams were interrupted by the sound of boots running after him. He turned, and found himself staring into a bright red face, lit up by anger, and a ferocious black moustache stretching, it seemed, from ear to ear.

'By God, it's robbery,' shouted the man. 'You've found oil there, haven't you? By God, I tell you, it's robbery.'

'Who are you, sir?' said Alan, putting some distance between himself and the man.

'Have you or haven't you, sir?'

'Have I what?'

'Found oil, dammit, oil.'

'You're one of the Anglo-Persian geologists. Is that right?'

'Yes, that's right. Pardon me. George Reynolds. Pardon me.'

Some of the heat left Reynolds' face and he held out his hand. Reynolds was a thickset northerner with a face that must have been ruddy at the best of times. He held himself compact and powerful, like a piston ready to fire. Alan shook the outstretched hand warily.

'Have I drilled for oil there? No.'

'I didn't mean that. A seepage. A trace. Tar in the water. Gas springs. Bitumen pits. A smell, for heaven's sake.'

Alan swallowed and brought something from his pocket. It was a small waxed canvas pouch containing a small handful of sand. He offered the pouch to Reynolds, who put it to his nose and sniffed. It was Ameri's sand. The smell had worn off since being carried around in Alan's pocket for the past few months, but all the same, it was unmistakable.

'I knew it. The fault. The others didn't see the fault. I tried to tell them, but they wouldn't listen.'

Secretly Alan began to be amused at Reynolds' fire-and-brimstone approach to life, but he kept himself cool. 'They're probably right. Geologically the fault is certainly there, but that doesn't mean anything about the presence of oil. I found the oil sand in the exposed strata, far above where any oil might still be today. It's a very long shot. A very, very long shot.'

'Yes.'

Reynolds was reluctant to hand back the pouch. He was standing in the gutter of the street, and a delivery van honked him to get out of the way. Reynolds sniffed and sniffed.

'Not too much sulphur there.'

'No, not much.'

Reynolds kneaded the sand with his fingers, letting it trickle between his fingers.

'Light. It feels light. Not too tarry.'

'I think so too.'

'It would refine well.'

'Yes.'

Reynolds handed back the bag, without taking his eyes from it. 'You'll drill there, of course.'

'Yes.'

'With your seventy thousand?'

'That's all I've got.'

'You'll need more.'

'Probably.'

'Much more. Very much more.'

'Probably.'

Reynolds nodded, his gaze transfixed by the bag. 'If there is a field there, it could be a big one.'

'It could be.'

'Well then. I'm sorry I came out shouting.'

'Don't worry.'

Re nolds was half on and half off the pavement. The street was busy, and every delivery boy and motorist shouted and honked. Reynolds was oblivious.

'Yes, well, sorry anyway. Goodbye. And good luck.'

He shook hands once again. He gripped Alan's hands as though he was grappling a drill pipe. He walked away heavy-footed, as though dragging himself off to punishment. Alan watched him go, thinking what a peculiar man Reynolds must be, then he turned and began to walk to Waterloo Station to catch the train down to Hampshire.

He hadn't gone far before the running of heavy boots disturbed him once again. Without turning, he said, 'Well, Mr Reynolds, what am I accused of this time?'

Reynolds stood in front of him, puffing. 'No, it's not like that. I'd like to work for you. If possible. In Persia.'

Alan smiled – laughed – and extended his hand to his first employee.

66

'Hi-yip! Hi-yip! Hi-yip-yip-yip-yippee!'

The teamster cracked his whip over his horses, fighting to keep them climbing the vertical bog that passed for the road up into the hills. Tom, born horseman that he was, wanted to take the reins and try himself, but the teamster knew his horses and the trail. In the back of the wagon, an assortment of huge steel plates jolted and shook like portable thunder.

'Hi-yip! Hi-yip! Hi-yip!'

The teamster's voice was losing confidence, as rapidly as his horses were losing theirs.

'I'll get out,' said Tom, jumping out into the mud.

One of the wagon wheels was snagging on a rock. Tom tried to shift the rock; couldn't, and put his shoulder to the wheel instead. The wagon heaved itself over the obstruction and beyond. Tom slipped and slithered up the track after it.

He was still a member of the honourable society of boot-leggers, but his business methods had undergone some necessary improvements. For one thing, his Canadian supplier now dispatched regular caseloads of whisky without any need for Tom to go and collect them. For another, the wooden boxes were now marked as containing boot polish, or condensed milk, or hair oil, or tooth powder – or anything in the world that would interest dogs not at all. And, since Tom didn't like to leave things to chance, he'd also taken the precaution of making friends with the senior US customs official at the border and ensuring that that excellent man had as much whisky as he needed to drink, and that his wife could finally afford the mink coat she'd always wanted.

Profits from the business were strong – a hundred dollars a week or more – but Tom's heart still belonged to oil.

At the crest of a rise, the teamster pulled up his sweating horses and waited for Tom to catch up.

'Jesus! Heck of a place to find oil!'

In the hills beyond them, the landscape was studded with oil wells. There were now a dozen producing wells that Tom knew of, but it seemed like another well was striking every week. Tom still hung out with Lyman Bard whenever he could and it was pretty clear from Bard's excitement that he was expecting to make his own strike any day soon.

'It's a perfect place,' murmured Tom.

'Which one's yours?' The teamster waved his whip in the direction of the oil wells as he clicked with his teeth to make the horses walk forwards once again.

'Huh?'

'Which one's yours? Which well?'

'I don't have a well.'

'You don't?' The teamster looked baffled. 'I thought . . .' He gestured behind him where the plated steel continued its deep grumbling.

'You thought right. They're oil storage tanks – least they will be once we bolt 'em together. We'll set 'em down over there, I reckon.' He indicated the spot.

For a minute the teamster drove in silence. Although they were over the worst of the hills, the track was still atrocious and needed careful driving. The teamster was lost in thought.

Eventually he said, 'I don't figure it.'

'Figure what?'

'You got tanks but you ain't got oil?'

'That's right.'

'No well?'

'No.'

'No crew?'

'No.'

'No nothing?'

'Just tanks.'

The teamster was apparently happy to accept the answer in silence, but before long Tom realised that the man was shaking. Tom glanced sideways. The man was shaking with laughter. Tom grinned. The teamster began to chuckle out loud.

'No oil, just tanks, huh?'

Tom chuckled as well. 'You got it right there.'

Reassured that Tom wasn't about to take offence, the teamster's laugh grew louder. 'No oil? Hey, don't worry.' He flicked his whip at one of the many streams. 'There ain't no shortage of water. Hey? Ha! Ha, ha, ha!' He threw his head back and yodelled with laughter.

Tom laughed with him; threw his head back, hat in his lap, wind in his hair, letting his laughter fill the whole wide-open prairie sky.

'You're the craziest son-of-a-bitch I ever saw,' said the teamster. 'The craziest or the dumbest.'

'Uh-huh,' said Tom, letting his laughter slowly subside. 'Uh-huh. Either that or the smartest.'

67

The oil business needs money, plenty of it. To drill: you need money. To collect the oil once you've found it: you need money. To pipe it: money. To refine it: money. To ship it: money. To market it: money, money and more money.

That's why oil companies grow so big. Whoever heard of a small oil company? Whoever heard of an oil company worth just seventy thousand pounds?

'We're mapping the field now with the American seismographs. Rather jolly, as a matter of fact. Let off dynamite and listen for the echo. Oil sounds different from everything else, apparently. It must be wobblier, I suppose. Something like a giant trifle.'

The Anglo-Persian field manager, Chandos Hughes, was a pale-faced public schoolboy who was seemingly untouched by the fact that he was now stuck out in the middle of the Persian desert about a million miles from Eton and Henley and Royal Ascot and all the other things that had once made up his life.

'Lots of jolly nice new rigs, as well,' he continued. 'New rotary tables mean we can drill to a thousand feet in about a third of the time it used to take us.'

George Reynolds nodded. The sun was burningly hot on the dry plain, and Reynolds took out a huge white handkerchief to mop his forehead. 'Blast the heat,' he said.

'Blast the . . . ? Gosh, yes, it is hot, isn't it? Lucky devils at Abadan have got refrigerators full of cold drinks. We poor desert rats do suffer rather.'

Reynolds pointed towards a heap of metal pipes lying in the dust. 'What's that? That looks ready for scrap, doesn't it?'

'Lord, yes. That's one of our old percussion rigs. Not zoom-zoom-zoom –' Hughes made a drilling motion with his hand – 'but rather bash-bash-bash. Literally dropped a thumping great weight down into the hole and smashed the rock underneath to smithereens. Imagine digging a well that way! Must have been a fearful old bore. Bash-bash-bash-bash-bash. Hard enough with a proper rig . . .'

Hughes rambled on. The sun blazed down. The battered old percussion rig shimmered in the heat. The drill bit was about twelve feet high, eighteen inches wide, and must have weighed well over a ton. The tangle of pipes showed little sign of rust – this was the desert, after all – but the hollow tubes were filled with sand and there were heaps of mouse droppings by their mouths. Hughes blathered on. Reynolds hardly bothered to listen. He was twenty years older than Hughes and had loads more field experience.

And besides, he hadn't come to learn anything. He'd come to steal.

The Americans were world leaders in oilfield technology. They'd offered to provide the very latest equipment, guaranteed to reach up to nine thousand feet in favourable terrain. The price was thirty-two thousand pounds.

British technology was less advanced, but Alan had found a Glasgow firm that could build equipment to his specification and ship goods free of charge to anywhere in the British Empire, at a price of twenty-seven thousand pounds.

But Alan had seventy thousand to cover *everything*. Not just equipment, but getting it set up, drilling, storing, piping, refining, shipping, selling.

He'd done his sums again and again. He didn't have twenty-seven thousand to spend. He had seven.

It was a night without moon. A slight wind blew out of the east and sent black waves slapping against the side of the little boat. The boat rode at anchor and showed a single dark-shaded lantern gleaming from the masthead.

'Are you sure we're in the right place?' asked Alan in Persian.

The boatman grinned and spat. A squirt of blood-red betel juice went over the side into the water. 'Sure, *aqa*, sure.' The boatman was an old man. Hossein Nasr, who had made his living from the Caspian Sea ever since he'd been a boy. Sometimes he caught fish. Sometimes he smuggled. It was all the same.

Alan rubbed his hand against the rough wooden side of the boat. He disliked the sea and there was something vaguely comforting about the familiar presence of wood. The crossing had taken eighteen hours and they were now only a mile off the coast of Lenin's Russia. A short distance to the west lay Baku, the biggest port in Azerbaijan, but more importantly by far, the heart of the Russian oil industry. The civil war was still dragging on, but it had become fairly clear that Trotsky's Red Army would annihilate all opposition. Stories were beginning to filter out of Russia about Soviet atrocities, and the fate of the kulaks, the Russian landowning class. Alan didn't believe everything he heard, but he knew that the Reds wouldn't look kindly on an aristocratic English spy anchored within spitting distance of Russia's most valuable industrial asset.

Nasr rooted around in a locker and came out with some flat bread, spiced meat cakes and a wooden bowl of goat's milk yoghurt. 'Eat, *aqa*. You must relax.'

They ate. Alan was surprisingly hungry and let himself gorge. They broke the meat cakes into pieces and used the flat bread to dip them into the yoghurt. It tasted like the best food in the world. When the shout came, Alan didn't even hear it. Only when it was repeated, did his heart suddenly stop beating in his chest. He held his breath.

Nasr listened to the cry, then called back in a strange singsong whisper that crept far over the water without ever seeming to gather much force. An answering whisper came back and Nasr turned to Alan with a grin. 'It is my friend, *aqa*. Peace be with him.' Alan breathed again.

For a while there was silence, but Nasr lifted the shutters from the lantern and let the light beam out openly for a moment or two. Then he replaced the shutters, and dropped down to the little seating area in the bows of the boat. He spread out carpets over the wooden planking, arranged some pillows, and brought out the hubble-bubble water pipe that he'd set alight an hour or so before. The charcoal was glowing in the bottom, but he added more and blew on it to make it glow yellow and hot.

Then there was a gentle bump at the side of the boat. Invisible hands made the two boats fast, and a couple of figures sprang over the side.

Nasr leaped up and embraced the two men, kissing them cheek to cheek three times. There was a quick babble of conversation in a dialect that Alan had difficulty in following: Persian mixed with a scattering of Russian and perhaps Armenian. There was a clink of bottles and glasses. The three men moved to the carpeted area and the hubble-bubble, and Nasr indicated that Alan should follow them. The newcomers were dressed in dark coats and boots, the universal dress-code for their trade. Though their skin had a Persian dark-ness, both men had the solid build and square, heavy faces of Mother Russia. Alan shook hands; then, feeling like a fool, embraced the newcomers cheek to cheek. He could smell onion and vinegar on their breath, tobacco and sea salt.

The four men sat down. The Russians had brought two bottles of vodka and some tiny vodka glasses. Alan shot a glance sideways at Nasr. Alcohol was forbidden to followers of the Prophet, and Alan had never seen Nasr partake of anything stronger than betel juice or tobacco. He needn't have worried. Islam was obviously less important for the moment than being good neighbours, and the hubble-bubble and vodka turned colleagues into friends.

After half an hour, the talk turned very slowly to business. Alan began to understand the Russians better than he had done at first, but Nasr still had to act as interpreter.

'The Revolution will set free the proletariat,' said the senior of the two Russians solemnly, 'but times are hard.'

Alan said how he had passed through Baku on his first journey out to Persia, and how impressed he had been with its prosperity and industrial power.

The Russian shook his head. 'Once, yes, once it was a great city. But now . . . People are hungry. They are afraid no one will buy their oil. They are afraid they will starve.'

Alan knew Easterners well enough by now to be aware of the proper reply. He said how much he admired the people of Baku, how he would gladly do anything he could to help relieve them of their distress.

The conversation then passed quickly to business. What did Alan want? How much could he pay? Would he pay in paper or gold? How could they be sure that Alan wasn't a Revolutionary spy?

Alan handed them a list, drawn up in Persian and Russian, of his requirements. He handed them a bag of thirty golden sovereigns as a token of his seriousness. He spoke of delivery needs and timings. Nasr listened like a hawk, and took over as soon as the nitty-gritty of delivery was discussed. What Alan wanted was going to require heavy shipping to deliver. The usual smuggler's stock-in-trade of alcohol, silk, fur and tobacco was all small and easy to handle by comparison. Nasr was voluble and insistent. Brokering this deal would make him enough money to retire on, a wealthy man. Screwing it up could easily mean that he'd be shot dead by a Russian coastguard, or simply be tipped overboard into the ocean. The Russians became voluble too, their voices thickened with drink and excitement. Alan was unable to follow what was going on.

He moved to the side of the boat and dashed a couple of handfuls of stinging salt water in his face. He thought of George Reynolds and the task they'd set themselves.

He thought of Lottie, confused as to who she really was: wartime Lottie, loving, serious and committed? Or peacetime Lottie, superficial and flirtatious? The thought tormented him, as ever.

He turned his attention back to the conversation. Nasr and the Russians were finishing. Far to the east, a glimmer of grey lightened the blackness. It was time to be gone.

68

The tank stood at the bottom of a small dip, lapped all round by coarse prairie grasses. No pipes led down into the dip. The tank's steel sides boomed hollow and empty. There was room inside for three thousand barrels of oil, but right now it held three thousand barrels of nothing.

Men from the rigs round about came to stare, snigger and laugh.

'Hey, pal! You better watch out. You got yourself a leak right there. Can't you see the nothing spilling out?'

'Hey, mister. You wanna fill her up with water? I fancy a swim, me.'

Another joker took his coat and shirt off and pretended to get ready to dive in.

Tom let them laugh. It was one of the first warm and sunny days of spring. He ate sandwiches and joked with the men who had come to gawp. He brewed coffee on a kerosene stove and handed it out in tin mugs to anyone who wanted some. But it wasn't long before Tom's lunch was interrupted.

A heavy-set man with big Victorian whiskers came to stand in between Tom and the sun. Tom recognised the man as the head driller on one of the first wells to have struck oil.

'This your tank?' said the man bluntly.

'Yep. You want some coffee?'

The man shook his head rudely. 'What you planning to put in it?'

'Sugar. I'm clean out of milk.'

'The tank, for Chrissake, not the coffee.'

Tom shrugged. 'It's called an oil storage tank, so I figure I oughta use it to store some oil.'

'I got oil.'

'Hey, good for you. Congratulations,' said Tom, without sarcasm.

'And you got a tank.'

'Sure have.'

'I'll give you a penny a month for every barrel of oil you store for me. Just till we can get a pipeline up the valley. Three or four months, maybe.'

'It's good coffee,' said Tom. 'Real fresh. I can't persuade you?'

'Three thousand barrels, is it? A penny a month. Three months. That's – what? – ninety bucks. Call it an even hundred.'

'No deal.'

'No deal?' The man was non-plussed. 'You got no oil.'

'Not a drop.'

'I'll give you a hundred and fifty. Right now, I'm pumping oil I can't hardly use. I'm burning it off mostly.'

'Now that's a shame.'

'One eighty?'

'Nope.'

The day wore on. Word of Tom's tank spread quickly. But by the end of the day, nobody was there to laugh at him, nobody was pretending to strip off for a quick swim.

Instead, a cluster of men squatted on the rocks round Tom's little camp site. The situation up on the oilfields was pretty extreme. More and more oil was being struck, but with the road down to the valley all but impassable, the oil that was pumped was next to worthless.

When Tom announced he was there to buy oil, he had half a dozen eager sellers.

257

'Tell you what, boys,' said Tom, as the sun began to slope down towards the hills, 'we'll have an auction.'

'An auction? How d'you figure that? We only got one buyer.'

'It's gonna be a special kind of auction. Here's what I have in mind.'

And he explained. Tom's idea was a kind of reverse auction. He'd offer to buy a thousand barrels of oil at twenty-five cents the barrel. At that price all six oilmen were eager sellers but Tom wasn't yet ready to do the deal.

'Now, anyone here willing to sell me a thousand barrels at twenty-four cents the barrel?' he said.

The man closest to Tom looked like he'd been socked in the jaw. He sat heavily down on a rock.

'Holy shit,' he said, 'we're going down.'

But he raised his hand anyway. So did the others.

'Six buyers at twenty-four cents?' said Tom. 'Who'll sell at twenty-three?'

The six men raced to raise their hands. Tom picked the man who'd moved fastest.

'Yours at twenty-three,' he said. 'Who'll sell at twenty two? . . . At twenty one? . . . At twenty? . . . At nineteen?'

As the last gold vanished from the horizon, the men were still there. Still glum, still shocked, still bidding.

69

'It'll never get up,' said Alan.

'It will,' said Reynolds.

They looked down at the truck, shimmering in the heat below. The khaki cab was covered in dust, knocks and scratches. It looked like an old prize-fighter after a losing bout.

'They overheat. Even without a load, most of the trucks need to stop a couple of times to cool off.'

'It'll get up.'

They squinted down at the truck. It was carrying the twelve-foot drill bit that Reynolds had seen in the desert. Anglo-Persian had refused to sell any of its equipment to its upstart competitor, not even the equipment that was good only for scrap. That had been as expected. When Reynolds had finished his reconnaissance, he and Alan had ridden out to the local Bakhtiari chieftain. Alan explained how certain materials had been left to rot by Anglo-Persian, and how he personally had a great use for those materials.

The chieftain had furrowed his brow. He'd ordered lemon sherbet and the slaughter of two young lambs for a feast. Then, once a sufficient volume of gold had changed hands, the chieftain had agreed to act. The very next week, he'd ridden out to the drilling site with a great troop of men, mounted variously on horses, motorbikes and trucks. The men had swirled around the camp, fired off a few shots to indicate that they weren't to be trifled with, then stolen everything that Alan had asked for.

Around the same time, the Russian smugglers completed their part of the transaction. Alan's cash had been enough to buy a complete set of drilling tools, storage tanks, temporary pipelines, and various other sundries. The equipment had been delivered by a tramp steamer with Russian Soviet documentation claiming that a cargo-load of grain had been delivered. Some of the Russian-made stuff was brand new; much of it already well used. Alan had more than a suspicion that some existing working installations had been simply dismantled and shipped out – right under the noses of the Revolutionary Red Guards.

With all the equipment assembled, the next task had been to haul it down to the Zagros: an immense labour. Roads were mostly nonexistent. Bridges were absent where spring floods had washed them away. Mules got lame and trucks gave up the ghost. And so they'd built rafts and rope bridges. They'd levelled mountain paths. They'd planted dynamite beneath falls of rock. They made and carried with them a mobile forge, so that they could improvise replacement parts for their battered trucks.

And now it was all almost here. Below them, the truck ground its gears and began the ascent. The air was giddy with the heat and the temperature inside the engine casing must have been unthinkable.

'A bottle of cold beer says it'll make three stops or give up completely.'

'A bottle of beer if it doesn't make it in one.'

There was no beer in the Zagros and no way of making it cold even if there had been. So far, since they'd begun work in Persia together, Alan owed Reynolds seventy-five bottles of cold beer, while Reynolds owed his boss sixty-one. The truck ground its way up the hill. The slope was steep and though Alan had road-gangs working on the track pretty much all the time now, the terrain was a mixture of gritty sand and sharp rocks and the track simply disintegrated under the pressure of the heavy tyres. The truck negotiated the first bend and seemed to waver a moment.

'It's stopping.'

'It isn't.'

The driver found the right gear and continued on up. The drill bit on the rear looked like some giant molar dragged from some dinosaur's jaw. It glinted dirtily in the sun.

'How are your sums?'

For the last few nights, the lamps had been burning late in Alan's tent as he figured out the total cost to the start of drilling. Back in London, Reynolds had advised him that doing things Anglo-Persian style would end up costing more than forty-five thousand pounds – or more than half their available funds just to get their equipment in place for the start of work. The truck ground on. A sudden lift of air brought a smell of petrol fumes and hot oil.

'Good,' said Alan. 'We'll come in just over fourteen.'

'Fourteen? Fourteen thousand pounds? By God, that's an achievement.'

Alan nodded with a smile. 'Not just that. There was a whole case of cold beer in it for me, as I remember.'

Reynolds acknowledged his debt with a glower and a tug at his moustache. 'The truck's still going, though.'

It was true. The truck was close enough now that they could hear the din of its engine bouncing around the craggy slopes. Alan shook his head. He couldn't understand it. Every truck overheated on this last slope. Every one. Most of them needed to stop and cool off with their hoods up for at least a couple of hours. But the truck with its massive load had already run much further than the others had.

'If it does get up, we can start drilling tomorrow.'

'If? If? It will get up. I've told you.'

Alan shook his head. 'It won't.'

Reynolds chuckled. He knew something Alan didn't.

'Ice in the radiator?' asked Alan.

'Where would I get ice from?'

'Freezing water then.'

'No.'

'You've speeded up the fan.'

'Yah!' Reynolds didn't even condescend to answer that one. The air was ninety-eight degrees in the shade. You could send a small gale through the engine and not help it at all.

'Then it'll stop.'

'It won't.'

Behind them the derrick cast an increasing shadow on the dust. They were going to start drilling not half a mile from the spot Muhammad Ameri had first pointed out. The well was already christened Muhammad Ameri No. 1 in the American fashion, and Ameri himself had swept into camp eight days previously with forty mounted warriors to inspect the work and to remind Alan who had first brought him to the valley.

Meantime, there was plenty of work to do. Punching a well using the old-fashioned percussion method would be devilishly slow work, but slow didn't matter, as long as they could manage steady.

The truck was only a little way beneath them now. Through the open cab window, Alan could see the sweating driver, dressed in loose Persian robes and a bristling growth of hair on his upper lip that (for once) put George Reynolds' moustache to shame. A piece of melon rind lay discarded on the passenger seat. There was little more than a hundred yards to go now and the slope was easing. Reynolds had been right . . .

The melon rind. The image stuck in Alan's mind.

The truck clawed its way over the lip of the hill and levelled out. The drill bit became horizontal and the ropes that held it began to slacken. Melon rind.

Reynolds chuckled. 'I'm looking forward to that beer,' he said.

But Alan didn't hear him. He was running to the truck. The driver was getting out of the cab, amidst the cheers of his companions. Alan reached the truck and snatched open the hood.

The engine was hot, all right, but not boiling. A gigantic watermelon, split down the middle, had been jammed over the radiator. When Alan put his hand to the melon it sizzled and spat with the heat and even the outer rind was scorching to the touch. Reynolds had arrived next to Alan, panting in the sun.

'Oh, yes,' he said, 'a cold beer will do me fine.'

70

The driller let the whisky hum its way down his throat.

'You got yourself a sweet bottle there,' he commented.

'It's the last one,' said Tom. He was no longer running alcohol. Profits from the business had become large enough that competition between rival providers was being settled with fistfights and shootouts. Tom wanted no part of that – and besides, his only interest in whisky had been to get himself a start in oil.

'Shame that. Drank some moonshine recently, pretty much turned me green.'

Tom made no reply. His campfire crackled and subsided. The night sky spread out a million stars, like a jeweller anxious to make a sale. Behind Tom, not one but four oil tanks lay groaning full of oil.

The driller reached for more whisky and continued his story. Tom listened with half an ear.

'So, anyways, this guy Casey has gone down pretty near six thousand feet. The drill is running through a layer of crumbly brown shale, dry as a bone, shale like he ain't never seen before. No money to continue on. Backers are refusing money, telling him to go to hell. Old Grandma Halstead, whose land he's squatting on, she's telling him to go to hell. Casey swears there's oil, there. *Swears* it. Anyhow, he hears about a

264

hole two miles north that's hit oil. He runs along, asks to see their drilling log. Begs them. They tell him to go to hell. Round about this time, everybody's telling Casey to go to hell. So he steals it. One night, he busts in, reads their drilling log: "5,700 feet, brown shale – unusual type, easily broken. 5,750 feet, brown shale – same. 5,780 feet, sticky brown shale, stringers of oil sand. 5,800 feet, oil sand . . . oil sand . . . oil sand."

'Well now, Casey reads this here log book and figures his drill bit is roundabouts a hundred feet above a field every bit as sweet as anything that John D. Rockefeller could dream of. So what does he do? Heck, what would anyone do? He sells the coat off of his back. He sells his watch. He pretty much sells the tongue out of his mouth. He gets together enough money to drill one more weekend. Sunday evening, there are gas bubbles coming up. Indications of oil. The riggers go crazy. Old Grandma Halstead's bringing out chicken pie and moonshine whiskey like deliverance day has come early. By this time, everyone had always known there'd be oil there and no one's telling Casey to go to hell no more. Ten feet more and they strike it big. Near enough two hundred barrels a day, with Okie crude up at near one dollar twenty the barrel.

'That's the only way to make money in this world, I reckon. Find yourself a drill and a patch of land. Go see what's down there.'

The driller reached for the whisky bottle again. Tom rolled onto his side and threw another log on the fire.

'Did you ever drill for yourself?' he murmured.

'Me? Sure. A coupla times. Never struck, though I came closer than a tightwad to his wallet.'

Tom nodded and swallowed some whisky himself. He'd hung around the oilfields long enough to know the pattern. Everyone had stories about people like old Casey So-and-so. The people telling the tales swore they were true. Maybe they even believed them. But if you asked them the magic question – 'Did you ever drill for yourself?' – the answer was always the same.

More than a half of the older oilers had sunk a wildcat well at some time in their lives. Every single one of them had missed a fortune by only a few hundred yards. 'Neighbouring block turned out to be some of the richest acreage in West Texas.' 'The field came to an end, right there at the boundary fence. Far side gushed like the Niagara Falls. My side, drier'n a dead coyote.' 'Ran outa money, but if we had've gone on another two hunnert feet, would've smacked right into the Tannawassa sands, the richest oil deposits in that part o' Californey.' And so on and so on.

Tom's liquor business had financed three of the oil tanks. A regular bank loan had brought in enough cash to buy a fourth tank, a six thousand barreler, with enough left over to let Tom buy as much oil as he needed.

As he'd expected, his first auction had been his worst. That first evening, the price had ended up at fourteen cents a barrel. Tom refused any further deals for twenty-four hours, then began buying again. The guys with surplus oil had thought about things overnight. Their maths looked simple. They could burn oil and get nothing. Or they could sell the oil to Tom Calloway and get something for it, no matter how miserable the something. The second auction had ended down at eleven cents. The third down at six and a half.

Right now, Tom had around fifteen thousand barrels of oil, purchased at an average price of slightly more than ten cents. He slept up on the hills amongst his tanks, protecting his precious oil against thieves or vandals. He missed seeing Rebecca – missed her with an odd intensity at times – but aside from that, he was happy.

'Pipeline will be here soon,' said the driller.

'Three weeks, or so they say.'

'What'll you do when it comes?'

'Sell, of course.'

'You should get plenty. Maybe one dollar the barrel . . . Sheez!'

'Maybe.'

'What you gonna do when you sell out?' said the driller. 'There's some land over Stone Creek way looks pretty rich to me. Wouldn't mind making hole over there, see what there was.'

'Stone Creek, huh?' said Tom, not exactly excited by the tip, but never one to pass up the possibility of good information.

'Right. Listen.' The driller rolled closer to Tom, speaking in a whisper in case the mice and the rabbits and the owls and the prairie grass would overhear him and broadcast the news to every oilman west of Pennsylvania. 'Got a friend's been over there. Prospecting. On the quiet. He ain't seen nothing, but he can smell it. Got the nose for it, see. We're just looking around now for the money to start drilling. Wouldn't let you in on it, 'cept I can tell you're a real oilman, an' all.'

Tom's interest, small to begin with, faded away to nothing. He yawned and lay down. His coat was rolled up to make a pillow. Beneath the coat there was a flat packet that rustled as Tom moved his head.

'Thanks for the tip,' he said. 'I'll think about it.'

'It's all about the smell, you see. Some folks can smell it, other folks can't. It's simple as that.'

'I guess,' said Tom, not keen to argue.

But it was horseshit. Obvious horseshit.

Oil that lay ten feet underground couldn't be smelled, never mind oil five thousand feet down. For all the stories about Casey So-and-So and all the rest of them, Tom had never met anyone who had drilled and made money. There was a reason why the big guys stayed big and the small guys stayed small.

Information.

Simple as that.

Information about where oil was likeliest to be found. Information based on geology and seismology and clever men making complex calculations. Information about available land and prices and refinery capacities. And that was why

Tom listened to the driller, but didn't get excited. That was why he spent his days thinking out his next move.

And that was why he had a flat packet underneath his pillow that rustled when he moved.

71

The Persian summer was fading into autumn, but they were in the midst of a mini heatwave, which brought back all their fiercest memories of summer. Mules and horses slept lazily in the shade. Those men who were not immediately required to work loafed under cotton awnings thrown up by the ever-resourceful tribesmen. The timber derrick stood idle, and the drilling crew (three Poles who had worked in America, two Russians and a gifted young Persian) bickered in four languages over a game of cards. The sun hammered down.

In one corner of the drilling site, the heat intensified into something almost solid. Even twenty feet away there was a wall of heat. Beyond that point, every step forwards carried you to a whole new contour of temperature. It was almost literally like stepping into a roasting oven.

Alan entered the furnace.

At the rear of the miniature forge, a Persian boy worked the bellows with his feet. Every minute or so, he dipped a wooden ladle into a pail of water that sat beside him and poured it over his head. By the end of the minute his hair had dried off and was ready for another drenching.

At the front of the forge, the heat was a horizontal punch that never lost its force. Reynolds laboured away over a metal tube that had become badly kinked. Reynolds' face was never less than ruddy, but right now it would out-crimson a tomato, outblaze a field of beetroot. All along his well-waxed moustache, globules of sweat hung like beads on a party frock. The shirt was glued to his back.

'My turn,' said Alan.

'Almost done, laddie.'

The metal tube was a key component in the Russian-made boiler. The boiler supplied power to the rig. No tube, no boiler. No boiler, no drilling. No drilling, no oil. This was the boiler's seventh breakdown inside two months.

Reynolds finished his work of banging the incandescent metal into shape. Alan held the tongs and allowed Reynolds to work the metal with both hands. Eventually it was done. Alan threw the tube sizzling into a bucket of cold water, and both men ran from the heat and doused themselves in the river. The Persian boy working the bellows emptied the rest of the bucket over his head and ran to get the quid of tobacco that he'd been promised.

Reynolds drank a small ocean of tea, as Alan took the tube between his feet. He began work with a metal file to get the tube to an exact fit. It was a nightmarish way of working, fabricating sophisticated parts with a crude forge and a collection of metal files, yet the alternatives were limited. Basic metalwork could be done in Karachi: a mere fifteen hundred miles away. But for more complex operations, there was nothing for it but to telegraph the specifications to England and have the parts built there and shipped out.

Reynolds watched Alan at work.

'Half a day, laddie, and we'll have the boiler back in action.'

'For another week.'

'Aye, well, I'll be satisfied with another week's progress.'

Alan half-laughed. Reynolds' stubborn determination to sink the well was second to none. Setbacks, disappointments, breakdowns and calamities were all in the day's work to him.

'Yes,' said Alan, 'me too. As long as we get some more fuel.'

Further away from the rig, there was a stir in the camp. The first whoops and yells of greeting went up. A couple of rifle shots were fired wildly into the air.

'That'll be the truck with the fuel now,' said Reynolds happily. 'We start drilling again tomorrow.'

'Let's hope so.'

The supply of fuel they'd had for the boiler – a mixture of coal, coke and wood – had all gone into feeding the furnace. They now had a nearly functioning boiler but no fuel to fire it. From the rocky valley walls, the sound of a truck motor began to echo. These days, the road up to the drilling site had been improved and a large supply of 'patent Reynolds radiator coolers' – watermelons, in other words – now lay in a stream at the base of the slope. It was eight weeks now since they'd last had a truck fail on the final slope, and some of the wilder Persians liked to run truck races down into the valley and back, complete with mounted escorts, random gunfire, and huge forfeits to be paid by the losers.

Alan filed patiently at the tube. Reynolds was already looking for something else to do. His colossal impatience filled the camp, and infected others. Alan had noticed how the Persian tents had gradually formed themselves into neat army-style lines under Reynolds' brusque supervision. The rabble of men they'd started with had now become a well-disciplined body. They supplied the camp, mended the road, ran the forge, prepared food, supported the drillers, and protected the camp from attack. They had even learned enough mechanical skills to begin repairing engines and fabricating spares with almost no supervision.

The truck approached.

'Fuel,' said Reynolds. 'Lovely fuel. I'll get it unloaded.'

Alan nodded. He was busy. If he stopped filing for five minutes, then drilling would be delayed by five minutes. He didn't stop.

The truck came over the lip of the hill, then gunned its engine and tore into camp in a racket of screaming gears and gleeful whoops. From the back, a couple of men began unloading goodies: fresh fruit and veg; three live goats; a very scrawny sheep; tobacco; a sack of rice; another sack of wheat flour that they'd use to bake flat bread. There was no sign of fuel.

Reynolds was over arguing with the men, but one of the tribesmen, a youngster called Ahmed, came running up to Alan. Ahmed was exceptionally proud of his increasing command of English, which he'd been learning from the Polish members of the drilling team.

'Well?' said Alan. 'What news?'

Ahmed's face broke into a vast grin. 'Three bloody goat. One bloody no-hope sheep. Plenty goddamn tobaccy.'

'And the fuel, Ahmed? What about the –' Alan silently swallowed the swearword that had been about to come out. 'What about the fuel?'

Ahmed puzzled over the English. Alan was about to say the same thing in Persian, but Ahmed saw his intention and vigorously shook his head.

'Few-ell? Few-ell?'

'The fuel. Coal for the boiler. Fuel to put inside the boiler.'

'Ah!' Ahmed's face brightened into a smile, brilliant as daybreak. 'Ah, *few*-ell, *few*-ell! Yes.' He put his shoulders back and head up, as though making a formal statement to a military authority. With huge pride visible in his face, he said, 'Today, *aqa*, no goddamn few-ell.'

72

Tom sold.

Not at a dollar the barrel – he'd never expected that – but at eighty-three cents the barrel, after all transportation costs. No longer needing the tanks, he sold them too. He paid off his loan. It was slightly over a year since he'd set foot on Ellis Island, telling the pen-pushers that he'd come to America to drill for oil. Back then they'd laughed at him: him and his forty-eight bucks. They wouldn't be laughing now. When all was said and done, Tom would walk away from Wyoming with near enough eleven thousand dollars to his name.

But before he walked anywhere, there was one person he needed to say goodbye to. He found her at her two-room apartment over a bakery store. It was just gone one in the afternoon and she was still in her dressing gown, having a couple of eggs for breakfast. What with his recent business commitments, it was a little over seven weeks since Tom had spent any real time with her.

'Hey, Rebecca. I just wanted to call round, say I'm off.'

She looked at him carefully and brought another forkful of egg up to her mouth. Good morning,' she said slowly.

'Sorry. Good morning. Afternoon. Whatever.'

'You're off?'

'Uh-huh.'

'Off to where? Off for how long?'

Although Rebecca had been in the States much longer than Tom, her accent had almost not shifted at all, whereas his accent and vocabulary was becoming daily closer to those of the oilmen he lived next to. Most people meeting him now would have guessed he was from somewhere in New England and would have been genuinely surprised to find he was from Old England, and not so long ago either.

'Off-off. I got some money now. Enough to drill with.' Tom checked himself. His last statement had fallen a little short of the truth. 'Well, almost enough, I guess. But enough to give it a go.'

Rebecca stared curiously at him. Tom was still standing up, hat in hand, his bag at the door.

'Are you coming in or going out?'

'Huh? Going out, I guess.'

'You don't even want a cup of coffee?'

Tom hesitated. He was uncomfortable in her room. There was only one bed in the apartment – a monstrous old brass dinosaur – and Tom well knew what it was used for and how often. The sight unsettled him. When in town, he'd come to like and depend on Rebecca's company and conversation, but whenever he could he arranged to meet in a public place: a restaurant or bar. But now was a time to make an exception. He threw his hat on the bed, took his coat off, and sat down.

Rebecca stood up, found a clean cup, and poured him out some coffee, adding cream and two or three spoonfuls of sugar. Quite early on, she'd seen through his guard to something important about his experience in prison.

'You were very short of food,' she'd announced over a meal together. 'You must have been very hungry.'

'Yes.'

'Starving?'

'Yes. Starving.'

'Nothing from the Red Cross?'

'No.'

'Am I upsetting you?'

'No. I don't like to talk about it, but it doesn't upset me. Why would it? It's over.'

'Hmm.' Rebecca had grunted, the way she always did when she didn't like one of Tom's answers. 'But the war ended soon enough to save you?'

'No, not really. I decided to escape rather than starve. They caught me and shot my friend. They could have shot me, but didn't. The camp commandant sent me to work on a farm instead. There was food there. I survived.'

'I see . . .' Rebecca stared at him, and put her hand out to Tom's arm, which was curled round his plate of food as though defending it from assault. 'It's all right now. I'm not going to steal it.'

For a moment, Tom resisted angrily. If he wanted to curl his arm round his plate, it was up to him. The muscles in his arm knotted. She kept her hand there, pulling his arm away, the warmth from her skin bleeding through his woollen jacket. There was a brief struggle of wills. Then he'd given way. He moved his arm. There was nothing now to guard his plate. There was a rush of blood into his forearm, as though he'd been keeping it tense for the last five years. He panted with a mixture of feelings he didn't recognise.

Rebecca continued to gaze. Then she nodded. 'That was brave.'

'What do you mean, brave? It wasn't anything. I just moved my arm, for God's sakes. Who the hell cares where I put my goddamn arm?'

Rebecca had made no answer, but ever since then she'd been highly sensitive to his feelings about food. Without even asking, she'd begun adding cream and sugar to his coffee. The brew was richer than he'd liked at first – or, rather, richer than he'd thought he liked. But it suited him. He began eating more sweet things, more creamy things, more of the food he'd have killed for in prison.

They drank their coffee and ate some warm rolls from the bakery down below.

'Nice,' said Tom, with his mouth full. 'Do you mind?' He helped himself to more coffee.

'You're welcome. I have more cream in the icebox.'

She wasn't too careful about tying her dressing gown and her long dark hair was loosely held at the back, making a kind of halo round the slightly oversharp features of her face. She had the smell of a woman only just woken up. Tom felt intensely attracted by her. When she was in her prostitute's get-up – low-cut blouse, too much make-up, a skirt that showed plenty of leg – he had felt both drawn to her and disturbed, but the disturbance had always won out. To this day, Tom hadn't had sex with her, setting some kind of record in terms of his friendships with women.

'I'll miss you,' she said at last. 'I probably oughtn't to, but I will.'

'Gee, thanks. That's a heck of a compliment.'

'I'm pleased you didn't stay with your bootlegging. In a way, I never thought you would stick with it.'

'Uh-huh, and did you ever think you'd stick *your* job for this long, Fräulein Lewi?' He pronounced her name the way she did, husky and Middle European.

She flushed. 'I can't remember saying anything to you which deserved that,' she said. 'I think you'd better drink your coffee and go. Perhaps you were only trying to save me from missing you at all.'

'Sorry. That was a stupid thing to say. I didn't mean it.'

'You did mean it.'

Irritation flashed in Tom. She was always like this, Rebecca, never able to leave a thing alone.

'OK, so I meant it. It's a dirty job and you know it. I think you're better than it and I sure as hell don't like you doing it.'

'I know your opinion. And I'll do whatever I want.'

Tom grabbed his hat and his bag. 'Right. You do whatever you want. You always have done, always will.'

276

He left, letting the thin wooden door slam shut hard behind him.

He strode angrily down Main Street heading for the station. Dammit, that woman irritated him. If she weren't a cheap little hooker in some cheap little oil town getting ridden by any young roustabout with a few bucks in his pocket, she could be . . . Tom didn't know what she could be, but he knew she bothered him.

He got to the station. The train left in forty-three minutes. He bought a ticket and wandered over to a candy stall to look over what was on offer. He glanced at his watch. Forty-one minutes. She was right about his sweet tooth, though. Tom always now liked to carry a packet of something in his pocket, just like a spoiled seven-year-old. He bought some peanut brittle and munched on it . . . Thirty-seven minutes.

All of a sudden, he made a decision. He left the station and went running back to Rebecca's apartment. He didn't knock on her door, just barged on through. She never locked it when she was at home.

She was still there, still alone, reading an old murder-mystery novel and finishing the last of the coffee. She looked up startled, as her visitor crashed in.

'A lot of people like to knock before entering,' she commented.

'Come with me. Don't stay here. Pack your things right now and move out. There's a train in half an hour. We'll be on the West Coast tomorrow.'

'Come with you? What does that mean?'

'It means leave all of this –' Tom swept his hand round the room, but particularly including the bed in his gesture – 'and come with me.'

'Are you asking me to live with you? Like man and wife?'

Tom was thrown by the question. He had no idea what he meant, he just thought it would be a good idea if they left town together. 'I don't know. Not like man and wife. Not like anything. Let's just leave.'

Rebecca had a very mobile mouth and it was fluttering with something now: amusement, fondness, a touch of mockery perhaps. Her deep eyes were impossible to read as always.

'That's a very well-thought-out proposal.'

'It's not a proposal, it's just . . . Look, the hell with it. You want to come or not? The train's going to be leaving soon.'

'Right. And I believe there'll be another one along in the same place tomorrow.'

'I'm not leaving tomorrow. I'm leaving now. You don't want to come, that's fine. I was only asking.'

He turned to leave, but Rebecca had stood up and come close to him. He could smell the coffee on her breath, feel her warmth, and see the soft skin curving down to her breasts. He was intensely aroused.

'Dear Thomas,' she said, 'don't apologise. It was very sweet of you. You are a good man, even if you don't always know it.' She was facing him and holding his shoulders. As so often with her, her deep eyes searched his face for the answer to some question. She took a step forward, rose on tiptoe and kissed him full on the mouth. It was a long, passionate kiss that sent his desire for her driving urgently through every fibre of his body.

'Thank you for coming back. God bless you. And good luck.'

And that was how he remembered her. Standing at the door, barefoot, in her dressing gown, smelling of sleep and coffee, the print of their kiss still warm on her mouth.

73

The first sign of trouble was a dose of 'Basra belly' that laid half the men in camp prostrate. The latrines were stinking and crawling with flies. Alan felt he'd emptied his guts out four times over, and the two Russians in the drilling crew had been caught threatening the Persian cook with a firearm, apparently accusing him of sabotage. Only George Reynolds was wholly unaffected, and he set about having the latrines hosed down with meltwater from the snow-capped mountains and keeping the drilling going as fast as possible.

Because the meltwater was being diverted to the latrines, the camp's drinking water had to come from some water butts set out by the cooking tent. The water should have been boiled first, but probably wasn't. It should have been kept very separate from any food or water brought up from the markets round Shiraz, but again it probably wasn't.

Bash-bash-bash or zoom-zoom-zoom?

No contest. The percussion method of drilling was vastly slower and more cumbersome than the modern rotary method. On the other hand, with the money that they had at their disposal, there was absolutely no alternative; and in some ways, the more rudimentary the technology they used, then the easier it was to fix when it broke.

The massive drill bit had long ago been christened Mother Hubbard by English-speaking oilers, but the Polish members of the crew referred to it as the Mother-bloody-Hubbard, the Matka Hubbardski or just plain Mamusiu. Whatever its name, the bit was raised on a pulley system driven by an immense camwheel, then dropped. Then raised and dropped. Then raised and dropped. After a while the chippings at the bottom of the hole dulled the impact, and the Mother Hubbard was lifted out of the hole, set to one side, and a bailing tool dropped down instead. The bailing tool brought up chippings, until the base of the hole was reasonably clear, and the Mother Hubbard was set to work once again.

Progress was slow, but roughly constant. They were down eight hundred feet so far, and the chippings that came up did nothing to rule out the existence of oil lower down.

'I smell it,' said Reynolds, tapping his almost luminous nose. 'I can smell the oil in this valley.'

After the diarrhoea had abated, there was a day of normality. They drilled eighty feet. The Poles and the Russians managed to go the whole day without arguing. Alan felt light-headed but otherwise fine. Two trucks came up from Shiraz, bringing a ton and a half of prime steam-coal, some more goats, and ninety-five bales of hay, which would keep the camp's livestock going when the summer grass began to run out.

The next day was worse.

Once again, dawn brought a queue of men outside the latrines, Alan amongst them. His diarrhoea was completely watery and quite violent, but almost entirely painless. A couple of the men complained of vomiting, but diarrhoea was the one common symptom. Alan noticed that while all of the Westerners were ill, except the steely Reynolds and one of

280

the Russians, the casualty rate among the Persians was much lower, perhaps only thirty per cent.

'Feeling all right, old man?' asked Reynolds.

They didn't 'old man' each other much, and Alan could tell from Reynolds' question that he was concerned.

'Perfectly. Just a case of the galloping trots. Last night's lamb, I expect.'

'Maybe.'

'It was fairly beastly.'

'Yes, I suppose. Better to rest up, though.'

Alan shook his head. The boiler had a safety valve, which seemed to release steam much too easily, and the pressure was often insufficient to drive the lifting gear. Alan and Reynolds had devised a way to jury-rig the valve so it would hold the pressure better and it had been Alan's job today to begin the fabrication.

'Well, take care, old man. These things can rather knock one for six.'

An understatement. By the end of the day, it was obvious that this was no ordinary outbreak of Basra belly. The fourteen men who were taken sick were losing up to two pints of water every hour. The latrines were once again disgusting and once again Reynolds' energies were taken up with keeping hygiene controls in order.

He personally supervised setting up the water butts and saw to it that they were scalded with boiling water. He then forced the kitchens to boil cauldrons full of water for a full ten minutes before emptying the cauldrons into the butts. Once the butts were full he summoned Ahmed, gave him a pair of revolvers and ordered him to shoot dead any man who threatened to contaminate the water. Ahmed took his orders with immense seriousness and more than once put his gun to the head of a man who approached the water butts intending to rinse his hands or bathe his face in them.

By evening, Alan's eyes were shrunk into his head. His fingers were wrinkled and his lips cracked and bleeding.

Despite the warmth of the day, he had stopped sweating and it took a Persian boy to keep him cool by keeping a fan trained on his chest and head. Reynolds had cancelled all work for the day and had been in and out of Alan's tent like an anxious nursemaid.

'For God's sake, old fellow, I'm perfectly all right,' said Alan. 'I've had this kind of thing before.'

'No, you haven't, laddie. This isn't diarrhoea. This is cholera.'

74

Californian sun is different from the sun anywhere else.

Californian sun is Friday afternoon sun. It's a sun with a big glass of gin and tonic and nothing to do but wait for dinner. By the time it gets to California, the sun has blazed down on Australia, Asia, Africa, Europe, the Atlantic Ocean and forty-nine out of fifty American states. Now it just needs to beam down on California, and apart from little old Hawaii and a few sun-soaked islanders, it's all done for another day.

Of course, just like anywhere else, the sun in California means nothing at all. If your luck's out, your luck's out. The sun won't make a blind bit of difference.

The evening slanted down in the west, with a big red sun about to fizz down into the Pacific beyond Santa Catalina Island. Tom pulled the brim of his flat cap down over his eyes as he approached the rig. A hand-painted sign said 'Alamitos No. 1, Signal Hill', but the rig was silent and the drill motionless. The boiler had developed a fault and its innards were spread out over a dirty cotton sheet as the drilling crew worked to fix it.

'That O-ring is shot,' said Tom, pointing. 'I'd be happy to go get you a new one.'

'No hirings, son. Sorry.'

'I've worked out in Wyoming. I can handle a rig.'

'I'll bet you can, son, but we ain't hiring. Sorry.'

'I'm not overanxious about pay.'

The driller – a well-known toolpusher named O. P. 'Happy' Yowell – had been wiping his hands on an oil-spattered rag. Now he looked down and saw he'd just been spreading oil ever more widely across his hands and arms and he threw down the rag in annoyance.

'Listen, son. This is Shell Oil, not one of your two-cent independents. If you want to earn some money making hole, then go find yourself somebody who's hiring. If you want to hang around the rig here hoping to take a gander at our cores, then to hell with you. You ain't going to see 'em and nor is anyone else neither. Motherogod, I swear you're the fiftieth person we've had poking round here. We're just drilling a discovery well, son. That's all. It's just another goddamned well.'

Tom got the message. He wasn't surprised. When a driller gets close to where he thinks the oil is, he takes the time to take cores. That means, roughly speaking, he sends down a coring tool, which works pretty much the way an apple corer does. The coring tool cuts out a cylinder of rock and brings it right up to the surface. That way you can see what you're drilling through. If you're getting close to oil, there'll be signs of it written into the rock.

Tom took a last loving look at the rig, then walked away down to the beach. The sunlight was still tilting in his eyes. He was deep in thought.

When Tom had been camped up by his oil tanks, he'd made it his business to acquire information. Not the worthless sort beloved by most independent drillers, but the quality sort on which real decisions are made.

He'd bought maps, studied existing fields, refreshed his

geology. He'd kept the papers beneath his pillow, enjoying the rustle of them as he moved. He'd read and thought and thought and read – and finally one day he'd obtained a geological survey of the Pacific coast. He opened the survey wide on his knees and finally saw what he'd spent his life looking for.

Two fists held together.

Knuckles uppermost.

The left-hand edge of the left-hand fist: Newport Beach. The right-hand edge of the right-hand fist: Beverly Hills. That line of knuckles marked out a whole chain of topographic highpoints: Reservoir Hill, Seal Beach, Signal Hill, Dominguez Hills, Rosencrans, Baldwin Hills, Inglewood.

Tom had guessed that none of them was much to look at. Low hills scraped together from shale. A few frowsy palm trees. Streams full of silvery sunfish and turtles. Cucumber farms, melon patches, avocado groves. Houses, roads, shops, sand. Not a lot.

But that line of highpoints had one thing in common. Each knuckle lay over a well-known oilfield.

Each knuckle, except Signal Hill.

Tom thought again and again of the core that Shell was about to take. If they were getting close to oil, then Tom had to get his hands on some drilling rights before land prices went crazy. If they weren't getting close, then there was no way Tom would drill there, no matter what the geology looked like.

In essence, his problem was simple. He had to see that Shell Oil core. He *had to*.

But how?

75

Under horrible conditions, Reynolds kept the camp running.

The Persians had mostly had exposure to cholera in the past, and their immunity was stronger. But that still left seventeen Persians, as well as the three Poles, one of the Russians and Alan. Properly treated, the disease could be controlled. Without proper treatment, the disease was usually lethal.

Reynolds did what he could. He boiled water, added salt and sugar, and forced all the victims to drink at least a pint and sometimes a quart of fluid every hour. If any man resisted or dared to complain, Reynolds would have the patient held down by a pair of burly tribesmen as he personally forced the water down the man's throat. He continued the treatment right through the night, and into the next morning.

The ravages of the illness were very severe, but no one further came down with the disease, and those who were sick didn't appear to be getting any sicker.

No one except Alan.

Alan had never had a particularly steely stomach. Often enough during the war, he'd hurriedly eaten some poorly cooked food and suffered for it the next day. Right now, although he did his best to drink what was put in front of him, his throat was so parched and swollen that he could hardly swallow. Where other men were drinking pints, Alan was taking only sips. His weakness was growing worse. Reynolds was acutely worried.

He went over to one of the trucks and rooted around its hydraulics system for a suitable tube. He found a decent length of rubber pipe, had it boil-washed for half an hour, then sucked clear water through it for twenty minutes. This done, he went back to Alan's tent.

'Look, I've never done this before, old man, but I think it's high time I learned. I'm sorry if it hurts.'

He passed the tube into Alan's nose.

'There's meant to be a hole in here somewhere, but damn me if I know where.'

The tube scraped around in Alan's nose, looking for an exit. Alan's nasal membranes were dried out and painful, but he just gripped the edge of his blanket and said nothing. Eventually, Reynolds found what he was looking for. The tube slipped suddenly far into Alan's nose and down the back of his throat.

'Ha! Can you breathe, laddie?'

Alan nodded.

Reynolds was triumphant. He fixed a funnel to the tube and began to dribble the salt-and-sugar water into the funnel. He began with just a teaspoonful every minute, then increased the rate, until a teaspoonful was entering the funnel every ten seconds. Twice Alan began to retch, but on neither occasion did he actually vomit.

'Ha!' said Reynolds again, relief starting to glimmer in his eyes.

The next morning, he came into Alan's tent.

'How are you feeling?'

Alan attempted a smile. It was a pretty feeble attempt, but it crinkled the lips just enough to cause a thin trickle of blood to come from one of the deep cracks.

'Righto. I'm sending you to Abadan. Anglo-Persian have got a hospital there, proper doctors and all the rest of it. It'll be a pretty lousy journey, I'm afraid, but there's nothing to do but try.'

Alan nodded. Abadan was a long way away, and the truck journey would be brutal. If he made it to Abadan alive, his chances of recovery were fair. If not . . .

Alan moved his hand, as though writing.

'You want to write? Don't worry. I'll look after the camp while you're gone.'

Alan closed his eyes, waited for a little strength, then shook his head. He made the writing movement again.

'Oh no, old chap. I'm sure you won't need to . . .' Reynolds petered out. He knew Alan well by now, knew better than to argue. 'I'll get pen and paper. Pen, paper and witnesses.'

Alan nodded.

Reynolds brought along writing materials and the two Poles who were best able to walk. They hauled Alan up on his sackcloth pillows and propped the paper on a board on his knees. Watched by everyone present and in an awful shaky hand, Alan wrote, 'Last Will. Sound mind. Concession to George Reynolds. Also money. Everything else (not much!) to Mother and Father. Love to all, esp Charlotte Dunlop. Alan Montague.'

Everyone in camp was silent as Alan was carried over to the truck. The Poles and Russians removed their caps and bowed their heads towards the ground. Alan was conscious, but only just. He felt like the guest of honour at his own funeral.

76

Down on the beach, there was a man with a couple of dogs, friendly faced mongrels with scruffy white coats and stubby little tails. The man wasn't just playing with them, he was getting them to do tricks. Up – down – sit – lie – stand – stay – roll over. The dogs complied quickly and barked enthusiastically once they had completed their routines. Tom liked dogs and he liked this pair as soon as he saw them.

Then the man changed his game. He took a brown paper packet from his pocket and unwrapped it. Tom couldn't quite see what it was, but it looked like a bit of beef bone or a knuckle of pork. The man rooted round on the beach and collected together some stones. Then the game began. The man rubbed the piece of meat on one of the stones, then tossed that stone along with two or three others into the long grass high on the sand dunes. As soon as he gave the command, the two dogs raced away after the stones, searching for them among the dunes. Twenty seconds of intense silence followed, then sudden motion. One of the dogs had a stone in its mouth and was racing back towards its owner. The other dog, annoyed, chased alongside, barking frenziedly, trying to get the first dog to release its treasure.

The game was repeated a few times.

Tom watched closely. When the man threw the stone that

had been rubbed with meat, Tom marked the fall with care. Every single time, it was that stone and no other that the dogs retrieved, sometimes one of them, sometimes the other. They never once missed the stone or brought back the wrong one.

The man began to get bored and threw the last of his stones into the sea. The dogs chased off into the surf and began fighting over a stick of driftwood.

Tom approached the man.

'Nice dogs.'

'Yep. They sure are.'

'You got 'em well trained.'

'They more or less train themselves. They're only pups.' The man whistled and both dogs shot towards him, leaving the beach neatly printed with their pawmarks. 'Good boy, Corin. Good girl, Pippa.'

Tom bent down to fondle the smaller of the two dogs behind her ear. He received a couple of salty licks in exchange.

'Nice trick that, with the stones.'

'Yeah. They ain't strictly speaking retrievers, but I ain't never seen a retriever do any better 'n that.'

'Nope, nor me. Can I give it a go?'

'You want to throw something for 'em?'

'How about this?' said Tom. He took a pocket knife from his coat and opened it out to reveal a thin smear of greyish oil around the hinge. He picked two stones from the beach. Both of them were flattish and smooth, but one of them had a rusty iron ore stain running through the centre. Tom wiped the red-coloured stone with the oil from his knife, then let both dogs sniff the knife all over. 'Ready, folks?' he asked. The two dogs ran backwards ten feet and began yelping with excitement. 'Go on then, fellers.' Tom threw the stones, hard and far into the dunes. He himself would have had the devil of a job finding them. It would be an exceptional dog who could find either stone, let alone pick out the right one.

'You didn't use a scrap o' meat,' said the man. 'I always

use a scrap of meat. That's what they want to retrieve for, see. They want meat. It's only natural.'

'That's true,' said Tom. 'I should have thought of that.'

The dogs were invisible and silent. Every now and then, the dune-grass was stirred by something other than the sea breeze and once Tom spotted a stumpy white tail wagging intently amongst the blue-green stems.

'See, I told you,' said the man. 'It's their animal nature. Wipe a bit o' meat on the stone an' you're working with their animal nature.'

Tom wasn't listening. His gaze was concentrated on the dunes. All of a sudden, the silence was broken. A yelping went up. The grass was shaken violently as though a sudden gale had blown up, two feet wide and forty feet long. The two young dogs exploded out onto the beach. The bigger one, Corin, was tumbling the other one, Pippa, to the ground in an effort to get her to release her prize. He was out of luck. Although Pippa was knocked over four times on her journey back, she arrived, panting, back at her master's feet and dropped a stone, wet and slobbery, into his hand. The stone was flat, smooth, with a distinctive rusty stripe down its centre.

'Well, I'll be jiggered!' said the man.

Tom turned to him with his broadest smile.

'I have a proposition,' he said.

77

The lurching of the truck was acutely uncomfortable. Alan hadn't the strength to hold himself steady and he didn't even have the muscle tone to bounce with the truck as it crashed over rocks and potholes. Reynolds had wanted to accompany him, but Alan had insisted absolutely and categorically that he should stay in the drilling camp until the very last trace of disease had been eradicated.

Instead of Reynolds, Ahmed was Alan's escort, as well as the two tribesmen who took it in turns to drive the truck. Ahmed attempted to keep the salt-and-sugar solution draining down the funnel, but the careening of the truck proved far too violent. Every hour they stopped for ten minutes. Ahmed used the pause to send more water down the funnel, but he was less skilful than Reynolds and perhaps Alan was in too weakened a condition to tolerate much fluid in any event.

The truck jolted down into Shiraz, then bounded along a rough track to Bushehr, before heading north towards the malarial flatlands around Abadan. The journey took three days. By the end of it, Alan was unconscious most of the time. His bowel continued to leak fluid that was now almost as clear as glass.

When his stretcher was carried solemnly into the Anglo-Persian hospital at Abadan, the chief doctor shook his head.

'It's no use, these people,' he complained in a high, whining voice to his Indian assistant. 'They will insist on bringing me patients in this condition, then seem to be surprised when they die. I mean, look at the fellow. And that tube down his throat's been taken from some kind of motor-vehicle. It really won't do, won't do at all.'

Alan was conscious at this point and heard every word. His lips were too broken now to move at all, but if they had been able to, they'd have echoed the thought in his brain. 'Christ have mercy on me.'

78

Tom lay with his back against a sun-warmed boundary wall, watching cottontails and jack rabbits squabble; ground squirrels loping along; trapdoor spiders digging tunnels into the sand. But most of all he watched the scene where, a hundred and fifty feet away, the Shell Oil derrick reared up against the skyline.

On the rig, the drilling crew were lifting the pipe section by section. Tom counted the sections as they came out.

'We're getting closer, Pips,' he said.

Pippa – or Pipsqueak, as Tom immediately renamed her – was turning out to be a lovable little rogue. She'd watched her previous owner walk away down the beach, richer to the tune of fifteen of Tom's dollars, then simply turned to Tom, gave him a lick and voted him in as her brand-new full-time unpaid dog-slave. She trotted round with him by day, snuggled close to him at night, and stole food from his hand in the serene conviction that there was no such thing as theft between dog and master.

Pipsqueak yawned, then scrabbled to get into Tom's pocket, where she could smell warm bacon. He pushed her away. Another section of pipe rose from the well.

'Any time now.'

The derrick was about a hundred yards from the truckstop

at the top of the hill. Today was the day that Shell Oil was taking its core, and half the local community had bets on whether or not the core would show signs of oil. A couple of heavies stood at the base of the rig, ready to keep prying eyes away, with fists if necessary.

The next section of pipe came up. Pipsqueak had given up trying to get at the warm bacon, and had fallen asleep with her nose pressed blissfully up against the magic pocket. By Tom's reckoning, there was just one more section before the corer itself. He shook Pipsqueak awake. 'Rise and shine, sweetheart.'

The little white mongrel yawned and wagged her stump of a tail.

The last section of pipe rose from the hole. Up at the truck-stop, a big car was parked, its nose already pointing down the hill. A man in a dark business suit leaned against the fender and watched the scene. He was the man from the Shell laboratories, there to take the sample off for analysis.

'OK, Squeaker, get ready.'

The black ants on the drilling rig had their corer now. They bent over it, taking superstitious care to bring the sample out whole. They sniffed at it, of course, but that meant nothing. If it was as full of oil as a sponge in your petrol tank, they'd have sniffed it. If it was as empty of oil as a bucket full of nothing, they'd have sniffed it just the same. Oilmen always sniff their cores.

Tom nudged Pipsqueak to make her stand. He stood up himself and strolled closer. A dusty trail connected the rig to the truckstop. Tom walked to within forty yards of it, then stopped. He bent down and put his hand on Pipsqueak's collar.

The riggers on the drilling platform wrapped the core in a canvas bag, then lowered it carefully to the ground. The two heavies now enjoyed their moment of glory. They heaved the bag up – it was a big core, two feet long and eight inches in diameter – and began to carry it between them up the path. Given the level of interest in the well, Tom guessed that the two heavies would escort the sample all the way to the laboratory and a Shell Oil safe inside.

'OK, Pips, don't you let me down now.'

Pipsqueak began to feel the tension acutely. Her mouth was open and panting, and every now and then she punctuated her pants with a long-drawn-out whine of excitement.

'Nearly, Pips, nearly.'

The two heavies were ten yards up the path. Twenty yards.

'OK, Squeaky, OK.'

Thirty yards up the path. In a moment's time they'd be as close to Tom as the path would bring them. Tom's mouth was drier than sand, drier than dust. One of the two heavies dropped his end of the bag and readjusted his grip. They started up again. They were forty yards up the path, halfway to their precious truckstop.

'Go, Squeaker, go.'

Tom released his grip on Pipsqueak's collar. The little dog raced away. She was a stumpy little thing with a big dose of terrier in her exceptionally well-mixed ancestry, but Tom could see that there was something faster too: a whippet maybe, or possibly one of the larger poodles.

She ran over the stony grass: a white blur. The two heavies saw her coming and grinned. People always grinned when they saw her. It was one of the nice things about having her.

Within a few seconds, Pipsqueak had caught up with the heavies. She hurled herself at the canvas bag and sniffed it as though trying to inhale the entire sample. The heavies became instantly suspicious, and began to drive her away.

Too late.

Pipsqueak was in heaven. She dodged the boots and fists, threw her head up to the brilliant sky, and barked and barked and barked. Tom's cracked lips broke into a brilliant smile. 'You treasure,' he said, 'you little gem.'

He let out a come-to-me whistle, and Pipsqueak tore joyously back to him through the dust. When she arrived, Tom's hands were full of bacon and all of it was for her.

79

The cholera germ isn't eternal. If it doesn't kill you quickly, it doesn't kill you at all.

For one week, Alan hesitated between life and death. Fluid ran through him like one of the Hampshire chalk streams of his youth. But the cholera bug had missed its chance. The outflow of liquid began to slow down. Alan began to be able to drink normally. He sat up in bed. He was terribly thin, and his face was hollow and dark. His pale blond hair was pricklish with sweat and dirt, until one of the nurses came to wash it for him. He was weak but on the mend.

When the doctor made his rounds that evening, he asked Alan how he was.

'Perfectly well, I believe, Doctor. I owe you my deepest thanks.'

'Yes, I believe you probably do. The native chappies who brought you in dished out some pretty rough treatment in that truck of theirs. Shouldn't wonder if they'd forgotten you were in the back.'

Alan disliked the little doctor. He was the worst sort of small-minded colonial prig, who understood foreigners all the less for living among them.

'Ahmed and the others did their damnedest to get me here

in one piece. If it hadn't been for them, I'd be as dead as a tent-peg.'

'Hmm.' The doctor produced a thermometer and thrust it at Alan, who obediently popped it under his tongue. With his patient prevented from speech, the doctor began on a litany of complaint: the poor food, the difficult climate, the unreliable servants, the absence of 'entertainments for the educated mind'. Alan wondered what the doctor had been expecting when he'd signed up for Abadan. The ballet?

The doctor pulled the thermometer out. '. . . nothing more to life than cricket. Hello! Temperature's up. Only half a degree, but . . .'

The doctor began to feel Alan's chest, and examined his pulse, eyes and tongue. 'Any feelings of fever? Chills?'

'A little chilled, perhaps. Part of convalescence, no doubt.'

You've been taking your quinine, of course?'

'Quinine?'

'Of course. Abadan is a mudflat lying at the head of an extremely warm marsh. The place is a devil's kitchen for malaria.'

Alan was silent for a moment. 'There's no malaria in the mountains and no mosquitoes,' he said. 'I've never needed quinine.'

'Ah!' said the doctor, as he solemnly shook down the thermometer.

The doctor's 'Ah!' was right on the mark. That night Alan's temperature rose to a hundred and one degrees. The following morning it hit a hundred and four. Alan had a headache that split his temples. He slipped in and out of a feverish sleep. For the first time since he had demobilised, Alan began to dream about the war. Or rather, since dreams only come to people with a reasonable grip on reality, the war returned to seize Alan. Tom was there in a million forms. Tom alive but dying. Tom pleading for help. Tom in captivity. Tom wounded. Tom in no man's land. Tom caught on the wire. Tom falling under fire. Alan kept trying to find his twin and bring him home but, every time, the nightmare intervened, to leave the two men just as separate as before.

After two nights and a day, the high fever came down, the delirium subsided, the headache weakened. Alan thought he'd conquered the disease in double-quick time, but the doctor was prompt to disillusion him. 'It's the way it works. Two days on, three days off. The intervals between attacks are no picnic, but the attacks themselves are sheer bloody murder.'

And so it was. There'd be two or three days of reprieve when Alan felt lousy, but at least he felt sane and lousy. Then his fever would rise, the crashing headache would return and the delirium came to smash all sense of reality. During these periods, Alan tossed and moaned in his bed, crying out in his sleep. And all the time, the delirium had only one theme, war, and one character, Tom.

Alan didn't mind the illness. He knew malaria was unlikely to kill him and physical suffering no longer meant much to him. But the dreams obsessed him. Alan had spent four years grieving Tom's death. Four years coming to terms with it. He'd made progress. He'd learned how to find joy, love, and hope. He never forgot Tom, but was no longer disabled by his loss. Until now. It was as though the dreams had stormed in to remind him that he would never get over it. And so Alan lay beneath a cloud of fever, sweating, groaning, and thinking constantly of his lost brother.

During his intermissions, he wrote to Reynolds telling him that he was going to be just fine. He wrote home to his parents, telling them that he was a little sick and had been advised to rest for a few weeks by way of precaution.

He wrote to Lottie, telling her the truth, telling her about his dreams and hallucinations, telling her about the drilling back in the mountains. Each time he finished a letter to Lottie, he reread it, signed it, then put it aside. He would burn them all later. But it wasn't the same as it had once been. Did he mean anything special to her? He didn't know. In Piccadilly, when they'd met, she'd treated him like just another man in her infinite circle of friends. Were his letters addressed to a forbidden sweetheart or to a wartime fantasy? He didn't know. He wanted to harden his heart, to forget her, or at least allow her to fade into the past. But he couldn't do it. He couldn't when he was well and he couldn't now he was sick. So he wrote his letters to Lottie, dreamed of Tom, and slept the light and muddled sleep of the fevered.

80

The veranda had once been green, but time and sunshine had picked the paint almost bare. A rusting screen door was shut tight against the flies, only there were holes in the mesh as big as grapefruit. A line of ants wandered through the gap in the bottom of the door like it had been built for them.

Tom rapped at the frame. 'Mrs Hershey? Hello?'

No answer, but maybe a movement from within.

Tom unhooked the door and opened it. He stood in the doorway, and called again. 'Hello? Mrs Hershey.'

There was another movement. As Tom's eyes adjusted to the gloom, he saw a big white shape on a broken-down couch in the centre of the room. The shape looked like a laundry basket loaded with dirty wash. The laundry basket belched, then groaned.

'Mrs Hershey, my name is Tom Calloway. May I come in?'

Tom's senses adjusted to the musty gloom. There was a smell of alcohol and puke. Violet Hershey sat upright, rubbing her soft fat neck. Her skin was grey and unwashed. Her hair looked like it had been cut with pliers six months before, then left to grow into a mat.

'No, sir, I ain't got nothing. There ain't nothing here to steal. Ain't no use poking round in this house.'

'Ma'am, I understand you own some land hereabouts. I

was wondering if you'd be interested in making some good money out of it.'

'I ain't got no land. I ain't got nothing to steal. I ain't –' The moan turned off abruptly, as Hershey slowly adjusted to the shock of being woken up at two in the afternoon. 'Who the hell are you?'

'My name is Tom Ca –'

'Mister, I don't give a damn who the hell you are. Ain't you even going to help an old lady up?'

Tom went over to offer her an arm. She didn't want an arm, she wanted a whole body lift. The smell of alcohol and puke grew sickeningly intense. Tom hauled her to her feet. Hershey dragged herself to the bathroom where she sat on the can with the door open. When she came out, she looked a little more awake, a little more alive.

'You going to fix me a drink or do I have to get my own?'

Tom looked around. The kitchen was more squalid than he fancied going into. The gloomy parlour was crowded with old bits of furniture, none of it worth a cent more than firewood, but nothing obviously like a drinks cupboard. Dust and sand from the beach had blown in through the gaping door and windows, and now covered everything. The floor crunched as Tom walked. Then he saw it: a clear glass one-gallon container of the kind that drugstores sometimes used to dispense root beer. Tom pulled out the stopper and smelled. It was pure grain alcohol.

'Prohibition Bourbon, that's what I call it,' cried Hershey. 'Prohibition Bourbon.'

Tom found a filthy glass on the floor, shook a couple of ants out of it, and filled it half full of liquor. He brought it over. Hershey wouldn't reach out her hand to take it. 'My arm,' she whined. 'Aches like a hooker's puss.' He bent lower, then lower still. 'Ha!' cried Hershey in triumph, as she snapped upwards to plant a fleshy kiss right on Tom's lips. 'Ha! Men! Only after one thing.' She swallowed her drink like it was ginger beer and held the glass out for more. Tom refilled it, but planted the glass on a table where she'd have to reach for it.

'Mrs Hershey, I'm an oilman interested in drilling for oil on your land. If you agree, then I'll pay you forty bucks an acre every year, starting from today. If I hit oil, you'll get a fifteen per cent share in the royalties.'

'Oh, I've had promises before. I've had offers. But when it comes to –'

'But first of all, I need to verify that the acres in question belong to you. It's not that I doubt –'

'Oh, go on, take advantage. My late husband of bloody memory, bleeding mem – . . . Oh, dang it all to hell-an'-horseshit, I mean blessed memory – he looked after them things. He was a good man, mister, no matter what you say. But now I'm on my own, defenceless, I don't care to keep account of all them technilegalations. I got my mem'ries and nobody can take them aways.'

As she babbled, she groped beneath her couch and brought out wads of paper. She threw them at Tom, but her throw was feeble and the papers just tumbled over the floor. Tom collected them up, taking care to avoid too much contact with her filthy skirts or the grit-grimy floor. The papers were mostly trash. Laundry tickets, shopping lists, unopened letters, invoices, some papers relating to the hire-purchase of a Model T Ford and other papers connected to its subsequent repossession. There was also a valid land purchase order, declaring the twenty-seven acres on Signal Hill to be the legal property of Mr Josiah Brand Hershey. The date was 1899. It figured. The land in question was farmed by a pair of elderly Japanese, raising cucumbers, melons and an acre or two of scraggy avocados. Only thing was, Japanese weren't allowed to own land under California law, so most of the farmers hereabouts leased their land from white landowners. The rental income from the land was probably all that kept Hershey afloat.

'This'll do,' said Tom, waving the document. 'Strictly

speaking, I ought to take this down to the county courthouse and have the county clerk verify this on his books, but this is a deal between friends, right? There's got to be trust.' His tone was warm and friendly.

'You didn't ought to call him bad names, mister. He had his bad points, I'll grant you, but he was a good man and you didn't ought to have said all them things.'

'No bad names, ma'am, only a deal between friends.'

Tom let himself act magnanimous, but in truth he was only protecting his interests. The county courthouse was alive with leasehounds and promoters. If he went to court to verify the lease, then by the time he got back to sign the deal with Hershey, there'd be two dozen other people trying to sweet-talk her into selling drilling rights. Tom smiled a broad trust-me smile. He thumped a stack of dollars on the filthy table. 'Ma'am, if we cut a deal here today, then these dollar bills are going to stay behind with you.'

'I want to count 'em.'

Tom knew that if he handed her the dollars they'd disappear in a flash into her dirty bosom. 'First we deal.'

'I only want to feel 'em. I'm only an old –'

'Ma'am, you can take them to bed and chew on them, only first we have to strike a deal.'

'Eighty dollars.'

'Eighty dollars an acre? That's way too much. I can go to fifty.'

'And I know all about Shell Oil, don't think I don't. I know there are people who'd take advantage of an innocent old woman. I know –'

'Mrs Hershey, Shell Oil is drilling an exploration well. It's called that way because no one knows what they're going to find. If you –'

'There are folks up on the hill who are millionaires, just from selling one little patch o' dirt. Mill-*ee-on*-aires. And you offer me a ratty little sixty dollars an acre.' Hershey started to cry, big round tears plopping from her cheeks.

304

'Mrs Hershey, you know perfectly well that's nonsense. If you want to be a millionaire, you need to sign a good deal with a capable oilman. Nobody gets to be rich if they don't strike oil.'

'Oh, I've had promoters in here. Young men. Charming men. They've promised –'

'I'm not a promoter,' said Tom, losing his patience. 'I'm an oilman. I have papers here. We can sign them now or you can leave them. If you leave them I won't come back. If Shell Oil sinks its well and comes up with nothing but dirt, then you won't make one red penny out of your land, and you know it.'

'I'm just a lonely old woman. I'm just –'

Tom plonked the papers down and looked at his watch. 'I'm going to leave in one minute from now . . . fifty seconds . . .'

Mrs Hershey blubbed and sucked at the last of her drink.

'. . . forty seconds . . . thirty seconds . . .'

'I don't have my glasses. I can't read those tiny little letters. I know you lawyers. I know . . .'

'. . . twenty seconds . . . fifteen . . . ten . . .'

Hershey stopped crying and grabbed the papers. 'Sixty bucks an acre, twenty per cent royalties, and a six-month no-drill-no-deal clause.'

Tom laughed. Hershey had obviously learned something from the promoters who'd visited. 'Sixty bucks an acre it is. The termination clause you want is already there.'

'And twenty per cent royalties. Twenty-five. I'm all on my own. I'm –'

'Fifteen per cent. Take it or leave it.'

Hershey looked coy again, wondering whether another serving of tears would squeeze more money out of Tom. The stack of dollars on the table riffled a little in the breeze. The ants paused for a moment in the doorway to let the new sand settle before they continued to ransack the house. Hershey decided against tears. 'I'm just an old woman, living here on my own. I'm –'

Tom stood up. He picked up the contract. He picked up the dollars. 'So long, Mrs Hershey. Thank you for your time.'

His footsteps crunched on the sandy floor. The screen door screeched as he pushed it open. Pipsqueak, who had been busily cleaning her paws, looked up and shook herself. 'Let's go, girl.' They walked away.

They hadn't gone fifty yards before there was a commotion behind them. Mrs Hershey had crashed her way to the door and was leaning over the rickety rail of the veranda, hollering at them.

'OK, mac! Sweet Jesus! Fifteen per cent. And don't forget, I'm busting a gusset for ya.'

81

The air cracked and rippled with rifle-fire. Wild teams of horsemen tore up the valley, wheeled round and descended, robes fluttering, pistols blazing, knives flashing in the sun. Not to be outdone, the truck drivers drove frantically alongside, risking an axle every time they plunged into a pothole or struck a larger-than-average rock. Men and boys hung to the sides of the trucks, holding on with one arm, and waving shirts or flags or firearms with the other. By some miracle, however, the only actual blood lost that afternoon belonged to a pair of juicy young lambs, slaughtered with immense ceremony by the fat Persian cook and two of his assistants behind the cooking tent.

George Reynolds showed his delight by pumping more blood than ever into his crimson face, and shaking Alan's hand as though intending to detach it.

'By God, laddie, it's good to see you! By God, it is! The camp hasn't been the same, not the same at all.'

Alan took his hand back. He was fifteen pounds lighter than before his illness and his strength wasn't yet what it had been. He greeted every single one of his men by name, hugged them close in the Persian manner, and asked each of them the questions they were burning for him to ask (Husain, and how was his shoulder? Mohammad, and how was his driving coming along? Ahmed, and hadn't his goddamn bloody English improved!)

And yet when the feasting and the jubilation had begun to subside, something like an air of gloom began to settle over the camp. The well was down to fifteen hundred foot, but progress was becoming slower with each passing day. More to the point, Reynolds had been observed shaking his head, and muttering and losing his normally unflappable temper.

'I'll not beat about the bush, laddie,' he said, taking Alan into his tent. 'Take a look at these samples.'

One of the few advantages of the percussion method of drilling is that, because you have to keep clearing the hole with a bailing tool, you end up with a complete record of the rock you're drilling through. Reynolds had collected and labelled all the samples collected on the drill to date.

'Here's the sandstone layers we drilled through to begin with. No surprises there. Then capstone. Solid honest-to-God capstone, hard and impermeable. I tell you, laddie, I was so excited I almost stopped drilling, so that you could be here for the fun of the oil strike.'

Alan looked sharply at his partner. 'And?'

'And I decided not to stop. I went right on. We got through the capstone and we arrived at this.'

He passed a sample bag to Alan, who opened it. It was sand. The sand that had once been a sea floor, the sea floor they had been drilling to reach. The sand was as dry as million-year-old bones.

There was no oil.

Not a drop, not a trace, not a sniff.

82

Pipsqueak heard the roar and woke with a bark.

Tom, who'd been dozing, leaped awake with a shock.

The scattered inhabitants of Signal Hill pulled their coats over their shirtsleeves and went tearing out into the gathering dusk.

The Shell rig had struck oil. Struck loud enough to wake a town. Struck hard enough to shake the ground. The rig was a magnet that drew all life to it. And why? Because oil isn't just a commodity like cocoa or nickel or pig-iron. Oil is fuel. It's warmth and movement and light. As a matter of fact, it's pretty close to life itself – and the nearest darn thing to money the earth provides. And here it was. A huge great jet of the stuff, whooshing into the air and slapping down on the earth from a hundred and twenty feet or more. People on the windward side had their faces, beards and hats glossed over with the fine black spray. Nobody minded. Kids and adults ran forwards to get their heads wet, palms open to gather in the precious juice. One man even kneeled beneath the fountain, bare-chested and face pointed up towards the black rain, that fell as if by magic.

The rig was a magnet because everyone, right down to the smallest child, understood what had happened. On this extraordinary night, the whole world had changed for ever.

It wasn't even like winning the lottery; it was better than that. The lottery, you have to buy a ticket. With the lottery, in the end, you know it's just a matter of luck. Everyone buys a ticket. A certain percentage get lucky. If you could go on long enough, you'd get your own piece of luck.

This wasn't like that. This was like being fingered by God. And God didn't just present you with a bland little cheque covered in zeros – this was a gift for men – real men, hard and shrewd – to profit from. The lucky ones were those who owned land up on Signal Hill that night, any land at all. Overnight, they'd become backyard millionaires, or would be if they could figure the angles. People's minds turned to royalty percentages, lot sizes, drilling concerns. Some people would be presented with an opportunity like this and fritter it away. They might agree to fifteen per cent when they could take thirty. They might sign up with an all-talk-no-money promoter. They might be seduced by the numbers and end up selling a million-dollar well for a cheesy hundred thousand bucks.

While the Shell men slaved to get the rig under control, the frenzy went on. People continued to gather. Now it wasn't just the residents of Signal Hill, it was people from further away: Long Beach, Wilmington, Huntingdon Beach. These were the envious ones. The people who didn't find themselves sitting on a quarter-acre block of Paradise. They looked on too, but their mouths were tight, and they held their kids away from the fountain of dancing black.

With Pisqueak in his arms, Tom also looked on. All his life, he'd been waiting for this. His Hampshire childhood, then war, prison, hardship, the all-American experience of starting with nothing and working for everything. All of it, every last hour of it, however sad or terrible, was leading up to this monumental moment. He breathed deeply. He would gamble everything. He would win colossally – or lose everything he'd staked.

And over them all, the winners and losers, the dreamers and the jealous, the thick black jet continued to spout.

83

'It may only be a pocket.'

'Maybe.'

'Or a false bottom. It may be nothing more than a fold in the rock, laddie.'

'Yes, maybe.'

Since Alan's illness, Alan and Reynolds had become closer. Previously, if they'd ever used each other's names, they called each other Montague and Reynolds. These days, Reynolds only ever called Alan 'laddie', and if Alan called Reynolds anything, he called him George.

'Look at the valley walls. There's folding, perturbation, upheaval on a massive scale as well as some quite violent local disturbances. The plain truth is that round these parts the strata are all to bug– – pardon me, all to cock. There's no telling what's up, what's down. We could go down another hundred feet and hit a gusher.'

Alan drummed his fingers on the folding table, crunching on the pile of dry sand brought up from the bottom of the well. They were talking by the light of a kerosene lamp. The kerosene was brought up by truck from Shiraz, and the Shirazi merchants obtained theirs from the Anglo-Persian works at Abadan. They were using their competitor's oil from two hundred miles away, and for all they knew they were sitting less than a mile above a massive oilfield of their own. The smoky yellow light threw Alan's gaunt shadow next to Reynolds' stocky one on the sloping canvas wall. Alan's drumming fingers appeared in huge relief.

'Yes, George, but we have to consider all the factors. It's getting harder and harder to sink the well. The weight of the cable inside the hole is now many times the weight of the old Mother Hubbard at the bottom. No matter how much we patch up our boiler, we have to recognise that it's reaching its limit.'

'Well now, that's true.'

'And the geology might still be favourable, but the odds have shifted against us.'

'Well, that's true too.'

Alan's fingers still drummed in silence on the billowing tent wall. George Reynolds stroked his thick black moustache. Since beginning to drill, he'd allowed it to grow ever longer and more piratical, as though competing with the Qashqai for some Best-Moustache-in-Camp prize.

'But even that's not my main concern,' said Alan.

'No?'

'Money. It's costing a lot to maintain the camp, but I don't see any way to reduce expenses. We needed every man we had last week just to clear the road after the landslip . . . The fact is that we're going to run out of money sooner or later and we have to make every penny count. Every day. Every hour.'

'Aye.' Reynolds sighed heavily. 'Laddie, I didn't tell you this before, but my Auntie Enid died recently – no, don't worry, I hardly knew the old bird, lived in Leicestershire on a farm, hoarded money like a magpie. Anyway, she left me five thousand pounds, I understand. It's there to drill with, if you want it.'

'That's very handsome of you, George! My thanks, indeed!'

'No, laddie, don't be silly. You can give me my share if we hit anything, and we can be beggars together if we don't . . .

312

You know that I'd sooner strike oil in this valley than anything else in the whole world.'

'Yes, yes. Me too.'

They were silent a moment. Alan had spoken the truth, or almost. Apart from Lottie, finding oil had become the only thing still important to him since Tom's death. He wondered if there was any business in the world quite like it: a business that stole your soul away, a business that could make fond romantics of the hardest heads. Reynolds' offer was a splendid one, but five thousand pounds would keep them going three months at most. Winter was setting in and drilling through the short and icy days would be quite hard enough, even without a failing boiler.

'I told you about Mickiewicz, did I?' said Reynolds interrupting.

'No.'

'He says he can't drill tomorrow. Another saint's day apparently. A religious holiday.'

'Saint Halina of the Numberless Excuses, I expect . . . What did you say to him?'

'I told him you'd have a word with him in the morning.'

As the Poles' morale had begun to drop, so the number of their religious holidays had begun to multiply.

'Would you say Ahmed is ready to become a full-time rigger?'

'Yes, I would . . . I suppose.'

'Yes, I think so too. Also Ali-Baba.'

'Ali-Baba? Ali-Baba? Well, maybe. At a pinch.'

'We're pinched, George. The Poles don't want to be here and I don't feel like forcing them . . . I'll tell them they can take the rest of the year to glorify their blessed saints.'

The long silence lengthened. By night, the Mother Hubbard was left on a slack cable at the bottom of the long hole. With a bit of breeze like tonight's, the loose wire slapped against the winch and pulleys and sent a low moaning out into the night. It sounded like the moan of a dying well.

'We'll move her, George. First thing tomorrow. We'll move the derrick and drop a well three miles further up the valley. The Muhammad Ameri Number 2.'

Reynolds was silent for a while, then began to nod in agreement. It was a solemn moment.

They had enough money for two, possibly three, wells and their first one had just failed.

84

Other men might have waited for morning. Not Tom.

Alamitos No. 1 drew oilmen to it like sailors to a mermaid. The oil-slippery ground by the Shell rig became a market-place for ideas, deals, offers and handshakes. Two blocks from the gusher, an enterprising barber lit up his shop and sold hot coffee at fifty cents the cup, while his wife handed round home-baked carrot cake and refused all payment. Tom hung out on the sidewalk outside. He was already half-famous. People pointed him out. 'That's him, English Tom, the guy with the land parcel down on the hill.' Drillers came to him and presented their credentials.

'Evening, mac. I heard you got some land.'

'I have.'

'The way you see it, would that be producing land?'

Tom explained where his land was – not the best location, but not bad – and the amount: twenty-seven acres. When he mentioned the size of his acreage, men stopped dead in their tracks. No one had twenty-seven acres. Apart from Shell, who hardly counted, *no one* had that much land. And that was the moment when the conversation would change tack. It wasn't the rigger asking questions of Tom, it was the rigger pleading to be considered.

'Well, sir, I'm mighty pleased to make your acquaintance.

My name's Dave Larzelere, you might of heard me spoken of as the Duster on account of some bad luck I encountered round down Torrey Canyon way, but I'm a fair hand with a drill and I reckon there ain't too many rigs I can't handle, and I wouldn't mind mentioning that any poor luck as I might have had in the past is good an' finished, seeing as the last two wildcats I worked on turned out to be producers, and pretty good ones at that . . .' The Duster spat on the ground, wondering if he'd said too much or not enough. His spit was brown and gluey and it balled up in the dust. Like many oilmen, he was addicted to chewing tobacco, since the smoking sort was dangerous anywhere near a producing well. 'And, anyways, I was wondering if mebbe you'd be needing some help any time soon?'

Tom rejected some men and accepted others. He wanted experience – he knew he was still short of knowledge – but most of all he wanted eagerness. He couldn't offer much by way of wages, but he peeled off percentage shares in his oil rights and handed them out like they were diamond mines, which in a way they were.

By two in the morning, he had a team of drillers: tough, experienced and as hungry as he was.

The next item was money. To sink one well would cost around twenty-five thousand bucks. By cutting down on wages and handing out royalty interests, Tom could cut that figure down to maybe twenty-one or twenty-two thousand. That still left a ten-thousand-dollar gap between what he had and what he needed.

No problem.

There are promoters and promoters. Some of them are all-mouth-no-money, first cousins to outright fraudsters, men so hopeless they wouldn't find a nickel in a packet of gum. Tom stayed clear of these. He asked big questions, tough questions about rigs and equipment and investors and distribution contracts. He used his interrogation to winnow away the losers, until he was left with the real men, architects of oil deals, men who could put together a business transaction from a concrete cell. Tom found a man he trusted, and by six o'clock in the morning, he had made the arrangements he needed.

He should have been tired, but he wasn't. He'd spent every penny he owned, but he had something better. He had land. He had a rig.

And he could smell the oil.

85

Winter came.

Some days, when snow was falling, it was impossible to drill, and Alan let the men keep to their tents, watching the valley disappear beneath its mantle of white. In the morning when the snow had stopped, they would be up before dawn to chip away at the ice that snagged the cables and clogged the pulley. They'd shovel fuel into the rickety old boiler, and stand around it, drinking their morning tea, grateful for the warmth. They went to bed fully dressed except for their boots, and even their boots they tucked into their bedding, to keep the ice from caking them during the night.

They began to have accidents. One of the Persian riggers allowed the heavy bailing tool to fall on his foot, and he lost three toes and could no longer walk without a stick. Even worse, one of the trucks, attempting to get up the hill in vile weather, rolled over and killed one of its occupants. They held a burial service up at the camp, laying out the dead man like the effigy of a saint and burying him with a Koran folded over his stomach to keep out the devil.

The Russians were thoroughly used to such weather, and worked at their constant unhurried pace irrespective of climate, but the Persians suffered acutely. The tribesmen usually spent their winters down in the lowlands in their family compounds. The idea of working outside in these conditions appalled them, and nearly a third of the men employed simply disappeared till the camp seemed empty and joyless.

Alan caught four men smoking opium. He disciplined them and confiscated their drug, but the men were moody and sullen, and four days later, when the supply truck came up from Shiraz, he smelled the odd meaty smoke and found the men grouped round an opium pipe with dull eyes and vacant faces. He did nothing while they were still under the influence, but the next morning he asked them to take their belongings and leave. The mood in the camp grew brittle and depressed.

And yet, despite everything, the Muhammad Ameri No. 2 continued to make progress. They passed each milestone with a modest celebration: two hundred and fifty feet earned lashings of tea, sugared almonds and tobacco. Five hundred feet earned an open fire built with their precious coal, and two young kids spit-roasted over the blaze. They were at nine hundred and thirty feet now and the camp was abuzz with plans for the thousand foot extravaganza.

Meanwhile, Reynolds and Alan met each night to examine their latest rock samples, and to compare them to the ones they'd taken from the Ameri No. 1. As usual – perhaps as always – the geology was inconclusive.

'We'll just have to go down until we find it,' said Reynolds.
'Or until we run out of cash.'

And day by day, their cash resources dwindled, the rock samples were unhelpful, their chances of failure grew.

86

There are important moments in life. Marriage. Baptism. Death. The first kiss, the first sex, the first broken heart. But however important these things feel, they're not such a big deal. They happen a million times to a million people every day. Everyone has 'em. They're nothing special.

But most people aren't oilmen. Most people haven't assembled land, a rig, and a crew of riggers all in the same place at the same time just five hundred yards from a producing well.

Tom had.

He'd had to wait forty days before getting his rig (bought from some bankrupt exploration venture in Indiana), but they'd got it set up in double-quick time and now, at six o'clock on a rain-spattered evening, they lowered the drill to within three foot of the sandy earth. This was bigger than marriage. This was bigger than birth. This might – just might – turn out to be an oil well.

'Hold up there, guys,' said the Duster, producing two brown paper bags with a pint of moonshine whiskey in each. 'We gotta do things properly from the drop.'

He handed round the bottles and each of the men took a long slow draught, before spitting some on their hands and running their hands solemnly round the fishtailed drill bit.

Earlier that day, Jeb Flecker had heated the forge up to white heat and hammered the blade of the bit so sharp you could have shaved with it. A bit didn't need to be anywhere near that sharp, of course. After a single minute twisting in the soil, the edge would be lost in any event. But each of the drilling crew owned one per cent of whatever came up, and the superstitious intensity of that gang was greater than anything Tom had seen, even in wartime.

Tom took his swig, rolled it round his mouth, spat on his hands, and baptised the blade. He swallowed the drink. It tasted of fire, blue-flamed and intense; the true illegal spirit of Prohibition. For some reason the taste made him think of Rebecca Lewi. He felt a sudden pang of longing for her company. Annoyed with himself, he spat on the ground and passed the whiskey bottle on round.

The Duster took the bottle and nodded at Pipsqueak.

'She's in the crew.'

'Yeah, I guess.'

'So.' The Duster waved the bottle.

'So?'

'So she's gotta drink.'

Tom thought of objecting, but the swell of opinion was against him. He wiped his dirty workman's hands on the seat of his overalls, then bent to lift Pipsqueak to the bottle. The Duster splashed her with the fluid, and she spluttered indignantly but her tail wagged harder. Tom then passed her beneath the drill bit, like a lamb of sacrifice. The men nodded approvingly. 'She'll do,' said the Duster, meaning the rig, not the dog.

'Then let's get moving,' said Tom. His voice was quiet, almost reverential. He had chosen his tone just right.

The drillers knew what to do. The boiler was fired up. The pressure was right, the rig was strong and level. First, they raised the massive lifting block that caused the drill bit to lower to the ground. The Duster brought it to rest on the sand as gently as a mother kisses a baby. He nodded. 'Boiler

Bob' Colvin threw the valve that passed pressure through to the kelly. The kelly turned. The drill pipe turned with the kelly. The bit twisted into a rapid blur, drove down into the soil, and was buried. Tom let out a sigh, that was one-quarter pain and three-quarters bliss.

He had just spudded in his very first well.

87

Spring 1921.

It was still cold, but the valley floor was clear of snow, and the river running through it was high and dangerous with meltwater. A couple of their goats lost their footing when the bank collapsed, were swept away, and found drowned two miles downstream. Everywhere in the camp, the ground was being churned into slush. The winter fight against cold had turned into a new fight against mud.

The Muhammad Ameri No. 2 had failed.

They hadn't struck oil. They hadn't found signs of oil. The chippings that came up from the well bottom gave Alan and Reynolds no hope. If they'd had time and money, they'd have continued, of course. But they didn't. With every day that passed, their money was draining away and time was measured in money. As Reynolds said, 'If we don't move now, we may as well not move at all. We simply won't have the cash to sink a third well to a proper depth.'

The derrick stood a hundred feet high. As well as the derrick, they'd have to move the boiler and pump-house and camwheel and lifting tackle and cable. Even a short move would require all the men to labour for a week.

323

'Time to get a bloody move up,' said Ahmed.

But Alan was unhappy about something. He squinted up at the glinting snowline, he rubbed his chin (newly shaved in boiled snow-water), and pulled slowly at a half-eaten flat-bread that was the day's breakfast. He had put on weight since his illness the year before, but he was still thinner than he had been. His face had lines that had never been there before, not even during the war.

High up on the valley wall, a chain of bedraggled calico flags was beginning to poke through the snow. Alan had put the flags up there last year, marking out the strata of oil sand that Ameri had found. Because the strata were exposed, there was no chance of finding oil in any quantity, but you could at least trace the line where the oil had once been.

The line of flags was further evidence in favour of Reynolds' impatience to move. The flags were never more than two thousand feet from the top of the ridge, and sometimes as little as eleven hundred. If the same logic applied on the valley floor, then oil should be found at between eleven hundred and two thousand feet. They'd driven the first well to eighteen hundred, and the second one to more than two thousand. Everything in logic said they should move the well now, and get cracking on their third and final hole . . .

Eventually, Alan made up his mind. 'No,' he said. 'We leave the derrick where it is.'

'What? Great Scott, laddie! There's no use in giving up. We've still got cash enough to –'

'We're not giving up. We're going to carry on down.'

'Good Lord, haven't we been through this?'

'Goddamn boiler not wanting any more down,' said Ahmed helpfully. 'Lousy useless damn-fool bugger.'

'Down,' said Alan decisively. 'George, look up at the flags there. What do you see?'

'I see an oilfield at eleven hundred to two thousand feet in depth. There's no sense in going deeper.'

Alan nodded. 'That's what I've always seen too. That's why

I was so sure we had to move the well. But maybe we've been seeing the wrong thing all along. Maybe the valley is giving us the clue we need and we've been too blind to see it.'

Reynolds grunted. He didn't like detective novels. He didn't see that there were any two ways about it.

Alan used his flatbread to point at the left-handmost flag. 'That flag is at least four miles from us and I got a real whiff of oil from that site.' Then he pointed right, far up the valley. The line of calico flags tapered out of sight as the valley curved. 'That way, the field stretches for another three miles at least. I imagine the field goes further still, I just couldn't get to it because of rockfalls from higher up.'

Reynolds nodded. This was baby stuff. He knew it all.

'So what do you see? What are the flags telling us?' Alan asked.

'That there's an oilfield between eleven hundred –'

'But what size of oilfield? Big or small?'

'Lord's sake, lad, if we ever hit the damn thing, it'll be enormous. What, seven miles long, by Lord knows how many wide! I didn't leave a comfortable berth in London just to find any old tiddler.'

Alan nodded. 'Precisely. Exactly. The field – if it exists – is enormous. It shouldn't make a blind bit of difference where we stick our well. If there's oil here at all, it's beneath our feet right now.'

He spoke in a voice of absolute authority. It was a voice he'd acquired as a leader of men on the battlefields of France and Flanders. Nobody who'd ever heard him use that tone had disagreed. Nobody was going to today. Alan took another bite of his flatbread and tossed the rest aside.

'We go on down.'

88

How many times and with how many women had Tom had sex in his life?

He didn't know. The answer was a lot, of course, but he'd always felt it would be contemptible, ungentlemanly in him to count.

His first girl had been Susan Risinghurst, an apple-cheeked farmer's daughter in Whitcombe. His most regular lover had been Laura Cole, a shop girl that he'd become close to in London before the war. His first foreign conquest had been a French woman, Amélie, about whom he remembered virtually nothing. His most disastrous one had been with Alan's Lisette, that awful August morning in Saint Tess.

But of all the pretty, laughing, dimpled crew, there was only one girl who regularly entered Tom's dreams at night and his imagination during the day. Only one: and one of the very few that Tom had never even tried to have sex with.

Rebecca.

He couldn't get her out of his head. He loathed the thought of her profession. He remembered being infuriated by her intense stare and intrusive questions. What was more, to put the matter at its very lowest, he wasn't even sure he found her attractive: with her narrow chest, overdefinite nose, and deep-set eyes.

But that wasn't the point. The simple fact was that he couldn't get her out of his head. One day in early spring, he handed the well over to the Duster, walked down to the railroad depot and caught a train out to Wyoming.

He was determined to find her. It felt nearly as important as finding oil.

~

When he arrived there, nothing had changed. Downstairs, the bakery still ran its business. Upstairs, the door still needed a coat of paint. A ribbon of linoleum still peeled away from the wall.

Tom knocked.

No answer.

It was still early. She wouldn't – thank God – still have any clients at this hour, but there was no chance that she was already up, dressed and gone out. Tom knocked again, long enough and hard enough to wake anyone inside.

No answer.

He leaned against the door and felt it bulge against the frame. He tested the weight and strength of it, then crashed into it with his shoulder. The door bowed in the middle and sprang open.

The room was empty. Not just empty of *her*, but empty. There was a table there, a couple of chairs, and the bed, stripped of all its linen and looking more than ever like a great brass beetle in the corner. Even the smells were gone. The room didn't smell of Rebecca any more, it just smelled of old carpet and stale air.

For fully two minutes, Tom stood like a block, frozen.

The tiny kitchen and shower room were both empty. There was nothing in the place at all: not so much as a coffee cup. Dazed, Tom was about to leave. Then, on a sudden impulse he dropped to his knees and looked under the bed. A cheap suitcase lay on the floor, shoved away against the wall. Tom reached in and dragged it out.

As he pulled the case out into the light, something fell from its top surface: a paper-bound exercise book. Tom opened it. Two columns of figures straggled down the pages, marked in pencil. Each row was neatly labelled with a word, written in Polish, or simply a date.

Tom tried to read the Polish, but didn't get far. Of the two twins, Alan had been the linguist, not Tom. The figures were no more comprehensible. The first column seemed to contain random amounts, some of them marked by a minus sign, the others apparently positive. The column on the right was marked '*Dlug*'. The number in the *dlug* column started out large at the top of page one, then fell gradually, ending up at zero on the ninth page of the book. The figure zero was ringed twice in red. All the following pages had been left blank.

For a few seconds, Tom stared.

Then, in a moment, it all fell into place. *Dlug* meant debt. Rebecca had kept accounts to track the money she earned and the money she still owed. When the money had been paid, her job was over.

Tom reached for the suitcase, but he already knew what he would find: Rebecca's working clothes. He broke the lock on the case. There were a couple of dark red dresses, with their low-scooped necklines. There was a black lace choker, a tube of lipstick, some stockings, a glimpse of more dark lace. Tom slammed the case shut and stood up abruptly. He felt an odd mixture of sexual excitement, loss, confusion and anger. More than ever, Tom felt the urgency of his desire to find Rebecca. The urgency and the uselessness.

Tom kicked the suitcase away from him back under the bed. Then, hating the idea that anyone else might find it and get a kick out of it, Tom crawled back down on his knees to lug it out again. He'd take it down by the railroad track, cover it with kerosene and do the job properly.

But not the book.

Tom needed a memento of the woman he wanted. The

clothes represented the part he'd always been ashamed of. The book represented . . . Well, what the hell did it represent? Rebecca must have been the only whore in the continental United States to use double-entry bookkeeping. He flicked back through the pages, taking pleasure in the sight of Rebecca's handwriting. As he flicked, some dates caught his eye. For instance, 17 December 1919 was followed by the sum of nine dollars fifty cents in the first column and a corresponding reduction in debt in the second. Income. Tom was looking at Rebecca's records of income.

The sight sickened him again. He was about to throw the book into the suitcase and leave it to join the rest of the prostitute trash on a trackside fire, when something caught his eye: 24 December 1919. A long line had been drawn across the page, and both columns had been left blank. December 24 was Christmas Eve, the day Tom had asked her to sell whiskey for him.

He'd offended her deeply that night, but the long line told a story. She hadn't made one red cent of income that night, her big brass bed had had only one occupant.

Tom quickly flicked to the other dates when, as far as he could remember, he'd enjoyed a bottle of wine with her. On each occasion, there was the same thing. A long line drawn across the page and not one penny of income earned. Tom breathed out with a sigh. So he wasn't alone in feeling something for her. She too had felt something for him.

Tom looked up, startled by a sudden feeling of emptiness.

He was standing in the exact spot where she had kissed him that one time, when he'd burst back into her room to ask her to leave. He remembered the surprise of that kiss and the intense joy it had given him. He had returned today to ask her again to leave with him. Leave as man and wife. This time, he'd have given her time, he'd have done it properly, not been rushing off to catch a train.

He'd have done a lot of things, if only he'd been in time to catch up with her.

Would have.
Would have.
The most useless words in English.

89

Summer 1921.

The Persian sun baked the sky to brittle whiteness, while the burning earth turned to dust beneath it. The camp had mostly emptied of people now, and the bare dozen that remained worked like dogs from first light to well beyond the last lick of fire on the western horizon.

Since Alan had decided not to move the derrick, progress had been desperately slow. It was far too late to undo the decision – money was running through their hands all the time – but their disappointment was as bitter as the wind-blown dust that entered their clothes, their food and their bedding.

The Ameri No. 2 now stood at two thousand seven hundred feet. As Ahmed had predicted the lousy goddamn boiler didn't want to go down any further, and breakdowns and stoppages were now an all but daily occurrence. On many days they made no progress at all. On other days they went five feet, sometimes ten feet, once and only once seventeen feet. Alan and Reynolds had stopped their meticulous sample collection. If they hit oil, they hit oil. If they missed, they missed. Things were *inshallah* – in the will of Allah – and rock samples wouldn't help them much either way.

The shortage of money made economy increasingly essential. Kerosene lamps were permitted only for matters directly related to work. Food was now restricted to rice, flatbreads and vegetables, except once a week when a couple of chickens would be shared among everyone. Fuel prices in Shiraz had risen because of bandit activity in the mountains, and fuel was desperately needed up at camp.

Nobody spoke the word, but they all knew that failure was creeping closer by the day.

Alan shifted his weight and grimaced. His hands were blistered where the boiler had scalded him, and his legs and back seemed to be fused in a permanent ache these days. He tweaked back the tent flap to encourage cool air to flow inside the baking canvas, but it was a fond hope. He turned back to his figures. Whichever way he did them, the answer was that they'd have to quit drilling in twenty-six days.

Reynolds' heavy tread came along the little path leading to Alan's tent. Reynolds puffed as he walked these days, and when he was sitting alone, his face often looked sad.

'Evening, laddie. I'm not disturbing you?'

Alan reached for his cigarettes, gave one to Reynolds and lit one of his own. He drew deeply on the blessed tobacco and waved his papers. 'Doing my sums.' The tobacco was bad for his war-damaged lung, but he allowed himself the pleasure all the same.

'Got the right answer yet?'

Reynolds meant: have you found us another two hundred drilling days? It was a joke between them. Alan shook his head. 'Twenty-six days, unless the fuel comes cheaper tomorrow.'

'Twenty-six days . . . That's a hundred and twenty feet, if we're lucky.'

Alan nodded. 'If we're lucky.'

There was a pause. For Alan, no oil meant no Lottie. For Reynolds, it meant that the grand finale to his professional life had ended in a bust. He'd return, wifeless and childless, to a poor man's London. They had twenty-six days to change their futures.

'How badly do you want to go home, George?' said Alan, at last.

'Want to go home? By Christ, I'd give my – Why? Why d'you ask? What d'you mean?'

'I thought if we turned up penniless at Abadan, they'd hardly let us starve.'

'Hardly, no, of course not. Good God, man, you haven't been saving money for our return journey, have you?'

'Only a little, only a very little.'

'To hell with that, laddie. We can shovel coal on a steamship from India, if we have to. No, no, no, no, no, I don't want to go home that badly.'

Alan laughed. 'Thirty days, then. A hundred and fifty feet.'

'A hundred and fifty feet. We strike at one forty-nine, eh, lad?'

'*Inshallah*, George, *inshallah*.'

90

Oil changes everything. It changes everything, everywhere, always. It changed everything on Signal Hill.

There were forty-two wells there now, and more coming every day. The once dozy Hill rang with noise. Normal life collapsed. Who needs a five-and-dime store when you could have an oil well? Why grow cucumbers, when you could lease your land for treble the cash? Even the air had lost its previous sea-scoured clarity. The boilers spewed steam, trucks threw up dust; gas jets added smoke, soot and fire.

To some, Signal Hill was a picture of hell. To Tom, it was the next best thing to paradise.

Or almost: Signal Hill might have the oil, but it lacked Rebecca. There were times Tom wasn't sure which one he wanted more.

They'd drilled down two thousand feet when a drill pipe buckled. It was now stuck down a hole eighteen inches wide and a third of a mile deep, and until the pipe was shifted they could make no more progress. They cursed but there was nothing to be done. They pulled up their drill, sent down a fishing tool, and fished for the pipe. They hooked it, brought it up, lost it, fished for it again, caught it, and brought it to the surface. They lowered the drill again, but they had lost time. A team who had begun drilling eight days after them, struck oil ahead of them. Nine hundred barrels a day and no problems with pressure.

The fever mounted and Tom was caught up in the tension. Anxiety and hope became two rats that gnawed at his belly, day and night. When his clothes became dirty he just left them. He forgot to shave. He never left the well.

The men worked like no drilling crew Tom had ever heard of. To a man, they were too superstitious to be openly hopeful, but the expectation was tearing them apart. Dawn had barely lifted the lid on the eastern horizon before the full crew was there, beneath the derrick, getting the boiler stoked up and the lifting blocks in position. Evening had pretty long gone in the west before they were done, lifting pipes into racks and prettying the rig ready for tomorrow.

But though they worked like demons, they spoke like milk-sops.

'Even if we make a strike, the well'll lose pressure when all them other wells get going. Most of them folks on the hill ain't never seen a field drilled proper.'

'Yeah, but we might be off-field here. You don't know. No way to tell. I drilled wells in West Texas, dusters every one, but not one of 'em more than a coupla hundred yards from a producer.'

'That's the Duster for you.'

'Hell, I ain't too sure about our casing. We got well casing made out east. I don't reckon it's right for this kinda sandy-type rock.'

All the same, certain types of conversation apparently didn't break the rules of superstition. For instance, the Duster might spit tobacco juice onto the ground and say thoughtfully, 'S'posing we strike – just s'posing, of course – what kind of control gear d'you reckon we'll need? I'm wondering about pressure and flow rates. What d'you figure? Two thousand pounds per square inch, and what?

Guess around a hundred barrels a day? Mebbe a little less?'

'Mebbe more. Alamitos One's still doin' nearly twelve hundred, and pressure's showing no signs of slacking off.'

'That ain't even so much. Bolsa Chica One down at Gospel Swamps came in at twenty thousand barrels a day. I once rigged with a guy who drilled down there. Said it just about blew the hair off of his head.'

'Twenty thousand barrels a day, at eighty cents a barrel, less maybe twenty cents production costs, that's . . . hell, that's something . . . Not that we're going to get that, o' course. Me, I'd be pleased just to strike at all.'

'Damn right.'

'Hell, if we get forty barrels a day, that's still a producer, ain't it?'

'Hell, yes, that's a producer.'

The men agreed that forty barrels would be a stunning result, though in truth the disappointment would have all but killed them. Nor was Tom exactly calm about things. This was his well. Every good thing, every bad thing in his whole life was now staked on succeeding here. Success on a grand scale would redeem everything that had been wrong in the past. Failure would pretty much annihilate Tom beyond hope of recovery.

But it didn't matter. Nothing mattered. So long as the spinning pipes continued down into the earth. So long as the drill bit ate its way deeper and deeper. And so long as the oil was there.

So long as the oil was there.

91

It was their thirtieth day.

Their money was finished and so were their hopes. The well now stood at nearly three thousand feet – perhaps the deepest well yet dug in Persia – and it remained drier than dust.

They were left facing a simple truth. They had done their best and failed.

As if to symbolise their failure, their last two goats had dropped dead in the night and lay soft and peaceful in a little hollow near the derrick. Alan was so upset, he almost wanted to bury them.

He doled out the final week's wages. The tiny crew that remained had turned into a superbly efficient and tightly knit bunch. Nobody much wanted to take money at this stage, and even the two phlegmatic Russians had tears in their eyes as they hugged Alan, Reynolds, and everybody else. Ahmed's stream of swearwords turned dark and Persian, and became mixed with enough blasphemies to merit the death penalty in certain less tolerant countries. The camp was dismantled and loaded onto the last remaining truck. The derrick, boiler, pipes and drill bits were left standing in the wasteland as a monument to what could have been.

The seven remaining horses were saddled and mounted. The other men clambered onto the overloaded truck for the journey down. Everything saleable would be sold in Shiraz and the proceeds given away in payment of various debts.

Alan – clean-shaven and washed, though in clothes now so tattered that an English tramp would look down on them – walked over to the rig, alone. He laid his hand on the cable, which was slack now, the huge Mother Hubbard lying in the darkness half a mile below ground. No oil meant no Lottie – neither the beloved one of wartime memory, nor the bright, flirty, superficial girl he'd encountered in a rainy London street. Either way, no Lottie seemed like no life at all.

Alan went next to the derrick and scratched at its timbers. Touching wood: it had been a superstitious gesture common to all soldiers, and there had been countless times when heavy shelling or sudden gunfire had caused Alan to reach for a bit of revetting or mud-soaked duckboard. He pulled off a splinter of wood and wandered over to the hollow where the two goats lay dead.

Their eyes stared upwards, already glassy. Flies crept on the exposed eyeballs. Alan sniffed, but the mountain air was clean and bright. He put out a finger and closed the eyelids on the two dead animals. Their eyelids were tougher than human lids and they resisted his finger. Alan applied more force and closed the eyes. The flies buzzed angrily away. It was time to go.

He walked back to the men, put the truck into gear and began down the hill.

It was the end of an era.

The horsemen went quicker than the truck, and were soon out of sight down the twisting valley. Alan steered the truck cautiously down. In places, the slopes were very steep and the lack of men had meant that the track was in a terrible state of repair. Even the hairpins were potholed and loose-sided.

Each journey became a battle of skill as well as a terrifying game of odds. Alan appeared to be concentrating hard, but twice he misjudged a bump in the road, and twice the truck jolted precariously towards the edge. Reynolds would have said something, but Alan's hands were white on the wheel and his face was set like a mask. Another couple of minutes went by. Then Alan made yet another poor turn and Reynolds spoke.

'Are you all right, laddie? Perhaps I should take a turn at the wheel?'

'I'm fine.'

Alan spoke, and even as he spoke, he let the truck drift into a soft-sided mudslip that hadn't been properly cleared. They rolled gently but unstoppably towards the edge. The truck slithered to a halt, its front left wheel spinning slowly in space. A couple of feet further, and they'd be dropping down a forty-five degree slope, a thousand feet long, and littered with rocks the size of houses. The six men in the cab felt their hearts stop as they watched to see if the vehicle would continue its roll. It didn't. Alan turned the engine off and let it die. All the time, his attention had been so keenly directed elsewhere, it was almost as if he hadn't noticed the near-tragedy.

'By Jove, that was a let-off,' said Reynolds. 'We'll all get out, from the back, of course, rope the truck fast, get it unloaded, and –'

'The goats,' said Alan. 'Have you thought about the goats?'

'The goats, lad? Never mind –'

'No, George, pay attention. The goats. Why did they die?'

Reynolds laughed softly. He was worried that the mission's failure was proving more than Alan could handle. 'They just died. People die, goats die. It happens to –'

'Nothing just dies,' said Alan sharply. 'You have to die of something. What did the goats die of?'

Reynolds stared at Alan. Then it clicked. 'Oh, by God, lad! Oh, by God!' He stared wildly for a moment. Both men were now infected by whatever it was that had Alan in its grip. 'Out of the truck,' said Reynolds. 'Now.'

Everyone piled backwards out of the teetering truck. Reynolds dug into their equipment and hauled out ropes and planks. With Alan and Reynolds both snapping orders as though they were two parts of the same machine, the truck was belayed to the cliff face, planks and rocks were used to give the wheels bite and to lever the huge beast back on to safe ground. But that was almost the easy part of the manoeuvre. The next stage was to turn the truck so that it was pointing back up the hill. The road was too narrow and the surface remained appalling. Nevertheless, they managed, and Alan was at the wheel again, driving furiously back up the slope. This time, every lurch into a pothole brought no silent gasps of horror. Every man on the truck was agog to know what was so urgently drawing the two Englishmen back.

A light breeze was blowing down the valley by the time they arrived back, and a small fire was burning itself out in the boiler.

'Fuel,' said Alan. 'Get fuel.'

'Come on, lads, look sharp.'

The puzzled men began to gather the few sticks or pieces of coal that were still lying around the camp, but Alan and Reynolds were way ahead of them. The two men tore into the truck. They ripped off its waxed canvas cover. They put a pipe into the fuel tank and began to siphon out the petrol. When the others got the picture, they joined in. Tents and clothing joined the fuel heap, latrines and tool cupboards, even the folding tables and chairs that had been their only comfort for so long. As soon as the pile looked large enough, they ran to the derrick to get it ready.

Like a dervish, Alan began loading the boiler. The little fire crackled and grew. Alan threw on petrol and the flames leapt up, as the water in the boiler began to heat. The Mother Hubbard was made ready.

'Go on, you lousy bloody no-good son-of-a-desert-bitch,' muttered Ahmed in fervent prayer. The boiler began to hiss. 'Don't break us down, you bugger. Don't break us now.'

Only Alan was silent. The pressure mounted. They threw the camwheel and pulley belts into action. There were nigh on three thousand feet of steel cable down the hole now, as well as the massive Mother Hubbard. Every turn was a stretch for the aching machinery.

But it worked. The winch ground its way round. Far down beneath the earth, the Mother Hubbard raised herself for one last strike. The camwheel lifted her, lifted her, lifted her.

'Go on,' said Reynolds. 'Go on.'

The camwheel completed its turn. The Mother Hubbard dropped, its massive weight smashing into the hidden rock.

'Again.'

They worked like seven devils. The drill bit rose and fell, rose and fell.

'Now bail,' cried Reynolds.

They winched up the Mother Hubbard, and sent their bailing tool down.

'Quickly!'

Their fuel pile, which had looked so vast just a few short moments before, was rapidly disappearing.

They bailed the well fast and imperfectly, but they wanted to clear the worst of the chippings before beginning to smash away once again. When the chippings came up, Alan snatched them, cleaned them off against his leg, and dropped them into a basin of water. For him, this well wasn't just about oil, it was about Tom and it was about Lottie – the past and the future. He and Reynolds hung over the bowl like it was the Delphic oracle. Air bubbles clung to the sides of the rock and rose to the surface.

'Come on, come on.'

Reynolds put his work-hardened hands into the bowl and swept the bubbles from the side of the stones. They bobbled up to the surface, popped and vanished. And then an odd thing happened. Chippings that were definitely free of air bubbles began to grow new ones. Little pinpricks appeared on the side of the stones, then grew into pinheads, then bright round bubbles. Alan jogged the basin and the little bubbles winked their way to the surface. Both men leaped up, wild hope in their eyes.

'Keep going!'

'Load the fire there, will you!'

They lowered the Mother Hubbard cautiously to within a hundred and fifty feet of bottom, then released her. Far below ground there was a thundering smash, as the rocky surface was split open once again. The drillers drilled, but the boiler began to fail. The fuel had burned brightly, but for too short a time. Once again they were out of luck.

'The tyres,' said Alan. 'Who the hell left the tyres on?'

They ran to the truck and stripped its tyres, its seats, the oil sump, the hydraulics cables, anything flammable they could find. The truck looked like a skeleton picked clean by a mountain lion. The boiler pressure climbed again. The Mother Hubbard rose and fell.

They worked until it was time to bail once more, but the boiler fires were sinking again. The winch tried to lift the Mother Hubbard one last time, but couldn't do it. Once again the well was abandoning them to failure.

'The derrick,' said Alan. 'Strip it.'

The wooden derrick was sturdily built of seasoned timber that had orginally been imported from the forested uplands around the Caspian. Alone of their decrepit equipment, the derrick itself had stood robust and strong. But not now. They began to tear away its timbers. They left the most obviously structural ones, but removed nearly everything else. Alan and Ahmed climbed high into the derrick until, to Reynolds' viewpoint on the ground, they looked like a couple of insects – one dark, one pale gold. The two men smashed away at the crosspieces with their steel mallets, until the nails gave way and the wood fell tumbling to the ground. And every piece they removed, every beam and every plank, was hurled straight into the boiler.

The flames bit into the singing wood. Alan clambered down from the derrick, drew more water from the river and added it to the boiler. He had worked harder than any of the men present, but fatigue belonged in a different lifetime. The boiler fire bit into the water, and the pressure rose.

'All right, let's do it.'

Alan threw the winch into action. It had to raise the Mother Hubbard and all the cable three thousand feet. It wasn't clear if the derrick would stand the strain. Everybody stood well back as the winch wound round. The derrick physically bowed under the effort. Nobody had ever seen the derrick move before, not by so much as an inch, but now there was a clear six- or eight-inch bend in the main supporting timbers.

'Go on,' said Reynolds.

'Go on,' said Alan.

'Go on, you pig-headed old sod, go on,' said Ahmed.

One thousand feet of cable wound in all right. Two thousand feet. It seemed as though the derrick was standing the strain. Then the winch began to make a groaning sound, as if it wanted to give up. The derrick seemed strong, but the winch wailed and groaned. There was nothing anyone could do but watch. The cable wound in slower and slower. The boiler was giving out ample pressure, but something in the cobbled-together chain of machinery was giving up. They could actually hear its death throes.

Two thousand eight hundred feet. Two thousand nine hundred. There were literally only a few feet left on the cable, the very top of the Mother Hubbard had just become visible emerging from the well, when it happened. The cable broke. The flying wire snapped and shot through the air in a lethal whiplash that luckily caught no one. The derrick snapped upright for a moment, then the winching gear buckled and fell. It smashed through one of the key remaining timbers, and the derrick itself collapsed down like the useless thing it had suddenly become. And meantime, while all this was happening, the Mother Hubbard, all one and a half tons of her, was zinging her way down through the well, ready to smash one last time into the stubborn rock.

In sudden shocking silence they heard the impact. It crashed up from the bottom of the well, muffled by its journey through half a mile of rocky tube.

Then nothing, just silence and the subsiding hiss of steam from the boiler.

Silence filled the valley.

And then a sound they'd never heard before. A deep boom from the centre of the earth. A boom followed by other rumbles, which merged gradually into one continuous thunder.

'The boiler,' screamed Alan. 'Put out the fire.'

They hauled water like they were crazy. They slathered water over the boiler until it had fizzed out, cold and black and dead.

And then it came.

Oil.

Bounding out of the ground in a jet that hosed seventy feet up into the air. Thick, black, wet, stinking, sulphurous oil. The seven men were sprayed with it. Their hair, clothes and eyes were thick with it. The oil that had eluded them for so long was running in thick streams through the dust. It was filling the rocky hollow where the goats had been found dead that morning – the goats that had been poisoned by the release of lethal natural gases from the well.

The seven drillers danced like maniacs in the inky jet. They splashed each other with the magical substance. They rolled in it. They caught it in their hands and hurled it up into the air.

The date was 23 August 1921, the day of Alan's twenty-eighth birthday.

92

Some strikes blow your hair off, others just puddle up from underground. But though everyone loves to see a gusher, the picture postcard pretties miss the point. A strike's a strike, and all that matters is how many barrels and how many bucks.

They pushed the well quickly to just short of three thousand feet.

It was time to go carefully. They quit drilling and lined the hole with steel well-casing. They cemented the top of the well-head to protect against groundwater inflow. They replaced their nine-inch drill bit with a tiddly six-inch bit for the final phase.

At this point, Tom let the Duster personally supervise every detail of the operation. They ran the the drill down at half normal speed. With every new length of pipe they added, they murmured prayers and touched wood and crossed fingers and muttered blessings.

Further up the hill, six wells had now passed three thousand feet. Each one of them had gone on to strike oil. Flow rates were good. Field pressure remained strong.

One morning, Boiler Bob came to work wearing a crucifix

round his neck. No one mocked him. A couple of the men even let themselves touch it for luck.

~

It came just before dawn on 23 August – the day of Tom's twenty-eighth birthday.

The land breeze had died down and the sea wind hadn't yet risen but, all the same, the men were chilled and the steel pipes were cold to the touch. The Duster wanted to get drilling right away, but Tom kept a clearer head. The drill bit on the well floor was old and dull and it was time to lift it to replace it with a newly sharpened one. He gave the orders. The Duster agreed. The men threw the lifting gear into action and stowed the pipes as they came up. Three thousand feet is a hundred lengths of thirty-foot pipe, or a little more than thirty lots of the ninety-foot sections that they stowed inside the derrick. They counted down to zero, as the derrick filled with pipework and the Pacific Ocean began to glint with gold.

They reached the last ninety-foot section. The first thirty feet came up clean, but the last sixty were slathered in an oily black liquid.

Tom looked at it incredulously. He was still cold and his brain was working slowly. His first thought was that they had hit some kind of problem. The pipe shouldn't look black, it should be covered in the mud they used to lubricate the bit. And then he saw the faces of the team. Like him, they couldn't take it in. But the evidence was unmistakable. Standing in the bottom of their well, they had sixty feet of oil.

One by one, their faces changed to certainty, as though something holy had just happened before their eyes.

They'd done it.

The well had struck. They only needed to go a little deeper and the pressure would be sufficient to pump the oil to the surface. For just a second or two, the sacred silence persisted – and then shattered.

'Oil! We got oil! We –'

'Sweet Jesus, we hit it! I knew –'

A couple of the men began to scream and shout, but the Duster was savage.

'We ain't got nothing to yell about,' he shouted. 'If you ain't got oil at the wellhead, you ain't got squat. I seen wells where they got oil at the bottom and ain't never seen nothing but coyote shit up top. I seen wells –'

He fought his team to order and they obeyed. Tom was left to himself.

For all Duster's yelling, Tom knew he had a producer.

Oil. He had oil. Five years after being taken prisoner by the Germans, two years since landing in America as an impoverished cattle hand, he'd actually made the strike that he'd dreamed of so long. The world changed, the past was erased as he drank in the moment. The entire earth became shinier, gentler, more colourful.

Tom was in love with California, in love with America, at peace with every living thing.

After so long, he was a man beginning to live.

93

Nobody forgets the day they strike oil and for Alan there were two things in particular that would make the moment live for ever.

The first was Tom.

He and Tom had always dreamed of this moment – 'kings of the world', to use Knox D'Arcy's phrase. With Tom dead, Alan had known his destiny lay in Persia. A promise made had become a promise fulfilled. Alan was satisfied, but also a little empty. A man can't live for ever in the past he shared with a man now dead, and Alan had his future to think about.

And the future was uncertain. Certainly he was on the road to wealth, possibly even very great wealth. He had been unable to marry Lottie because of his poverty. Now that he was rich . . . what?

Perhaps she had forgotten him, or was in love with someone else. Perhaps, even, worst of all, but perfectly likely, she wasn't just in love with someone else, she was engaged or even married. Perhaps he would return to England to find her happy, healthy, pleased to see him – and already surrounded by a husband, a home, even her first child . . .

Alan literally didn't know what to do with the infinite possibilities. Should he be pleased to be returning to England and Lottie? Or should he be terrified? In truth, he was both.

That night, as he snatched a couple of hours' sleep (three-quarters frozen because everything soft, warm and comfortable had joined the final cataclysmic blaze), he was both happy and anxious, eager and frightened, lovesick and broken-hearted.

94

With excruciating care, Tom's men deepened the hole, but superstition had gone clean out of the window.

'You see the sign in the barbershop up the hill?' said Boiler Bob. 'You see it? Guy's got a gusher in his backyard. He locks up shop, hangs a sign on his door, says "Cadillac Salesmen, Please find me at home." That's gonna be me, huh? "Cadillac salesmen, come call on me at home!"'

'Have a whole fleet of damn Cadillacs!'

'I'm gonna get my own wildcat rig, if we do good here. Go up coast a little. I got a friend, a trendologist, he's got the strikes all mapped out. Drilling with him wouldn't be like wildcatting at all. Not that we'd ever hit nothing like this, though.'

Slowly they punched deeper and deeper. They ran down a perforated casing, which would protect the bottom of the hole from cave-in, but which would let the sweet God-sent oil flow into the well. Then, delicate as anything, they pushed a little deeper.

There was a physical change in the pipe. A low rushing became audible.

'*We got OIL!*' screamed the Duster. This wasn't just a strike, it was a strike that he owned a piece of.

And then it came: oil bursting up from the ground,

running over their shoes, covering the sleeping Pipsqueak in a tide of black. The world seemed better and better. Somebody produced a huge bottle of moonshine, and they drank whiskey in huge delighted mouthfuls as they wrestled to get the wellhead into place. Tom needed to move out of the way, but more to the point, he wanted to enjoy the moment alone.

'Hey, girl, hey, Pipsqueak.'

He carried his bedraggled dog a few feet from their beloved well. She licked him with long salty licks, as he rubbed the pink inside of her ears.

'Maybe it's all been worth it, eh, old girl? Even rough stories can have a happy ending.'

If licking was agreeing, then the Squeaker agreed. He stroked her. For some reason, at that moment, Whitcombe House sprang forcefully into his mind. He remembered Sir Adam and Pamela and Alan as though he had seen them yesterday. For a second, no longer, the thought of them brought nothing but warmth, even love – but the moment passed. He thought about his next steps. He had twenty-seven acres. He could get at least two dozen rigs on it, even more in time. Higher up the hill there were places where the legs of the derricks interlaced on the ground, but Tom didn't even have to squash 'em up close. He had twenty-seven acres of the most valuable land in America.

The crew got the wellhead in place, fixing it with massive bolts set into the cement. The wellhead was made fast. They threw a valve. The flow of oil out onto the ground was turned off. All that was left was to hook the well up to a pipeline and start to count the money. Duster let the crew begin to celebrate, but Tom was in a land of his own.

He climbed ninety feet up the steel ladder that ran up the outside of the derrick. He hung out as far as he could to let the oil-perfumed air run through his hair.

He was happy. Maybe for the very first time since being taken prisoner in 1916, he was truly happy. The ghosts of his past, the betrayals, the hardship and dangers – everything was rubbed out by this one huge, magnificent success.

He turned his head down to survey his acreage. Pipsqueak had caught the prevailing mood and was hurtling round the field in a blur of dirty white. Tom smiled. He already knew where to plant the wells that would follow this. He knew where to run the pipeline, how to sell the oil, how to raise new capital.

And that was when he saw it. His destiny. His demon. A pasty-looking man in a shiny suit and thin-soled city shoes running across the dirt acres, dodging drill pipes and slush pits and sucker rods and well-casings. He looked like nothing at all. He looked like a cheap city suit a thousand miles out of place. But it wasn't how he looked, it was what he was saying. And what he was saying was something Tom would never live to forget.

'What the hell are you boys doing here on *my* land?'

95

When oil decides to spout, it *spouts*. And when the men who tried to make it happen then go and try to stop it – well, sometimes you'd wonder which was the harder job.

For nineteen days, the oil had burst unstoppably forth.

To begin with, Alan and his men had tried to cap the well-head, to block it with rocks or chains or bits ripped from their defunct drilling equipment. They'd tried, but the effort had been useless. The oil shot from the ground so fast that nothing short of a landslip would have covered the hole.

Quickly, then, they'd turned their efforts to their next task: building a reservoir big enough to hold the oil. The dozen exhausted men made little progress, though they worked all through the night and into the next day. Relief only came when some of their former comrades, fearing the worst, had come back to look for signs of the truck and found an oil well instead. With astonishing rapidity, the valley had filled with Qashqai tribesmen: some of them the men who had worked alongside them the year before, others rounded up by Muhammad Ameri, who had heard the news, and ridden in to survey 'his' well. At this stage, no one worked for pay. They worked because the valley was filling with oil, and everyone knew that unbelievable riches lay in store for the people who could catch it.

For nearly three weeks they'd laboured. Using bits of truck panel for shovels, even their bare hands, they'd diverted the course of the river, and set out to build a huge dam across the valley for the oil. All this time, they barely slept. They worked like donkeys. They ate nothing but boiled rice, which they cooked in cauldrons five miles up the valley and brought down stone cold, for fear of the spark that could blow the whole valley higher than heaven.

Then they were done. The flood of oil hit the dam and began to fill the reservoir. There were a few minor leaks, but nothing that couldn't easily be repaired.

And meanwhile, stores began to flow up from Shiraz, everything on credit, nothing too hard to find for the suddenly rich *Farangi*. Eventually the oil-smeared labourers even managed to cap the wellhead. They brought a truck up the valley, filled it with rocks and cement, dragged it by hand to the wellhead, then toppled it over. The oil still came out, but the jet was no longer the force it had been. After another three days, and another three hundred sacks of cement, the wellhead was capped.

On the shore of their black and foul-smelling lake, two oil-blackened dervishes embraced each other. One was short and powerful. He had a nineteen-day-old beard, but his moustache was much older and better kept than that. His face was as black as a coal-face by night, but beneath the black there were glints of red. The second man was tall, upright and exhausted. His once-blond hair had turned the same deep black as everything else. His pale eyes seemed out of place in their filthy surroundings. Both men stank of rotten eggs from the sulphur in the oil, but neither man noticed or cared.

'I'll miss you, laddie.'

'Yes, I'll miss you too. God knows, I'll even miss being here.' Alan looked around the rocky valley, home for so many months. 'Cold rice and oil sauce.'

'Aye . . . Well, you'll have a job facing you in England. A damn sight harder than hitting oil here, I make no doubt.'

'Yes.'

Alan was returning to England. His job there would be to turn his lake of oil into a company. He'd need money, investors, shares, directors, accounts and managers. It was vital work, but also difficult, and both men knew that Alan would infinitely have preferred to be staying, as Reynolds was, to supervise the works on the ground.

'Is there anyone at home you'd like me to call on for you? There's so much one can't quite say in a letter.'

'Aye, there's my mother and father, if you wouldn't mind. They're a pair of nervous ninnies, so –'

'So I'll explain to them in great detail how cushy our life has been out here –'

'The fine houses, the pleasant climate –'

'The ease of drilling, the diversity of amusements –'

'The helpful and attentive local officials.'

Both men laughed.

'And you can call on Sir Charles Greenaway for me,' said Reynolds. 'You can tell him that there's an oilfield, vast in its possible dimensions, in precisely the spot I told him it would be. You can remind him that I said seventy thousand pounds for the right to drill there was criminally low.'

'I'll tell him.'

'And then this.' Reynolds produced a sheet of paper. It contained the name and address of somebody in London, and the words 'PSALM 104 VERSE 15 STOP REYNOLDS'.

Alan looked at him questioningly.

'If you wouldn't mind sending this telegram for me, please . . . I believe there are facilities at Abadan.'

Alan nodded. 'Psalm one-oh-four? I'm not sure I remember how that one runs.'

'Well, there's to be no peeking at your Bible, laddie. If I wanted you to know how it runs, then I'd sing it to you.'

The two men embraced again. A mile away in the distance,

a pair of long-legged Arab horses danced impatiently, their hoofs muffled with rags to avoid the danger of sparks from their shoes. Alan would ride quickly down into Shiraz, then make his way to Abadan, and either hop aboard a passing oil tanker and ride through the Suez Canal directly home, or, if no tanker was expected soon, make the more arduous journey overland via Istanbul.

It was time to leave.

Alan felt as though the easy part now lay behind him. He faced the future with foreboding.

96

At times during the war, Tom had put his hand out to a man, perhaps a soldier lying out in no man's land, perhaps a man leaning up against the wall of a trench. He'd put his hand out, expecting to find a human being, then the body rolled over, the head had no face, and the skin was as cold as death.

This moment was like that. It was a leap of horror, the touch of a corpse.

The man came running across the dirt. Once his thin-soled shoes slid on some slush-pit mud and sent him sprawling, but he kept on coming. He was bald-headed, spectacled, out-of-place, furious.

Tom climbed slowly down the ladder. Pipsqueak, who'd been hurtling round the field, now threw herself at the man, leaping at his ankles, snapping and growling. The men in the drilling crew stopped their celebrations and fell silent, looking alternately at the newcomer, who was picking his way over a pipeline trench, and at Tom, who was still forty or fifty feet up the ladder.

Slowly Tom descended.

The man arrived at the foot of the rig.

'What in . . . ? What in hell's name . . . ? Jesus Christ, boys, who gave you permission to drill here?'

The man was panting and out of breath. He looked like he was about to have a heart attack. He sat down on a section of well-casing and tried to recover himself. There were now more than a hundred derricks on Signal Hill, and the air resounded with their noise, smoke and stink. The newcomer was clearly unused to it. It was almost as though he was waiting for the noise to stop before coming to the point.

'This is my land,' said Tom. 'That's to say, the drilling rights are mine. Signed it up with old Ma Hershey. You can take a look at the contract, if you don't believe me.'

'Hershey, the old witch! She doesn't own this land no more. She doesn't own doodley-squat. She doesn't even own that little rathole she lives in.'

'I saw the title deed. It was all in order.'

'Order, yeah, but in order when? Hershey hasn't owned this piece of land for fifteen years. Her old man used to run cattle here, or tried to, but he mortgaged the land to pay for his drink, and the drink ended up swallowing the land. Couple of Japs farm it now.'

'And you're who?' Tom's voice came over all aggressive – needlessly so, since aggression would get him nowhere. He swept an oil-stained hand through his oil-stained hair and did nothing at all to improve his appearance. He checked his voice and added more gently, 'I mean, who do you represent?'

'Pardon me – good girl, good girl –' Pipsqueak had begun pulling angrily at the man's laces and he tried to shake her off without hurting her. The man's heart had slowed to a few hundred beats per minute, and he mopped his face with a huge white hanky as he stretched his leg out and surveyed the view. 'Pardon me, I'm Walter P. Faries, down here from Bakersfield, Bakersfield Thrift Savings Bank . . . Damnation, is it always this rackety and hot? A man can't hear himself talk, let alone talk himself think. No, no, I mean a man can't think himself . . . Oh hell, you know what I mean.' He blew out his lips in a long puff as he slowly recovered his breath.

Tom's face flickered with hope. 'Of course, I can see you're no oilman, Mr Faries. Just supposing you can prove title to the land, I'd be most happy just to switch around that contract. Address all those royalty cheques to you instead of Hershey.'

'Lord, no, I'm no oilman, and don't want to be one neither. It's a wonder to me how you boys can stand all this.'

'I've figured it all out. Where to site the wells, where to lay the pipelines, how to get it to the refinery cheap and easy. There's a lot of pitfalls in this business. It's not just finding the stuff.'

'It's a wonder this hill isn't pumped dry already.'

'Not really, Mr Faries. We've only just struck today, and we're ahead of most of these drillers round here. Now we've got oil, we can begin to raise some real capital to get new wells sunk. In a town-lot scramble like this one, you need to drill fast and pump furious.'

'Capital . . . that'll be my side of things, I guess.'

'That's right, Mr Faries. An oilman and a banker, the ideal partnership, I reckon.'

'I reckon so. That's what I been figuring.'

Faries took off his shoes and shook sand and gravel out onto the dirt. His sock was glued to his foot with sweat. He massaged his feet, wiggled his toes, and put his shoes back on with a sigh. A sudden bolt of wind brought the rough heat of a natural gas flare down the hill and a shower of forge-flung soot. He blinked.

'If you want,' said Tom, 'we can go someplace quiet right now. Sort out the paperwork. Have a lawyer look over it. I'll need to get your land title checked over at the county courthouse. All being well, we can switch the contracts round within a day or two.'

Faries' gaze had been locked into the middle distance, staring at nothing. Now, at last, he heard Tom speaking to him. His gaze changed, and he focused, blinking, on Tom.

'No, no, no. I'm sorry. No. God, my brother would knock the hell out of me if I went and did anything like that. He's an oilman, see? Been in the business thirty-five years, would you credit it? He's going to drill here. Right here. Got it all figured out, so he says.'

97

It was a new look Alan Montague that presented himself at the immense black front door to 49 Berkeley Square.

His blond hair had never recovered from the nearly three weeks it had spent beneath a thick shampoo of stinking crude. Reluctantly, he'd had his hair cut to within an eighth of an inch of his scalp at Abadan, and spent many vain moments in front of the mirror hoping that it would grow back fast enough not to embarrass him in time for his return. His moustache and beard he had shaved off, of course, and, though he'd expected to let the moustache grow back, he found that he preferred himself completely smooth-shaven. He'd also washed himself three times daily, until the shades of black had finally left his skin. He'd carved at his nails with a penknife until they looked almost clean and white. He'd bought a suit of clothes with borrowed money – everything was borrowed now – and hoped that European fashions hadn't long passed him by.

His efforts had been a passable success. He was certainly clean enough. His hair was very short, but it gave him a military appearance that made him look younger and not unattractive. His clothes were newish and reasonably well-fitting, though they'd never have passed muster at Savile Row. He raised his hand to the great brass knocker and brought it crashing down.

He had never been so nervous in all his life.

The door swung open. A butler, as tall and solemn as a column of marble, stood behind it.

'Sir?'

'I'm . . . My name is Alan Montague . . . I'm hear to see Miss –'

Alan's nervousness extended to his mouth. He actually found it difficult to find words, let alone say them. He felt as though he must be shaking like a leaf, though in fact he was doing nothing of the sort.

'Alan Montague to see Miss Dunlop. Yes, sir. If you would like to follow –'

The butler had turned and was beginning to lead Alan down the long cool hallway towards the drawing room when there was a minor explosion. Running feet, the fast light tapping of a woman's shoes, a rushing of skirts. Alan turned towards the staircase leading from upstairs. It was Lottie. He hardly had time to see her face. She flung herself at him, arms around his neck, lips pressed hard against his.

'Oh, Alan, darling, darling, dearest Alan, my love,' she said, when their need for air finally forced them apart. 'My darling, best, bravest, most favourite oilman.'

'Lottie, dear, good Lord, how did you . . . ?'

Slowly and deliciously, in the ponderous old drawing room, they began to reintroduce themselves.

Alan spoke of Persia, the long months of exploration, the sale of his concession, the return to Persia, the first dry hole and a little of the agonies connected with the second. He said nothing of his cholera and nothing of the malaria that had followed.

'Darling, you were so brave. And what was the climate like? Was it very beastly?'

'No. Not at all. It was chilly in winter and a little too warm in summer, but not unpleasant. Spring was delightful.'

'Oh, dearest, now I can't believe a single word you've told me. Daddy is the best of chums with old Charlie Greenaway, who says the weather out there is perfectly frightful.'

'Well, it was rather trying at times.'

'Pig.'

For the first ten minutes, Lottie seemed like an exotic bird of the jungle: very wonderful, but very strange. Her beauty was dazzling. Her hair had the colour of a Persian sunset: crimson and gold, seen through a smoky cloud of dust. She wore a simple green frock, but the skirt sat higher up the calf than Alan had ever seen worn by a decent girl. But it wasn't long before the shock of her newness wore off. When she laughed, the end of her nose bent down as he always remembered it. There was a tiny scar that drew a thin white line across her right-hand eyebrow. She was just the way he'd always remembered her: completely different and exactly the same.

They discussed all the most important topics in turn. Alan's hair ('Horrible, darling. You look like a drill sergeant'); the loss of his moustache ('Don't even think of growing it back. It was like kissing a hairbrush'); his clothes ('Those trousers are simply laughable, my dearest. Your legs are like two little pencils. We'll get you some Oxford bags first thing in the morning'). And then, of course, there was Lottie's life.

'Parties, darling, mostly parties. Mummy and Daddy became terribly upset about me being a nurse. As you know, I adored it, but they just couldn't see how I was ever going to get married if I was knee-deep in bandages all day long. Well, I wasn't going to be bullied, of course, but then some of my dearest friends among the soldiers died or moved back home and I realised I wasn't really needed any longer. So I came home. Daddy kept throwing whacking great parties for me, hoping that I was going to get married to one of his dreary City people. I couldn't tell him that I wouldn't even think of marrying a banker when I jolly well meant to marry a strapping great oilman.'

Alan swallowed. 'Lottie, my dear, may I ask you a question?'

'What a silly thing to ask. Apart from anything else, you just did.'

'That night we bumped into each other. In Piccadilly. You were with your friends. We said hello and you invited me to join you all for a drink.'

'Yes?'

Alan swallowed a second time and licked his lips. 'Look, I thought about that meeting every single night in Persia. I couldn't see . . . I couldn't see that you could still have had any tenderness for me . . . You seemed so distant, so light. It was almost as if –'

'You *are* a nitwit. What was I meant to have done? I didn't know you were going to hit oil, did I? I had to think jolly quickly and I decided the best thing was to pretend I'd forgotten you. I thought that would give you the very best chance of getting over me. And personally, I think I did rather well at it. Pretending that is, not forgetting.'

Alan smiled and stroked her arm. The hairs on her arm were auburn too. It would take a lifetime to get to know her properly, a lifetime he now hoped to have . . .

'Oh, darling, I've been forgetting,' she interrupted. 'Daddy's here, in his study. He's raring to meet you. Oil's *in*, apparently. All the rage in Leadenhall. Oh, and I think this might be a good moment to mention the fact that you're dying to marry me.'

The interview this time could hardly have been more different.

'Montague, my dear fellow! Splendid! Splendid news! Many congratulations!'

'Thank you, sir. I may take it then that you give your approval?'

'My approval? I hardly think you need my approval.'

'It's just that last time, sir, you were . . . a little less enthusiastic.'

'I don't follow you. Oil comes out of the ground whether I approve of it or not. Probably just as well, eh?'

'I see. Oil . . . Yes, I was actually speaking about another topic even more precious to me. Your daughter, sir, and I have loved each other for some time, and –'

'Good golly, man, of course, of course. Couldn't ask for a better husband. Of course you must marry her. Sooner the better.' Egham Dunlop turned to some papers on his desk. The map of the world was still there on the wall behind him, though with slightly fewer pins in it than before. Dunlop was still a powerful man, but Alan noticed that he had aged a little since their last interview. They all had, even Lottie . . .

'As a matter of fact,' the banker interrupted Alan's reverie, 'I've been looking over some figures. How much d'you think you'll need?'

'Excuse me, sir?'

'How much money? Will a million be enough or d'you need more?'

Alan flushed. 'I hadn't thought . . . I didn't intend to ask for a penny, sir. Though I may be a little short of funds at present, I have no doubt that, following my recent good fortune, I shall be able to keep your daughter in a manner –'

'No, no, no! God's sakes! You'll damn well keep Lottie like a princess, but she's hardly going to cost a million, is she? How much for the company, man, the company? Oil stocks are burning hot at the moment. If you want to raise money, now's the time to strike. As I say, I can see you getting a million without much trouble. Two million might be pushing it, but I wouldn't declare the thing impossible . . .'

Back with Lottie immediately afterwards, Alan gave her the good news. By this stage, Alan was happy beyond happy. He'd arrived at the house not knowing if Lottie still remembered him, and he would leave it engaged and with her father's blessing. He was in a kind of blissful delirium, as though the air was champagne. But even amidst the champagne, there was a question he needed to ask.

'Lottie, darling, how did you know everything? I mean, I didn't tell anyone about finding oil. I didn't tell anyone I'd be coming here. Yet, you knew about the oil and everything seemed so . . . well, expected.'

Lottie threw back her head and laughed. '"He bringeth forth grass for the cattle: and green herb for the service of man."'

'What?'

'Don't interrupt. I haven't got there yet. He bringeth forth grass and all that, so that "man may bring out of the earth oil to give him a cheerful countenance". Psalm a hundred and four, verse fifteen. And you're an atheistical old goat for not knowing.'

'Psalm one-oh-four . . . Reynolds! Reynolds sent you . . . You and he . . . The pair of you have been in league all along. I don't believe it!'

'Well, I was hardly going to let you stride off into the Persian desert with no way of knowing what was happening to you, was I? I asked Charlie Greenaway if he knew anyone who could keep an eye on you for me and he said that one of his best chaps had just gone off to work with you. He was rather cross about it, actually. So I met up with George. I thought he looked terribly ferocious to begin with, but he turned out to be a perfect sweetie. He sent letters to me every month, addressing them to a friend of mine so you wouldn't suspect. He told me all about how you were getting on and all about how you – dear, dear man – wrote infinite letters to me that you never sent. Obviously I wanted to know the very first minute you'd struck oil, hence the telegram. Personally I don't know why he didn't choose psalm one hundred and fourteen, verses seven and eight: "Tremble, earth at the God of Jacob; who changeth the flint stone into a springing well." Not that you'd have known either way, Mr Goat.'

'He didn't mention, I suppose . . . he didn't say anything about . . .'

'About your cholera? Yes he jolly well did. And your malaria. I told Charlie Greenaway that if his blasted doctors had let you keel over from some horrid little mosquito, I'd've come along and shot the lot of them. The doctors, I mean. I shouldn't think I could hit the mosquitoes.'

'Oh dear, my love! He shouldn't have told you.'

'No!' Lottie's tone changed abruptly. Her voice was suddenly forceful, even steely. 'If we're to be married, then we're going to be damn well married. That means knowing everything, even the bad things. Especially the bad things.' Her voice softened again and she put a hand on his arm. 'I'm not very easily shocked, you know.'

'No.' Alan's heart slid a little further in love. 'You are a remarkable lady. I'm very lucky.'

He kissed her.

And on that evening of blissful delirium, there remained just one last important ritual. Lottie pointed out to Alan that, technically speaking, he had completely forgotten to ask her if she wanted to marry him and, 'For all you know, I might say no. I do like to be consulted, you know.'

Alan sank to one knee. He took her hand in his.

'Dearest Lottie,' he began, 'will you make me the happiest man in the world . . . ?'

98

Lawyers did what lawyers do.

They fought, they argued, they dragged things out. Tom's attorney told him he'd win for sure. He babbled about the irregularities in the mortgage documentation, about statutes of limitations, about protection of widow's rights in the sunshine state, about *ipsis dipsis* and *locus fatuus*. Tom's attorney promised victory and delivered defeat.

Walt Faries struck a deal with Duster Larzelere and the others, and they all switched round to work for him. The Duster and the rest were sympathetic. They preferred Tom to Faries, but they had to go where the money was. They were apologetic but determined.

Tom tried to recover something. He'd drilled the well, after all. The derrick and rig were his, even if he'd had to buy them with promises and prayers. But he lost. He lost everything. He ended up owing more than he possessed, and would have been declared bankrupt except that his creditors didn't bother to hound him for money they knew he didn't have.

On the last stupid day of the last stupid hearing, Tom owned the clothes he wore, a small white loving mongrel with a soft spot for bacon, and two dollars fifty-five cents.

He stumbled out into the sun, a pauper.

There were more than four hundred wells on Signal Hill

now, four hundred producing wells. America had seen oil booms before, but never anything like Signal Hill.

Take the cemetery. Everyone had agreed that it would be quite wrong to drill beneath the cemetery: blasphemy and desecration. But there's blasphemy and then again there's the crime of unAmerican stupidity in the matter of money, and it didn't seem like any way to honour the dead to leave them floating over a sea of perfectly saleable oil. So the next-of-kin all clubbed together and built oil wells round the holy yard, whipstocking their drill pipes sideways into the land beneath the graves. Tom had met a guy selling shares in his Auntie Flo. He said it was his auntie that lay dead up there, so it must be his oil, and if anyone wanted a piece of it they'd have to buy shares in Flo. It seemed like everyone in the whole world had made money out of Signal Hill.

Everyone but Tom.

There were tears in his eyes as he sat down on the courthouse steps, trying to figure out what to do next. He felt like he'd lost all his motivation. All through the troubled, difficult years he'd kept himself going. All through war. All through prison. Through all the betrayals and poverty and hard work. And now he'd failed. Spectacularly failed. He felt as though he didn't have the puff to get up and start all over. He felt worse than he knew a man could feel.

Pipsqueak, a loyal heart in an absurdly small body, gently but insistently forced her head between Tom's arms, put her face to his, and licked his mouth and eyes. And that was when he heard a voice, a woman's voice, husky and East European.

'Tom?' it said. 'Is that you?'

PART FIVE

Speculation's all the go,
With rich and poor, both high and low,
And everybody's in a boil
For some Petroleum Oil:
Love for gold will long increase,
We hear of raids and talk of peace,
But best of all, it's worth your while
To come where 'I've struck Ile'.

from 'I've struck Ile'
by Frank Wilder

99

The year is 1929.

The hit record of the year is 'Happy Days are Here Again' and the tune seems to capture the spirit of the age. People have never been so free. The economy has never been so strong. The stockmarket is hitting all-time highs. Life is good.

But across the world, there are clouds on the horizon. A communist demonstration in Berlin ends with more than thirty dead. The parties of the German far right are increasingly restless. Further east, in Russia, Stalin has eliminated opposition to his rule as the biggest country in the world is passing into one-man dictatorship. There is terrorism in the Balkans, riots in India, unrest in Europe.

Clouds on the horizon.

Outside a large white stucco house in Chelsea, a man in a new black suit hesitates. He checks the number of the house against a piece of paper he carries in his hand, then moves to the door and knocks loudly. It is eight fifteen in the morning.

The butler's sick and the under-butler's busy so a maid comes to the door. The tradesmen's entrance is round the back, and whoever has the impertinence to knock so loudly while the family is at breakfast is in for an earful. The maid has her mouth open ready to remonstrate, but there, on the step, is a gentleman. His face is the colour of a chestnut, and his moustache would make a bank clerk look like a pirate – but, nevertheless, his class is obvious from his dress and the maid says nothing fiercer than, 'Good morning, sir, may I help you?'

'Indeed you may, lassie,' says the man, 'if this is the house of Alan Montague and his good lady.'

'Yes, sir.'

'Ha!'

The man makes as though to enter. The maid is flustered.

'I'm sorry, sir, the family is at breakfast. Perhaps if you'd like to wait in the library? And who should I say . . . ?'

'No, lassie, no. It's quite all right. The breakfast room is downstairs, I take it? I don't think Mr or Mrs Montague will mind an unexpected call from an old ruffian like myself.'

He winks at the maid and moves down the gleaming hall towards the stairs. The maid runs along after him, excited. Strictly speaking, she ought to stop him, but there's something unexpectedly kindly in the gentleman's manner, no matter how brutal his exterior may seem. The man leads the way, the maid hurries along behind.

East Texas.

A country of sandy soil, rolling hills covered with sweet gum and pine trees, and in the valleys there are fields of stunted corn and broiling sweet potatoes. It's difficult land to make a go of, and on a roasting hot day in summer even the chickens look at the horizon, longing for a change of life.

The village, Overton, is nothing. It's a whistle stop on the Missouri-Pacific mainline, with not a single paved street to boast of. On the edge of the village – outside the village would be more accurate – there's a little house standing in the shade of a bois d'arc tree. The house is a poor one, wooden built, just two rooms from the look of it.

On a washing line behind the house, there are a couple of shirts hanging out to dry. Men's shirts, not too well washed. You'd guess the house had no woman to keep it, but there are signs that it wasn't always so. One of the shirts has been mended almost invisibly under the armpit. The stitches are tiny, neat and even. No man ever sewed like that, certainly not the man who washed the shirts.

And one other thing. There's a photo that stands on the windowsill. It's a photo of Tom, but not him alone. There are two other people in the picture: Rebecca Lewi, squinting in the sunshine, and, in her arms, a tiny baby, six months at a guess. Tom has his arm around Rebecca. She has her head back, laughing at something beyond the camera. The snapshot isn't of terrific quality, and red Texan dust has blown in through the window, covering both frame and photo. All the same, if you look up close enough, you can see Tom's hand and Rebecca's too. They're wearing rings, wedding rings. But the photo speaks of the past. Right now, the shack has a sad feel to it. Sad and alone.

It looks and smells like a wasted life.

And Guy?

What of Guy, the eldest son and heir to Whitcombe House?

His military career appears to have stalled somewhat. His staff work during the war seemed to have destined him for high things, but peacetime has been less kind. Briefly in charge of a detachment of British troops in one of the African colonies, Guy returned home after an unexpectedly short stint. There were some mutterings in the press about a supposed failure to command the troops in a soldierlike and resolute manner. Guy's own version of events – insofar as he bothers to give it – blames weak soldiers, poor communications, difficult weather conditions, and a half-dozen other unlucky circumstances. He is now a lieutenant colonel at the military academy at Sandhurst, so perhaps things haven't turned out too badly.

As for Guy's domestic life, he passes it in a way that continually surprises his more strait-laced younger brother. The parties, dances and extravagances continue. Only last year, Guy surprised his entire family by announcing his engagement to an American woman, Dorothy Carter, whom he promptly married three months later. Nobody quite likes to say it, but his new wife seems rather dull, and quite unlike the sort of girl whom Guy has usually fallen for.

Is Guy happy?

Well, maybe. Alan isn't too close to him and Guy doesn't confide much in his mother or father. In any case, Guy seems to have settled and that much at least must be a good thing.

100

The man stopped just before the breakfast room and turned to the maid. He winked at her, held a finger to his lips, then tiptoed silently to the door.

The door was slightly ajar, and the man could see through it into the room. There was a man, his wife, and two small children, a boy and a girl, aged probably five and six respectively. The father was in animated discussion with the boy about the merits of boiled eggs, and whether or not the things were best enjoyed by being eaten or by being spread over every available surface with the back of the marmalade spoon.

The man outside watched for a second, then crashed the door open with a terrific bang.

'Good morning, good morning, good morning!' he boomed. 'Any kedgeree for your Uncle George?'

'George!' cried Alan and Lottie simultaneously, both delighted.

Alan leaped to be the first to embrace him, Lottie moved more slowly, but won out by getting a much longer hug. Her relative lack of speed was explained as she stood up: a pregnant bulge round her belly giving her five months' worth of reasons for caution.

'Great heavens, George, we weren't expecting you back for another fortnight at least.'

'Ha, I flew back, would you believe it? No more Red Sea steamers or those blasted Turkish trains. Came straight back: Abadan-Baghdad-Tiberias-Athens-Genoa-Amsterdam-London. Got back last night, in the devil of a rainstorm – pardon me, dear, pardon me – but wasn't properly home till I'd banged on your door here.'

Lottie stood up, wanting to see to George's breakfast, but both men protested vigorously and forced her to sit, and it was Alan who got to call for tea and kedgeree and bacon and kidneys and egg and sausage and kippers and tomato and mushrooms and more toast and more tea and another dish of butter and marmalade, and raspberry jam made with fruit picked from the kitchen garden at Whitcombe House.

Alan and Lottie delivered their domestic news. Little Eliza was thriving, and was already happy on horseback and a pleasure in the classroom. Little Tommy was a menace to everything within reach of his destructive little hands, but was nevertheless regarded as a jewel and a treasure. The third little treasure was expected within four months; the pregnancy had been a trifle compared with the other two; and in all other ways, their world was as happy and as harmonious as they could possibly want it.

Then there was a pause. A nurse came in to fetch little Tommy. The nurse shot a disapproving glance at the newcomer. It was strange enough the family taking breakfast together in this way, but to entertain an unannounced arrival over breakfast with the children present was almost disreputable . . .

Alan and George looked at each other, and Lottie caught the glance.

'Oh, don't be so silly, you two,' she said. 'Of course you're dying to talk business and of course you should get on before the pair of you burst like almighty great balloons. And before you think of retiring to talk oil wells and pipelines and bandits and explosions, then you should jolly well know that I'm going to follow you and listen to every word.'

The men laughed, and the next three hours were spent over

the decaying breakfast table going over every detail of the current state of the company, which Alan had christened Alanto Oil – the name born from its two spiritual founders: ALan ANd TOm.

The enterprise had expanded beyond recognition since the day, eight years back, when Alan and George had burned their last belongings to bring their boiler to one final, magnificent blaze. Egham Dunlop had been true to his word and his profession. Alan had drawn up careful estimates of how much money was needed. Dunlop had sounded out market sentiment. And then, fingers crossed, they'd gone to the stockmarket for the eye-popping sum of two and a half million pounds sterling.

They'd used the first tranche of money to drill step-out wells a mile or so away from Ameri No. 2. Every well they dug (and they used the most up-to-date American drilling equipment this time, working at speeds unrecognisable to the original pioneers) struck oil. They hadn't even mapped the full extent of the field, but they knew it was not less than nine miles long and not less than two wide. They threw up vast storage tanks in the mountains to hold the oil they were beginning to pump. Meantime, two dozen road engineers recruited from the army in Britain and India began to survey a pipeline route down from the mountains. They mapped out the route with steel rods and calico flags. Then, as the first sections of pipeline arrived from Glasgow, they purchased eleven thousand mules and hired enough men to work them. The men and mules hauled, dragged, heaved and cursed the nine-inch pipes into position. Muhammad Ameri, leading a troop of Qashqai, generously offered to protect the new line from bandits – that is to say, from himself. Alan and Reynolds negotiated with humour and patience and ended up agreeing to pay two dozen tribesmen with rifles to watch over the pipeline, and (more significantly) to award Muhammad Ameri a three per cent ownership of Alanto Oil, to be held in perpetuity for the benefit of all Qashqai.

On a more personal note, Alan rode out to Ameri's tent and handed him a small sculpture of the oil rig, fashioned in gold, and labelled in English and Persian: Muhammad Ameri No. 2.

The growing company didn't neglect its other duties. It built schools and hospitals at both ends of the pipeline. In its first year, the hospital at the Shiraz end of the pipeline cured almost six thousand cases of trachoma, carried out two hundred operations to remove cataracts, extracted three and a half thousand tonsils, and began a long programme to wipe out the waterborne diseases of dysentery and cholera. The schools also prospered, teaching basic literacy and numeracy to children, technical skills and hygiene rules to adults. In the school up at Shiraz, the literacy class contained forty-two children under the age of ten – plus Ahmed, who had decided that 'it's no bloody use being so goddamn bloody illiterate'.

A refinery was built on the shore of the Persian Gulf. In the City of London there was resistance to the idea. Although Anglo-Persian had done the same, many people considered it lunatic to site the new company's most complex and valuable industrial assets in some of Persia's wildest countryside.

Alan, the managing director and principal shareholder, listened to all the arguments and dismissed them. As he confided privately to Reynolds, 'God put the oil in Persia, George, not England. If we can't give something back to the Persians in exchange, then so much the worse for us.'

The young company was growing quickly into a great one. They still had their fun, of course. Explosion, flood, plague, riot and fire were all part and parcel of the game. But the oil was flowing now. They'd moved two hundred thousand barrels in their first year, four hundred thousand in their second, and were hoping to shift two million in this, their fifth full year of operation. Already, they were beginning to scout for further sources of oil. Iraq was their best bet. Other countries in the Middle East were also targets.

Alan and George talked. Lottie sat with some embroidery,

dreamily stitching, half listening to her two favourite men, half listening to the tiny life growing inside her belly. The breakfast things were cleared. Tea made way for coffee. The silver cruet set, which the maid had cleared, was brought back so that Reynolds could arrange salt, pepper and mustard pots all over the table to explain certain new complexities in the arrangement of the cooling towers at the refinery.

Life was good; blissful, in fact. Would it – could it – always stay this way?

101

The evening sun was skimming the tops of the pines. In the clearing beyond the derrick, a hog-nosed skunk loped through the brush, took a long and arrogant look at the labouring oilmen, then trotted forwards, confident that whatever the humans were up to, it was nothing to touch the pleasures of being a skunk.

It was Saturday evening, and the men usually knocked off early. They hauled another section of drill pipe from the well, unscrewed it, stacked it, and looked up. Perfectly on time to meet their gaze, an old Ford motor, a Tin Lizzie, came bumping down the track, its black sides clothed in the brick-red dust of the area. A man got out and approached Tom.

Tom spat tobacco juice on the ground, wiped his hands, and walked out to meet the man.

'Doin' OK?' drawled the man.

'Not bad,' said Tom. 'Two hundred and fifty feet this week, pretty good considering the cave-in we had Tuesday.'

'Done better if you didn't have no cave-in.'

'Done better if we had a rig instead of a rust-heap, and riggers instead of a bunch of cowpokes.'

'Never heard a good driller blame his tools the way you do.'

'That's because you've never even seen a good driller. Wouldn't know what one looks like. Before me, that is.'

'Yeah, well, you want to go drill for the Rockefellers, you go drill for the Rockefellers. They won't give you a piece of the action, though.'

Tom spat again and walked away. He picked up his jacket from the patchy grass beside the rig, shook it free of dust and insects and pine needles and put it on. He gave a whistle, and a scruffy little white dog with an enthusiastic tail came running from wherever it was she'd been sleeping, to greet her master. Tom's face broke into a broad smile of welcome, as he bent down to accept her licks. The act of smiling made him look younger. He looked more like the man who had stepped off the boat at Ellis Island, less like the man who had failed on Signal Hill.

The man in the Ford had pulled out a fat calfskin wallet and a red-bound notebook, and was counting out some money. 'Hey there, Pipsqueak. You still in charge here? Forty-five bucks.'

He held out the cash and Tom took it.

'I been trying to find a better boiler for you,' said the man. 'Nothing harder than drilling without a good head of pressure.'

'You could try buying some fuel instead. We've been stoking it with green wood and the damn stuff smokes but won't burn.'

'Well, that's part of the pleasure of independence, ain't it? I'm meeting a guy in Houston next week. A guy with some interested investors, maybe. Like I say, if we raise some new money, we can get on and sink this hole.'

'How many interests you going to sell, Titch?' said Tom. 'You already sold more than a hundred per cent and you sold a lot of them to me.'

'We hit oil, then no one'll be complaining. Not even you, bud.'

It should have been the end of the conversation. Tom had his week's money. Titch Harrelson had the other men to pay. But Harrelson was slow to walk over to the riggers who were waiting for payment. 'Course, if you wanted to get a lead over them Houston investors, I could let you in ahead of them, make a special rate for you.'

'Forget it.'

'Now's the time to be investing. We shouldn't be more than a thousand feet or so from the Woodbine. Plenty of oil in the Woodbine, I reckon.'

'Right. Another thousand feet and we'll hit the Woodbine. Full of saltwater and broken promises.'

'You want to work on a salary the rest of your days, that's up to you. Like I say, I got investors coming.'

'Yeah.'

Tom had heard it all before. The promoters, the talkers, the salesmen. Lies, promises, fantasies. He felt a familiar mixture of feelings. He had grown disgusted at the gap between the hundred-dollar descriptions and the ten-cent reality. He'd worked on a dozen independent wildcats these last few years, all of them the same as this. Worn-out equipment, local farm-hands recruited for the heavy work, the project always teetering on the edge of financial collapse. Industry wisdom was that you had to drill forty-five wildcats for every one that hit oil, and those were the odds for the industry at large. The odds facing independents were worse than that because they couldn't afford to buy access to the sweetest drill sites and because they often ran out of money before drilling deep enough. Here in East Texas, there wasn't a single indication of oil. Not one. A few wildcats had been drilled and nothing had ever been found. When guys from Big Oil saw wells like this, they slapped their thighs and promised to drink every barrel to come out of the hole.

But Tom's disgust had another source. Himself. He knew the odds. He knew the set-up. And yet time after time, he couldn't resist the lure. Perhaps *this* new well would strike it big. Perhaps *this* new promoter-geologist really did have a patch of land with potential. So time after time, Tom spent money he didn't have buying worthless chits of paper in worthless enterprises. Sometimes he worked whole months for paper instead of money. In California, he'd become famous as 'the only man to lose his shirt on Signal Hill', to quote a newspaper headline of the time. He'd become obsessive about trying one more time and succeeding. Each well was a new horizon. Maybe this time, maybe, just maybe . . .

Harrelson paid off the farm-hand riggers. Three bucks a day was dirt cheap, even for these poverty-stricken parts, but if the rain wouldn't come, the harvest would be feeble, and three bucks a day doing something useful was better than no bucks a day scratching at dust and praying for rain . . .

Harrelson wandered back to Tom, pushing his wallet away in a side pocket.

'Give you a lift?'

'Nope. No need.'

'Anything I can do to cheer you up? Hey, what you say, you come over tomorrow, eat some chicken with me and Mrs Holling? She's been saying she hasn't seen you for a while.'

Mrs Holling was the landowner on whose land they were drilling. Harrelson sponged off her shamelessly, lied to her endlessly. Tom assumed that they slept together, but didn't know it for a fact. Although Holling's husband was dead, Harrelson technically had a wife and family a hundred and thirty miles away in Dallas.

'It's OK. I got plans.'

'The hell you have. How could you have – educated man in a shithole like this? No sign of that wife of yours, I guess?'

'No.'

'Shame that. Mrs Holling thinks the world of her. Look, quit stalling. We'll see you tomorrow. Round about six.'

'Yeah, OK.'

'And hey, look, I didn't mean to bust your balls over that cave-in. Could have happened to anyone. And look, I feel bad. I owe you. I'm going to sign you up for some more interests, before I ever get to those wise guys from Houston. I'll sign you up for another half per cent, free, gratis and for nothing. No. Don't say nothing. It's yours. You deserve it. Hop in the car. I'll give you a ride back.'

Pipsqueak jumped into the car with a bark, then Tom followed her in. He'd never owned a car. Never come close. Too poor to find the three hundred bucks. He felt ashamed. The Ford's suspension was built for a giant with iron buttocks. Tom was jolted so badly, his head almost hit the windscreen post. Another half per cent would be nice. In theory (and he knew that the well had been sold out at least twice over), Tom now had a ten per cent stake in the property. If there was oil there, he'd have ten per cent of it. His luck had been so bad, so long, it had to turn some time. The car hit a particularly vicious pothole. The engine stalled and died. Harrelson gazed out into the road. He didn't try to restart the car. Tom realised he'd let the engine die on purpose.

'Hell's name, goddamn it!'

Tom knew he was meant to respond, but didn't. Harrelson waited a moment, then went on without a question from Tom.

'Aw hell, bud, I just realised I might've spoken out too soon. I made a promise to Ed Manninger that I wouldn't give any more interests away without payment. Wouldn't care nothing for that, of course, but he made me write something down. I'm worried that that half per cent I just gave you wouldn't hold up in a court of law.'

Silence.

'I'm real sorry about that, Tom. I should've thought before speaking.'

Silence.

'I meant it about dinner tomorrow, though. Chicken. A man gets tired of hog and hominy.'

Silence.

Then: 'How much?' It was Tom asking.

'Oh, you wouldn't have to pay anything like the Houston guys. I mean, you been central to this whole enterprise. That's why I feel bad bawling you out for a stupid cave-in.'

'How much?'

'Let's say two hundred bucks – hell, no. Forget it, forget it. Hundred and fifty. Thirty a week for five weeks. You should have it all paid down by the time we make a strike.'

'I can't live on fifteen a week, Titch.'

'Hell, you don't have to. Ain't I trying to offer you a chicken dinner?'

Silence.

In the gathering darkness, a big grey bird flew with heavy wingbeats across the roadway in front of them. In the distance, they could hear a thousand-wheeled freight train come clattering towards them through the night.

'OK.'

'That'd be thirty a week for five weeks.'

'I said OK.'

Silence.

'Starting now, bud. I can't get to the paperwork till I got an instalment. Plus I promised the boiler guy he'd have thirty bucks advance this Monday.'

Hating himself, Tom took the grainy grease-shined dollars from his pocket. He divided them into two piles and handed the bigger one to Harrelson.

The freight train was close now and it sounded like thunder.

102

Night.

Alan lay with his face pressed to the ground. The soil was muddy, and he could taste wet clay on his lips, smell it oozing up his nose. Overhead, the night sky was screaming in pain. Shell bursts turned the air to metal, while the horizon around was tongued and spattered with fire.

Alan pushed himself forward using toes and elbows. His right hand held a revolver, which he was careful to keep out of the mud. His left hand slipped and rolled on something that had a different wetness to the wetness of everything else. Alan knew what sort of thing that was: a head, an arm, a torso. He didn't want to look, but a German flare burst above him and he caught a brief glimpse of some torn human fragment, before he snatched his gaze away and looked forwards.

Tom was there. A hundred yards ahead.

Typically brave, typically impulsive, typically disobeying his typewritten orders, Tom was making his way through the wire.

Couldn't he see he'd never make it? Alan wanted to rush forwards and haul him back, but he knew that to stand up here was to die. He urged his limbs forward, but he found himself in a nightmare breaststroke on a slope of liquid clay. He was shouting something, or felt like he was, but the clay in his mouth clogged the words, or perhaps the shells had simply deafened him.

Way ahead of him, Tom's dark figure stood up beyond the wire. He was shooting. Attacking the German lines single-handed. He was crazy. The war had turned him crazy. As Alan watched, the figure sank down. Not suddenly, but slowly, softly. It seemed like he was sinking into something. Alan stood up to run towards him.

The noise was deafening.

The air split.

He woke up.

Lottie was awake and stroking his forehead anxiously. When Alan's eyes opened and came into focus, her gaze softened and her anxiety faded.

'Sorry, darling, was I shouting?'

'Yes.'

'Another dream.'

'I know.'

'I do apologise. Perhaps I should sleep in my dressing room. The last thing that a woman in your condition needs is –'

'Darling, please don't be a fathead.'

'I'm serious. You need a full night's –'

'I need a husband who isn't a fathead.' Lottie sat up in bed, and arranged the pillows behind Alan so he would sit up too. 'Your dreams are becoming more frequent and they're becoming worse.'

'They're not –'

'Yes they are, at least if the amount of shouting is anything to go by.'

'But still, they're only dreams. As soon as I wake up, I feel –'

'Perhaps, but I don't only love you when you're awake. I've had enough of you ignoring the problem.'

Alan rubbed his eyes. The dream didn't quite fade upon

waking. It was still there with him now. A kind of nameless horror, the memory of those awful offensives, death everywhere, and Tom sinking like a shadow to the ground. He gazed around the room: the heavy red-tasseled curtains, Lottie's things gleaming silver on her dressing table, photographs of their children, of Lottie and her parents, of Alan and George in Persia. The two worlds fought for mastery, and the daytime world began to win. But Alan knew that as soon as he lay down to sleep, the contest would start again and the war would return. He hadn't told Lottie, but he dreamed of the war every night now, it was just that he didn't always end up shouting.

'It's not a question of ignoring it, dear,' he said. 'There's nothing to be done about it. That's all.'

'Perhaps not, but we haven't tried.'

Alan looked at her. She had the blooming skin of pregnancy, as well as the misty look in her eyes that showed that a part of her attention was always somewhere else. He stroked a length of short auburn hair from her cheek and raised his eyebrows.

'I have the name of a doctor,' she said. 'He studied with Dr Freud in Vienna, but apparently he's not in the least intimidating. A friend of mine saw him and said he was very helpful, very understanding.'

'What's his name?'

'Dr Westerfeld. John, I think. He has a practice in Harley Street.'

Alan nodded. 'A doctor? A psychiatrist, I suppose? I'm not sure. I really don't think –'

'Darling, you're being a nincompoop.'

'I'd go if I thought there was any real –'

'Why is it that men are so brave about some things and such cowards about others? If it doesn't help, then don't go back.'

Alan swallowed. His blond hair was gummed to his scalp with the sweat of the dream. She was right, of course. It was only his discomfort at the idea that stopped him going. And if he was being absolutely honest, there were times, even during the day, when he felt inexplicably out of sorts. Even that morning when Reynolds had so splendidly burst in on them, Alan had felt it. For the most part, he'd been happy, full of joy at seeing Reynolds again, full of excitement for Alanto's progress in Persia. But, even as they'd built refineries out of mustard pots, he'd felt oddly disconnected, a kind of weary disenchantment with everything. With Reynolds, with Alanto, with oil, even with Lottie.

'Very well. You're right. I'll see him, but I'll also move into the dressing room. I won't have you disturbed.'

'I'll miss you.'

'I'll miss you too.'

Lottie nodded. Alan kissed her, saw her snuggle back down, then padded silently to the single bed in his dressing room next door. He got into bed, turned the light off, and closed his eyes.

Sleep came.

His lips were caked in clay. The bitter, mineral taste filled his mouth. He raised his eyes. A short distance ahead, Tom moved purposefully towards the enemy.

103

Ten wasted years.

Tom didn't kid himself. There are different ways you can succeed. You can make money. You can build a career. Or if you're a bust at work, you can always find love, start a family, be content.

But Tom had failed in all ways, all dimensions. He had watched the rise of Alanto Oil in Persia, and resented it bitterly. He read about other men's successes in America and resented them too. Wherever he turned, he saw happy families and loving couples, and he resented them all.

More than a decade since the war ended, Tom had nothing to show for it, nothing but loss.

Take that day in April 1922. Tom had been left penniless on the steps of the Long Beach courthouse. He'd had two bucks, a little change, and a loving white mongrel. He'd felt desolate and shattered. Then came the voice: 'Tom? Is that you?'

It had been Rebecca. She'd paid off her debts in Wyoming and come out west to Los Angeles. With her debts cleared, she was starting out afresh, working as a typist for some Hollywood studio. She'd read in the papers about Tom's story

– that awful headline about the only man to lose his shirt on Signal Hill. She'd at once wanted to come and find him.

It had been a shock to see her. She was instantly familiar. Olive-skinned, thin, angular, Tom (despite his prior doubts) had found her deeply attractive without quite making it to beautiful. Until he'd got to her eyes. They were different from anything Tom had known in a woman. They were dark, perceptive, piercing but never hostile. It was her eyes that Tom recognised at once, as though he'd seen them just yesterday.

She'd come as a friend, but by the time Tom had spent the best part of his two bucks fifty-five cents on buying her lunch, they were well on their way to becoming lovers. The months passed. They lived together. They slept together. They were very nearly happy.

Yet Tom found it almost impossible to settle. He had to take jobs as a lowly rigger, when just a short time before he'd been on the verge of millions. He was living in a one-bed apartment paid for by his ex-prostitute lover, when his one-time twin was the Managing Director of the world's youngest and most exciting oil company. The land that he'd drilled on – old Ma Hershey's twenty-seven sandy acres – had turned the Faries brothers into multi-multi-multi-millionaires. Tom blamed his luck incessantly. He became angry and vengeful towards the world. He resented Rebecca's contentment. He resented her.

The strain showed.

He spent too much money on idiot oil ventures. He stayed out drinking. He occasionally (just occasionally) slept with women other than Rebecca.

And so it finished – or should have done. But one evening, in spring 1923, just about one year from their meeting on the courthouse steps, Rebecca had an announcement to make. She was pregnant. Tom was shocked, but honourable. He asked her right away to marry him, and he did it graciously and even gallantly. They were married quickly and quietly, and their baby – Mitchell – was born six months later.

Mitchell was a strong little lad, with powerful lungs and his parents' dark hair. Tom was extremely fond of 'Mighty Mitch', but his feelings for his son didn't compensate for a difficult relationship with the boy's mother. Tom somehow felt that a shotgun wedding wasn't the same as a real wedding, and his womanising grew more frequent. Meanwhile, his work life went from bad to worse. Up and down the Californian industry, Tom was known by his nickname of 'Twenty-Seven Acres' or just plain 'Twenty-Seven'. Each time he heard the name, he fought the man using it. He fought with fists and bottles and, once, even a rigger's handspike. Within the space of twelve months, he'd been fired by Standard of California twice, Union Oil twice, Shell and Gulf once each.

The troubled family moved to Texas, hoping that Tom could leave his reputation behind and settle down. The nicknames grew fewer, but Tom still found a settled life impossible. News of Alan's growing successes followed him round and gnawed at him. An ordinary life with ordinary successes and failures was impossible when Alan was living an extraordinary one in England. Even the name Alan had chosen – Alanto; Alan and Tom – seemed to Tom like a carefully chosen insult. He followed news of the company's growth with obsessional care, and everything he learned pushed him further into anger and self-loathing.

He drifted away from the big companies, preferring to work for the little guys. He was paid less and he squandered more. Each failure fed the fire for another attempt. Each attempt led directly to another failure.

Twice Rebecca had moved away, taking Mitchell with her. The first time she'd been away for just five weeks, the second time for eight months. On both occasions she'd taken herself off to a farmer's widow who'd been kind to her when Tom was working the oilfields of the Gulf Coast. She'd stayed there, helped out the old lady, looked after her growing boy.

Both times, Tom had hesitated between an angry restlessness and the hope of rescuing something valuable from his disintegrated family life. The second time especially, during that long eight-month gap, he'd stormed around, taken jobs and lost them, stuck more capital than he possessed into the most wild-eyed and even fraudulent oil schemes going. He'd begun drinking more than he should and ended up brawling in moonshine joints where the men he brawled with were big fisted Texan cattle ranchers who gave every bit as good as they got. But eventually, both times, Tom had become sickened at his own attempts to ruin his life. Twice he had crawled out to Rebecca to woo her back with promises of reform and pleas for patience. Twice she had accepted.

But just two months earlier, as Tom's reforms had evaporated again, Rebecca's patience had finally snapped. She'd left him once again, for the 'absolute last and final time'. She wanted to save Mitch from his father. She wanted Mitch to be proud of his parents, not ashamed. Tom was on his own now, bitter and despairing.

Ten wasted years.

~

The car dropped Tom in the dirt yard, beeped a farewell, and was about to swing off into the night. Then, on a sudden impulse, Tom leaped forward, forcing Harrelson to stop the car.

'Jeez, bud. You don't want to jump out like that. I almost ran into you.'

'One question. Just one question, Titch. You promised some money to that boiler guy. When did you make your promise?'

'The boiler guy? Who cares? He's nothing. You leave the business to me and I'll –'

'Just tell me. When?'

'It's no big deal. I promised him just now. Just before coming down to pay you and the boys.'

'How much?'

'For God's sake, pal! What is this? You worried the boiler guy is trying to take a topslice off of our profits?'

'Quit stalling.'

'Jesus! He's asking a coupla hundred, but he'll take less. We haven't shook on anything. Hey – get a good night's rest and we'll see you tomorrow. Right?'

'Right,' said Tom, hollowly.

The car beeped again and vanished into the night. Behind Tom, the little wooden house stood empty, when it ought to have contained a wonderful wife and a healthy sleeping child. Tom had no reason to go inside. He had no reason to do anything at all.

104

'Well?'

'Well?' echoed Alan. 'Do you examine me?'

'Yes.'

'Should I take off my jacket?'

'If you like.'

'You don't need to listen to my heart or anything?'

'Yes, but not with a stethoscope.' Alan looked puzzled, and Dr Westerfeld hastened to end the mystery. 'This is your first encounter with a psychiatrist, I take it?'

'I saw some nerve specialists during the war, but nothing like this, no.'

'And you're both a little nervous and wondering whether you're being had?'

'Yes.' Alan laughed with the first start of relief.

'Yes, well, I wonder that myself at times . . . I will examine you, or rather I will ask you to examine yourself, your heart. All we do here is talk. You will wonder how on earth talking can bring about any change and I'm not entirely able to answer you. I can only tell you that with some of my patients, our little talks have brought about profound changes. I hope that they will do the same for you.'

Alan nodded. 'Even so,' he said, 'I'm not sure I even have a problem. In my waking life, I'm as sound as a bell.

I work hard, I have a splendid family, I enjoy my life.'

Westerfeld's Harley Street room was furnished like a gentleman's drawing room. He had offered Alan the choice of reclining on a chaise longue or sitting upright in an armchair. Alan had taken the chair without hesitation. Outside the shuttered windows, there was a burr of traffic rolling up Harley Street.

'And?' said Westerfeld. 'You are perfectly happy, have a splendid family, but you have come to see a psychiatrist.'

'And . . .' Alan sighed. 'It's only dreams, but –'

He was interrupted by Westerfeld vigorously shaking his head. 'No, no, no. Not "only". Not "only". We believe – that is, Dr Freud and his followers believe – that dreams are a clue to our unconscious selves. Selves more powerful than us, more primitive, less civilised, more passionate. I am a doctor of dreams. Please tell me about your dreams, but never describe them as "only" dreams.'

So Alan took a deep breath and began. He spoke about when they had started. The cholera, followed by the malaria. The hallucinatory nights. The daily deliriums. The dreams that had started then and followed, first of all sporadically and now nightly. All night, every night. As he spoke, something of the intensity of the experience communicated itself in his words. He sat forward, lean fingers grasping the arms of the seat.

'During the day, let me be clear, do you experience anything untoward? Buzzing in your ears, tremors, fear of bright lights or sudden noises?'

'No.'

'Any nervousness or anxiety that you can't explain?'

'No.'

'Sudden excitability? Angry outbursts? Anything like that?'

For a fraction of a second, Alan hesitated. Then: 'Nothing at all.'

'Nothing? You don't sound sure.'

'Well . . . nothing that I could exactly complain of.

Sometimes I feel a kind of dullness for no reason that I understand. A kind of ache here.' Alan struck his chest over his heart.

'Dullness – sadness, perhaps?'

Alan was about to say no, when he felt a jab of emotion similar to what he was trying to describe, only stronger. It *was* like sadness. 'Yes, possibly. I've certainly never thought of it like that before.'

'Indeed . . . Please continue. You were telling me about your dreams.'

Alan spoke more about his dreams. How they had once been simply about war and how they were now about Tom. All night, every night. Westerfeld asked about Alan's relationship to Tom, and raised his shaggy eyebrows higher and higher as Alan explained.

'In these dreams, does Tom die?'

'I assume so.'

'That isn't what I asked. I asked whether he dies. Whether you see him die.'

'I see a blaze of fire. I see him sinking down.'

'Do you see him die?'

Alan pondered. It was a strange question, but perhaps doctors of dreams had a professional obligation to be strange. And as he thought, the answer came to him, crystal clear, like the sudden illumination of a falling Very light.

'No. It's very odd. He almost dies a hundred times a night, but I never quite see him die . . . No, that's not it. He never dies. In my dreams, he's always dying, never dead. I don't know why. It makes no sense.' Alan sat back.

Westerfeld was nodding vigorously. He was chestnut-haired, with a squirrelish face and shaggy eyebrows that joined in a single bar above his nose. With his great repetitive nods, he looked like a nodding toy of the sort that might be sold in the Hamley's toy store. 'Good, good.'

'You can make sense of it, doctor?'

'Oh, yes. Remember, your unconscious is a primitive,

childish sort of beast. It has little to do with the logic which says that a man mown down by bullets must necessarily be dead. Your unconscious is trying to tell you that it doesn't accept Tom's death. Not now. Probably not for a moment since the night when Tom was lost. Hence your dreams.'

'So we must tell the beast to grow up, to accept reality.'

'Oh, no.'

'No?'

'Far from it. The unconscious won't grow up, but it'll talk to you, if you let it. Talk to you in dreams, the way it always has.'

Alan smoothed his hair, and brushed his hand over his upper lip, just as he'd done in the days when he'd worn a moustache. He hadn't done that for years. It was a gesture from the past, a gesture from the days of war. He had been taken aback by Westerfeld, but was pleased. He couldn't quite have said why, but a boyish excitement was beginning to beat in his heart.

He stood up to go.

'Doctor?' he said. 'Am I . . . ? I mean, do you . . . ? Look, I've never thought worse of a man for suffering shell shock. Some of the best men under my command suffered from it, and I had a bad case of nervous exhaustion myself. But if you think –'

'Not shell shock, no.'

'You're sure?'

'Listen, Montague, as soon as I see a man your age inside this consulting room, my first thought is shell shock. I all but assume it. In the Great War we sent men into conditions that were unsupportable. In a literal, medical sense: unsupportable. That's why I asked about the buzzing, the tremors, the fears of loud noises.'

'Well, I'm clean on that front, thank God.'

'Yes, you're right to.'

'To . . . ?'

400

'To thank God. If a man's mind is shattered by warfare, there's nothing that I or anyone can do for them. Nothing at all. Sometimes I think the men that died were the lucky ones.'

105

Tom had known nervousness before. When he first trod the muddy duckboards leading to the front line. When he first crept into no man's land under enemy fire. When he planned his escape attempt with his long-dead friend Mitch Norgaard. When he presented himself at Ellis Island, seeking admission to the United States.

But he'd never known anything like this. He was appallingly nervous. His mouth was dry. His hands sweated profusely and as often as he wiped them on his flannel trousers they gummed up again with sweat. It was a Sunday afternoon, cool by the standards of southern Texas, and Tom wore a dark suit with a respectable black hat and tie.

He walked up to the front door of the farmhouse. It was a biggish two-storey affair from the prosperous days of the last century, but the white paint was beginning to peel and where the boards were bare, they were weathered and brittle.

Tom knocked.

A maid answered, let him in, showed him into a velvet and lace parlour, and let him stew there on the edge of a feminine little couch, twisting his hat between his hands until the brim was beaten out of shape and the crown was soft. Then footsteps, and the door opened.

'Ah! Mr Calloway!'

It was the old dame, the farmer's widow, still in black some twenty years after her husband's death.

'Mrs Elwick, good afternoon.' Tom stood up, standing as awkwardly as a lowly cattle hand in the presence of his boss's wife.

'I expect you have come to persuade Rebecca home with you.' She said 'home' in a nasty way, a way that implied what Tom called home was what most decent people would call a cesspit.

'Yes . . . No . . . Not exactly. I wanted to see her.'

'You should have called ahead.'

'I should have done. I was worried, maybe . . .'

'You were worried she wouldn't wish to see you, and little wonder.'

Mrs Elwick nodded, birdlike, took a little look round the room as though to check whether Tom had soiled the carpet or stolen the porcelain. 'Wait here, please.'

She went.

Half an hour passed. There was an ormolu gilt clock on the mantelpiece, and Tom counted the ticks as a way of holding on to his small amount of self-possession. Then more steps. Tom stood up. His head swam. The door opened. It was Rebecca.

She was wearing a black dress with starched white cuffs and collar. The dress gave her a severe look, accentuated by a pair of gold-rimmed glasses that she took off as she entered.

'Becca!'

'Tom! You shouldn't have come.' Rebecca's voice wasn't unkind, but it was grave and measured, like a mind made up. 'I had asked you not to.' She remained standing.

'I know, hon, I . . .' Tom's voice trailed away. His wife was still standing. She had left him to wait for half an hour. Defeat already nagged at him. 'I can leave.'

'No, you're here now.' Rebecca sat down, but not close to him, not in any way that invited contact. 'I apologise for keeping you. I was with a client.'

'A client?'

The word sounded strange, given their surroundings. The only clients that Tom had ever known Rebecca to have had weren't exactly the sort that Mrs Elwick would make welcome. For that matter, Rebecca's outfit, which made her look like some kind of Puritan Wall Streeter, wasn't exactly the kind of thing to pull in the punters.

She smiled. 'Not like that. I used to help my father out with his bookkeeping. My father and some of his friends. I studied a little to learn how these things work in America, then advertised for clients.' She shrugged, as though her resourcefulness were commonplace. 'It was surprising to me how many of the ranches and other businesses round here have their finances in a total mess. It's been a pleasure to help them.'

Tom gaped, remembering the book of accounts he'd found in Rebecca's empty apartment eight long years before. But he'd never known that she knew bookkeeping well enough to make a living at it. 'How come I never knew that? You never said.'

'You never asked,' she replied, with some sharpness. 'You think because you want to hide your own past, you can't ask me anything about mine. I don't want to speak to you about things you don't want to hear.'

There was a short, difficult silence.

'Sorry.'

The silence continued a moment or two.

Then: 'Perhaps you're right, Tomek. Perhaps it would be better if you left.'

Tom's hat should have bitten the bullet and surrendered then and there. The battering it took in the next half-minute was indescribable. Tom twisted and wrung it between his fingers. It had arrived at the house a brand-new hat. It would leave it a cheaply millinered corpse.

'Hear me out, hon. This time, I promise . . . hell, Becca, I don't suppose you think too much of my promises.'

'Not much.'

'So no promises.'

'OK.'

'I just wanted to tell you about where I am, what I'm doing.'

Rebecca nodded. If Tom had been calm enough to notice, he'd have seen emotion flooding her eyes. He'd have seen that, although her voice was steady, she was breathing fast and deeply.

Tom handed her a white card. 'This is my new address. If you want to get hold of me, I'll be here. It's a bit of a dive, but as soon as I can save for something better, I'll let you know.'

Rebecca took the card and her eyes registered surprise. The address was no more than ten miles away: a settlement thrown up around a Texaco drilling site.

'You're living here?'

Tom nodded.

Rebecca looked back at the card. There was a second question in her eyes and Tom knew what it was.

'I've taken a job with Texaco,' he said. 'Starting Monday. I ain't gonna . . . I mean, I'm not going to work for any hooey and hokum promoters any more. This job with Texaco, I'm starting as an ordinary rigger, but I've got more experience than some of their drillmen. I'll get ahead pretty quickly.'

'Honestly? You're working as a rigger? For Texaco?'

'They're OK. They're not stuck up like Standard or Shell. It's an OK outfit.'

Rebecca nodded, silently amazed. Three things amazed her. First, Tom had moved close to her and Mitch, rather than trying to persuade them back to him. Second, he had demoted himself. He was a highly capable lead driller and to take a rigger's wage was almost an insult – and Tom had never been the slowest person to resent an insult. And third, Texaco. Whatever Tom said about it, they both knew that it was a major oil company. He'd get a wage, decent working conditions, and nothing else. No 'lease action', no 'percentage of wellhead crude'. No promises, no lies, no worthless slips of paper – in short, no dreams.

'I missed you,' he said. 'I'm not going to live without you both again. I'll make it work this time. It's been . . . every time till now it's been my fault, no matter what I said in the past. It'd break my heart if you didn't want to see me.'

Rebecca came and sat next to him on the couch, taking the hat gently out of his hands and laying its battered remains on a mahogany sidetable. She took his hand.

'What's all this about, Tom?'

'It's about you. You and Mitch. I couldn't bear to have him grow up ashamed of his daddy.'

'We've always been around, Mitch and I. What's brought this on?'

Tom sighed. 'Age, maybe. Age and wisdom.' He smiled and they both laughed. 'OK, not wisdom, but maybe a little break from idiocy. I felt ashamed. I realised I was better than . . . than all of that.'

She laughed again, kindly. She was always kind.

The truth was this. The final straw had been that last night with Harrelson. The boiler man needed money. It most probably wasn't a down-payment on a new boiler. Most likely it was a debt unpaid from the last one. Harrelson could have paid him off then and there. He had a fat calfskin wallet that still had notes in it after he'd paid Tom and the riggers. But Harrelson didn't need to do that. He could play Tom so easily that he rolled up that afternoon absolutely confident of taking a hundred and fifty bucks off him, having already promised away the first thirty. Tom was just a way of paying Harrelson's lousy debts.

Tom had known Harrelson for a crook, but this was something worse. Harrelson had no intention of finding oil. He honestly didn't care. He'd sell 'shares' in his well and live off the proceeds. When the well was dry, he'd disappear, leaving Mrs Holling in the lurch, amidst a forest of unpaid debts and unkept promises.

Tom's disillusionment was complete. He'd sat down on the wooden step of his veranda, listening to insects grating in the trees. By accident, he put his hand on something behind him: Mitch's toy train gleaming softly in the dark. He brushed the dust off it and rolled the wheels on his palm. As he did it, Pipsqueak nuzzled up close as if trying to build a family from just the two of them. Tom felt a sudden rush of homesickness. Mitch, Rebecca and him. It hadn't been such a great family, but, by God, it had been one.

For the first time ever, the thought occurred to him that he could forget about making his fortune. He could forget his tangled feelings about Alan's success. He could forget about everything except making his wife and children happy and comfortable. And what the hell? They were both still young. He wanted another baby. A girl for preference, but either would be great. For the first time in his life, the old, old dreams of oil were falling silent, the old betrayals no longer important. It was time for something else to take their place.

He touched his face with his hand where a falling lifting-block had grazed it. Rebecca reached her hand out and touched him in just the same spot. Her hand was as soft as a cloud of butterflies.

'I'm pleased you came,' she said.

And so was he.

106

The Rolls-Royce Phantom was a beautiful silver-green affair, polished to a lovely shine, the leatherwork gleaming and smelling of beeswax. It was a damn stupid car to take into the East End of London.

'Just park it here, would you, Ferguson?' said Alan. 'And if you can keep the nippers from wrecking it, then I'd be grateful – and impressed, I might add.' He gave his driver a pocketful of coppers, in the hope that Ferguson would be able to bribe acceptable behaviour from the crowd of urchins who were already gathering round the car. 'I'll try to be quick.'

The street was made up of two rows of working men's houses, jammed up against each other, thick with the smell of coal-smoke and privvies. None of the houses had a number on the door, and Alan asked one of the urchins to direct him. The boy took a longing glance at the car, turned his back on it long enough to jab a dirty fingernail in the direction of a door, said, 'That's me Auntie Min,' and went back to adoring the Rolls.

The door, which wasn't shut, was pulled fully open before Alan could knock. A poorly dressed woman of about fifty bobbed and curtsied on the step, while in the back a man was yelling, 'Get out of here, you little bleeders! And take that bleeding Stumpy, while you're at it. We've got a bloody

408

gentleman, an' all.' The woman finished her bobbing and the man finished his yelling. The house fell into a silence of expectation.

'Good morning. Mrs Hardwick?'

'Mrs Hardwick as was,' said the lady, quickly. 'Mr Hardwick laid down his life for his country, sir, an' it's Mrs Jephson now, sir, begging your pardon.'

'May I come in, Mrs Jephson? There was something I wanted to ask.'

Alan was taken into the tiny front room, where a small child was trying to sweep away the last of the breakfast things before being ejected by a toe of Mr Jephson's boot. The room was astonishingly dirty. The walls had once been papered, but much of the paper had peeled off with the damp, and the gaps had been plugged by cut-out pictures from magazines: the Tiller Girls, the Prince of Wales, Josephine Baker, Rudolph Valentino, Greta Garbo, Clara Bow. Someone had even taken some ordinary sheets of notepaper and cut them into intricate doily shapes and pinned them out along the filthy shelves.

'Sorry, sir. Sorry, sir,' they both kept saying.

'Please,' he said, 'I should apologise for arriving so unexpectedly. Please don't let me put you out.'

The man and the woman arranged themselves. He pulled on a black-stained jacket indicating his trade as a coalman. He stamped heavily on a gigantic cockroach ('Pardon, sir!') and sat down. The woman tucked in her skirt where it was stained or patched, leaving a thin strip of threadbare material stretched tightly across her legs.

'I was trying to trace a fellow by the name of Hardwick, Edward Hardwick. The War Office gave me this address.'

'Why yes, sir,' said the woman, 'that's Stu – That's Shorty you want, sir. Shorty's what we always called him, sir, before the war.'

'Is he here now?'

'Why, yes, sir, only . . .'

The two looked at each other.

'He was caught quite bad in the war, sir. He ain't too pretty to look at, though the boy's just as good if you could only look inside.'

'I'm sure he is, Mrs Jephson,' said Alan gently. 'There were a great many good lads caught badly. I was there myself.'

The couple looked at each other awkwardly, then Mr Jephson rose. 'I'll fetch him out. I believe he may be out for a breath of air,' he added, in what seemed like a ludicrous imitation of Alan's manners.

There was a bit of thumping out back. Mrs Jephson tried to rearrange her skirt again, but there was a limit to how little black material was needed to cover a pair of quite ample thighs. Another huge black cockroach waddled across the floor and they both stared at it as though mesmerised. Then a door slammed, Jephson puffed, and he came in with the one-time Private Edward 'Shorty' Hardwick held lop-sided in his arms.

Shorty Hardwick had no legs, hence his new name, Stumpy. He looked dishevelled. His shoulder and hair were white with cobwebs and a disintegrating lime mortar. His face was dirty with the dirt common to all children of the East End. He smelled vaguely of excrement. For a second or so, Alan gaped rudely before realising what had happened. In the haste to clear the downstairs room for its grand visitor, the Jephson kids had hauled Stumpy out of his normal seat and leant him up against the wall in the only place they could think of putting him: the privvy.

'Shorty Hardwick, is it?' said Alan, extending his hand. 'My name's Alan Montague, Captain Montague as was.'

'Sir. Yes, sir.' Stumpy brought his hand up to his forehead in something like a salute.

'No, no, never mind that. We're all in civvies now.'

'Yes, sir.'

'Look, I'm trying to track something down and I have reason to believe you may be able to help.'

'Yes, sir.'

'It was in France. August nineteen sixteen. The night of your infinitely courageous assault on the gun posts –'

'Machine guns, sir. Two of them, there were.'

'Exactly. Two of them. You were under the command of a Mr Creeley, I believe. Is that right?'

'Yes, sir. A proper gentleman he was. Picked me an' Bobby Stimson because he didn't want to kill anyone as had a missus.'

'Quite, quite. Now what I want to know is this. You were there when Mr Creeley was hit, I take it?'

'Yes, sir.'

'Please can you tell me, as exactly as possible, what you remember of that moment. I'm particularly concerned to know whether Mr Creeley was killed outright or whether he might just have been severely wounded.'

'Oh no, sir. He copped it all right. It's a wonder that any of us survived. They hit us pretty hard. I lost both my legs,' he added, in case Alan hadn't yet noticed.

Alan winced at Stumpy's matter-of-fact tone, but pursued his line of questioning. Dr Westerfeld had been right. His dreams had been burning to tell him that Tom hadn't died. His dreams were almost certainly wrong, but, with Westerfeld's encouragement, he realised he would never have an easy night until he'd got to the truth of the situation. And so he'd gone back to the curt official dispatches of the time. He'd found the names of the two privates that had gone with Tom. He'd used War Office pension records to find (to his surprise) that one of the two had lived, although horribly wounded, and had used the same records to trace Hardwick's address.

'Please. If you could tell me exactly what happened?'

Stumpy was no storyteller, but, with patience, Alan got to the bottom of it. The three men had crept close to the first gun post. They had no real chance of taking it, unless by some fluke the Germans panicked at the first Mills bomb and fled. But before anything could happen, they were seen. A hail of German fire broke out from appallingly close quarters. 'Stimson, sir, he disappeared in front of my eyes. Like in a sausage machine he was. Must have had maybe ten thousand bullets inside him, I wouldn't be surprised.' Shorty – as he then was – had also been hit and had crashed to the ground. He'd lain there horribly wounded, resigned to that staple of Great War deaths: the slow bleeding away in a shell-hole, within sight and sound of British lines. 'I thought I was a goner. Tried to remember all them things the padre said about going on living after you'd snuffed it, but I can't say as how it made a lot of sense. I fainted. Don't remember anything else, till I found myself in Field Hospital, screaming bloody blue murder, sir, pardon my French, only they were short of morphine, sir, and the buggers hurt me bad, getting my legs trimmed off all neat and even, like.'

Rescued by some RAMC corporal who'd earned an DCM and a sergeant's stripes for his deed, Stumpy had made a slow but complete recovery. But the strange thing was that, when it came to Tom, his account almost precisely followed Alan's dream. 'There was heavy fire, sir, horrible heavy. I saw him sinking. I know he must have been hit. Not like Stimson, sir. Stimson pretty much came apart as I was looking. But hit pretty bad. Must have died, sir. Nobody could of survived it.'

And that was that.

A hail of fire – Tom sinking – probably dead – then nothing. It was just as in the dream. Nothing was resolved. Alan felt a crease of tension running across his stomach as he took in what he'd been told. He stroked his non-existent moustache to conceal his agitation – that old wartime gesture once again.

'Thank you. You've been most helpful.'

'Oh yes, sir, not to worry. Pleased to be of help, sir.'

In the horrible little room, Alan caught sight of a photo: it was a young Shorty, in private's uniform, a long pale underfed city-faced boy, almost certainly underage.

412

'Listen, Hardwick. I do a spot of work now and again for the Infantryman's Artificial Limb Board. We're always on the lookout for deserving cases. Have you ever been measured up for a pair of legs? They're not as good as the real thing, but a lot better than nothing at all.'

'Oh, no, sir.'

Stumpy's face was white and the silence in the room became almost holy as the family waited in awe.

'Well, if you don't mind, I'd like to send you to a fellow who's the very last word in artificial legs. What d'you say?'

'Oh, sir!'

'I'll make an appointment for you and send a car to fetch you there. Will that be convenient?'

'Oh, sir!'

'Good man.' Alan nodded. Once Stumpy Hardwick was Shorty Hardwick once again, Alan would find a job for him somewhere in Alanto Oil. He wondered about making a gift in cash, but decided that the right moment would be later, not now.

He stood up to go. He shook hands with Mr and Mrs Jephson, who were both rooted to the spot and dumb. If he had been the risen Christ, he could hardly have made a greater impression.

Ferguson had kept the car safe from malicious hands by driving round and round the block with a different carload of kids each time. The queue for an encore now stretched out of sight down the street. Alan drove back in silence.

To his surprise, he wasn't mostly thinking of Tom. That would come later. At night, by day, with Lottie, with Dr Westerfeld, he'd turn over every possible angle connected with Tom, until his head and heart ached with the effort. But now his head was full of something else altogether: an anger that took his breath away and left reason bleeding in the gutter.

His mind filled with the names and faces of the men he'd known in France. Tom: dead. Fletcher: crippled. So many others dead or lost or maimed or blinded, it sometimes seemed a wonder there were men enough to people England. He saw Lottie's bloody apron as though it was yesterday. He saw Stumpy Hardwick's childish face light up at the thought of a pair of hollow steel legs. He heard that 'Oh sir, oh sir,' until the big car nosed out of the City into the West End, where the din of traffic swallowed thought.

107

Up in New York, the stockmarket descended with a crash that was heard across the world. Across America, the economic ripples began to shatter and split the glass-bubble economy of the late 1920s. But in one small cottage in Texas, work remained steady, income remained adequate, life became good.

Early on in spring 1930, Tom was working for Texaco, managing to hold down the same job for nine months on the trot – the first time he'd managed that since serving as a British officer. What was more, not once during those nine months did he let himself slip. He didn't womanise. He didn't brawl. His drinking was moderate. And best of all, he didn't hand over so much as ten dollars to any snake-oil salesman promising untold riches from any 'sure-fire wildcat' (as if that weren't a contradiction in terms). After six months of exemplary behaviour, Rebecca, still working as an accountant, trusted him enough to let him back.

Of course, nobody, still less Tom, reforms overnight.

He was helped by the fact that the drilling site was old and well-developed. The tarts and bars and whorehouses that are part and parcel of any oil-boom town had moved on elsewhere. The girls that remained looked drained and listless. And this was Texaco he worked for, one of the big guys. Its rigs sat on a block of nearly three thousand acres. Anywhere Tom moved, he was on Texaco land. The promoters who tried to chisel out a living by parting small-time investors from their cash couldn't work without leases. The promoters were up in Oklahoma. They were there chasing shadows in California. They were out there scratching amongst the pines and corn fields of East Texas. The one place they didn't hang out were the prime oilfields of the Gulf Coast.

But Tom, definitely and certainly, was making progress. He was still working as a rigger – a senior one now – but he genuinely didn't mind the loss of position. He looked forward to the end of drilling every day and hurried off to the Elwick farmstead to catch Mitchell (now six years old) before he went to sleep. He played with his boy and taught him baseball, having hurriedly learned the game himself first. He helped him with his alphabet and his numbers. He stayed around as Rebecca bathed the child and put him to bed.

And then there was Rebecca, the miracle of Rebecca.

It was only now, after so many years, that Tom learned what a jewel he had accidentally come to possess. She was wise, she was kind, she had an astonishing inner strength and purpose, like her own in-built compass needle. In a strange way, Tom had never really thought her beautiful before now. When he saw her these days, he didn't even see her imperfections: her slightly too bony face, the wrinkles that spread their net out from the corners of her eyes. He only saw his one true love, a woman with grace in every movement, a woman who mixed love and laughter with her more serious virtues.

And Tom became younger. As a young man, he'd been charming, even dazzling. He could spark laughter from a woman with a handful of words. His own smile had been enough to ignite one in response. But then, following war and prison and his long succession of American failures, he'd lost even his desire to please. That had returned. These days, he and Rebecca *laughed*. If there was one thing they remem-

416

bered about that time, other than the infinitely absorbing detail of Mitchell's boyhood, it was laughter. Tom grew his hair long again, plunging his head into the water butt on his return home each evening to rinse it of the day's oil and mud. And that was when it started each evening. She'd push him under water. He'd respond by shaking his head at her like Pipsqueak drying off. They'd splash and play and laugh, and then the laughter didn't really stop until they climbed into bed that evening. They made love often and their lovemaking was wonderful.

One more nugget of positive news: Rebecca's parents had finally made their move, away from Vilnius and the dangers of life there, all the way to Leipzig in Germany. Her father had set up a pharmacy: smaller than his Vilnius business, but already doing nicely. Her mother, a dressmaker, was as busy in her new surroundings as she ever had been in her old ones. They were well settled, with friends and a synagogue that welcomed them. There were unpleasant undercurrents in their adopted country, of course. But there was unpleasantness everywhere. The point was that they had resettled. They were happy. They were safe.

But even in Paradise, people grumble, and Tom and Rebecca grumbled in theirs.

They were renting a cottage hard by Mrs Elwick's farmhouse. If they made noise, it was disapproved of. If they horsed around with water in the garden, it was disapproved of. On Sundays they were expected to attend church morning and evening (no matter that Rebecca was as Jewish as Yom Kippur) and to sit through a very long and dull English-style roast dinner.

It was time to move, but they were short of cash.

'You go and ask her to give you lessons in Christian deportment, while I'll nip upstairs and snitch her jewels.'

'They're all paste. I bet they are.'

417

'*Paste!*' cried Tom in a high-pitched imitation of Mrs Elwick. 'How dare you say any such thing, you ungrateful little flapper!'

They laughed. It had been a hot day, Mitch was in bed, Pipsqueak snoring at his feet, and the two adults were taking it in turns to bathe naked in the waterbutt behind their cottage. Tom had arranged some wooden palings to shelter them from prying eyes, but even so, they kept their voices low to avoid attracting attention. Rebecca bobbed her head below the surface, took a big mouthful of the cool green water and spat it out on Tom, who dunked her for her trouble.

When she rose again, she wore a more serious look.

'How much do you think we need to buy a place of our own?'

'Well now, that's all be depending on what exactly you were looking for.' Tom's accent was now a deep Texan drawl, with every vowel split into at least three long-drawn-out parts. 'We can offer you a wide selection of shacks, dives, dumps, hovels and holes. Only thing we don't have in at present are sties and flophouses.'

'Seriously.'

'OK, seriously now, our dumps aren't too good at the moment. And the termites have pretty much gotten to the last of our shacks.'

Another green jet of water came Tom's way. 'Hopeless, absolutely hopeless.'

'Them damn termites.'

Rebecca rinsed her hair back from her forehead, rested her forearms on the side of the butt and her chin on her forearms. 'Three thousand dollars for somewhere decent?'

'Yeah. About three thousand. I want to get away from Mrs E, but I don't want Mitch to grow up in squalor.'

'And how much do we have at the moment?'

'Why, hon –' Tom was Texan again – 'I'm a mill-ee-on-ay-er. I got you, haven't I?'

'And in dollars?'

'One thousand one hundred and sixty-eight.'

Rebecca grimaced. Even with her income, which was the equal of his, it would be a long haul to independence.

'Tomek?' It was a trick she sometimes had of switching his name into the soft East European syllables of her birth.

'Yes?'

'We do in theory have a little more than that.'

'Not in the bank we don't.'

'No, not in the bank.'

Tom looked at her enquiringly.

'You have the most beautiful eyebrows,' she said, tracing them with a wet finger. 'The most gorgeous mouth. I'm a lucky girl.'

'Lucky-ish.'

They kissed.

'No, really . . . Look, do you think there's any way on earth you could get money back from that creep Harrelson?'

'Ah!'

Tom jerked his head up and back, and sucked his breath in. He had a mixture of feelings. One feeling was it was a good idea. Tom had stuffed Harrelson's pocket with cash in exchange for worthless paper. It would be nice to see some return from that, and doubly nice if it meant giving his family a chance to start out in a place of their own. But then, on the other side, Harrelson's stupid dry-hole wonder was all that remained of Tom's fantasies and dreams. In theory, if Harrelson ever struck oil, Tom had a big slice of it. It was a stupid daydream, but Tom still clung to it when the ghosts of failure hung too heavy round his bed.

'Ah, jeez!'

'Would you be able to make him give you anything?' asked Rebecca.

'Well, not strictly speaking, there wasn't any kind of refund scheme, of course . . .' Tom trailed off. His stake in Titch Harrelson's hopeless well was his only chance of making something of himself. Tom followed developments in the oil industry closely and he was familiar with every detail of Alanto's success: oil production in Persia expanding all the time; exploration projects in Iraq; marketing networks in Europe and Asia. Tom felt sick at the thought of it. And all he had to boast of was his stupid ten per cent of a barren well. Perhaps the time had come to put his last feeble hope behind him. '. . . Of course, I'm sure I could get *some* money from the guy.'

'You could?'

Tom sighed. He had a difficult admission to make. 'He sold that well so many times over that pretty much everyone this side of the Mississippi owns a piece of it. I'd only have to threaten him with the courthouse and he'd give me something to buy me off. He'd have to.'

Rebecca listened in silence. It was *her* money and *her* life that Tom had wasted, as well as his own. She was entitled to be angry, but all she said was, 'The money. Does he have it?'

'Titch? Hell, no. Course not. But he can get it. That's the way he works.'

'How much did you give him?'

'Give him? Nothing. I invested it, of course.' Tom laughed uncomfortably. His pained feelings on the subject were still close to the surface, and this was his second confession within a minute. 'In cash and in lieu of wages, I guess the old bastard took around four thousand dollars.'

'Oh, Tom!'

Tom had always been vague about his earnings, and Rebecca had never quite guessed exactly how much cash had been frittered away over the years. She was shocked, but it no longer mattered now that she had her husband back.

Tom was sunk in thought. The water on Rebecca's back had dried off, but her hair still fell back from her forehead in a smooth unbroken sheet just as it had done when she rose from the butt. Tom reached for a quid of tobacco and began to chew on it, a habit he tried to keep confined to the rig but without complete success. His dark-veined mahogany spit began to speckle the ground.

'If you can't do it, dearest, then you can't. Whatever happens, I don't want to start fighting again.'

'No . . . no.'

Tom spat again, crushed the tobacco into a pellet between his teeth and laid it aside. He couldn't get Alan and Alanto out of his thoughts. If Alan had failed in Persia, how much easier things would have been! He took a deep breath. 'I'll do it,' he said. 'If I can't manage it on my account, then I'll manage it for Mitchell and you.'

'You're sure? You could think it over.'

'No. Next week's not a bad one to take off. The rig's been listing a tad and we've got to quit drilling for a week while the construction crew levels it out again.'

That was true, but it wasn't the reason. Tom felt a burst of resolve that shoved away the ghosts. It was better to act now while he was in the grip of his decision than to wait and let it fester. Rebecca suddenly shivered violently in the water. She'd been in too long and the evening had grown cool. She stood up, beautifully naked, and climbed into an old piece of curtain they used as a towel.

'I love you,' she said.

'Me too. I love you too.'

Her deep dark eyes roved over him as they so often had before. 'You're a brave man. It's not an easy thing to do.'

The wind blew and she shivered again. She felt a sudden chill. They were happy here. Things were good. Was it craziness on her part, sending Tom back to the heart of his addiction? Right or wrong, she was playing with fire.

108

Alan sat at the foot of the bed. Lottie sat up against a mountain of pillows. Her white nightgown hung half open. It was 12 March 1930. Their third child, Polly, born four months earlier, had fallen asleep during feeding, her tiny mouth still closed over her mother's nipple. Lottie softly drew the baby away and closed her gown. She smiled.

'You're not tired?' asked Alan.

'It's three in the morning, my love. Of course I am.'

Alan caught hold of Lottie's foot beneath the bedclothes and massaged it. His wife was the only woman he knew – or rather, the only rich woman – who took care of her newborns herself, going to the extraordinary lengths of breast-feeding them, even at night. Even now, on their third baby, Alan wasn't sure if he admired Lottie for it, or would rather she stopped.

'You must take care of yourself too,' he said.

'That's precisely what I am doing.'

'We could have someone just for the nights, if you wanted.'

'Yes. If I wanted, I could.'

Alan shook his head and smiled. He'd be as likely to strike oil in Piccadilly as he was to change his wife's mind. He didn't know why he bothered.

'You weren't sleeping either,' she commented.

'I was sleeping lightly and heard you wake. That's all.'

'Are you still dreaming?'

He glanced at her sharply. It was the first time for some while she'd mentioned his nightly dreams.

'Yes,' he said. 'Or rather no. Yes and no.'

'How clear. I'm so pleased I asked.'

Alan laughed. 'It's odd. I was trying to explain it to Westerfeld earlier. The dreams themselves haven't changed in the slightest. I dream every night. Always about Tom. Always about the war. Always about Tom sinking down in a storm of fire.'

'Oh, darling!'

Lottie's voice was full of concern, but Alan shook his head. 'But you see the odd thing is this. The dreams *have* changed. I used to wake up in nightmare. Now I don't. It's not exactly that my feelings have changed, it's more that they've completely disappeared. I feel as though I'm watching a news-reel whose basic truthfulness I don't actually believe for a minute.'

Lottie stroked her baby's tiny head. Little Polly was beginning to snore, puffing milky bubbles from the corner of her mouth.

'What does Westerfeld say?' she said, keeping her voice low and gentle for Polly's sake.

'He says my unconscious can't accept that Tom has died. He wants me to . . . to contemplate the possibility that Tom is still alive.'

'Good heavens! You really think he might be?'

Alan shook his head. 'No. Of course not. For months now, Westerfeld has been on at me about this and I still can't help thinking that I'm in the right. Quite apart from anything else, if Tom were alive he'd have come and found me by now. The war's been over long enough, after all.'

'Yes.' Lottie allowed the conversation to lapse for a moment, before apparently changing the subject. 'I didn't tell you, my love. We're very lucky to have had Polly with us at all.'

'Well, of course we are . . . Why? What? What are you saying?'

'When Polly decided to come out, she managed to get all knotted up in the umbilical cord. It had wrapped itself round her neck. All the effort I was making to get the little minx out into the world was just knotting the cord tighter round her throat.'

'Good Lord! I had no idea! I . . .'

Alan had never once been present when his wife had given birth. He'd never asked and never been told about the gory feminine details.

'That's perfectly all right. I had a doctor and a midwife who knew exactly what they were doing.'

'Thank heavens!'

'Yes. And it made me think. It made me homesick for the time when I was a nurse.'

Alan swallowed. He half-guessed what Lottie was driving at and he wasn't sure he liked the idea. 'You can't want to . . . I mean, you don't surely . . .'

'No. I do.'

Alan gulped again. 'In what capacity?'

'Not babies, if that's what you mean,' said Lottie. 'Part of the reason I liked nursing was that I liked the soldiers I met. I felt for them then. I feel for them now. For instance, that chap you told me about – what was his name? Shorty somebody or other? The one you sorted out with some new legs?'

'Hardwick. Edward Hardwick. The legs are jolly good, apparently, only they make a kind of whizzing noise as he walks.' Alan grinned. Edward Hardwick was now one of Alanto's newest clerks. 'They call him Clunky now.'

Lottie grinned back, before getting serious again. 'There are thousands like him. All over London. All across England. Their country neglects them. The poor devils can't afford to pay for help. Well! We aren't poor and I hope we're not neglectful.'

Alan shook his head. 'No, I hope not.'

'Daddy's given me lots of money. Money I hardly need. I

should like to set up a hospital in the East End. For ex-servicemen and their families. We'd offer the best possible help, free of charge.'

Alan was quiet a moment.

He loved Lottie and loved his domestic life with her. If she ran around setting up a hospital, their life would change. He was busy already. She'd become equally busy. Their peaceful family life would never be the same.

'And your job would be . . . ?'

'Getting the place established.'

'And then?'

'I know the difference between a good nursing staff and a bad one. I know what works. I'd be in charge of the nursing side. If every now and then, I wanted to put on an apron and go onto the wards, then I expect I'd do just that.'

Alan smiled unhappily. 'I expect you would.'

'And you're wrong, you know.'

'Wrong?'

'You said the war's been over long enough. And it hasn't. You still suffer it in your dreams. There are thousands of Stumpy Hardwicks longing to become Clunky Hardwicks. There are other men who can't breathe properly. Or who wake up every night screaming. Or who are blind or deaf or still in pain from a wound that's never properly been attended to. For that matter, the war's not over for the people of Germany, because we still find it necessary to punish them savagely for a crime they themselves had no say in.'

Alan sighed. Little Polly let out a milky burp with a sigh of happiness and slipped further down onto her mother's belly. One tiny hand stayed flat between Lottie's ribs, as though to keep her from moving. Alan reached out and smoothed the hair away from Lottie's face.

'I expect you're right,' he said, concealing his continuing unhappiness at his wife's proposal.

She smiled. 'And Westerfeld is right,' she said. 'You do think Tom's alive. You've never let go.'

'My love, I –'

'Say it.'

'You're as bad as Westerfeld.'

'I jolly well hope I'm worse. Say it.'

'Say what?'

'That Tom's alive.'

'But if I know perfectly well that he isn't, why –' He would have continued objecting but he could see from Lottie's face that there wouldn't be much point. So he said it. 'Tom's alive.' He felt like a fool for saying so.

'Not like that. Properly. As though you mean it.'

'Tom's alive.'

'Again.'

'Tom's alive. He's alive. Tom's living, not dead. Tom, my brother, my –'

But he couldn't go on. Like a ten-thousand-barrel gusher, his emotions blasted to the surface, smashing obstructions to smithereens. Alan Montague, Managing Director of Alanto Oil, holder of the Military Cross, father of three, sat on the edge of his wife's bed and wept like a baby.

Lottie waited until the storm of weeping had passed, before saying gently, 'Tell me, my love, no matter how unreasonable it sounds: what is it you want?'

'I want to find him,' said Alan.

'Of course you do. So do it.'

109

Harrelson was behind the shack, kicking around in the long grass.

'That's no way to search for oil, Titch. You gotta drill for it.'

'Hey, bud! Welcome home! You sure took off sudden.'

Tom shrugged. Harrelson kicked around until he swung his foot into a tangle of devil-grass, when he began hopping around and swearing as he extracted the barbed little seed heads from his leg. 'Jeez, goddamn the . . . Listen, didn't we have a fishing tool here sometime?'

'Shed over there. Behind the lumber,' said Tom, pointing.

'Shit, you might have told me. Been kicking around here half an hour.'

Harrelson went to the shed and came out with a rusted-up fishing tool, the sort you had to use to fish a broken pipe from a well.

'Drilling's going well then?' said Tom smiling. With a decent rig like the one he worked on at Texaco, he didn't experience boiler breakdowns, hole cave-ins, pipe twist-offs, drill ruptures. At Texaco, he'd never even seen a fishing tool.

'The fuck it is.' Harrelson spat. 'Since you blew out of here, the whole damn thing's been one lousy break after another.' Tom noted Harrelson's anger with interest. Perhaps he'd been wrong about Harrelson. He was a hustler and a crook, of course. There was no doubt about that. But perhaps there was a little piece of him that also cared about finding oil. Tom liked that.

'I want my money back, Titch.'

'*What?*'

'You heard.'

'Ain't no damn money coming anybody's way. Not mine, pal, and definitely not yours.'

Harrelson was a biggish man, but soft and paunchy. Tom was not as heavy, but his muscles were trained as hard as whipcord on the rigs. Tom put his hand against Harrelson's chest and pushed him without roughness but with plenty of force up against the corner post of the little shed.

'Titch, you stole my money, like you stole everybody else's. Some of it you put in the well. Most of it you put in your pocket. I want the part that wound up in your pocket.'

'Jesus Christ, Tom, Jesus Christ.' Harrelson put his hands to Tom's arm, pushing it back, and Tom, after resisting a moment, dropped his grip. 'You used to be a believer, pal. You was one of the guys I could rely on.'

'You find me the money or I'll go to the law. They're poor folk around here, the ones you take from. You took from me long enough. And maybe it's time you stopped taking anything at all.'

'Hell . . . Jesus . . . You sure got religion since you hoofed it outa here.' Harrelson rubbed his chest, as though Tom had hurt it, which he certainly hadn't. 'Never knowed you to be a crabapple annie before.'

'The money, Titch, the money.'

'How much d'you want?'

'What you stole.'

'I got expenses, pal. Costs you wouldn't know about.'

'French frills for Mrs Holling?'

'Hey. I do what I can.'

'Get me the money, Titch.'

428

'Yeah, yeah, OK. I got the message.'

'And no forgetting it.'

'OK.'

Tom nodded and stepped away so that he was no longer in Harrelson's face. The tension dropped. And the moment that had privately terrified Tom had turned out to be easy. Now that he was here, he saw how stupid the whole thing was. He had no urge to stick with Harrelson, no temptation to gamble one last time . . . He was proud of himself, eager to get back to his beloved wife and son.

'OK, Titch.'

'Sheez.'

Tom pulled some tobacco from his pocket and offered some to Harrelson, who took it gratefully. They both chewed in silence for a moment.

'Listen, bud, no shit, I'll get you some money.'

Tom nodded.

'But I got a bunch of no-hopers working the well for me now. We're on Number Three. Two was a bust. And Three – shit, you know how we decided where to site this one? We was moving the rig when the sill collapsed and the rig just dropped down in the dirt. We couldn't move it no more. The timber yard wouldn't stand us ten bucks for a new sill, so there we were. Nellie Holling Number Three.'

Tom laughed. That didn't happen on fields managed by Texaco.

'While you're here, bud, do me a favour and lift that end of pipe out. The one which got busted yesterday. The cowpokes I got now could fish a hundred years and not fetch it up.'

'No problem.'

'And take a core. The idea was we would take a core. We're at three thousand two hundred feet, pretty near.'

'I need to be back with my folks in seven days' time. You're going to get me the money in six days. Between now and then, I'll do what I can.'

'We should be down on the Woodbine now. Oil sands.'

'Yeah, yeah.'

'Hell, if we don't hit nothing, then I'm out of the game. Nobody can say I didn't try.'

There was something hopeless in Harrelson's look, something dejected. It wasn't Tom's demand for money, it was the failure to find oil. For almost the first time in their mutual acquaintance, Harrelson moved up in Tom's esteem.

110

The military records bureau was on the fourth floor. It was tiny, just big enough for a thin metal desk and a pair of thin metal chairs, marked 'WAR OFFICE', as though someone might want to steal them. A lieutenant colonel stood smoking in the window, his back turned.

Alan knocked at the open door.

'Excuse me, I'm looking for –'

The officer turned. The first thing Alan noticed was that the man had only one arm, the left empty sleeve pinned loosely to the tunic. The second thing Alan noticed was the face: a face he knew well, almost the first face he'd seen on the front line in France. A dark moustache, a lop-sided smile, the muscular slope of the shoulders.

'My God, Fletcher!'

'Montague!'

Alan felt shock, then surprise, then delight. Similar emotions crossed the other man's face. Fletcher bounded across the room, throwing the cigarette away from him as he did so. 'Bloody nice to see you again. Very damn bloody nice surprise.'

The two men shook hands with real warmth. Fletcher looked older than before – older and without the same dangerous muscularity that he'd once enjoyed. But his face was still young and his grip still powerful.

'Must be a bit of a bloody shock to see my ugly mug, what? Probably thought you'd escaped the sight of it?'

'Not at all.' Alan smiled. His right hand rose to a loose civilian salute. 'It's the very best sort of surprise.' He almost literally had to bite his tongue to keep himself from adding the once-obligatory 'sir'. 'You're well, I take it? You look . . .'

'I look like a bloody cripple, Montague. You probably think you ought to fling tuppence in my hat or buy a box of matches off me. But at least I'm not dead, eh? That's the main thing. You look all right. Limbs all present and correct.'

'Yes. They patched me up.'

'Talking of patching, it's not your wife, is it, who's . . . ?'

'That's right. The hospital for the war wounded in the East End. She's just bought the premises. Now it's all down to the builders to get the place fitted out. There's a colossal need for such places, you know.'

'Yes. I do know. As a matter of fact . . .' Fletcher's face reddened a little with embarrassment, 'I heard about the project. Sent along a little donation – very little, of course – nothing compared to what – anyhow – thought it best – probably shouldn't have said – bloody fool.'

'Not at all. You're very kind.'

'Yes, quite, quite.' Fletcher grunted away his embarrassment and abruptly changed the subject. 'How's that other fellow? Friend of yours. Creeley. Worst dressed subaltern in the King's Army. Is he . . . or was he . . . ?' Fletcher petered out, trying to remember if Creeley had fallen in the general slaughter.

Alan smiled thinly. 'That's why I'm here, actually. Creeley was sent to storm some guns. Machine-gun posts. Properly fortified.'

'God, yes! The brig's idea, wasn't it? Thought the bloody war was God's way to win him promotion. He got it too. Promotion one day. Heart attack the next. Fell face first into his plateful of beef. So I heard, anyway. Probably balls. Anyway, you were saying?'

'Missing, presumed dead,' said Alan softly.

'Presumed dead . . . I'm sorry. He was a damned good soldier, Creeley. One of the very best. A bloody joke on the parade ground, but in the field . . . You too. Damned good. I was lucky.' Fletcher's hand strayed to the stump of his left shoulder and gripped it hard.

'Thank you. Tom would have been pleased.'

Fletcher nodded and moved his hand. 'Yes, I was lucky.'

'The thing is, I'm not sure Creeley was killed.'

'Hmm? Really? I remember those posts. Say what you like about the Boche, they knew how to use a gun.'

'True. Only one of the men that went with Creeley did survive. He was badly wounded, but alive. I think it's possible that Creeley survived too. Survived but taken prisoner.'

'A prisoner of war, eh? That's why you're here? To find out?' Fletcher waved his single arm round the tiny room and the corridor outside. 'War Office Records, eh?'

Alan nodded.

Fletcher's expression grew more serious. 'Prisoners of war. *Yes*. Well, look, strictly speaking you've come to the right place, only . . .'

'Only?'

'Well, we've got two sorts of lists here. There are reports from the front at the time – "Lieutenant Creeley, jolly good sort, missing, presumed dead," that sort of thing. Trouble is, the reports were pretty bloody stupid then and they haven't got less stupid with age. Like the rest of us. Plenty of the chaps we presumed dead turned out to be captured. Plenty of those we thought were captured turned out dead. Waste of bloody time.'

'I understand.'

'And then again there are the fellows we took back from Fritz following the Armistice. Our lists were jolly well meant to be complete. I mean, we needed to know who we had and who we'd lost. Bloody desk-soldiers in the War Office wanted to know because of pensions and that kind of thing, not to mention wanting to know which of our chaps had survived.'

'Survived?'

'Yes . . . I suppose you know what the camps were like, do you? They were no bloody holiday camps, that's for sure.'

'I'd heard something.'

'Well, not much perhaps. Our lords and masters didn't want to whip up hatred of the Boche, just as we were supposed to be making peace with him. Can't say I agreed. The only thing worse than a Hun is a bloody Frenchy. Though come to think of it, the only thing worse than a bloody Frenchy is a . . .'

Something in Alan's expression caused Fletcher to let his analysis of international relations die away. Fletcher shrugged. The shoulder that had lost the arm was completely stiff. His shrug was lop-sided, half easy, half destroyed. The whole of England was like that now.

'Any case,' he continued, 'whenever we entered a camp, we took names, ranks and numbers. So did the Frogs, naturally. But you see, in some cases, the camps had pretty much fallen apart by the time we got there. Not much point in keeping your camps full of prisoners if you've just lost the bloody war. Not much point in worrying about records either, come to that.'

'So some prisoners just walked away?'

'They'd have been damned hungry, you see. Bloody Boche wouldn't feed 'em properly – couldn't feed themselves properly by the end, mind you – so if I'd been in prison, I'd probably have buggered off myself. Holland. Switzerland. France. Whichever was closest.'

'When you say hungry . . . ?' Alan's voice wasn't quite steady. He was thinking of Tom. Tom hungry. Tom ravenous.

Fletcher knotted his jaw, trying to tone down his language for Alan's ears. When he spoke, his voice was an odd mixture of gruff and gentle. 'Not just hungry, starving. Some of our chaps came back weighing seven stone, six stone, bellies sticking out all full of air and wind . . . We lost maybe one in eight of the men taken prisoner, mostly from lack of food.'

'One in *eight*!'

'And of course, you see, Creeley would have been "missing, presumed dead".'

'I'm not sure I follow.'

'Food parcels. The Red Cross didn't feed dead men. Not their job. Sorry.'

'I see. I had no idea.' Alan's voice was a whisper.

'And . . .'

'And?'

Fletcher's face looked ever grimmer. 'Our poor bloody boys, you, me, Creeley, everybody, we were shot to pieces on the Somme. Nineteen sixteen. August. That meant Creeley would have needed to survive two years. More. More than two years. More than two years on not enough food to feed a baby. I'm most awfully bloody sorry.'

And that was that. They continued to sit and talk. They remembered past comrades, past ordeals, past horrors. They smoked their way through Fletcher's cigarettes and turned the air blue with smoke. They promised to meet up again and perhaps they would.

But Tom.

No amount of reminiscing could change the truth about Tom. He had almost certainly died under the guns. If he hadn't, he'd have been taken prisoner and left to starve. The chances of his having survived seemed a million to one against.

111

Harrelson wasn't kidding when he talked about cowpokes. Big raw-boned men with wide sleepy faces. They worked the drill hard but steadily, never shifting one second from their pace. When they took a bite to eat, they talked about cattle and crops and farm prices and banks and repossessions.

Tom fished the broken bit first go. The bit had sheared off almost in half, the break clean and sharp at the edges. The cutting edge was so blunt that a baby could sleep on it. Tom looked at the bit and wondered what triumph of cowpokery had managed to stick a drill that bad down a well this dicey.

He set up the corer, and sent the long, poorly conditioned tubes down into the earth. Half a mile deep, thirty-foot section by thirty-foot section. The lifting tackle on the rig was close to exhaustion and there were many stages in the process where heavy parts had to be lifted entirely by hand. The cowpoke-riggers swung their thirty-foot sections of pipe without complaint, like God had written rules against the use of machinery.

Harrelson came by the rig three times to invite Tom round to dinner. The first couple of times Tom refused. He didn't want to watch Harrelson and Mrs Holling pawing each other under the table. He didn't like the widow's mock-genteel chatter about whatever rubbish she was reading in the movie magazines when, outside her house, the whole of East Texas lay under a cloud of depression, which had been bad enough through the twenties, when farm prices had fallen through the floor, and had only got worse since the stockmarket had crashed and the economy was junking itself. Most of all, he didn't want to sit through an evening of Harrelson's attempts to buck him up and get him back on board with the project, money and labour and everything.

But the third time Harrelson came by, Tom couldn't refuse. Harrelson was lonely. The part of him that was an oilman – not a crook, not a snake-oil merchant, not a seducer of older women – the oilman part of him was lonely. His wells had failed. He wanted comfort.

So Tom said yes.

The dinner was awful. Mrs Holling had been crying before Tom arrived. The food was badly cooked. Conversation sputtered like a gas flare on a dying well. The next day, Tom would take his core. Harrelson had promised him fifteen hundred bucks, and Tom would head off home. They'd never see each other again.

This was the end of the end.

112

The tune hung on the air, sentimental and melancholic, instantly familiar yet impossible to place. Alan paused, listened, then remembered. It was a melody he'd last heard on an icy February night, ankle-deep in freezing mud, shell-fire on the horizon, and the soft German voices floating over on the breeze.

He smiled – or rather half-smiled, half-grimaced – before making as if to move on. The deputy ambassador to Germany, Aude Hartwell, looked sharply across at his companion.

'Sounds familiar?'

Alan nodded. 'February nineteen sixteen, I last heard the song.'

'Under less pleasant circumstances, I expect.'

'I should say so.'

It was an understatement. The Berliner Tiergarten in April 1930 was as far as possible from that cold February night. The band in the bandstand were dressed in vivid scarlet jackets, sitting where everyone could see them. There was no more hiding from an unseen enemy. No more waiting to see if you could kill them before they killed you.

Hartwell continued to read Alan's face. 'Your first time here?'

Alan nodded.

'Odd, isn't it? Everyone thinks so. We spend four years teaching our people to hate the Boche, then we actually come here and find they're perfectly agreeable. I'd far rather be here than Paris, to tell you the truth.'

As they crossed the park they chatted about tennis and cricket and the summer racing season in England; and Hartwell wanted to hear news of Sir Adam, an old friend of his, as well as of Pamela and Guy.

'How is Guy? Ever the gallant soldier, I expect?'

Alan paused.

He'd seen Guy shortly before leaving London for Germany. It had been after dinner one night and Guy had been drunk – but even so, the scene had made an unpleasant impression. Guy had wanted to play cards with Alan for money. Alan had refused. Guy had been bitter about it. It appeared that he'd made some ugly losses in the American stockmarket crash and he seemed quite preoccupied with the subject.

'Listen, Guy,' Alan had said, 'if you and Dorothy are feeling short, you should ask. You know perfectly well that Lottie and I have money to spare.'

Guy had refused angrily, as though Alan had been attempting to pity him. When Alan had asked how he and Dorothy were finding married life, Guy had answered, 'Not too inconvenient, considering.' It had been a loathsome evening and Alan shuddered at the thought of another.

He answered Hartwell's question briefly, then changed the subject. The diplomat could take the hint. He said, 'Look, Montague, you haven't come all the way to Berlin to chat. How can I be of service?'

Alan cleared his throat. 'You remember Tom Creeley, of course? The boy who was –'

'Lord, yes, I remember Tommy. I was down in Whitcombe House, just after the funeral of Queen Victoria, spring, oh-one, it must have been. Tommy – he couldn't have been a day over ten – what, seven, you say? – was fascinated by my pipe. Found a ruse to send me off down the hall, and when

439

I came back the little rascal had my pipe in his hand, coughing himself black and blue.'

Alan smiled. It had been a dare between them which Tom had won – or would have done if he'd been able to puff without choking. 'Yes, exactly. You know he was lost in the war, I take it?'

'Yes, of course. What a dreadful loss! Especially for you, perhaps, though I know your father and mother were fearfully cut up as well. Couldn't have been more grief-stricken if it had been you.'

'No . . . Look, this is going to sound damned stupid and it quite probably is. But Tom's body was never found. I think it quite possible that he was captured, not killed.'

'I see. Of course, if he never showed up afterwards, then it probably amounted to the same thing, poor devil.'

'Yes. But still I'd like to know.'

'Yes, naturally.'

There was a pause.

'I'd say he was like a brother,' said Alan after a moment, 'only that doesn't really say it at all. He was more than a brother. We called ourselves twins because we were born the same day, only it went deeper than that. We were . . .' He shrugged. Even now, after so many years, he had no words for the depth of his connection to Tom. 'I don't know, all I do know is that I won't be able to rest easy until I know what became of him.'

'I understand.'

'Thank you.'

There was a short pause, as Hartwell allowed Alan to overcome his feelings. Then: 'You've tried the War Office, I take it?'

'Yes. And the Red Cross. I think I've done everything I can from England.'

'So you'd like me to see what I can dig out here. Of course, I'd be happy to . . .' Hartwell trailed off with an air of concern.

440

'Will it be difficult?'

'Perhaps, no, I don't know. I'll have to look into it. I'll say this for the Germans, they do love a bureaucracy.'

'It's just you seemed a little anxious.'

'Yes . . .'

They had reached their restaurant and they ordered before returning to the conversation. Here on the Ku'damm, the country's difficulties were more evident than they had been in the park. There were groups of unemployed men loafing on street corners. Election posters hung on walls and trees, many of them already ripped up or defaced. There was something brittle in the atmosphere, something hostile. Alan felt almost as though Tom was still there, still in Germany, caught up in the dangerous currents that eddied around.

Hartwell spoke of the elections. The National Socialists were set to make heavy gains, as were the Communists.

'The reds are something of a known quantity, at least, but it's these movements of the right which are causing us to tear our hair out in the embassy.'

'They're dangerous?'

Hartwell sighed. 'They don't hold power, not at the moment, and their Herr Hitler is a comical little fellow, really, like a bad cabaret turn . . . But it's a nasty situation. You don't meet a single German out here – not one – who thinks that Germany's eastern frontier was fairly determined at Versailles. You don't meet a single German who's happy about paying reparations, when the country has nearly five million men unemployed. You don't meet a single German who thinks it's right that a great nation at the heart of Europe should be forbidden to arm itself. I don't know that *I* think it's fair, as a matter of fact, not that I'm allowed to say so . . . That's why I don't know how far I'll get finding out about Tom Creeley in prison camp. There's a lot of hatred in this country – some of it focused, some of it just swirling in the air. Questions about British prisoners of war may fall on sympathetic ears or they may not . . . There, look there.'

Alan looked. Two young men in brown shirts with red and black armbands were walking along the pavement just outside the café window. They were chatting and smoking. A little further ahead there was a middle-aged lady struggling with some awkwardly packaged shopping. She was dark-haired, dark-skinned, probably Jewish. Hartwell's face was grave and his attention fixed rigidly on the two young men.

He was right to worry.

By the time the two men were level with the woman, she had more or less got her shopping under control. One of the young men deliberately jogged the lady's arm, spilling her packages. The other man kicked the packages into the gutter with his toe. Alan leaped up with a flash of anger, but Hartwell's hand restrained him from doing anything further. The two young men jostled the woman off the road and went on their way. Alan thought, but wasn't sure, that one of the men spat on her as he left.

113

The cowpokes hauled on the tackle like they planned to do it all day every day for the rest of their lives. Their rhythm hypnotised Tom. Just as they did, he raised pipes without urgency, stacking them in ninety-foot sections inside the derrick, counting them off as though life was just a question of pipes.

Harrelson shambled about on the ground below, lonely and unhappy. He'd started the morning, saying, 'Any smells up there, boys? You getting any smells? I'm pretty sure I got something down here just now.'

But there had been no smells, no excitement, no suck of oil, just the steady rising of pipes. Harrelson had a suitcase in the back of his Ford. Tom guessed that was the last of his relationship with Mrs Holling, and now it was back to the wife and kids abandoned back in Dallas. Around lunchtime, Harrelson produced a parcel wrapped in a white linen cloth.

'You boys hungry? Mrs Holling made me something to eat.' He hefted the parcel in his hand. It was heavy. 'I reckon I'm gonna need a little help here.'

Tom and the cowpokes clattered down from the rig. Harrelson unwrapped the parcel. It was a huge ham and chicken pie, eighteen inches in diameter and five or six thick. 'Jesus Christ,' said Harrelson mildly. He cut into it. The pie crust was far too thick. Below the evenly browned surface, it was virtually dough. The meat inside was completely raw, and the juices ran pink and bloody from the cut made by the knife. Harrelson finished cutting the slice, but laid it on top of the crust, like something from a funeral.

'I don't reckon that pie'll be too good to eat,' said one of the cowpokes, observantly. 'It needs more cooking, I'd say.'

Harrelson took the pie to the edge of the clearing and dropped it. It thumped heavily down. A trail of ants diverted course and began to run up the cut side of the pie and over its surface. Meantime, lunch was lunch and the riggers unwrapped their lunches, sharing with Harrelson. They ate in silence.

Tom watched in silent astonishment.

The rig stood idle.

At midday, with only a little more than a thousand foot of pipe to lift before the core came up, the rig stood idle. Tom couldn't believe it. He'd never seen a rig idle, not at midday, not unless there was a problem somewhere with the apparatus. And they were taking a *core* – and a core close to the level of the hypothetical oil sands. It was unbelievable, just unbelievable.

Nobody spoke.

After lunch, it was back to the pipes. The boiler had lost pressure during the break and it took twenty minutes of stoking to get a head of steam back. Then one by one the pipes rose. Big fat flies buzzed on the air. The warmth made Tom sleepy. He counted the pipes up, to know how close they were getting to the core.

Nine hundred and ninety feet. Eight ten. Six hundred. Three ninety.

Harrelson was sitting down with his back against the side of the Ford. He was pretending to watch the core come up, but he'd fallen asleep. His head had tipped sideways and his hat had caught on the door handle. The noise of the rig drowned out other sounds, but from Harrelson's juddering chest, Tom guessed that the snoring was pretty bad. At least Mrs Holling could look forward to quiet nights.

Two hundred and ten feet now. Just seven lengths of pipe underground.

Tom could do his thirty times table in his head, upside down, blind drunk, in the dark. It sometimes seemed he'd been rigging all his life. He enjoyed the work. In a year or two, he was pretty sure he'd make it to head driller at Texaco. He knew he was good enough, it was just a question of seniority. He'd get a raise too. He'd buy Rebecca something good, something nice.

Thirty feet.

Tom had got to thirty feet of pipe without excitement. It was just unbelievable. He nudged one of the cowpokes.

'Go give Titch a kick, would you? It's his damn core. He ought to see it.'

The cowpoke clambered down the steel ladder. Tom smiled to himself and shook his head. He'd spoken to the stupidest of the cowpokes, the one who'd been so swift to identify the problem with the pie. Harrelson would be lucky not to get a boot in the ribs.

The last pipe rose.

Sure enough, Harrelson got a kick, though not a hard one. He woke up blinking and for a few seconds snatched around on the dirt searching for his hat. He found it on the car door.

The core came up.

The coring-barrel is designed so that flaps close as the tube rises, thus protecting the soil sample from contamination by soil from higher levels. The flaps were jammed and Tom gave them a kick. He was still half looking down at Harrelson, who was adjusting his hat and putting on his dignity like it was a suit.

Tom looked down at the core. It was sand, greyish and coarse, compacted by the weight of rock above it to something that you could crumble with a thumb, but only just. It was sand of the sort that Tom had seen a hundred times, on a hundred rigs, in a hundred places.

Except that this time, the sand was blotched with thick black gobbets of something that looked like caked blood.

The blotches weren't blood, but oil.

114

The factory was derelict, high-ceilinged and spacious. Tall windows blinked out on to the glittering Thames. A scrap of an old notice gummed to the wall proclaimed the building's former use: 'Jones & Palmer Bearings Co. Ltd'. Alan glanced at the notice – then stared. He tore the peeling old paper from the wall and stuffed it in his pocket. For twenty minutes or so, he mooched around, gazing at the traffic on the river, feeling disconsolate at his wife's new occupation, but irritated at himself for minding. When eventually Lottie was done with her architect, he walked over to her, brandishing the paper.

'Hello, darling!' she said, with a kiss. 'Sorry to be so long. My architect is a sweet man, but he can be a dreadful ninny. Not that I care. Our hospital is going to be simply wonderful.'

'Look,' said Alan, after greeting her. 'Jones & Palmer Bearings. That's what this factory used to make.'

'Bearings? Little steel balls? I can't say I –'

'During the war,' said Alan. 'They used to fill certain types of shell with little steel balls. The idea was that the balls would cut the enemy barbed wire. They didn't, of course, but there were plenty of places where the ground was fairly solid with the things.'

'I'm still not sure I . . .'

'Well, it rather closes the circle, doesn't it? From shell blasts

447

to shell victims. I should think the building's jolly glad to be turned into a hospital.'

Lottie nodded. 'I hope so.' She was dressed in a long brown coat and strong brown walking shoes, suitable for the dilapidated floor. Only her absurd little grey feathered hat dented her business-like appearance. Her face looked suddenly grave. 'You don't mind, do you? All this, I mean?' Her hand swept around the soon-to-be-converted shell.

'No, my love. I'm pleased to see you so enthused.'

'Oh!' Lottie sounded disappointed. 'So you *do* mind?'

'I didn't say that. I said –'

'You nincompoop, I know what you said. Any old fish-wife could have heard what you said. It's my job to know what you mean.'

'Well, I do mind, I suppose. But only a bit.'

'Hmm! I suppose that means quite a lot, really. But I'll bring you round.'

'If anybody could, you will.'

'You said you had news? Was it . . . ?'

Alan opened his wallet and held out a pink telegram slip. The sender was Aude Hartwell in Berlin. The text of the message read: 'FOUND HIM EXCLAMATION STOP THOMAS CREELEY HETTERSCHEIDT PRISON CAMP ADMITTANCE SEPT SIXTEEN STOP FULL DETAILS SOONEST BY MAIL STOP'.

It took Lottie a second or two to read and understand the message, then her face lit up in delight. Her smile broadened out, the tip of her nose bent down, the little white scar over her eyebrow tightened as it was pulled back. Alan knew his wife's face so well. He didn't want her to be this busy practical-minded woman. He wanted her to remain simply his wife and the mother of his children. He wanted to take her home now, to lie in each other's arms and kiss, as they had done in Hampshire during the war, as they had done every day since Alan's proposal of marriage.

Alan shook himself from his trance. Lottie was speaking,

asking him questions, eager to know what he was doing next.

'I've spoken with Hartwell by phone,' said Alan. 'It appears Tom *was* taken prisoner that day on the Somme. The German prison records indicated that Tom was wounded in the leg, but he obviously recovered reasonably well, since he was well enough to make an escape attempt the following year.'

'Oh! How like him!'

Lottie half-laughed and Alan did the same. 'Yes. That was Tom all right. But, you see, the odd thing is this. When the Allies took over the camp, Tom wasn't there. There was no record of him dying. The camp records continued to have him on their register, but he was gone. Not there. Vanished.'

'Oh my darling! It's just like your dreams all over again.'

'Isn't it? He just sort of disappears into the gloom.'

'So what will you do? Golly! I don't suppose you've thought . . . ?'

And Alan laughed again. He was only able to be so self-possessed with Lottie now because he'd already experienced his own storms of emotion upon reading the telegram and speaking with Hartwell. He'd been amazed – delighted – shocked – disappointed – upset – ecstatic – almost everything, in fact. But no matter how great had been the shock, his brain had been working pretty much perfectly.

'So what will you do?' asked Lottie again.

'What *will* I do? Nothing. Nothing at all.'

'Nothing? But –'

Alan reached out and and gently squashed Lottie's nose with his forefinger.

'Don't be a clot,' he said. 'It's not what I will do that counts. It's what I've already done.'

115

Big fat flies buzzed on the air. The cowpoke riggers looked down at the core like they'd looked down at the pie. The silence seemed to go on for ever. Down on the ground, Harrelson was standing like a man frozen.

'Is that oil?' asked one of the riggers.

And then Tom did the single cleverest thing of his entire life. It was the sort of thing you'd think of days afterwards but never actually think of doing on the spot. Except that Tom did. Straight away. Without giving away anything in his face or the way he spoke. Without even pausing, he just came out with it.

'Screw it!' he yelled, kicking the core hard in apparent frustration. 'Screw this goddamn stinking stupid flea-bitten lousy pisshole of a well.'

'There a problem?' The stupidest cowpoke spoke mildly.

'Goddamn lubricant's leaked. Gotta do it again. Stupid goddamn son-of-a-bitch.' He kicked the core barrel again.

'We gotta take another core?'

'Yeah.'

The cowpokes looked at the tired apparatus. 'We gonna start right now?' They would honestly have been willing to empty the core barrel, re-arm it for another trip down the well, and start hauling pipes all over again until the fall of night.

'No. Screw it. Tomorrow. If I spend another hour on this rig I'm going to puke.'

One of the cowpokes bent down. He dug his thumb into the sand, exposing oil deep down inside. 'You sure this ain't oil?'

'I'm damn sure it *is* oil,' said Tom. 'Premium grade Texan oil. It's been all the way through a Gulf Oil refinery and come out the other side in a shiny red can marked "For Lubricant Use Only".'

'It spilled, huh?'

'No, it just got homesick for underground. Go on, beat it. Scram. I'll close down.'

The cowpokes melted away. One of them went over to the huge pie still standing like a millstone on the ground. He nudged it with his toe and looked at it sadly, before heading home like the others.

Harrelson came over to Tom.

'Lubricant spilled, huh?'

'That's right.'

'Bad?'

'Uh-huh.'

Harrelson sighed deeply and sat down in the shade of the rig. He wiped his face with a white handkerchief.

'Shame that.'

'Yeah.'

''Cept that a core barrel don't use no lubricant.'

'Nope.'

'Nothing 'cept mud.'

'Nope.'

Tom brought the core down for Harrelson to see. Both men hefted it in their hands. They probed it with their fingernails. They smelled it. They crumbled it between their palms. What was there to say? It was oil.

When the car turned up, Rebecca was working in the little cottage garden behind the house, while Mitchell was scooping water from the butt, in an effort to teach worms to drink. The car – a battered old Tin Lizzie, filthy with dust – shot up to the front of the house and stopped with an angry bark from the engine. Whoever had been driving it, raced up the garden path and in through the front door.

'Mitch, you wait here a moment –'

'I'm going to make them swim!' said Mitch with delight as a new idea struck him.

'No darling, worms don't like swimming. What about making Mommy some nice mud castles?'

She supervised Mitch long enough to make sure that the worms would escape their swimming lessons, then hurried inside.

It was Tom.

Tom crazy, Tom possessed.

He was snatching everything that had any saleable value at all. He had clothes, crockery, a blue vase that Mrs Elwick had given them, a clock all rolled up in their bedroom quilt. When Rebecca found him, he was hesitating over her thirty-dollar wedding ring on the windowsill, where she'd left it while she was out gardening. Pipsqueak, who had tried to welcome him home with her usual explosion of licks, barks and tail-wags, was cowering frightened in a corner of the room.

'Tom, what the –'

He stood up, leaving the wedding ring where it was. 'Your necklace, hon,' he interrupted. 'I've got to have cash now, as much as I can as fast as I can.'

'Tom! We need our money for the house!'

'Screw the house. Have a mansion.'

Rebecca saw one of their bank books lying on the side. She knew instantly that Tom had already drained their account of its last dollar and cent.

'You can't do this,' she said. 'The money's half mine. I earned it.'

'I'll pay it back.'

'*Tom*! Don't do this. It's not –'

'No, no, no. It's not like before. This is not what it seems. We're this far from oil, this far.' Tom held his finger and thumb two inches apart. With his other hand he groped in his pocket and pulled out some compacted sand, which he threw onto the bare table. The sand mostly looked like sand. There were some dark oily blotches in it, which could have come from anywhere.

A person's world can change utterly in a matter of seconds. Rebecca's world changed now. She knew there was no point in fighting her husband's addictive drive. She saw her dream of a new home vanish. She saw that Tom would never be able to escape the trap he'd built for himself. Her world turned to ash.

'If you go now, we're finished. You know that.'

He stopped and took her by the shoulders.

'We're only a few yards from striking oil. Feet, even. Doesn't that make a difference to you?'

'You always were only a few yards away. Only a few more yards.'

Tom snorted out through his nose. 'Not like now. See that?' He pulled away from her and poked the sand on their kitchen table. 'Smell it.'

'Don't go, Tomek.'

'I've got to. Right away.' He looked again at her necklace, wanting to ask her for it again and only barely restraining himself. Rebecca could see his fingers itching to take her wedding ring. 'I'll be back,' he added.

'Don't count on it.'

He pretended he hadn't heard her. 'I'll write you from Overton. Soon as I can.'

'I've let you back three times, Tomek. I swore I never would again.'

By this time, Mitchell had come in from the garden. His first impulse had been to run to Daddy, but something in the atmosphere scared him and he hung back, pressing himself into Rebecca's skirts, holding Pipsqueak into his little chest. Tom picked up the quilt by its four corners so it formed a grab-bag of all their household possessions.

'Bye, Mitch. See you soon. Be a good boy for your mommy.'

'Don't go, Tomek.'

'I'll write.'

Tom looked around the shabby little cottage one last time. There was nothing left to take. The room was almost empty, except for the wedding ring on the windowsill and the oil sand on the table. He tousled Mitch's hair and kissed him. He would have kissed Rebecca but she shrank from his touch. Ten seconds later, the Ford's engine clattered into a roar and tore off.

Away from Rebecca, out of her life.

116

Coppers are coppers are coppers are coppers.

Probably, if it were possible to go back to ancient Rome, or further back still to the first dawning of civilisation in Assyria and Sumeria, you'd find that their policemen looked exactly the same. Big-footed, heavy-shouldered, plain-faced, bent-nosed, put-upon, dogged.

Alan's first act on receiving the news from Hartwell had been to identify and then retain the leading firm of private detectives in London. The three men standing in front of Alan now didn't just look the part, they were the part. Between them, they had sixty-eight years with Scotland Yard. Sixty-eight years of hunting men and finding them.

The senior detective, Alfie Proctor, cleared his throat.

'On the fifteenth of April nineteen thirty, you supplied us with a list of some eighty-three persons believed to have been held in the Hetterscheidt –' he pronounced it Hetter-shit, with only the smallest glimmer of embarrassment – 'Hetter-shit prison camp in Germany during the last war at the time when your friend, Lieutenant Thomas-known-as-Tom Creeley, was also believed to be present.'

Proctor paused briefly, to let Alan acknowledge the facts. He did so with a nod and Proctor continued.

'As of today's date, the twenty-seventh of August, we have

now been in touch with sixty-one of the eighty-three persons. Of the twenty-two individuals we have not been able to find, six have died, four have emigrated to America (in three cases) or Australia, in the fourth case. We have so far been unsuccessful in determining the whereabouts of the remaining dozen, but will – if so instructed by yourself – continue to make enquiries.'

Alan nodded. 'Please do.'

'Of the sixty-one men we have been able to find, five were not available for questioning or were found not to be of sound mind, and were accordingly removed from our list of possible informants.'

Alan nodded again, more briskly. Why the hell couldn't the man just get on with it? Alan sighed. The man was a policeman, that was why. And because he was a policeman, he'd been able to find as many men as he had. Proctor turned a page in his notebook, as though he himself had no idea what the outcome of the investigation had been.

'Of the fifty-six men we have spoken to, nineteen had no recollection of Thomas Creeley or were positive that he was not present in the camp. The remaining thirty-seven had some recollection of him and thirty-two were able to pick out a photograph of him correctly from a set of five.'

'*Yes!* So he was there.'

'Yes, sir, he was there.'

'And . . . ? Did you . . . ?'

Proctor, at last having mercy, or perhaps just finding the pull of humanity stronger than his years in the police force, put down his notebook. 'Well, sir, it's funny. We know he was there for definite. There was eleven people who remembered him escaping and the stir that caused, and remembered in enough detail that we can be pretty sure they're not making it up – people do invent things, sir, not that they mean to, but just to be helpful, like.'

'Yes.'

'Now no one – at least, no one what I would call reliable

456

– remembers him being executed for the offence. It seems like the prison wasn't too harsh, not by comparison with some. But what's peculiar, see, is that no one really remembers him much after the escape. We've got six people swearing he was moved to a different camp, nine people saying he survived till the end of the war and was liberated like everyone else, five people saying he was sent to work on a farm and wasn't locked up with the rest of them or not near so much. Then again, we've got –' Proctor checked his notebook again – 'one person says he died in an accident down one of the coal mines, two people saying he was involved in a brawl over a bowl of soup and ended up dying of injuries, and one chap swearing that Creeley woke up with a vision of the Blessed Virgin Mary and all the hosts of Heaven, then died that night with a blissful smile on his face.'

Proctor closed his notebook.

Alan was blank with amazement. You could send three long-serving detectives to find and interview more than eighty men – and end up as uncertain as you began. At least the oil business wasn't like that. When you drilled for oil, you either hit it or you didn't. Alanto had expanded its operations to Iraq now, and so far had drilled unsuccessfully – but at least the answer was clear cut and unmistakable.

'Proctor, listen, what d'you make of it? As a man, I mean. I've heard your statistics, but what d'you make of them? In your opinion, is Tom alive or dead?'

'Obviously, sir, anything I ventured would only be an opinion, like.'

'Yes, yes, of course.'

'But in my opinion, sir, Tom Creeley did not die in Hettershit during the war.'

'He survived?'

'That is my opinion, sir. Yes.'

117

It was the toughest drilling Tom had ever done.

He spent his days working as hard as he could – and doing his damnedest not to drill down another inch. With excruciating care, he picked his most rotten drill pipes, spent his evenings filing them down in their weakest spots, then hoisting them carefully into place the next day. When the rotten pipe was deep enough, Tom would send a surge of power through the turntable, while at the same time letting the drill down as hard as he could. Twice he tried it. Twice he failed.

Then he waited for the wood-man to haul a new load of prime firewood. He got up a strong head of steam. He tried the same manoeuvre one more time, and bingo! The drill pipe buckled and snapped. Tom swore (but was delighted) and promptly began the horrendous task of fishing for the busted tube. Days passed. Tom was normally skilled at deploying a fishing tool, but this time the job took ages. The cowpoke riggers did what they were told to do, until Saturday evening when Harrelson forgot to come and pay them. The next Monday only half of them turned up. When Harrelson still failed to show, the riggers melted away. The rig was there and Tom was there, but there was no action at all.

Rumours of their failure spread across Henderson and

Overton and Kilgore and Longview. The well was a bust, just like everyone had always known.

The news even reached Rebecca, still living alone down south. She didn't cry, or at least not until Mitch was all tucked in for the night and soundly asleep. And then she did. Non-stop for three hours, in the house that had once been a home.

She was sure in her heart she would never let Tom back again.

Meantime Harrelson was busy. He went from farm to farm begging to lease new land for further wildcats. The farmers knew of Harrelson's failure. They laughed at him for dreaming, but he was offering good cash up front for their signatures on a contract. They signed up and they signed up cheap. On land that was drier than dust, any cash at all was better than nothing. Because of Tom's foresight in killing news of their discovery, Harrelson was able to buy the drilling rights to a block totalling almost seventeen thousand acres.

They spent their last cent.

'The car,' said Tom.

'Aw – Jeez – how can I get around without I have –'

'Sell it.'

So Harrelson sold his car and used the proceeds to acquire rights to a further four thousand acres.

'OK,' said Tom. 'Let's do it.'

They made their announcement. They went to the Overton village general store and told the storekeeper they'd struck oil. They told the guys over at Henderson. They told farmers and cowpokes and people they met on the street.

Word spread.

At the failed old rig, a crowd gathered. Harrelson begged firewood and firewood appeared as if by magic. The same cowpokes who had walked away a few weeks earlier returned. Although the rig was the same clapped-out old rig it had always been, although the cowpokes were just as stupid, although the well hadn't produced a single teaspoon of oil – there was something new in the air, something different, something a little brighter than sunshine.

Tom fished the broken clutter from the hole and began to ream the sides of the well. When the sides of the well were solid, he bored down another seventy-five feet. If he drilled too shallow, the oil would still be below the bit. If he drilled too deep, he might go clean through the oil to salt water, and ruin his chances of bringing the well home. It was the sort of moment that called for every ounce of Tom's hard-won experience.

He lifted the drill and lowered a recently invented drill stem tester. The device was like a core barrel, only it was intended to collect liquids, not solids. He lowered the tube. On its way down, the device struck a bulge on the side of the well and opened early. Tom was desperately anxious. He wanted to pump like crazy. He wanted to drill until oil spurted from the wellhead. But reason fought with instinct for control – and won.

Tom reamed the well a second time to smooth out its sides, then lowered the tester once again. The tester descended to the bottom of the well, opened on cue, and filled with liquid.

It was time to lift the tube.

They began to raise the pipe, but long before the bottom rose into view, a smell of gas came rushing up. On and on it came. Stinking of mud and sulphur, the gas belched from the ground. As the smell filtered down into the crowd, there was a burst of cheers and clapping. With an old oilman's superstitiousness, Tom felt a jolt of anger. How dare a bunch of farmers' boys bring bad luck by clapping too soon? He almost wanted to drive them away, but nobody was going to be driven anywhere and once again Tom's brain had to fight his impulses.

Then the tester appeared.

Tom made ready to open the tube but, even as he did so, the well began to show its hand. A deep vibration rose from far underground. The equipment on the derrick floor began to shake. The tall structure began to quiver with life. The heavy machinery was forced against the massive timber sills that held it in place, till every timber and bar of steel was taut with effort. The crowd, sensing something big was about to happen, drew back with an indrawn breath of wonder. Tom braced himself against one of the juddering timbers and cracked open the tester. Water and mud poured out over his feet, but the water and mud were shot through with oil.

Tom rose with a shout of triumph – '*Yes!*' – when the well delivered its own unmistakable verdict.

With a single violent burst, the rush of gas suddenly exploded upwards. Mud, water and oil were flung high into the derrick. There was a moment's deafening silence. Then another smaller bang, another eruption of oil-rich mud, then silence returned, except for the thin hiss of still escaping gas. High up in the rafters of the derrick, oil and mud and water began to drip down onto the ground.

The silence lasted a moment longer, and then the seventy-five people who'd been watching broke into spontaneous applause. Tom and his fellow riggers danced with glee. One of them scooped up a big pile of oily mud in his cap, waved it in the air, then dunked it down on his head, splattering himself from top to toe.

Tom, too, drank in the moment. *Oil*. He'd struck *oil*. The dream, so long held, with such difficulty abandoned, had finally come true. He hardly believed the truth of the black and stinking mud that still slopped down from the derrick.

There was still plenty of work to be done and Tom did what he had to do. But as he continued to work, he found himself oddly subdued. For one thing he remembered the Duster's dictum: 'If you ain't got oil at the wellhead, you ain't got squat.' And it was true. If the oil pressure was too low, you might never be able to coax the precious fluid half a mile vertically up to the surface. It wasn't just a theoretical risk; Tom, like the Duster, had seen it happen. So he was cautious.

But there was another bigger reason for his low-key reaction. He was older than he'd been at Signal Hill: older and wiser. He had a family: Mighty Mitch and wonderful Rebecca. His happiness depended on them now. Depended utterly.

And oil or no oil, he didn't know if he'd ever see them again.

118

Christmas Eve.

By four o'clock, a huge red sun was plunging below the horizon. Beech trees tangled bare branches against the bloody light and the footpaths were slippery with black leaves. In the field by the lane, something must have startled a group of horses, who began to gallop round the muddy pasture, throwing up divots of sodden turf.

Alan ran.

Twice his boots skidded badly. Twice he stayed upright only by grabbing at outstretched branches or a handful of wet grass. In the big house behind him, electric light blazed from the downstairs windows. The cottages he was heading for had no electric light and their windows were dingy and dark.

He approached the last cottage of the row: Jack Creeley's former home. How well Alan remembered it! It had been here that Jack had patiently taught his two eager pupils how to lay a trap for rabbits, how to hook or tickle trout from the stream, how to set bottles in the river as traps for crayfish. This same cottage had been Alan and Tom's entry into the real world of the village, infinitely far removed from the goings on at Whitcombe House. When there'd been something to celebrate – May Day, a wedding, somebody's return from the navy – Alan and Tom had climbed from their bedroom windows, down a drainpipe, over the kitchen roofs and down to the ground. Then they'd headed off to Jack Creeley's place and drunk a glass of beer with him before going on with him to the party. And what parties they'd been! Wild affairs of strong beer, fiddlers, dancing, a couple of oil lamps swinging from the rafters and nobody enquiring too much who kissed who by their smoky light. Tom had always been the leader of those night-time expeditions, but Jack Creeley had always been every bit as welcoming to Alan as he had been to his own son.

The pull of the past was strong now and Alan was in its grip. He put his hand to the door and knocked.

119

Maybe there are some businesses where luck doesn't play a part. Maybe there are some businessmen who can look themselves in the mirror aged sixty and swear that they got where they got through one hundred per cent skill and a lifetime of effort. Maybe there are businesses so dull – gravy-making, cotton-reels, fork-handles – that luck just doesn't come into it at all.

But oil wasn't like that and oil isn't like that and oil will never be like that. And if by any miracle the oil business changes, and the geologists and the computer guys and the hydraulic engineers and all the rest of them ever take the luck out of the industry – then the real oilmen will quit. The industry will still go on hauling oil, but its soul will be dead, its life ended.

From that first violent belch of oil into the sky, it had taken Tom and his crew one month, working solidly, to bring the well home. It had to be cased off using second-hand casing supplied under loan by the Standard Pipe and Supply Company. They had to bring in storage tanks – only three because they only had cash for three – and a proper well-head control system to take the place of the junk that was

465

there already. Tom moved cautiously and expertly, but the crowd that watched him grew by the day, humming with excitement. First there were hundreds of people. Quite soon there were thousands.

When everything was ready, Tom began to swab the well. Swabbing was a little like using a household plunger. The apparatus used a simple vacuum to suck water and mud up from the well. When the suction got strong enough, the oil would flow.

That was the theory.

Tom swabbed and swabbed, and brought up nothing but mud – but Tom was patient. He continued to work and one golden day his patience was rewarded. The well sounded a deep note, like a trombone playing in a bass register almost out of hearing. It was like a cry from the furthest reaches of the earth. Then the sound finished and a deep rushing began.

They extinguished the boiler and waited, but they didn't have to wait for long.

With a last violent motion, the well hurled a cap of mud and water into the air, followed by gushings and gushings of oil. The crowd went wild. One of the crewmen pulled a revolver from his pocket and began firing like a crazy man. Tom had to jump on the man and tear the gun from his hand, for fear the shooting would ignite the gas and blow the whole rig higher than heaven.

The oil continued to spew upwards.

It was a glorious sight.

Titch Harrelson should have been pleased – and of course he was – but for him, the oil strike was a dangerous blessing. He'd sold more interests than there were interests. One particular lease he'd managed to sell in its entirety eleven times over. 'I guess I was kind of enthusiastic,' he admitted unhappily. In the days when Tom used to work for him, Harrelson had boasted of owning leases to nearly five thousand acres of neighbouring land. But, as his lawyers and everyone else's lawyers began to dig down into the truth, it turned out that Harrelson had managed to leave himself with clear title to just two acres. The first handful of court actions began. The dreaded word 'bankruptcy' began to be spoken.

One night, Harrelson and Tom were eating cheese and crackers in a hotel room in Henderson. All evening Harrelson had been plucking at his lip and looking old and tired.

'You going to be OK?' asked Tom.

'Yeah, I guess.'

'What does your guy Manninger say?' Manninger was Harrelson's lawyer.

'Ed? Hell, Ed says . . . Ed says they's gonna eat me alive.'

'Are you talking about everything?'

'Could be. Could even be I lose everything.'

Tom shook his head. 'It was you who found the oil, Titch. No one'll forget who found the oil.'

'No, sir! That's right!'

For a moment Harrelson straightened and looked boldly ahead of him, but the moment was short. He plucked his lips and crumbled crackers on his plate. In some ways he'd been happier chasing oil than he'd ever been since finding it.

'I could take you out, Titch.'

'Huh?'

'Buy you out of everything. Give you cash, take over your debts, let you just walk away.'

'You would?' Harrelson lit up at the idea.

'We'd have to agree a price.'

'Yeah, sure, we'd have to agree something.'

Harrelson's desperation to leave his legal tangles behind him was hopelessly evident.

'You want to suggest a number?' said Tom.

'Huh? Sure . . . I mean, I'd want something to live on. Maybe do a little more wildcatting. Maybe . . . maybe . . .' He had no idea what amount to name. He just wanted to return to his old life as soon as possible.

'Would you settle for a million bucks?'

'A million? Sweet Jesus, pal! A million? You don't have –'

'You'd have to wait for most of it. Some of it I could get within a few days.'

And so they shook on it. Tom bought everything, all the leases, all the debts, for one million American dollars.

∾

Which left only Rebecca.

Tom drew up outside Rebecca's little cottage in a long black limousine. The noise alerted her and she came to the door, with a half-smile on her face and a touch of worry in her eyes.

'Hey, girl,' he said.

'Hey there.'

'Mitchell's OK?'

'Mitch is –'

Mitch answered for her. He came tearing round the house from the garden, followed by a disgracefully muddy little white dog. Except for a ragged pair of shorts and a coating of mud, Mitch was as naked as a peeled banana. He saw Tom, gave a shriek of delight and leaped into his father's open arms, as Pipsqueak hollered her approval to Tom's shin-bones. Father and son kissed and cuddled for a while, until Mitch was ready to wriggle off. Tom took something from his pocket and gave it to Mitch. 'Give this to your mom, would you?'

It was a cheque, payable to Rebecca, for an amount exactly equal to the money that had been in their account before Tom had emptied it.

'I said I'd repay you.'

'Thanks.'

She and Tom were still standing five yards apart from each other and hadn't yet touched. Tom couldn't tell from Rebecca's face how she felt about him. He'd sent her a telegram as soon as he was sure of his strike, but he'd had no answer. Even in the midst of his glorious success, he was desperately uncertain over the one thing that mattered most to him.

'And I got you something else.'

He tossed her over a small jeweller's box, which she caught neatly. She opened it. The box contained a fine diamond ring, with a single solitaire, large and exquisitely cut. She put the ring on and it was a perfect fit, glittering and glinting in the sunlight. Her smile broadened.

'I never had the money to buy you something nice before. I do now.'

'It's beautiful.'

'Really? You like it? It's not too . . . ?' He shrugged. 'I don't know. You like it?' For the first time since leaving Rebecca in such appalling style, Tom began to believe he might not have screwed up his life yet again.

Rebecca teased him with her eyes. She was enjoying his uncertainty, though only briefly. She flashed the ring at him. 'Have you gotten too big an oilman to give me a kiss?'

'Oh, Becca! Not if you're happy to be an oilman's wife.'

They came together and kissed. Mitch leaped up against them, hollering to be let inside. Tom put an arm down and hoisted him up, so it became a family of three kissing and cuddling. Pipsqueak leaped and hollered too, so then it became a family of four.

As Tom and Rebecca went to bed that night, with Mitch snoring away in a cot at their feet, Rebecca stroked her husband's cheek with her hand.

'Tomek?'

'Yes?'

'I'm proud of you,' she whispered. 'It was a strong thing you did.'

He kissed her hand. Yes, he had become proud of himself. Those awful failures of the past, especially Signal Hill and the wasted years that followed, were washed out by this one stunning success. The future would hold many challenges, but he was man enough to meet them. He was proud and deserved to be.

For what felt like the first time in his life, he was Alan's equal. Alan's *better*.

120

Bertie Johnson had become more than half blind. He had a kerosene lamp but didn't use it except with visitors. Feeling for matches with one hand, he tried to adjust the wick with the other.

'No, leave that,' said Alan. 'I'll do it.'

He screwed the wick clear of the guard, trimmed the sooty end, and set a match to it. The wick caught and burned. The light was hardly dazzling, but at least Alan could see. Bertie's downstairs room was clean and well stocked with wood. Bread and dripping lay on the table and there was a scent of apples.

'Merry Christmas, Bertie,' said Alan, once they were settled.

'Oh, and a merry Christmas to you, sir. It'll be a wet one, I believe.'

'You have everything you need?'

'Yes, sir, thankee.'

'You'll have something hot tomorrow?'

'Maggie Davis promised me a seat at her table. Pork, she has, I think. A nice bit of pork.'

'That's fine. With a bit of apple sauce, perhaps?'

Bertie Johnson chuckled deeply. He liked the thought of it. 'I'm hoping so.'

'Good . . . Look, Bertie, I came over to ask you a question.

About something that happened a long time back, or that maybe didn't happen at all.'

Bertie sat straighter at his little table. His hands had curved rheumatically with age and they were now almost fixed into position around a pair of invisible reins, just as he must have sat, hour after hour, when he was the village carrier riding his wagon into Winchester and back. There was something evasive in his face.

'Yes?'

'No one's to blame, Bertie. Whatever happened, there's no blame.'

'No, sir.'

'You remember Tom Creeley, of course.'

'Of course. Jack's lad. A fine boy.'

'Well, you'll remember that he went missing in the war and was presumed dead. I thought so. My mother and father thought so. Jack thought so too.'

Bertie nodded. His blind eyes didn't seek contact with Alan's face, but perhaps there was also a little stiffening of embarrassment? It was hard to tell. Alan continued.

'Now, for some reason, I never quite accepted that. I probably should have done, but I didn't. Anyhow, I began to look into things. I went to the War Office and the Red Cross. But I also asked a friend of mine who lives in Germany to help me. He looked into the German war records and it turns out that Tom did survive, after all. He was imprisoned in a place called Hetterscheidt and lived there until the end of the war. That's all I know so far.'

The old man nodded. His hands moved to the bread and the bowl of dripping. He crumbled the bread, but he was only fiddling. His eyes were filmy and white.

'Now, let me tell you what I think must have happened next. Tom had quarrelled with me shortly before he went missing and I know he'd had an argument with Guy. For a long time, I didn't think all that much of it. Tom was quick-tempered, and arguments came and went without much fuss.

But now I think a little differently. I think, for whatever reason, Tom must have been angrier than I understood. Perhaps he didn't want to see me. Perhaps he didn't even want to see my mother and father. But, you know, Bertie, the way I look at it, he'd have done anything to see his old man. I think he'd have come back here shortly after the end of the war, December 'eighteen or January 'nineteen. I think he'd have knocked on this very door and I think he'd have come in here and found you.'

Bertie was rigid as a gatepost. His opaque eyes stared straight ahead of him. His hands were still.

'I only want to heal old wounds,' said Alan gently. 'There's nothing done which can't be undone. Even now.'

'There are promises. Once made, they're not for breaking.'

'Even if they hurt the man who asked them?'

'A promise is a promise, sir.'

'And a man's life is a man's life, Bertie.'

There was a moment's silence. Johnson breathed out heavily and Alan knew he'd won.

'He came looking for his pa, all right.'

'And you told him the news?'

Johnson nodded slowly. 'Dead from the flu, like so many.'

'And?'

Johnson stared out into silence again, wrestling with his old man's conscience. 'He was angry. He went away again.'

'That same night?'

'Yes.'

'Making you promise to say nothing?'

'Yes.'

'Do you have any idea where he went to?'

'No. He didn't say.'

There was a short pause. A fire smouldered in the old man's hearth, and Alan threw some logs on it, poking it hard to get the flame to rekindle. When he stopped, the cottage filled with silence like a well.

For a moment or two, Alan felt the familiar disappointment.

No sooner had he got close to Tom, than Tom seemed to disappear in a blur. Gone, but with no clue as to where . . .

But the feeling lasted only a moment. Where on earth would Tom go? There was only one possible answer. America! As soon as he thought it, the idea rang with truth. It made so much sense from every angle. Tom, somehow, had always been American. Too classless for Britain, too energetic, too rebellious.

And oil. America was still by far the world's largest producer of the precious liquid. No place on earth offered so much to the independent oilman. If Tom had wanted to go into oil, where could he succeed like America?

So if Tom was in America, Alan would look for him there. There were ways of tracing people. Part of his brain grappled with questions of cost and practicality and timing. But he pushed such thoughts away. None of that mattered. Not now. Not any more. The world had changed; changed utterly.

Tom was alive and the world was good.

'Thank you, Bertie,' he said, 'and a very merry Christmas.'

121

Three months later, March 1931, Tom met up with Titch Harrelson in Dallas. Harrelson was already scouting around for investment in a new wildcat venture up near El Dorado over the state line in Arkansas. Much of his money was already gone, but the old wildcatter seemed ten years younger, drinking root beer and trying to get Tom to loan him money.

'Oil's getting too easy to find,' he complained. 'Prices'll drop.'

'Maybe,' said Tom.

'Maybe? Nuts! Look at our find. Look at what's happening in El Dorado – about to happen, I mean. Look at – heck, what's the name of that limey company? – made a big strike in the Mid-East?'

'Iraq?'

'How the hell would I know? The one next to Persia. Company name was Alonzo. Some dumb-ass name like that.'

'Alanto Oil made a big strike in Iraq?'

'Right. It's getting too easy to find. We ain't gonna see one dollar a barrel no more. Not in Texas. Not no place. Be lucky to get fifty cents, once El Dorado comes on stream.'

The rest of the conversation happened behind glass.

Tom felt numb at the news. Numb, then angry. It wasn't enough for Tom to make the biggest oil strike since Signal

Hill – and maybe the biggest oil strike in American history, period – but Alan had to go and do something similar in Iraq. The old resentments began to burn. Alan had started with birth, money, and a concession to drill in one of the world's richest oil countries. He'd found oil with his second well. His *second*! Who'd ever heard of a strike as sweet and easy as that? And now, when he wanted to expand production, what did he do? He turned up at another country, half-in, half-out of the British Empire and wangled himself a concession to drill there too. Where was the competition? Where the struggle?

The more he thought about it, the stronger the old anger burned. Tom would not – *would not* – permit himself to be outdone. The resolution was like a flame in his heart, strong, blue, focused, intensely hot. It was a flame that would find its target or incinerate its owner. Maybe both.

When he met up with Rebecca later that night, she was shocked to see him.

'You look like you've seen a ghost,' she said.

And she was right. He had.

PART SIX

There's 'Gull 'em & Skinner'
And 'Gammon & Sinner'
'R. Askal & Oily & Son'
With 'Sponge 'em & Fleece 'em'
And 'Strip 'em & Grease 'em'
And 'Take 'em in Brothers & Run'.

from 'Famous Oil Firms'
by E. Pluribus Oilum

122

June 1932. The Great Crash has ushered in the Great Depression. Hemlines are lower. Prices are weak. Dictators are powerful, and democrats fearful.

In the meantime, the oil business is proving tough. That's nothing new. It always has been. Always will be. That's why it's fun.

'Hello, George? What d'you have for me today?'

'Morning, laddie . . . hey, hey, my Lord, I'm not as young as I was.' George Reynolds walked in and sank gratefully into one of Alan's chairs. At sixty-three, he was almost ready to quit the deserts and mountains and settle back full time in England. The shares he'd owned in Alanto Oil had turned him into a rich man. He cared little enough for money, but Alan was pleased to see him comfortably off.

'Lord, is there such a thing as a cup of tea in this wretched country?' he asked.

Alan grinned and ordered tea for them both from his desk intercom. 'It'll be in cup and saucer, though,' he apologised, 'No samovars. No hubble-bubble. No iced sherbets.'

'Uncivilised brute. Any minute now, you'll be telling me you haven't slaughtered a sheep in my honour.'

479

Alan's smile continued, but the warmth of Reynolds' entry made him think of his dinner last night. He and Lottie had kept a long-standing engagement with Guy and Dorothy. The conversation had been awkward and cold. Guy had drunk too much and, for most of the evening, Lottie and Alan had been forced to talk to each other, as though their hosts had been absent. When finally the last awful mouthful had been forced down, and Alan and Lottie were in a position to leave, Guy accompanied his brother to the door.

'I suppose I ought to tell you, Dorothy is leaving me. We'll be getting a divorce, then she'll go back to America. Most bloody stupid thing. Marrying her, I mean. Sorry about this evening. You must have hated it. I did.'

In the car on the way home, Alan and Lottie had discussed, in quiet voices, whether a bad marriage was better than no marriage at all. Now, in Reynolds' presence, Alan realised the married state wasn't the important thing: the person was. A good man like Reynolds would find his peace in any circumstances. A flawed one like Guy . . . well, peace seemed to be beyond him in any situation.

'Now look, said Reynolds, extracting a lengthy telegram from his pocket. 'Good news, I think. Mussolini's torn up his oil contract with Shell, and wants to negotiate a new one with an "entity working for the consolidation of the fascistic reconstruction of the Italian nationhood", whatever on earth that means. Apparently, it means Mussolini was getting fed up being pushed around by Shell and he wants to deal with someone small enough to *be* pushed around.'

Alan stopped. For a moment it seemed like the world stopped too. There was a second or two of total silence.

'The Italian government has cancelled its deal with Shell?' He spoke like a man in a trance.

'Yes.'

'They're looking for a new supplier?'

'Yes.'

'They're asking us?'

480

'Among others. Yes.'

Alan breathed; not because he quite dared to, but because he'd been holding his breath since Reynolds had mentioned the telegram. The breath came out jagged, as though his lungs were still suffering from the war.

He was intensely excited, and little wonder. Alanto Oil produced crude oil on a massive scale, mostly from Persia, but now increasingly from Iraq as well. It refined as much of its crude as it was able to, but even so, its refineries were hard-pressed to cope. But refining wasn't the weak spot. Marketing was. Anglo-Persian, Shell, Standard – all had massive chains of petrol stations stretching right across the globe. Alanto Oil struggled to shift its oil and ended up selling at a discount. A huge contract with the Italians would be a vast breakthrough in the company's short history.

'Petrol?' he asked.

'Yes, but not only.'

'What else?'

'Everything. For instance, "petroleum fractions of high-octane composition as might be suitable for flight of aircraft not of passenger denomination",' Reynolds quoted from the telegram once again before handing it over to his boss. 'I assume that means they want us to fuel their filthy warplanes.'

'We'll tell him to get his aircraft fuel from elsewhere. He's welcome to petrol, but I'm not going to help him fly his bombers.'

But Alan's hands were shaking with eagerness as he reached for the telegram. He read and reread it with mounting excitement, then looked up. Fire glinted in his pale eyes. Quite unconsciously, his hand had formed itself into a fist, crumpling the telegram into a ball. He beat his hand softly against the table.

'We have to win this deal, George,' he said.

123

Tom stood in thick leather boots and a pair of goggles. They were outside beneath the sweet gums, because the refinery's tiny office was sweltering and oppressive. A greasy breeze moved between the trees.

'See now?' said the young chemist. 'This here's being sold as gasoline. It shouldn't ignite, not until we've got the temperature up another forty, fifty degrees.'

There was a dishful of fuel brewing over a burner, with an industrial steel thermometer recording the temperature. In the background, the pipes and cooling towers of the rinky-dink little refinery reached upwards towards an unblemished sky.

'You might want to stand back there, Mr Calloway. I wouldn't want –'

Too late.

The dish of fuel caught alight, and flames and smoke leaped upwards. The young chemist had known what was coming but, even so, he was startled. He jumped back, caught his foot on a table leg, and fell over, bringing the table and fuel dish after him. The blazing gasoline spilled over his leg and puddled right over the dirt and pine needles all around. The flames began to scorch upwards. There was shouting and screaming, though in the confusion you could hardly tell who was yelling, let alone what they were saying. A couple of acne-scarred lab assistants began swatting feebly at the flaming leg.

Tom was faster, and not just faster, he was better.

He ripped off his jacket and leaped towards the screaming chemist. One of the pimply youths was in the way and Tom threw him aside, the way a rodeo horse tosses a novice. Tom wrapped the leg in his coat and hugged it tight, until the flames were smothered. The chemist, ashamed of his clumsiness in front of his boss, began to pull his leg away, muttering thanks.

Tom ignored the thanks and the tugging leg. Gasoline flames have a nasty habit of leaping back into life as soon as oxygen returns. Tom carried the chemist to a butt of water and dunked him in. The man tried to climb out, but Tom held him back. 'You stay there till we can get a doctor here. Got that?'

'Yes, sir. Thank you, sir. Sorry, sir.'

'Can you get your pants off?'

'Yes, sir.'

'Then get your pants off.'

The man complied. His leg was burnt, but nothing too bad. He'd be fine.

Tom turned away to find himself watched by the company's Chief Operating Officer, who was doubled up with laughter.

'Testing out fuel quality, huh? We should use that in the ads, maybe. "Bites the pants, but spares the man." What d'you reckon?'

Tom spat. 'What you got for me, Lyman?'

Lyman Bard, the Chief Operating Officer, waved a telegram. 'I got good news, pal – least it's good news if I got this damn thing figured out straight.'

Keen to honour the memory of his friend from prison camp, Tom had named his company Norgaard Petroleum. It was quite an honour.

483

Norgaard Petroleum had grown fast and grown big.

There are big strikes and little strikes, and Tom's was about to prove one of the richest in history. The Black Giant oilfield – there was no other name for it – turned out to stretch from Upshur County in the north to the north-east tip of Cherokee County in the south. The field was forty-five miles long and between five to twelve miles wide: more than one hundred and forty thousand acres of liquid gold. The twenty-one thousand acres that Tom had leases on didn't all lie on the field, of course. Much of his land lay too far east, and no matter how many wells were drilled there, every single one came up dusters. But an even larger chunk of his land proved to be as sweet and rich as a Rockefeller daydream – fifteen thousand acres stretching all the way to Overton and beyond, with oil, beautiful oil, beneath every inch.

His dream had come true.

More than true. Better than true. Truer than true.

But Tom was older than he had been on Signal Hill. Older and smarter. He remembered Mitch Norgaard in prison telling him, 'It ain't enough to find oil, Tom, it's turning it into dollars that counts.'

Tom had been dealt a hand full of aces. But he still had to play them and a dumb move could cost him the game.

First things first. He'd hired a bunch of lawyers to settle the multitude of claims against Harrelson. He'd settled them as fast as he could, fast and generously. When the dust had cleared, he had undisputed title to all fifteen thousand acres of oil-producing territory, with debts (including the million he owed to Harrelson) amounting to around three million.

Three million in debt and not a penny in his pocket.

Tom didn't care.

He raised money, somehow, anyhow. It was simple enough. He had fifteen thousand acres of the richest land in the world and banks were dying to lend. With Rebecca handling the finance, Tom stood at the centre of the whirlwind. He planted rigs on his land like he was sowing corn. Within a matter of months his daily production was better than fifty thousand barrels a day. Fifty thousand barrels and income to match.

Meantime, all around, the world was going crazy. What had been tiny little farming villages turned into honky-tonk boom towns on a scale that made even Signal Hill look provincial. Farmers turned into hustlers, cowpokes into wild-catters. Fields of corn were left to rot, as no one could spare the time to harvest them.

But Norgaard's warning rang in Tom's ears – Norgaard's warning and Tom's own experience.

One day, with the oil price still strong and the oil rage still rising, Tom called a halt.

'A halt?' asked Rebecca, surprised. 'We have money for another nine rigs. More, as soon as I can get our next loan organised.'

Tom bent and kissed her on the top of her beautiful head. 'A halt. No more rigs. We ought to start selling.'

'Selling?' Rebecca furrowed her eyebrows. 'You are joking, I suppose?'

He smiled down at her. She had an odd way occasionally of sounding like an immigrant newly arrived from the boat. Partly it was her accent, which hadn't changed through all the time Tom had known her. Partly it was her English, which had remained oddly formal, even old-fashioned at times.

He bent his knees and whispered, 'Remember Wyoming.'

'Wyoming? . . . Ah!' A look of understanding grew in her eyes. 'So when do you want to sell?' she murmured.

'Tomorrow. We'll start tomorrow.'

And he did.

He sold quietly, but fast. He sold land. He sold leases. He sold rigs. He sold out.

He sold out when the market was still strong, when men were concerned about getting oil from the ground as quickly as possible. He got good prices. In fact, because the oil madness ran so strong, he got crazy prices.

But the flood of oil was constantly growing. As the flood grew higher, the market began to buckle. Back in 1926, Tom could remember the price of a barrel of West Texas crude rise as high as one dollar eighty-five. Four years later, when he'd struck the Black Giant, prices were round about a dollar a barrel. By the middle of the following year, the glut was so extreme that prices had collapsed down to fifteen cents, six cents, even occasionally two cents a barrel. In Wyoming, the price collapse had happened because there was no way of taking oil from the wellhead to the market. In Texas, the collapse had happened because there was so much oil that the entire world wasn't capable of soaking it up.

'And what next?'

Rebecca's question was simple. Tom's response was equally blunt.

'We buy, of course.'

Tom hadn't spent his entire life trying to get into the oil business just to sell out of it when prices dropped. So having sold, he promptly bought. He bought refineries. He bought pipelines. He bought makers of drilling equipment. He bought gas stations.

In fact, by now, the middle of 1932, Norgaard Petroleum was heavily invested in every part of the oil business except oil production itself. And, as the oil producers were losing their shirts, taking oil out of the ground at an average cost of eighty cents a barrel and selling it on at an average of just fifteen, Tom, superbly supported by Rebecca, was making money hand over fist.

Tom brushed pine needles from his pants. It was a relief, frankly, to be without a coat in this weather. He walked deeper into the shade to read the message. It was the same telegram as Alan had seen, in the same tangled English. 'Having regard to the inadequacies and defecations of the previous contractor (SHELL), the Secretariat of Fuel coming under the authorisation of the Ministry of Industry and Foreign Trade is inviting tenders for a new contractor . . .'

Lyman Bard watched in silence till Tom had finished, before spitting tobacco juice on the ground and saying, 'You think all ginzos are like this?'

Tom shrugged. 'Do we care?'

The telegram might have been sent from heaven. It was an answer to an oilman's prayer – especially one with a flood of East Texan oil on his doorstep. Tom was so excited his hands had actually been shaking with eagerness.

'Hell, they can't be. The Mob wouldn't've been nothing but a bunch of pussies if they'd've gone about their business like that. "Flight of aircraft not of passenger denomination" – Jesus!'

Just about the time that Tom had started selling his oil rigs, he'd run into Lyman Bard who'd been hanging round Houston as a drill-for-hire. After an evening spent drinking together, they were solid enough friends again for Tom to offer and Bard to accept the position of Chief Operating Officer in Norgaard Petroleum.

Tom sat on the ground and gestured back at the tea-kettle refinery, which he'd recently bought for two hundred dollars from its bankrupted owner.

'You reckon we can fix her up?' he asked.

'We can fix anything,' said Bard, 'but I can't see us wanting to.'

Tom nodded. 'OK. Scrap it or torch it. Whichever's cheaper.'

Bard assented with a grunt. There was so much over-capacity in the refining industry locally – and so much of it poor quality, like the junk-heap in front of them – that it had become profitable to buy capacity simply in order to close it down.

'The ginzos,' said Bard, 'what do we do about them?'

Tom read and reread the telegram with mounting excitement, then looked up. Fire glinted in his dark blue eyes. Quite unconsciously, his hand had formed itself into a fist, crumpling the telegram into a ball. He beat his right hand softly against the left.

'We have to win this deal, Lyman,' he said.

124

Alan hadn't given up. He hadn't forgotten.

He had hired a big American detective agency, Pinkerton's, to comb the continent for his lost twin. So far, they'd drawn a blank, but there wasn't a day that went by when Alan didn't think about it, when he didn't half expect to be reunited after so many years.

And one day, there was news.

It came over breakfast in the form of a cable from New York. 'ADVISE SUBJECT LOCATED MORE DETAILS FOLLOW STOP PINKERTONS'. The colour rushed from Alan's face.

'Tom!' he cried. 'At last!' He pushed the cable across the table to Lottie. 'I've found him!'

Lottie took in the message and looked up. 'Darling, congratulations! What wonderful news!'

Alan was already standing. He rang the bell. 'Yes, absolutely. Isn't it? I'll go straight out.'

'Go straight out? Where out?'

'Hmm? To New York, of course. I'll leave on the next ship sailing.'

A servant entered and Alan gave him instructions to pack a bag and book tickets on the next liner bound for New York. Lottie waited in silence as Alan spoke. The servant left.

'Darling?'

If Alan had been smart he'd have heard the warning note. But he wasn't and didn't.

'Yes?'

'Aren't you forgetting something?'

'Oh Lord, yes! I'd better tell Reynolds where I'm off to. He's up to his neck in this Italian oil contract.'

Lottie's voice tautened further. 'There's a fund-raising do at the hospital tomorrow night. And Tommy's birthday party two days later. *Our* Tommy's.'

The warning was clear enough, but Alan continued to ignore it. Ever since Lottie had got her hospital fully established, his worst fears had come true. She was spending less and less time with the family; more and more at the hospital. And Alan wasn't comfortable with the change. It was one thing for the young unmarried Lottie to have nursed the seriously wounded during a time of national crisis; it was quite another for a wife and mother to be doing the same in peacetime London. He didn't like the smell of war and suffering. He didn't like the thought of Lottie on the wards. He attempted to be polite, but ended up deceiving no one.

'Oh . . .' Alan's tone was dismissive. 'More fund-raising? Really? I'm sure you can handle it. I'll bring Tommy something back from America.'

'Or you could wait a few days. You haven't even spoken to Pinkerton's. Wouldn't it make sense to –'

The dining-room door opened again. It was Alan's valet with times of ships sailing from Southampton. Alan examined the list quickly.

'If I leave now, I should be in time for the *Caroline*. I'll be in New York before you know it.'

'Darling, you have a life here too. I jolly well do need you at my fund-raising do, as you perfectly well know. And little Tommy –'

Alan wasn't listening. 'Sorry, my love. I need to leave now. I'll telephone from the dock if I have time.'

'Alan!'

But it was too late.

Alan was gone, leaving Lottie white with anger at the table. He felt bad about it afterwards. Bad enough to scribble a note to her from Southampton and post it before the ship left. Bad enough to buy a silly little gift for Tommy and send it with the letter.

But not bad enough to delay his departure. Not bad enough to overwhelm his excitement at the prospect of finally locating Tom . . .

～

It was seven days later.

Alan was in New York, so newly arrived that there was still a glimmer of salt sea spray on his coat. Peter Oswald, the senior Pinkerton's investigator, grinned at his visitor. 'I can see you didn't waste any time,' he said.

'No, of course not,' said Alan. 'Not given the news.'

Oswald plucked at the trace of an old scar over the bridge of his nose. 'You mean that cable we sent you, I guess.'

'Yes.'

'Uh, well, strictly speaking that cable oughtn't to have been sent.'

'You haven't found him?' Alan felt the shock of disappointment slap into him, grey and chilling, like an Atlantic breaker.

'No, it ain't that. We got Tom Creeley for you, all right, only the thing is . . .'

'Yes?'

'Well, we done good. Too good. We haven't just found one Tom Creeley. We got ourselves six.'

'*Six?!*'

It turned out that Pinkerton's had indeed done much too well. They'd found a Tom Creeley unemployed and poverty-stricken in a shack near Albuquerque. They'd found a prosperous apple-farming Tom Creeley in Washington State.

They'd found a father and son Tom Creeley running a two-bit shrimp-fishing business in North Carolina. And just in the last couple of days they'd found two more Tom Creeleys, a Chicago one and a Canadian one working with illegal papers down in Portland, Oregon.

'Are any of them . . . ? Could any of them be my Tom Creeley?'

Oswald plucked at his scar again.

'Yeah, well, the thing is, that's why they didn't really ought to've sent that cable out. The only Creeley we got who fits your guy's birth-and-build details would be the North Carolina shrimp-fishing Creeley. The younger guy. The son.'

Alan nodded. He could already hear the punchline. It was with a hollow voice, he said. 'I see. But that can't be my man, because . . .'

The detective nodded. 'Right. We sent an operative down there. The father's clean. A bona fide father-son relationship we got there.'

'There's no chance your man might be wrong? It wouldn't be worth sending someone else? To double check?'

'Not worth a plugged nickel. We sent one of our best guys. This is a pretty regular type of search for us. I'm sorry.'

Alan nodded. He'd spent more than fifty thousand dollars with Pinkerton's so far. They'd placed ads. They'd checked phone books. They'd checked voting registers and police records. They'd combed the oil industry from Canada down to Mexico. It sometimes felt as though they'd poured all of America through a fine-meshed sieve – and after all that, they'd come up with nothing.

Alan was devastated. He thought of home and Lottie. He'd hurt her and hurt their son for what? For nothing. Once again, he saw Tom's shadow racing ahead of him, into the shadows. He wondered if he'd ever see Tom in his life again.

Hollow-voiced, he said, 'There's nothing more to be done, then? Nothing at all?'

Oswald shook his head. 'I'm sorry, I'd say there was nothing. At least, nothing except . . .'

Alan jerked his head up sharply.

'Yes? Except?'

125

'It's gotta be along this way someplace,' said Bard, as the right front wheel of his De Soto plunged savagely into a pothole and seemed to think a long time before making up its mind to come out again.

'Boy, am I pleased we took your car!' said Tom.

'Yeah, but the company pays – hell! – expenses, including – Jesus, would you look at that rock? – new goddamn suspension.'

'Need a coupla new axles, I'd say, only I don't remember reading anything about that in the company handbook.'

'Yah!' Bard growled his hatred of the Oklahoma dirt-track that was trying to pass itself off as road. The Wichita Mountains loomed black and humped in the middle distance. A thin wind rattled the dry grass. 'Who the hell would drill a place like this?'

They drove on in silence, interrupted only by the violence of the car's motion and a stream of muttered swearwords from Bard. Tom sat and thought about Rebecca. He'd become a real homebody now. He liked visiting his own oil facilities, but apart from that, he just liked being at home. At home with her. Who'd have guessed that he'd have turned out like that? The wanderer had come home. The thought made him grin.

Eventually the track levelled off and the road surface improved.

'All to see a lousy ginzo!' said Bard.

'You're sure he speaks Italian?'

'No, pal. Name like Marinelli, he speaks Swedish and eats . . . I don't know, whatever the hell they eat in Sweden. Reindeer.'

'And he's reliable, right?'

'I told you. He's not your regular type of ginzo. Neatest guy for reaming a well I ever saw.'

'Lyman, for Chrissake! I don't want him to ream wells for me, I want to know he's not going to play me for a sucker.'

They came to a fork in the road, neither direction signed. Bard hit the brakes angrily and grabbed the map on the rear seat.

'He's straight. I already told you.'

'OK. It's important.'

Bard spat out of the car door, then reached for a packet of cigarettes. His head, face and shoulders were covered in a fine grey dust. Where he'd lifted the packet of cigarettes, there was a dark mark left on the dashboard.

'OK, pal. I'll tell you how come I know he's straight. In return, maybe you could tell me why all of a sudden you want a ginzo.' He lit up and threw the match out of the open window into the dirt. 'Back in 'twenty-five, we was working a new-fangled type of electric well out here in Oklahoma. No boiler. No steam. Just electrics. We hated it. I mean the thing was unlucky. It looked wrong, sounded wrong. The well belonged to some dumb-as-shit New York consortium who probably picked the thing out of a book. Three thousand feet down, we get an escape of gas. We need to get the blowout preventer in, and fast. We're kinda jumpy, but it's going OK. Then the motor surges. It's hot. There are sparks. Big blue sparks crackling through the air. We stare at them like dummies. Then – boom! – worst possible time, we have a full-scale blowout. The works. Oil, mud, water, gas. I seen wells take before, but this was a scorcher.' He spat. 'Shoulda stuck with steam. Slam-bam-an'-go-to-hell.'

'Hmm.' Tom grunted and reached for one of Bard's cigarettes. 'But Marinelli survived, right? I don't have any use for a heap of Italian-speaking charcoal.'

'Yeah, he's OK. The guy was on fire, I run back in, haul him out. Don't really know why, only I did. And that's how I know he's straight. He owes me. Them Catholic boys remember that kinda stuff.'

'Excellent.' Tom's eyes gleamed with something dark. 'You saved his life and he knows it.'

'Yeah.'

Bard continued to wrestle angrily with his map, but Tom tapped him on the arm and pointed. Further down the valley, sticking up above the scraggy little oaks, there poked the unmistakable shape of a wooden-built oil derrick.

'That must be Marinelli, over there.'

'You still haven't told me why you want a ginzo,' said Bard, as he put the De Soto into gear and began to move off.

'I've got a job for him.'

'What kind of a job?'

But Tom just shook his head. He wouldn't say any more. Not yet.

But one thing he knew was this: there weren't many firms capable of meeting the requirements for the Italian contract. Norgaard was one of the leading contenders. Another one was Alanto Oil. Tom and Alan head-to-head. Tom and Alan in a battle for supremacy.

Tom grinned again, but not warmly this time. Savagely. Even brutally. If this was a game, he was playing to win.

126

Ellis Island.

Maybe now they've cleaned it up. Maybe now they've gone out into the North Atlantic and picked up an ocean gale and sent it screaming down the halls and walls and passages of the old immigration buildings until the place came to shine like it had been scrubbed with sea air and salt, and all the old smells had been rubbed out of it for ever.

Maybe.

Only more likely not. More likely the place still carries its smell of hope and anxiety; poverty and ambition; old oppressions cast aside; the stink of pork sausage, hard biscuit and dark European tobacco.

Alan walked stiffly along the corridors, feeling out of place and awkward. He was still conscious of his row with Lottie and he almost felt obliged to find Tom in order to prove her wrong. Eventually, he got to the right door: one marked 'James F. Galston, Immigration Records Officer'. Alan put his hand to the door and knocked.

Galston was a foxy little man with quick eyes and a nervous mouth.

'Yeah, sure, come in. Close the door, would ya mind? No, don't worry. On second thoughts, leave it . . . No, better shut, I guess. Sure, closed. That's it. Right. Great.'

Galston's office was little better than a cubicle with cardboard walls and a thin window set into an iron frame. The frame had corroded badly in the sea air and each time there was a puff of wind outside, the glass rattled.

'You want coffee? I can get Miss Jennings down the hall to fix you some co –'

'No, thank you, I'm quite all right.'

'Hey, sit. Sorry. I should have said. Sit! I didn't mean for ya to stand.'

Alan took the cheap little folding chair on his side of Galston's desk and moved some papers from it so he could sit. The chair was filmed over with the damp stickiness of the ocean. Alan sat. Something about Galston's staccato brittleness actually made him calmer, less hurried, more businesslike.

'Perhaps I should say why I came,' he said smoothly. 'As you know, I was given your name by a detective named –'

'Oswald, right. Pete Oswald. Sure. Pinkerton's. Right. Do a lot for them. When I can. Help 'em out. Good guys.'

'Yes. I spoke with Peter Oswald. I'm trying to trace a man whose name in England was Tom Creeley. I believe he arrived here in Ellis Island some time late in nineteen eighteen or, more likely, at some point during nineteen nineteen. Pinkerton's hasn't been able to find him under his real name and we suspect he must have changed his name, most likely upon entry to this country. Now what I wondered was –'

'Yeah, right, got you, regular type o' thing. Search. British male, right? Entry nineteen eighteen, maybe nineteen nineteen. Say 'twenty as well. Don't want to pin these things down too tight. Not unless you know. Right. For certain, I mean. You got a dob?'

'I'm sorry?'

'A dob?'

'I don't –'

'Hey, sorry, shoulda said. Dob. Date of birth. Technical term. Use it a lot round here. Dob. You got one?'

'Date of birth?' Alan half-laughed. Date of birth was easy. It always had been. The 23 August 1893. It was his own date of birth; his and Tom's; the terrible twins of Whitcombe House. Alan gave Galston the date, in the same even tone he'd used so far.

'Right, OK, good. We got a dob. British male. Assumed name. Entry date known, only approximate, but we got something. It's a heck of a search, yeah, a heck of a search. Did Oswald mention anything about . . . ? I mean, like . . . It's a big one.'

Galston's nervousness had gone into overdrive. He had found a broken matchstick in the litter on his table and was sawing at something brown between his front teeth, whilst fidgeting nervously with his trouser leg with his free hand. He looked like a panicked starling. For a second or two, Alan stared at him, amazed. Maybe taking bribes was a cultural thing, something they knew how to manage better in Persia than here in America. Alan covered his smile with his hand, then said, 'I understand this is beyond the call of duty. Of course, I'd want to reward you well for your effort.'

'Yeah, yeah, reward. Good way of putting it. That's very straight of you.'

'How much do you feel would be appropriate in this case?'

Galston's heart rate rose slightly until it entered the low nine hundreds. He sawed so hard with the matchstick that a bit of it broke off inside his gum, but his right hand was too busy with his trouser leg to do anything to get the splinter out. There was sweat on his forehead, though the room was barely even warm.

And then Alan's gaze travelled up and he saw it. Beyond Galston's agitated shoulder. Through the thin window in its rattly frame. Beyond the broad swathe of water where the chilly Hudson joined a cold Atlantic. The Statue of Liberty, torch raised, looking out to Europe, with her promise of a new future, new hope.

Suddenly, Alan knew Tom had seen this sight. He didn't

know what had driven Tom away from Europe. He didn't know why Tom had changed his name, changed his country, hidden from the truest friend he'd ever had or ever would have again. Alan simply knew that Tom had been through this port, that he'd seen that sight, that he'd taken that promise of liberty to his heart.

'Perhaps five hundred dollars would be sufficient,' he said in a distant voice, his attention still focused on the view beyond the window.

'Five hundred bucks? Five *hundred* . . . ? *Five* Cs . . . ? You wanna . . . ?'

Alan smiled. In Galston-ese that was a positive yes – and no wonder, since Alan had probably overpaid five times over.

But he didn't care. He didn't even look at Galston, so captivated was he by the sight of that noble statue. It was in that moment that he knew for the first time, as a matter of absolute certainty, that Tom was alive and that he, Alan, was going to find him.

127

Bard was woken up by a kick on the sole of his boots. He blinked himself awake to find Tom and Marinelli, already best buddies, laughing down at him.

'Hey, guys!' he said, swatting ants away from his trouser leg with his hat. 'You get anything fixed up?'

Marinelli grinned. His face was badly scarred. Any oilman would instantly recognise a man who'd been caught by a bad oil blaze. His white teeth looked oddly out of place in his red and black complexion. 'No, no. Not *any*-thing, we get *every*-thing fixed up.'

Tom was over by the De Soto beating grey Oklahoma dust from the rear seat. 'We better get going, Lyman. We gotta go by Gianfranco's place.'

'You're coming back with us?' said Lyman, in surprise. Even by Tom's standards, it was fast work getting a man to leave his job, home and family all at the drop of a hat.

'No, no, not with you. Not all the way. Only to the *stazione*.'

'The stat-see-oh-nee?' said Lyman, copying Marinelli's pronunciation. 'The railroad? Either of you guys gonna tell me what's going on?'

Marinelli laughed again and looked across at Tom, who nodded.

'I am going on holiday,' he said. 'To Roma. I stay in a nice hotel. I throw some nice parties. I make some friends.'

Bard was totally confused now. He looked at Tom, a little angry at the way his boss was playing with him. 'You wanted a ginzo to send on holiday?'

Tom laughed. 'In Italy, Lyman, a good friend is a talkative friend. Right, Gianfranco?'

And it was in that moment, for the first time, that Bard understood what his boss was doing. His boss was a genius. A double-crossing bastard maybe, but a genius for sure.

With a man like that bidding for the Italian contract, they almost literally couldn't lose.

128

'I'm sure Mrs Montague said to meet you in the West Wing, sir,' said the matron. 'Maybe she meant in amputations.'

The matron scurried around, looking for Lottie. Alan followed.

Lottie's hospital was now fully operational. The once-derelict factory buildings now hummed with busyness. The place smelled of clean sheets and medical alcohol and fresh air blowing in from the Thames outside.

As Alan chased after the matron, he saw ward after ward. Most of them were set aside for veterans of the war: the pale-faced boys that had fed the British Army's insatiable need for troops. There were men here who'd had limbs amputated in the war now being fitted for artificial limbs. There were others being treated for damage to eyes, ears, lungs, or throats. There were shell-shock survivors whose suffering was being taken seriously, in some cases for the first time. The British Army had cared for these men to the best of its ability a dozen years back, but the need for care was never-ending and the army's medical budget wasn't.

'Perhaps it must have been the East Wing after all,' said the matron.

Alan followed slowly. She was wrong again. Lottie wasn't in the East Wing, or the West Wing, or any of the wards in between. When they finally tracked her down, she was in a lung damage ward tucked away to the north.

'There you are!' said the matron.

Something about her tone was unconvincing. Alan shot her a glance, in time to catch a look passing between the two women. Alan understood it. The game of hide-and-seek had been prearranged. It was Lottie's way of making sure that Alan – finally – saw her hospital properly for the first time.

'I'm so sorry,' said Lottie, when the matron had left. 'I definitely said the North Pier. Quite clearly, I'm positive.'

'I'm sure you did.' His tone was touched with sarcasm.

Lottie glared at him and pushed past him to a small room marked 'LINENS'. The room was full of wooden racks, on which was stacked all the linen of the hospital: bedsheets, pillowcases, aprons, gowns, caps, dressings, bandages. Lottie folded her apron and put it away. Alan leaned against the racks and smelled the odours of starch and clean laundry. Lottie turned, but made no move to leave the room. When she spoke, there was a warning note in her voice.

'You've never seen the hospital before. We've been fully open for five months now and you've never done a proper tour.'

He opened his mouth. 'I've been –'

'Of course you've been busy. So have I. So too has everyone here. So has everybody in the world. But you could still have come.'

'Yes . . . Well, it looked most efficient. Most impressive indeed.' Alan played with the white belt of one of the aprons that hung down from its place above him.

'Oh, don't be such a pompous ass!'

'What?!'

'If you don't like it, you should damn well say so, not start speaking like some horrid little municipal inspector.'

'Well, of course I like it. I –'

'Really?' Lottie was angry now. 'Then why is it you've never come to look? Properly look, I mean. And why when you do come, do you start speaking as you never do normally?'

'Well, maybe I don't like it!' cried Alan. 'Maybe I don't! The hospital is all very well, but I never see you these days. You're always busy. Always rushing somewhere or other. I sometimes feel as though you've left the family completely.'

'*I've* left, have I? *Me?* You have your oil business, your trips overseas, your constant worrying over a brother you haven't seen for all of fifteen years, and *I'm* the one who's left, am I?'

Lottie put her hand to her head. She still had on the white nurse's cap she liked to wear while touring the wards. She yanked the cap off hard, accidentally pulling out a hairpin and releasing a long auburn strand of hair, which fell to an inch or two above her shoulder. She brushed it angrily away. Something in the gesture made Alan remember the girl he'd fallen in love with a decade and a half ago.

'Sorry,' he said.

'Why?'

'For shouting just now. I didn't –'

'Oh, for goodness' sake! For just a moment I thought you were going to say something sensible.'

Alan's anger flared again. He opened his mouth, but she waved him down.

'I couldn't care less about you shouting,' she interrupted. 'It was all those months of not shouting that I minded. If you are upset about something, you should jolly well say so.'

'Well, I suppose I am,' he said, suddenly glimpsing a ray of light, suddenly hoping that maybe Lottie was about to compromise. 'I mean you *have* been awfully busy. Of course I admire your work here, but –'

'But nothing. If you admire it, then live with it. I shan't give it up. I shan't work here any less than I want to.'

Alan swallowed. 'That's your final word?'

'Of course it is. It's time you accepted that the woman you fell in love with during the war is the same person who's involved here now.'

'So much has changed.'

'Really? Has it? Look out there.' Lottie swept her hand at the world beyond the linen room. 'The war isn't over for those men. It isn't even over for you. You dream about it. You feel obliged to chase the ghost of poor old Tom Creeley. Do you want to know the reason why you hate my hospital?'

'I don't hate it.'

'The reason is because you're still caught up in the war. You haven't escaped. And you won't escape until you acknowledge as much.'

129

Tom rolled sideways off Rebecca. He was panting and sweaty. She still had her eyes half closed, her arm still cradling his naked back. One of the utterly unexpected things about Rebecca was how much joy she took in lovemaking. Tom had never known a woman who gave herself more completely to the experience. He almost felt jealous of the depth of her feeling.

He groped for a cigarette. The bedroom was the only place he smoked them now and though Rebecca didn't usually smoke, after lovemaking was an exception for her as well. He lit cigarettes for them both.

She opened her eyes and propped herself up. Her hair was a dark and tangled halo on the pillow. Her breasts were unselfconsciously free of the sheets. She took the cigarette but didn't inhale at once. She gazed at her lover, then lifted her head to kiss him sensually one more time on the lips, hand tucked hard round the back of his neck. She sighed happily one more time and let herself sink back.

For the first few weeks of their lovemaking, back in California ten years before, Tom had steadfastly refused to ask Rebecca about her previous partners. But he could never lose the thought. She'd slept with hundreds of men, perhaps as many as a thousand. The thought had tormented him.

When he'd made love with her, he'd flung himself around like an acrobat, hoping that she'd tell him he was the best, that no one made love like him. She'd said nothing of the sort. Their lovemaking had become painful to Tom, and Rebecca's expressions of satisfaction had seemed wooden and conventional.

Then Tom could stand it no longer. He'd asked her outright. She'd been angry. 'Make love? Make love? I didn't make love with anyone. Not in all those years. Not once. I had sex. I got paid. I can't even remember one single night that meant anything to me.' She'd told him to stop treating sex like some kind of bedroom gymnastics and he'd slowly calmed down. Their sex had got better, but it had never really become sublime until those fondly remembered nights in the little cottage on Mrs Elwick's farm. Since then, it had been constantly wonderful. Sometimes quick, sometimes slow. Sometimes passionate, sometimes tender, sometimes with so much laughter that they ended up falling off the bed and giggling helplessly on the floor.

They smoked in silence. Rebecca watched Tom. Tom thought about work and the Italian contract, which was obsessing him. Bard's man, Marinelli, was already set up in Rome. He'd been given enough money to stay in a good hotel, to throw extravagant parties, and had already secured good friends in the Secretariat of Fuel and the Ministry of Industry and Foreign Trade. Marinelli had already dug out most of the details of Alanto Oil's intended tender offer. Tom was now preoccupied in finding ways to go one better.

The absolutely crucial ingredient of any bid was the price involved. All the oilmen knew that they'd have to beat the prices offered by the previous contractor, Shell. The question was, by how much? Tom reckoned most of his American competitors would pitch in at two to three cents less than Shell. The million-dollar question (and, as a matter of fact, the question was worth very much more than that) was what price Alanto would offer. The question made Tom tense up.

Though he had one hand curled behind Rebecca's shoulder, his attention was absent, his touch wooden.

'You are an evil stinking pig,' said Rebecca meditatively, 'and I think I shall never sleep with you again.'

'What?'

'You were thinking about work.'

'Work?'

'Don't deny it or I might feel obliged to bite you.'

'I *was* thinking about work. You're right.'

'I know.'

'How?'

'Everything. Everything about you. For instance –' She held her cigarette between her index and middle fingers and raised it to her mouth. Her posture shifted subtly and became more masculine, a careful imitation of her husband, but her mouth still held the looseness of sex and her eyes were soft. 'This is how you smoke when you're still thinking about making love.' She held the pose a moment to show him, then changed. She sat more upright. Her eyes went smaller and harder. She held the cigarette between finger and thumb with her other three fingers curled over the top. She dragged hard on it, and tapped the ash away with a brisk, dismissive gesture. 'This is how you smoke if you're thinking about work, and then only if it's not going well.'

Tom laughed. He was always transparent to his wife. 'Yeah. We've got a big deal on in Italy. It'll be worth a lot if we get it.' He scratched his nose.

Rebecca suddenly looked at him more intently. She too had now lost the dreamy afterglow of sex. '*And* something. Work *and* something. It's not just about money, is it?'

'Hey, come on! It's –'

'You scratched your nose. It's an evasive gesture with you. You do it any time I ask you about your past back in England, for example. You give me an answer that tells me nothing, then you scratch your nose and change the subject.'

'I just want to win the deal. There's way more oil in Texas

than we know what to do with and the Italians want to buy a whole load. The deal would be the making of Norgaard.' His nose began to get uncomfortably itchy and he had to fight himself to avoid putting his hand up to scratch it.

Rebecca continued to read him with her eyes. Then she put her hand to his chest and massaged him lovingly, ending with a long stroke that began at his collarbones and ended between his legs.

'Why not talk about it?' she said. 'Your past, I mean. It's gone. Whatever it was can't reach out to get you here.'

'No.'

She found his gaze and held it. 'I've worked as a prostitute, you know. I've been in debt. I've seen my brother die of tuberculosis. I've left my parents in another continent and I'm scared for their safety. What on earth do you think you could tell me that would shock me?'

'It's not about shocking you. I just don't want to talk about it.'

'I think you're dying to talk about it. I think your past burns inside you every minute of every day.'

'And I think you're wrong.'

'Who cares if you win the Italian deal? You know, it won't make any difference.'

'It'll make us a hatful of money. That's a difference.'

'That's not what I meant. I meant it won't make any difference to whatever it is that bothers you so much.'

'Nothing bothers me,' cried Tom, conscious that he was hardly speaking the full truth. 'I'm not remotely bothered.'

'Your past isn't outside of you. It's inside. You can't run from it.'

'I'm not running. I just want to win a contract, for Chrissake.'

Rebecca looked annoyed. She finished her cigarette briskly and stubbed it out. 'Will you win?'

Tom nodded. 'It's going well. We've got an excellent pitch. It's just a question of making sure we got the best prices.'

He didn't say anything about Marinelli, the news filtering out of Rome, his spy placed in the heart of the Italian camp.

Rebecca sat up and pulled her hair back from her head, hard enough to pull her skin tight around her forehead and ears. Then she dropped her hands, shook her hair free and dropped back into bed. She rolled on her side and began to play with Tom's nipple with her tongue and mouth. When she bit him, she bit just hard enough to inch across from pleasure into pain.

'It's inside you,' she said. 'Whatever it is, it sits inside.'

130

'A beautiful evening, no?'

Alan looked around. His memory for faces wasn't always good, but this face wasn't one you forgot in a hurry. It was red and black, badly scarred, almost certainly the result of an oil blaze at some far-off well.

'Beautiful,' agreed Alan, trying to put a name to the face, but failing.

'Cigarette?' said Oil-Blaze, holding out a case.

'Thank you, no.'

Behind the two men, a banquet was running its course. The Italian Secretariat of Fuel had thrown the extravaganza for the various foreign oilmen in town. Alan was the most senior oilman there, and rumour and intrigue had swirled around him all evening. The final bids on the Italian oil contract were required within a matter of days and Alan still hadn't decided what price to set.

Oil-Blaze lit a cigarette for himself and leaned on the balcony, copying Alan's posture. Beyond them, Rome glowed gold in the last light of the evening.

'It's crazy,' said the Italian, jerking a thumb at the ball-room behind them. 'Too much craziness for me.'

Alan smiled in agreement. 'You speak English very well. And you're an oilman. That means, I suppose, you've spent time in America.'

'No, alas. I would like to go. It is the home of oil, no?'

'Well, I've a soft spot for Persia myself, but I know what you mean.'

The din of the banquet didn't get any less, and Alan showed no inclination to go in. When the Italian lit a second cigarette, Alan accepted one for himself. The two men continued to chat idly about the dinner, the guests, and oil – inevitably oil.

'The air,' said Oil-Blaze. 'The next big market for oil. After Charles Lindbergh, we will have paying passengers across the Atlantic soon. No, really! I believe it.'

Alan laughed and disagreed, but the Italian – obviously passionate about aviation – was adamant.

'You must be very proud of Marshal Balbo, in that case,' said Alan, referring to the recent highly publicised feat of Italian airmanship. 'Ten seaplanes, all the way from here to South America! Astonishing. And only six men dead.'

'Bah! Six men! Is worth it.'

Alan laughed again and changed the subject. 'You seem very well connected.'

'Ah no! I have a little money. I make nice entertainments. I have some good friends.'

Alan nodded, as though indifferent, but the truth was that he'd noticed how the Italian officials had fawned around Oil-Blaze like bees around a honeypot.

Alan thought of Lottie. Early in their marriage, they'd come to Rome on holiday. It had been an enchanted time. Right now, it seemed there was little prospect of such togetherness again. He didn't care how unreasonable he was being, but he wanted the old Lottie back. He didn't want her to be running hospitals – still less to be changing dressings in some ghastly amputations ward. He leaned hard against the wrought iron of the balcony rail, feeling the hard metal across his waist, the cool air across his face.

Oil-Blaze was still talking, listing his friends and boasting of his connections.

Alan only half listened. In the room behind him, no doubt officials were being bribed, state secrets being whispered, quiet deals being done. Alan shook himself from his trance. He had work to do.

'I may need a little help finding friends,' said Alan with careful consideration.

'Ah, yes?'

'Friends to make sure that the Alanto tender offer receives the consideration it deserves.'

'You are right, you are right.'

'But it needs to be done discreetly. If it were to get out, our chances wouldn't be worth a plugged nickel.'

'No, no, but listen, perhaps I may be able to help . . .'

Evening drew into night. An arrangement was made. Money passed hands and more was promised. Oil-Blaze – Gianfranco Marinelli, to give him his proper name – turned out to be extremely helpful; extremely receptive to Alan's needs.

And by the time Alan went to bed that night, he was satisfied he had done everything he could to assure himself of success. He felt he almost literally couldn't lose.

131

It was 5.30 p.m., Texan time. The date was 19 September 1932.

At the offices of Norgaard Petroleum, things were winding down for the day. Except that today wasn't normal. Today wasn't ordinary. Today the Italian government was due to announce the results of the tender, and the entire company was breathless to hear the news.

First of all, there was bureaucracy. The Italian government was releasing the news in the US through their embassy in Washington. Some problem with the telegraph services there meant everything was held up. Lyman Bard had hung on the phone all day, as though doing so could make the news faster.

But at last, 5.31 p.m., his patience was rewarded. The telegraph began to chatter, the magic letters began to spill forth.

Bard ripped the telegram off the machine. He snatched one quick glance at it, then began to run.

He ran fast, he ran wildly. He ran towards Tom's office, skidding like a schoolboy on the polished parquet floors, grabbing at the walls to spin him faster round the corners. Colliding with a stenographer, he would have knocked her down, except that he put both arms round her, waited till she'd regained her balance, then shot off, planting a big kiss on her astonished forehead.

He reached Tom's office and hurtled in.

'We got it, we got it!' he yelled.

Tom knew instantly what he meant. Joy and relief burst through him like a flood. 'We got the deal? We got it?'

'Hold up, pal. This son-of-a-bitch is addressed to you. I ain't read it yet.'

'But you're smiling,' said Tom, grabbing unsuccessfully for the magic telegram.

Bard snorted with delight. 'OK,' he admitted. 'Maybe I peeked. I got as far as the "we are delighted" bit.'

Tom grabbed for the telegram a second time and got it. Marinelli had advised Tom that Alanto was bidding at three or four cents under Shell's prices, and Tom had placed his bid at six cents under, just to make absolutely sure. Winning wasn't a vast surprise, but it was sure as hell a nice way to end the day. Bard slammed down the intercom button on Tom's desk and called for 'Champagne, wine, whiskey, cake, and a whole damn chorus line of cancan girls.' He continued to whirl around the room, a one-man hurricane of pleasure.

Tom tried to ignore Bard as he focused on the telegram.

132

At exactly the moment that Lyman Bard was skipping like a puppy round Tom's office, it was 11.36 p.m. in England.

Alan was at home, where he'd given a dinner party that night. Things were winding up. Servants yawned discreetly. The kitchens had fallen silent. Outside the house, streetlights puddled on rainy tarmac. The guests had mostly gone home, taking their furs and their cars and their chatter with them. The rest were saying their goodbyes. All except Guy, who dawdled still.

'Not tired?' said Alan, wishing that his brother would leave.

'Not tonight.'

'The hours you keep!'

Guy was no longer an officer in His Majesty's Armed Forces. Further promotion had eluded him. A long spell in the field, probably in East Africa or North-East India, appeared to be the next step for him. Detesting the idea, Guy had arranged things so that he slipped sideways into a senior civilian position at the War Office.

'I'm used to it,' said Guy. 'Billiards?'

'Yes, yes, perhaps just one game, and then I really must . . .'

They took cigars and brandy up to the billiard room, where Guy set the balls up. 'A shilling a point?'

'Can't we just play?'

Alan was mediocre at best, whereas Guy was skilled. He generally played for money and generally won. There was a hungry intensity around his play for money, which Alan found difficult to stomach. Guy shrugged and began to knock the balls softly around the table. There was something almost hypnotic about the dazzling green baize, the dimness all around, the clicking balls. Guy finished knocking around and stood up to chalk his cue.

'I apologise for keeping you up. I know you want to get to bed.'

'Yes, it's just that we'll be very busy at the office tomorrow.' An understatement. The Italians should have announced the result of the tender today, but their embassy had closed before they'd sorted out their problems with the telegraph. The news was promised first thing tomorrow and Alan – and all of Alanto Oil – was breathless to hear it.

'There was something I wanted to speak to you about.'

'Yes?'

Alan was surprised. He and Guy weren't close, never had been. He could almost not recall a time in the last ten years when his brother had been urgent to talk to him.

'I understand from – well, from my driver, if you must know – he overheard a conversation here which implied you were looking for . . . for Tom.' Guy spoke Tom's name as though the person was known to Alan but scarcely familiar at all to Guy himself.

Alan's surprise mounted. Suppressing a glimmer of annoyance at talkative servants, he said, 'Your driver is perfectly correct. I am looking for Tom.'

'Tom is dead. He died in France.' Guy spoke the words stiffly, looking at his brother with a fixed stare, then he bent down and played three shots in quick succession, scoring twice with a neat cannon shot, then making a difficult pot.

Alan's irritation mounted. 'Tom is alive. He wasn't killed. He was wounded and taken prisoner. He spent the war at a prison camp in Hetterscheidt, near Düsseldorf. He left the camp in nineteen eighteen and returned to England.'

Guy licked his lips, which dried up again instantaneously. 'He's in England? How do you know this?'

'I didn't say he was in England. I said he returned here. He then left again for the United States and is living there under an assumed name. I know all this because I found it out.'

Something in what Alan had said caused Guy to relax just a little. He indicated that it was Alan's turn to play. Alan took his shot badly and set up an easy double pot for Guy. Guy took the shots, then a well-judged safety play, which left Alan with nothing to do.

'If he's in America under an assumed name, it would seem as though he's fairly keen to disappear.'

'Yes, but it's a two-way business, disappearing.'

'What on earth do you mean?'

'I mean he won't be disappeared much longer if I have anything to do with it.'

'He's under a borrowed name, anywhere in the United States. It won't be –'

'I'll find him.'

'It won't be easy.'

'I said I'll find him.' Alan suddenly realised he was quite angry. He had never forgiven Guy for volunteering Tom's services that terrible wartime night. Part of him had always held Guy responsible for Tom's death; counted him as little more than a murderer. He got a grip on his emotion and said in a quieter voice, 'I am obtaining a list of men who entered the United States through Ellis Island during the relevant period. British males of the right age. I have some good leads. I'll find him.'

Guy nodded. It was Alan's turn to play, but Guy bent down again and drove the balls round the table. There was something extraordinarily easy in his poise. Even in middle age, Guy was a handsome man. A dinner jacket suited his frame and face, the way it never did Alan's. Alan ran a finger inside his shirt collar, where a loose stud was chafing his neck.

'Perhaps it would be better to leave things alone. He wanted to go. It would be simple enough for him to find you.'

'For God's sake, Guy! This is Tom we're talking about! *Tom!* Do you really think I could know he was alive and not find him?'

'Whatever he may have done? Whatever caused him to run and hide?'

'What the devil do you mean?'

'Do you ever remember what I said to you that time you came to see me in hospital in Amiens? The time I got a bullet in my leg?'

Alan shrugged. He was angry. He knew Guy was bound to have some half-arsed justification for his murderous behaviour towards Tom. Right now, he didn't care. 'I don't give a damn,' he said.

'Do you remember where I was, when I was shot?'

'In a trench, I think you said. There was a war on, as I recall.'

'That's right. I was in a trench.'

Alan shrugged again, rudely. 'So?'

'So how is it that I was wounded in the leg?'

There was a short silence as Alan took in the question. Then he stepped back and, in stepping back, struck the light over the billiard table with his cue. The big brass light began to swing heavily across the table. Alan put up his hand to stop it but, not removing his eyes from Guy, he was unable to find it and the light continued to swing.

'Well?'

'I know why he vanished. I tried to tell you at the time.'

Alan groped for a seat and sat, not taking his eyes off Guy for a moment.

'Well?' he said again.

'I was running back from the front that day. The Germans had shelled the telephone exchange and our runners kept being killed. Brigade staff had no idea what was going on. I was sent to find out.'

Alan nodded. That much he knew.

'Coming back, I ran into Tom coming the other way. It was just after you and he . . . after you'd . . .'

'After you had sent me to find him in bed with Lisette. You can speak the truth. It won't hurt. Not now.'

'The truth?' Guy half laughed. 'The truth? Very well then. If you like. Tom shot me. He was angry with me – I can't say I blame him – but you know your bloody twin just as well as I do. There were no limits with him. None. He shouted at me, struck me, then shot me. He was pointing his bloody gun at my head and it was only because I knocked his hand that –'

Alan listened with a cold rage growing inside him. 'That's not true, I don't believe you. He wouldn't do that. He was hot-tempered, but he'd never –'

'You don't have to believe me.' Guy spoke bitterly. 'I know what you're like when it comes to the bloody gardener's boy. Just a moment. My briefcase is in your hall.'

Guy left the room. Alan closed his eyes and rubbed his face. With his eyes closed, it came back. The slippery chalk. The bursting shells. The greeny smoke. Alan realised he'd seen the scene that Guy was describing in his dreams. Not once, but hundreds of times. He'd never been able to see the faces of the people in his dream and so had never understood its significance. Alan felt sickened by his new knowledge.

Guy re-entered the room, holding a sheet of paper. 'There were witnesses. I kept a note of their names. I've no doubt that you and your brilliant detective skills will be able to find them. I think you'll find they confirm everything.'

Alan took the paper as though sleepwalking. He looked blankly at the names. Privates Hemplethwaite, Jones and Carragher. Details of regiment and company.

'That's why Tom vanished,' said Guy. 'He knew there'd be a court martial. He knew there could only be one sentence.

That's why I put his name forward for that bloody raid. He was done for either way. I thought it better for everyone, Tom included, that he died the hero. There's nothing pretty about death by shooting squad. I'm sorry, old chap, but that's how it was.'

133

The time: 5.39 p.m., Texas time.

Lyman Bard's caterwauling had quietened down for a moment and Tom was able to read undistracted.

'To Mr Thomas Calloway, Pursuing to the invitation issued by the Secretariat of Fuel coming under the authorisation of the Ministry of Industry and Foreign Trade . . .'

Tom blinked. His eyes skipped down the telegram, trying to find the meat. Here it was. 'We are delighted to inform you that your submission of tender relating to supply of lubrication products has been completely accepting, and hereby announce that . . .'

Tom paused, blinked, and read the sentence again. *Lubrication products?* He forced himself to read every syllable of the telegram. There was nothing about petroleum. Hold on. No. That wasn't right. 'Your offering of petroleum is thankfully not required.' *Not required?*

Lyman Bard caught sight of his boss's face. He became utterly still. The world was suddenly very quiet.

'Bad news?'

Tom didn't answer. Bard took the telegram and read it in silence. The English was horrendous, but its message was clear.

They'd lost.

They'd lost the contract to supply gasoline, fuel oil and kerosene, which between them accounted for more than ninety-nine per cent of the value of the contract. They'd won a trivial little deal to supply lubricants. The profits they'd make from the lubricants wouldn't even cover their costs in making their bid.

But that wasn't the worst of it.

The worst was this. The telegram stated that 'Norgaard Petroleum will be required to be working closely with the below-named petroleum supply company: Alanto Oil.' And there it was, in black and white. Tom had lost. Alan had won. It was the worst outcome in the entire world.

Tom sat like a statue at his desk. He knew this feeling. It was the oldest feeling in his life. It was Alan. It was the Montagues. It was Signal Hill. It was failure. The only difference was that this time there was someone to blame.

'The bastard,' he whispered. 'The bloody bastard.'

134

The time: 9.12 a.m., London time.

Alan hadn't gone to his office, but to the Italian Embassy in London. There had been some bureaucratic nonsense to delay them, but eventually he had got his hands on the precious news from Rome.

He'd won.

He'd won the contract to supply petroleum, kerosene, and fuel oil. It was a massive victory.

For a long time, Alanto had been a major oil producer, but a relative weakling in the matter of sales. Overnight that had changed. This one single contract had elevated Alanto into the very top tier of international oil companies. Alanto would be as strong in marketing as it always had been in production. A vast amount of work would be needed to consolidate the triumph. The profits from the contract would need to be reinvested to complete Alanto's transformation. But Alan wasn't worried about working hard. Right now, he wasn't worried about anything at all.

George Reynolds was next to Alan as he glanced at the news and tucked the telegram nonchalantly into his top pocket.

'Well?' said Reynolds impatiently. 'Well, laddie?'

'Well what, George?' answered Alan, as he began to saunter happily outside. 'I told you we'd win, didn't I?'

Later that day, 6.17 p.m., London time. More to the point, at a certain large white-fronted house in Chelsea, it was bath-time for the youngest member of the family.

As Polly splashed contentedly in the soapy water, Lottie made a determined effort to wash the bits of her that needed washing. Alan, just home from work, paused at the door. It was an outrage against the social order for a woman of Lottie's wealth and breeding to supervise her children's baths, but Lottie enjoyed doing it, and what she enjoyed, she did.

'Daddy!'

Polly, a happy-go-lucky girl of nearly three, smiled up at her father.

'Hello, Poll!'

He rumpled her hair and pretended to splash her. She shrieked. He took his hand away. 'Again, again!' she yelled. He pretended to splash her. She shrieked.

Alan smiled at his wife. 'Hello.'

She smiled back. 'Hello, my love.'

'Again!' yelled Polly.

'It was today, wasn't it?' said Lottie.

Alan nodded.

'Well?' Polly had found a lump of pumice stone and was trying to work out if she could fit it into her nose. 'No, darling,' said Lottie, removing the stone and offering a sponge instead.

Alan found himself wanting Lottie's full attention, but he realised he wasn't going to get it. He waited for an interval in Polly's quest for playthings.

'We got it,' he said. 'We won.'

'Oh, terrific. Well done.'

Polly's next game was filling the sponge with water and squeezing it out over the floor. Lottie removed the sponge and tried to interest Polly in a model wooden oil tanker, carved by George Reynolds as a gift for young Tommy some years earlier.

'You don't sound very interested. This is the most important news for Alanto since we first struck oil.'

Lottie straightened up. 'Really? And how interested are you in things that matter to me?'

'Do you want to know how we won?'

'I imagine you want to tell me.'

'We found one of the rival oil companies had a spy in Rome.'

Despite herself, Lottie looked interested. 'Don't tell me you decided to start spying on them? How unlike you!'

'No. At least not exactly. I let them spy on me. I was able to take advantage.'

By this time, Lottie was busying herself with Polly again and once again Alan felt cheated of his wife's attention. At the same time he knew that her complaint was reasonable. When Lottie had news about the hospital, Alan had only ever responded in the same excessively cool way.

Polly continued to splash. Lottie continued to play with her and wash her.

After a while, Alan said, 'This *is* big news for us, you know. I'm sorry I haven't always been . . . I suppose I've been a bit of a beast to you at times over your hospital.'

Lottie sat up again. 'Yes. You have.'

'Sorry.'

'Sorry as in sorry-but-you're-going-to-continue-being-a-beast? Or sorry as in you've-seen-the-error-of-your-ways-and-have-learned-to-love-everything-about-my-beloved-hospital?'

Alan grimaced. 'More like the first of those, probably.'

To his surprise, Lottie bent forwards and kissed him hard on the lips. 'Either way, it's an improvement, Mr Beast. So tell me, how did you catch your precious spy? Did you catch him flashing codes with a pocket mirror?'

'Not exactly.'

Alan laughed. It had been simple enough.

Knowing the importance of the oil contract, Alan had been on his guard ever since arriving in Rome. Already when

Marinelli had stepped out after him onto the balcony, Alan had been suspicious. Those suspicions had hardened when Marinelli had known everything about American aviators, but had failed to spot Alan's errors in describing General Balbo as a Marshal, referring to ten seaplanes instead of fourteen, and six men dead instead of the five actually lost. And then, when Marinelli – who'd claimed never to have been in America – knew instantly what Alan meant by 'not worth a plugged nickel', Alan's remaining doubts had vanished altogether.

From then on, it had been simple.

Alan had allowed himself to take up Marinelli's offers of 'help'. He had asked the Italian's advice on pricing his bid. At two to three cents under Shell's old prices, Marinelli had been happy. At four to five cents under, he'd been seriously worried. When Alan had suggested putting his bid in six cents under, the Italian was violently upset. It had been easy enough to guess from his reactions that his paymasters (whoever they were) were contemplating making a bid of five or six cents cheaper than Shell. So Alan had told him that he'd place a bid at three cents under, and had in fact placed his bid at seven cents under.

Even at what was fairly cut-throat pricing, Alanto had enough cheap oil to make a stunning profit with every barrel.

'Papa! Papa!'

In the bath, Polly wriggled with annoyance. *She* was the centre of the universe, not oil, and she considered it about time her father gave her the adoration she so plainly deserved.

'Now it's time for *meeeeee*.'

Alan and Lottie found each other with their eyes. Their argument hadn't disappeared by any means, but something had changed somehow. When Alan smiled, she returned his look, not just with her mouth but her eyes as well.

'Papa! *Papa*!'

Alan moved across to the bathtub. Polly broke into a vast grin of delight. The adoration was about to begin.

135

'In the name of Allah, the compassionate, the merciful . . .'

They were in a small aircraft in the grip of a hefty cross-wind, and the modern metal frame heaved and jolted with every gust. It was obviously impossible to kneel head to ground in the Muslim fashion, and the man next to Tom had to make do by knocking his head gently against his closed fist, as his left hand traced the lines of a prayer book open on his lap.

The plane lurched again and lost height at a stomach-losing pace.

Tom leaned to look out of the window. He saw the flat mud roofs of the old town of Tehran. He saw the desert beyond. He saw a handful of gardens, astonishingly lush and green in the surrounding dust. He saw a railway line, unfinished and unworked on, heading out into emptiness. Rebecca wanted him to confront his past, did she? Well, he was doing it now, though not in any way she knew about – or would approve of, if she did.

The plane lurched again.

The man next to Tom lost his place in the prayer book, and began again at the top. 'In the name of Allah . . .'

Jeez, thought Tom, was it as bad as that? Down the back end of the plane someone must have dropped a basket of limes, because a couple of dozen of the small green fruits came bouncing down the central aisle, bombing the legs of the passengers and even, in a couple of cases, hurtling through the open door into the cockpit.

Jeez! Tom wasn't religious in the slightest. Any tendency he'd ever had in that direction had been more than completely crushed by the experience of war, but this plane ride was enough to bring out religion in a plateful of rice. Out of the window, a windswept runway was rising to meet them at astonishing speed. There was a brief flash of mud-coloured houses, a handful of robed figures and an oxcart, a sudden glimpse of telegraph wires moaning in the breeze – then touchdown, bumpy and far too fast, but touchdown, blessed touchdown, all the same.

Tom let out the breath he'd been holding in. For the first time in his life, he was in Persia, the country of his childhood dreams.

136

The package arrived express from New York.

Alan knew what it was and ripped it open. Thirty sheets of cheap stationery, unfastened, Galston's nervous handwriting tilting down across the page. Names. Lists and lists of names: twenty-five to each page, times thirty pages, seven or eight hundred names in total. Each name: an English male, entry point Ellis Island, the year 1919 or 1920.

Abbott, Abrams, Ackerley, Adams, Adkins, Adshead . . . Right on down through the alphabet to *Yarnton, Yaxley, Yeats, Young, Zimmer.*

Next to each name, there were scribbled notes. The first name, for instance, read, 'ABBOTT – James – 88 – 1.6.19 – Ks Cit, Ks – Majestic.'

The first two digits represented Galston's precious dobs, though, annoyingly, only the year was given. Since most immigrants were in their twenties, there were a large number of names with their date of birth given as 1893.

The next three items represented date of entry, destination inside America, and vessel of disembarkation. Alan tried to think of a way he could use this information but came up short. As far as Alan could see, Tom could have arrived in Ellis Island anytime in 1919; he could have been bound for anywhere in America; and he could have arrived on any ship whatsoever. For all the enormous amount of work that Galston had put in, Alan guessed the information to be completely useless.

Which left names. Seven or eight hundred names, of which, at a guess, fifty or more would have a birth date in 1893. If Tom had altered his date of birth by even a year or two as well, then the list of possible names was even greater. But Alan had a better clue than that.

Pride.

Whatever had happened to Tom between August 1916 and the date in 1919 when he'd landed in America, Alan couldn't believe he'd have lost his pride. If Tom was alive, Alan was certain that his given name would still be Tom. Maybe, at a pinch Timothy or Trevor or Terence, but most likely just plain old Tom. It was true of the surname too. Creeley was Tom's name. It was his father's name. Alan couldn't imagine Tom becoming a Jones or Smith or Robinson: it would have been too much like running away.

So Alan turned to the Cs. *Cabot, Caffyn, Cahill, Cairns, Cairns, Calloway, Campbell* . . . One of the names leaped out at him. 'CALLOWAY – Thomas – 93 – 6.12.19 – New Haven, Ct – Calloway.'

Alan stared. There, near the top of the list, was a man, born 1893, first name Thomas, and the surname starting with a C.

After a long amazed pause, Alan checked the rest of the list. There were twelve names with the intials TC. Of those, five had the first name Thomas. Of those, only Tom Calloway had a birth date in 1893.

Hope began to grow sharp and alive. He turned back to Galston's hurried notes on Calloway – then noticed it. Galston had accidentally copied down the surname twice, once as the surname, the second time as the vessel of disembarkation. Alan's first reaction was disappointment. If Galston had got that wrong, he could have got the surname wrong. Or the birth date. Perhaps Alan would have to check all the TCs, just to be absolutely sure.

Then it clicked.

The ship! Galston hadn't made a mistake. Whoever Thomas Calloway might be, it was an assumed name, borrowed from the vessel that had brought him. The coincidence was too much. Alan had found a Thomas, born in 1893, and boasting a newly invented surname that started with C. Alan stared and stared and stared.

Sixteen years on from the day he'd lost him, Alan had finally found his twin.

137

It was thirteen years since Tom had first entered the United States of America and eight since he had become a citizen of his adopted country. He had honoured the flag (gladly). He had paid his taxes (grudgingly). And with the exception of the Eighteenth Amendment (the one that had outlawed the import, manufacture and sale of alcohol), he had respected the Constitution. He was, in every sense, a loyal American. An American and a republican.

Kings and monarchs revolted him. An English king had sent him to die. A German kaiser had tried to starve him. Tom would be happy if all the kings of the earth had been turned overnight into ordinary people: shoe-shine boys, oil-riggers, commercial travellers, bums.

And yet.

There's something about a king that can't help but touch a man. A king can make a man light-headed, make his heart run a little faster, make him feel hot and heavy in his own body.

Tom felt it as well. He felt it now. Because he too stood in the presence of a king.

138

It would have been the simplest thing in the world to get Pinkerton's to look for Tom Calloway. To look for and find. Only Alan hadn't done it. Just as he hadn't mentioned his discovery to Lottie. Not yet.

There was something he had to do first.

The station shrilled with the whistle of engines. White steam and black smoke eddied around the roof. Pigeons screamed and swooped.

Alan made his way up the platform towards a railway porter. He was a stocky weather-beaten man, smelling of tobacco and coal-smoke, but with a kind of rough geniality to him. Alan instantly recognised a type that had served the British Army well in France.

'George Hemplethwaite?' said Alan. 'I'm looking for a –'

'That's me. Hemplethwaite.'

The porter gave his answer with some reserve, as though people usually expected to pay for the privilege of knowing. Alan felt a sudden jab of nerves. He'd gone to the War Office with the names that Guy had given him. The War Office had been able to confirm Guy's records of regiment and company. Carragher, unfortunately, had been killed in the great German

535

offensive of 1918, but Hemplethwaite and Jones were alive and well, and Alan had been able to trace them without much difficulty. He was seeing Hemplethwaite today and would see Jones the following day.

'Yes, sir?'

'Good morning, Hemplethwaite. My name's Alan Montague, and I have come to ask you a question concerning an incident that took place in the trenches during 1916. You may answer in strictest confidence. This matter has nothing to do with any official investigation or inquiry. It's a purely personal matter and all I ask is that you answer my questions truthfully.'

'Yes, sir.' Hemplethwaite's tone became instantly bland and uninformative – the way any private spoke when asked anything sensitive by any officer. Alan recognised the familiar infantryman's stonewall straight away, but continued.

'The incident took place in August 1916. It involved two men. Major Montague and Mr Creeley. Do you know who I mean?'

Hemplethwaite looked sideways at the ground and wrinkled his mouth.

'Let me, once again, give you my word of honour that nothing you say is for any official purpose whatsoever. As I say, it's a personal matter, nothing more.'

Behind eyes that disclosed nothing, Hemplethwaite weighed the odds.

'And there's five pounds for you if your answers are helpful.'

Hemplethwaite grinned. 'Mr Creeley,' he said. 'Lieutenant in the Hampshire Fusiliers? Wasn't he the poor bugger that got done over with Shorty Hardwick and Bobby Stimson? Stupid bloody raid on the Boche machine guns.'

'Exactly –' Alan felt a violent jerk of emotion at hearing Tom's name spoken in that context – 'and Major Montague, as he was then, is my brother. Now what I want to know is whether you saw anything . . . anything unusual involving the two of them.'

'Maybe I did, sir, that would depend on what you was meaning.'

'Hemplethwaite, I understand that there may have been an argument. There may have been a shot fired. I want to stress that this is not a court-martial affair. Anything you say to me will go no further.'

Hemplethwaite nodded, turning Alan's words over to see if he could find any threat in them to himself. He couldn't. He cleared his throat. 'Well, sir, it was like this. The Hun was chucking stuff at us that day. I was bringing my Lewis gun up to the line, because George Davis, the poor sod who was there before me, got a bit of shell casing right up his arse – excuse me, sir, but that was where it was, two inches sticking out, four inches sticking in – and he hopped around so much his gun got all bunged up with dirt. Then there was a couple of other lads, Jones and Carragher, I think – it's been a while, sir, so I couldn't say for definite, like – shovelling out the trench. Regent Street they were calling it, I think, though it was a Jerry trench really. Anyway, they were shovelling it out, where a whizz-bang had knocked the banks in –'

'Yes?' Alan knew he should try to get the narrative in Hemplethwaite's own words, since he was much more likely to get the truth that way, but he could barely suppress his impatience. At the same time, he was grateful for Hemplethwaite's apparently perfect memory and stream-of-consciousness recall.

'Well, sir, anyway, as I was saying, your brother it would be, Major Montague, was coming running down the trench. The phone lines had been all smashed to buggery, sir, if you pardon the expression, and the runners kept on being shot that day. Bloody barrage, that's why the trench got into such a state. Anyway, top brass would have been all in a stew. That was why the major was up there, most likely.'

'Yes, yes. I know.'

A train came in beside them, with a hiss of steam and a

whine of brakes, followed by the clatter of doors and people. Alan wanted to move somewhere quieter, but Hemplethwaite stood as though rooted to the spot.

'Exactly, sir, that's right,' he said, ignoring the train. 'Well, your brother, he just about runs into Mr Creeley. I didn't recognise the lieutenant, myself, but Johnny Jones knew Creeley from way back, a right good 'un, he used to say, extra bloody shame about raid, if you ask me – it was always the good 'uns that went, sir, no disrespect – and he said it was definitely Creeley, swear to God and everything. They have a bloody great row. Your brother and Creeley, I mean. I don't know what about. There was shells still coming down. And I'd got the bloody Lewis gun caught in the revetting, sir, fucking great nail sticking out, remember it like yesterday, thinking I was going to get a whizz-bang down my backside before I'd got the bleeding gun unstuck.

'Anyway, there's me trying to free up the Lewis gun, but partly watching to see if there's going to be a bit of a dust-up, when, bugger me – pardon me, sir – Creeley whips his gun out and shoots old Major Montague – that'd be your brother, sir, I'm afraid – bang, right in the leg. Looked to me like he wanted to stick the bullet some other place altogether.' Hemplethwaite tapped the centre of his forehead. 'That was it. Creeley went scarpering off up to the front and Montague came hollering down screaming blue bloody murder . . .'

Hemplethwaite finished the story in his own inimitable style. Alan heard him out in a state of increasing shock. He'd seek out John Jones, of course, but he was already certain that the man would simply confirm the basic outline of Hemplethwaite's account. Tom had shot Guy. In cold blood and without provocation. Guy hadn't put his hand to Tom. He hadn't even touched his gun, still less drawn it.

On the train home that evening, Alan thought about Tom Creeley-Calloway, the twin with whom he had once shared his life. The man who now cared so little about his former attachments that he could live fifteen years in the United

States and not bother, not once, to send Alan a message saying he was alive and well. The man who was willing to shoot his twin's brother. The man whose darkness had outshone his light.

Alan felt infinitely sad. He felt as though an ancient friendship had dissolved. In its place, there was nothing but loss.

139

The summerhouse had no chairs, only carpets and cushions. The Shah, the King of Persia, was sprawled over two dozen cushions of silk and silk-velvet, massively embroidered and glinting with jewels. The cushions left for Tom were ample enough, but he didn't dare stretch out, and he didn't have the knack of sitting in a way that was either comfortable or dignified. The Shah looked arrogantly at Tom, saw his discomfort, and didn't care a straw. He was a big man, strong and military, and fully half a head or even a head taller than most of the men in his entourage.

'Calloway?' said the Shah. An interpreter by his side, pointlessly repeated the name.

'Yes, Your Majesty.'

'Norgaard Petroleum?' The Shah spoke the unfamiliar syllables with an accent so thick Tom hardly recognised them.

'Yes, Your Majesty.'

The Shah grunted and sipped on the iced sherbet that he had and Tom didn't. Despite his arrogant manner, the Shah had been an ordinary officer in the Persian Cossack Brigade. He'd risen to become colonel, and then, in 1921, led a troop of three thousand men into Tehran. He'd arrested some politicians, appointed his own prime minister and, after a decent delay, had himself crowned Shah of Persia, the oldest monarchy in the world. He was tough, uncompromising and decisive. In another life, Tom thought, he could have been a decent oilman.

'Well?' The Shah was blunt. 'What do you want?'

Tom had heard much about oriental codes of politeness. If you want to tell your adversary that he is the stinking son of an ox-driving dungheap and that you fully intend to cut his tongue out if he doesn't repay you the two kran and one abassi he owes you – then naturally you have to begin by honouring his ancestors and praising his hospitality. And if you've come to flatter a king, then heaven help you . . .

'Your Majesty, we in America have heard so much about the beauties of your kingdom and the richness of your land, particularly oil, that . . .' Tom's fine sentence sputtered to a premature close. He wiped his forehead, feeling uncomfortable. His old Persian lessons lay packed away in the back of his brain someplace. He couldn't find them. Alan had always been the natural linguist, anyway. Tom was just a tongue-tied, English-speaking, all-American oilman.

The Shah grunted again and looked impatient.

Tom tried again: the American version this time. 'Your Majesty, we would love to be able to drill for oil here. We think there's lots more to be found. We'd drill it fast. Pipe it fast. Sell it fast. We'd make a huge contribution to your treasury.'

'We have sold the concession.'

'Yes, Your Majesty.'

'You know this.'

'Yes, Your Majesty.'

'To Anglo-Persian and the other one. Alanto.'

'Indeed, sir.'

'So why have you come?'

Tom watched for a sign that the Shah would contemplate breaking an agreement. There was no such sign. A mountain breeze fluttered the corner of the tent. Tom saw a glimmer of silks and a woman's foot. He longed to be out of the tent.

He longed to see the woman's face, to smile at her, to begin a flirtation. Here in modernising Persia, women went unveiled. Men wore fedoras above their robes. A surge of recklessness seized hold of him.

'Your Majesty, Alanto Oil isn't paying you enough. They're robbing you blind – playing you for a patsy, as you might say. You've got some fine oil lands here, sir, and at Norgaard Petroleum we'd pay you a full price to drill 'em.'

There was some difficulty over translating this speech. 'Robbing blind' and 'play for a patsy' were terms that Tom needed to put into more conventional English before the interpreters could get a grip on what he meant. The Shah looked as black as thunder as his interpreters stumbled.

Then they were done. There was a moment's silence. The mountain stream burbled down its marble channels through the summerhouse and on into the garden beyond. Tom didn't know if he was going to be thrashed for his impudence or thanked for his honesty. Somewhere there was the laughter of women, quickly cut short. Birds called in the mountains beyond.

Then, eventually, the silence was broken. The Shah spoke again. The speech was short and didn't need much translation. It was two words long.

'How much?'

140

It was gone midnight by the time Alan arrived home. He'd been met off the train from Manchester by Ferguson, the chauffeur, at half-past nine, but Alan had been unable to face going straight home. He'd gone first to his club, then just driven the streets. It was long gone midnight by the time Ferguson dropped him at his front door.

'Good night, sir.'

'Good night, Ferguson. Sorry to keep you so late.'

'Not to mind, sir. Good night.'

Alan took out his house key and turned to the door. Ferguson was back in the driver's seat, and was putting the big car into gear, about to move off. Alan had a sudden thought and hurried back to the Rolls. He rapped on the window.

'Sir?'

'Listen, Ferguson, you don't by any chance know how to make cocoa, do you?'

'Cocoa, sir?'

'Yes. Mrs Montague loves the stuff and I haven't a clue how to make it. It's just I don't want to wake the kitchen staff.'

'Yes, of course, sir. I'd be happy to . . .'

A few moments later, they were downstairs. Alan was

hopelessly unfamiliar with his own kitchen. He didn't know where the milk was kept, or the cocoa, or coal for the range. Ferguson found each item in turn and set a pan of milk to heat.

'The trick is not to let it boil, sir. And stirring. It goes lumpy unless you stir it.'

'You're very domestic, Ferguson. I'm ashamed of myself.'

'Does Mrs Montague take sugar, sir?'

'Um . . . I've no idea. Is it usual?'

'I'll put some in a bowl. She can add it if she likes it. You'll have a cup too, I expect, sir?'

'Thank you.'

Alan found a tray and put it out on the table: his one contribution so far. The milk came close to boiling, Ferguson whipped it from the heat and made the cocoa. Alan thanked him again, saw him to the door, where they wished each other good night for a final time. Alan went upstairs bearing his tray. Lottie was sleeping, stretched out, holding Alan's pillow in her arms as though dreaming about the real thing. Alan woke her gently.

'My love, it's me. Sorry to wake you. I've brought cocoa.'

Lottie blinked – once, twice – rubbed her eyes – yawned – and sat up.

'Well, of course it's you. If you're sorry about waking me, then why do it? And I wasn't missing cocoa.'

'I wanted to talk.'

'My dear, you are very welcome to talk. It's the listening part I have an objection to.'

Alan kissed Lottie into something like compliance and settled the cocoa into her hands.

'You didn't wake up the kitchen staff, did you?'

'Of course not. Ferguson made it for me.'

'Good old Ferguson.'

'Yes . . . Listen, my love, I've got news.'

'Yes?'

'Big news.'

544

'I just said yes. Should I say it again?'

'Two things, actually. First thing. I've found Tom. I don't mean our son Tom, I mean Tom Creeley. My twin, Tom.'

Lottie took the news in slowly as though still needing to distinguish carefully between dream and reality. Then, with gathering amazement, she said, 'Darling, you mean you've found Tom Creeley? Alive? Here? Where . . . ?'

'I haven't *found*-found him. But I know his name. I know when he arrived in America. I have a firm of detectives who are sure to find him if I ask them to.'

'*If* you ask them to? *If*?'

'Which brings me to my second piece of news.'

'Yes?'

Alan paused. He suddenly didn't know how to say what he had to say.

'Yes?' repeated Lottie.

'Um . . . well, this sounds extraordinary. But true. Apparently true . . . The fact of the matter is that Tom shot Guy.'

By this time, Lottie was wide-eyed and wide-awake. 'Tom *shot* Guy?'

'So it would seem.'

'*Shot* him? Shot Guy? Just now? When? I thought you said –'

'No, no. Not now. In the war.' Alan took a deep breath and began. 'Tom and I had quarrelled. It wasn't the first quarrel of our lives, not by any means, but it was the worst. It was easily the worst. Guy had prompted the quarrel quite deliberately. He sent me to where he knew Tom was in bed with my girl – the girl I thought was mine, I hadn't realised she was . . . she was common property.'

Alan swallowed. He'd never mentioned this detail of his pre-marital life to Lottie before, but she simply shrugged. 'It was war,' she commented.

'Yes . . . Anyway, Tom would have been angry. Furious. It appears that he met Guy in the trenches during the Somme.

545

He argued with him, then shot him. In the leg. Here.' Alan indicated the spot on his own thigh.

'So Guy says?' said Lottie, gently suggesting that the truth might be a little different.

'Yes, so Guy says, but he has witnesses, dammit. I interviewed one of them today. He wasn't acting, I'd stake my life on it. There's another man I need to see, but he'll confirm Guy's story, I'm absolutely certain.'

'But, darling, Tom is supposed to have *shot* Guy?' Lottie's tone was incredulous.

'Yes. You must understand that Tom had a tendency to be . . .' Alan struggled to find the right word, 'to be overimpulsive.'

'Which is a polite way of saying that he could lose his head completely.'

'Yes. Of course, he'd never ended up shooting anyone before . . . although . . .'

'Yes?'

'Well, there was another time.'

'Another time? This isn't sounding good.'

'Earlier in the war Tom stole a motorbike and drove to Arras to threaten Guy with a revolver. He thought Guy was plotting to have the pair of us split up. He was probably right.'

Lottie's eyes were wide with astonishment, though she was careful over what she said. 'Twice? Once he threatened Guy, the other time he put a bullet into him?'

Alan nodded.

'Guy was a senior officer, presumably, when it happened?'

Alan nodded again.

'And there were witnesses?'

Another nod.

'Gosh!' said Lottie mildly. She knew as well as Alan what Tom's offence would have meant at court martial.

'Yes, "gosh" is about right.'

Lottie spooned the skin off her cocoa and began to drink. 'Ferguson makes excellent cocoa,' she commented.

'I'll tell him.'

'If I was being fussy, perhaps he could have used a little more cocoa powder. If I was being very fussy.'

Alan nodded.

'But no lumps. That's the difficult bit, getting it smooth.'

'Yes, dear.'

'Darling, how do you feel about all this?' said Lottie at last. 'You must be in rather a stew.'

'The devil only knows what I think,' said Alan. 'I've no idea.'

Lottie put down her cocoa. 'Will you promise to answer my next question honestly?'

'Yes.'

'Do you like Guy?'

'No.'

'Never have?'

'No. Never have.' Alan sighed. 'Look, I'm a different sort of person from him. I haven't ever quite approved of him. But in the end he is my brother. I don't want just to give up on him.'

'No, of course not. I didn't mean that . . . And Tom? You loved him, of course?'

'Yes.'

'Still do?'

'Still do.'

'And you approved of him? You said you didn't approve of Guy.'

'I admired Tom as I've almost never admired anyone else. As a matter of fact, I think you may be the only exception, my dearest. Tom was crammed with faults, I knew that. He was maddening, impulsive, foolish, quarrelsome, a devil with women – good Lord, he was no kind of saint. But there was something infinitely noble in him too. I always felt that, deep down, his goodness was a thousand times stronger than his darkness.'

He sighed deeply, and Lottie finished the thought for him.

'But now you're worried. You think perhaps Tom is only human, after all – and perhaps not even a particularly good one. He shot Guy in a mere temper tantrum. It was wartime, of course, and emotions run high – but still. Perhaps you need to recognise that Tom was a bit more flawed than you realised.'

'A bit more? A *bit*? It would be an unforgivable thing to do. Absolutely unforgivable . . . And then on top of all that, Guy thinks the reason why he left for America was fear of court martial. If that were true, it would make Tom a coward as well as a villain.'

There was a pause. Lottie sipped her cocoa. Alan sipped at his.

'And something else,' he said.

'Yes?'

'You've been right all along. I should have known.'

'Of course I have and of course you should, but perhaps you could tell me what on earth you're talking about.'

'The war. It isn't over . . . till – well – until it's really over. When I think of going to see you at the hospital, it's almost more than I can bear. The men. The soldiers. It's as though I see my entire platoon lying there again. The few that didn't die, that is. I hadn't realised till now. There are some things that never leave. The horror. The loss.'

'Oh, my poor love!'

She kissed him, and Alan felt as though some awful distance between them had suddenly collapsed and shrunk to nothing. He kissed her back, hard. He had fallen in love with Lottie because of her bravery and compassion. He felt he was about to fall right back in love with her, and for the same old reasons.

'You don't mind?' he asked.

'Silly.'

'If I ask very nicely, will you give me a proper tour of your hospital some day soon? A proper one. No need to send me chasing after matron this time.'

'I'd like that.'

'And a holiday. We need a proper holiday. Rome perhaps? Or the Riviera?'

Lottie nodded. 'Yes, please. Both. Very soon.'

'I love you.'

Lottie nodded, as though simply collecting her due. 'And by the way,' she said, 'since you're being so sweet, allow me to save you from making a colossal mistake.'

'Oh?'

'Don't give up on Tom.'

Alan's voice hardened. 'I don't think I have, only –'

'Only what? He shot Guy, who's always been vile to him. In wartime. In the midst of battle. You don't know the circumstances. You don't know what made him leave.'

'Cowardice. It looks like simple cowardice.'

'Don't be silly. Your Tom? A coward?'

'Apparently. Perhaps I trusted the wrong brother after all.'

'Oh, Alan, you can't mean it.'

'Why not? Guy's here. Tom isn't.'

'Find him. Don't give up now. Find him.'

'He hasn't bothered to find me. That's hard to swallow after all these years. After all I've done.'

'Find him, my love. You won't settle until you do.'

Alan shrugged. He had his annual visit to Persia coming up shortly. He'd think it over there, make a decision before arriving home.

He nodded. 'I suppose I will . . . probably . . . not for sure . . . I'll see.'

Lottie smiled and yawned. 'Come to bed, my love.'

141

It was nearly three weeks later. Tom was home from Persia, only to find Rebecca tear-stained and shaky, curled up on one of the big couches in the drawing room.

A letter, postmarked from Germany, lay on the table. In the cool high-ceilinged rooms beyond, Tom could hear the maids and servants moving around as quietly as they could, knowing that their mistress was upset. Out in the garden, Mitch and Pipsqueak were playing together, but even they seemed to be observing a kind of tactful silence.

'Hon?'

Rebecca said nothing, just let herself melt into her husband's arms. Tear channels had already flowed and dried on her cheeks, and new ones were opening up to accommodate the new rush of tears. Tom stroked her dark hair and high forehead. She seldom wore perfumes or scented lotions, but she always smelled good, something like warm skin and hair that's been dried in the sun.

'Hon?'

Rebecca's voice began – broke – then began again.

'My parents . . . They're OK, they're fine . . . But their rabbi, a good man, from Lithuania like them . . . A mob broke into his house. Tore up his holy books. Began to set the house on fire . . . He came home. Found them. Protested,

I don't know what. They set upon him. Kicked him. Beat him. Left him unconscious. Then . . . then . . . they left. The house was on fire. It wasn't possible to pull him out. He died . . . The newspapers afterwards accused him of murdering Christian babies. It was a matter of justice, they said. The people who did it received nothing. No punishment. No blame.'

Rebecca poured out her speech in broken bursts. Tom petted and soothed her. Eventually, it was possible to speak more normally, and he said, 'They must leave. There've been too many stories like this lately. We can pay for everything. They can come here and live with us. Or we'll buy them an apartment in one of the Jewish parts of New York. They can eat chicken soup and kneidlach and not even notice they've left.'

'I've asked them, I've asked a hundred times. They're getting old. They don't want to move again. They say . . . they say . . . they say it'll pass. They say it's just while Herr Hitler needs to prove himself a strong man.'

Tom was silent for a moment. The thought of Europe's ancient hatreds appalled him. They had ruined one genera-tion. It seemed that they were darkening the air for a second time in the space of twenty years. He felt the old anger that he associated with his time in prison. He never wanted to leave the United States again. He'd be perfectly happy never to leave Texas. His trip to Persia already seemed like half a lifetime away.

He reached for something to smoke, wanted a cigar, remem-bered Rebecca's distaste for them, and moved instead for a cigarette. He lit up. His thoughts of oil passed. There were more important things in life, after all.

'Your parents. Isn't there anything we can do for them?'

Rebecca shook her head.

'We could send money?'

She shook her head again. 'It would only draw attention. That's the last thing they need.'

The two of them fell silent. Across the globe, in a different continent, the fate of Rebecca's parents and millions like them was falling into the hands of dictators. There was nothing to do now. Nothing but pray.

142

Alan enjoyed his annual trip to Persia – or Iran, as the country had now begun to call itself. His visit to the oilfields up in the mountains was still to come, but he always began with an inspection of the refinery and shipping facilities down on the coast.

Now he was in a hotel built right on the shore of the Gulf, where Kharg Island bobbed blue on the horizon. He was shaving on the balcony with the help of a tiny wall mirror and a bowlful of soapy water, enjoying the sea air and the sparkling light. His war-damaged lung preferred the clean air of Iran to the soots and smokes of London. He breathed easily. It was a time of day that Alan relished. The rift with Lottie had been healed. His family was well. The only cloud on the horizon was the whole ugly matter of Tom Creeley-Calloway and the shooting incident with Guy. Alan didn't want to think about it. Not yet. He shoved the thought successfully to the back of his mind. He was at peace.

Then a frenzied little Iranian boy burst in on him.

'*Aqa, aqa,* the Shah is starting a war against us!' The boy went on to describe the atrocity in highly coloured language. The Shah had sent soldiers. No oil was flowing. The whole company was being closed. Shortly, there would be shooting and massacres and tribes from the north would swoop down, destroying everything in their path, with explosions, famine and plague following in their wake.

Alan finished shaving the right-hand side of his face and began slowly on the left. His face was getting its first real lines of age. In places he had to stretch out the skin to make a smooth surface for the razor. He told the boy to help himself to a couple of figs from the bowl on the table indoors and then to go and fetch him a cup of tea. The boy disappeared. Alan finished shaving and patted his face dry with a small square of towel. He wasn't too concerned about the boy's news. In Persia, minor incidents had a habit of being blown up out of all proportion. He ate some fruit and the boy returned carrying tea and a warm flatbread straight from the oven.

Alan drank the first and ate the second. The boy stood in a corner gazing at him in wonder. In an effort to reduce the staring, Alan asked the boy if he went to school. He did, and quite soon was absorbed in reciting his times table, before going on to show off his English.

'My name is Sadegh. I am ten years old. The weather is fine today. Thank you. Please. How do you do? I am over-joyed to hear it . . .'

Alan finished his breakfast and let the boy escort him down to the waterfront. The smell of salt and seaweed mixed with the smell of diesel engines and oil. Little blue waves ruffled the water, where white gulls swooped in search of food.

But the boy had been right.

At Alan's back, there was a line of Alanto storage tanks chock-full with oil. To his right there was a pumping station, a coil of thick rubber hose and a team of white-robed Alanto Oil workers. In front of him, there was an Alanto tanker, riding high in the water, waiting to take on oil.

But it couldn't.

And wouldn't.

Because in between the storage tanks and the tanker, there stood a double line of twenty-four soldiers, rifles held across their bodies. An officer stood motionless in front of them. Alan noticed that the soldiers were from a northern regiment, the Cossack Brigade, the Shah's own men. Alan wasn't scared by the rifles, but he was petrified by the piece of paper in the hands of the officer.

It was an order signed by the Shah himself. The concession was cancelled. With immediate effect. Without compensation.

Behind Alan, the boy had found a new piece of English with which to impress the illustrious visitor. 'The Shah make great big fight. He kill us all. I die. You die. He, she or it die . . .'

143

The great veranda sparkled with light. Silverware glinted on the table. Glassware imported from Venice shone brilliantly amongst the candles. Servants fussed over the place settings, adjusting plates and knives to the accuracy of one sixteenth of an inch.

Tom was throwing a dinner for some of biggest hitters in Texas's oil establishment. Tom was part of the Texan scene now. He was liked, respected, admired. He strolled over to check the table. The table setting was pretty much perfect, but he found a bunch of flowers beginning to brown in one of the stands. He called a maid over to ask her to change it.

'Oh sir!' she said, as if genuinely shocked. She removed the offending blooms and began a strip-search of all the other flower arrangements. Tom looked at her but didn't recognise her. He and Rebecca had a lot of servants now, but Tom still prided himself on knowing them all.

'Excuse me,' he said. 'What's your name?'

'Sarah Gutman, sir.' Her accent wasn't American. It was like Rebecca's, only much thicker. She had to frown with concentration to understand Tom's English.

'From Central Europe?'

'Germany, sir.'

'You're Jewish, of course?'

'Yes, sir.'

'Recently arrived?'

She didn't immediately understand the word 'recently', and struggled to find an answer.

'*Sie sind neulich angekommen?*' said Tom, shocking even himself by how easily the language of prison camp sprang to his lips. Prison must have been a better teacher than he'd remembered.

'*Ja, ja, neulich.* Three days ago, sir.'

Tom nodded. 'Thank you for doing the flowers,' he said. 'And welcome to Norgaard House.'

That night, as they were undressing for bed, Tom spoke to Rebecca.

'You hired a new girl, Sarah Gutman.'

'That's right. She arrived in New York as a refugee and drifted down here in search of work. I know we don't really need another maid.'

Tom shook his head. 'You were thinking of your parents, I guess.'

Rebecca stood in her evening gown removing a coil of pearls. It was rare that her husband could resist touching her when she stood undressing like this, but his mind was in a different place. 'Yes. My parents. Their friends. Their relatives. Their people. They're my people too.'

Tom plucked at his bow tie and brought it loose in a single practised movement. Rebecca had observed how easily Tom had taken on a rich man's role. Even from the first, he'd addressed servants as though he was used to having them. He wore a tuxedo with confidence. He could tie a bow tie without needing a mirror. She had long guessed that his life in England had been one of privilege, but her husband had never let himself speak of anything at all before his capture by the Germans. He was a mystery, a wonderful mystery.

'Good idea,' he commented. 'At least, it's something we can do.'

She loved her husband. This comment was so typical of him. He voted Republican, he hated unions, he had little time for Roosevelt (aside from liking the way the price of oil had come up off the floor), but injustice to one group at the hands of another got to him every time. The black servants in the house and the black workers in Norgaard Petroleum earned wages exactly equal to the whites. If the whites didn't like it, they were free to quit. More than once Tom had been threatened. He was a 'nigger-lover', a 'white-faced coon', he was 'unAmerican trash'. He'd had rocks thrown at his car and received warnings from the Ku Klux Klan. Tom ignored the rocks and scorned the warnings.

'Perhaps that's not all we can do,' said Rebecca softly.

'Hmm?'

'We could do more. Find refugees off the boat. Help them with money. It can be tough here, getting started, especially without good English.'

He glanced sharply at her, guessing that she had in mind her own troubled years after arriving.

'Sure.'

'We could hire somebody in New York. A kind of welcome-to-America person. They could handle the details for us.'

'Ah, honey!'

Tom screwed up his face. He was uncomfortable. Rebecca was puzzled. Tom wasn't mean with his money – far from it. Nor was he unsympathetic to the plight of the badly off.

'You don't want to help?'

'No, it's not that . . . It's just . . . I don't know. We left Europe, Becca. We left it because of everything like this. The hatred. The history. The injustices. I just don't want to get close to all that again.'

Rebecca had taken off her jewellery now, and had combed her hair out for the night. Now she slipped her gown off her shoulders and stood in her underwear in front of her dressing table. She wasn't sure what to say. She could simply have argued, but she didn't want something good to grow out of an argument. Instead, she stood quiet for a few moments, before saying gently, 'Isn't that the point, Tomek?'

'What? Isn't what the point?'

'That we left. That we were able to.'

'Ah, I guess.'

Tom had been slow undressing, but he speeded up now, flinging jacket, shirt and trousers to the bed in quick succession.

'We could begin slowly. See how it went.'

Rebecca went to hang up her dress, and passed close in front of Tom smelling of perfume and warm skin. He put an arm out to stop her, kissing her on the eyes and mouth. Beneath his shorts he was aroused and she stroked him tenderly.

They pulled apart.

'Nope,' said Tom decisively.

'No?' Rebecca was shocked at him and her voice showed it.

'No. If we're going to do this, let's do it. Why screw around? We could make a real difference. How about we set up some kind of fund? Help Jews from Germany come over here. Help them with cash, transport, jobs, everything. Heck, we could buy apartment blocks where they can stay until they find their feet. If the whole Hitler thing blows over, we can resell the property at a profit more than likely. Depression's kicked hell out of the market.'

'Oh, Tomek! Tomaszu, my love.'

Rebecca felt full of respect for her husband. If he decided he was going to help Jews from Germany, he'd do it. He'd fill whole ships with refugees. He'd house them, feed them, help them with their schooling and their job-hunting. He'd do it without vanity or desire for recognition. He'd do it because he wanted to spend his money like that and that was all.

'What do you say?' he said. 'A fund. Call it the Rebecca Calloway Foundation. Something like that. You run it. Start out with a couple of million bucks and see how it goes. If you need more, we got plenty.'

His lips asked one question, but his eyes, roaming all over the soft contours of her body, asked another.

'I love you,' she answered, saying 'yes' to both.

144

Alan had told Lottie that he'd think things over in Persia. He'd said to her that he'd use his time away to decide whether to go in search of Tom Creeley-Calloway. When he'd said it, he'd thought the decision might be a tough one. But as things turned out, it was easy.

Horribly easy.

On finding that the concession had been cancelled, his first action had been to sail up the coast to Abadan. Once there, he'd found Anglo-Persian in the same position as Alanto: no concession, no business.

'What the devil is the Shah playing at?' said Alan to the Abadan refinery manager.

'Raising money for his treasury, I expect. Apparently things have been stirred up by some American oilman who came here offering ludicrous amounts in exchange for drilling rights.'

'Drilling rights? We've got the only blasted drilling rights.'

'Absolutely. Damned Yanks.'

'Do we know which company was involved?'

'The company was a Texan outfit, Norgaard, I believe the name was.'

'And the oilman?'

'A chap called Calloway. Thomas Calloway.'

145

That was it.

Done. Finished. Dusted. Over.

Tom had found a new contentment. He'd come to America in search of everything and now, at long last, he'd found it.

Home? He'd come home the day he set foot in Texas. Oil? Norgaard Petroleum was everything he'd ever hoped for and more. Family? He had the best family in the entire world. And even the past felt settled now. Alan and the Montagues had done him great wrongs in the past, but, in overturning Alanto's concession in Persia, Tom had struck back in a way that seemed to settle the score.

Tom was at peace. If the Montagues never crossed his path again, he'd never again cross theirs. The accumulated bitterness of twenty years seemed washed away and done with for ever.

146

Alan lost his head.

Tom!

Tom had done this. He'd come to Persia for no reason except to smash the company that Alan had built in his name and memory. He'd done it from anger; from cool, malicious calculation; from some inexplicable desire for destruction. Over the years, Alan had wondered endlessly about the reason for Tom's long absence. He'd thought of everything. Everything except the one true reason.

Rage.

Even out here, on the burning Persian coast, Alan could feel the storm of Tom's unreasonable anger. Sixteen years in the making, Tom's fury was like a whirlwind storming round everything that Alan had spent his life creating.

Something inside Alan hardened and blackened. For the first time in his life, his thoughts turned to revenge.

The boardroom was silent. Twelve faces stared in silence. The Chairman, Egham Dunlop, nodded at his son-in-law, who stood up.

'You've heard the news,' said Alan, briefly. 'The Shah has cancelled our concession. We're not allowed to ship so much as a single barrel of oil out of the country. Though we still have access to oil in Iraq, it's nowhere near enough to meet our obligations. Within a matter of weeks, our stocks will be exhausted.' Alan smiled thinly. 'To put it mildly, gentlemen, our company is on the brink of disaster.'

Silence.

What was there to say, after all? Alanto's offices stood in a quiet street near St James's Park. The day was a foggy one, the sort that only London could produce: green and choking, harsh with the sting and smell of coal-smoke. Outside the boardroom windows, the leafless plane trees were hardly visible through the murk.

Then Dunlop spoke. 'We'll take it back, I suppose?'

Alan looked surprised. 'I beg your pardon, Chairman?'

'Take it back.' Dunlop tapped the map of Persia that hung on the wall. 'Give the Shah a whiff of gunpowder. Knock some sense into him.'

'I'm not sure that would be altogether . . .'

'We could send in a few Tommies. Land 'em here.' He tapped the map. 'March 'em here. Either sort out the Shah or put in one of our own chaps. Don't see why not. Who's going to stop us?'

'The Persian army, perhaps.'

'The Persian army! Phoo!'

'It has a hundred thousand men and Western armaments,' pursued Alan. 'Besides, I'm not sure –'

'A hundred thousand men, eh? Yes, but have they ever seen a De Havilland bomber in action? Have they ever tasted –'

'Perhaps the Managing Director would explain to us what he has in mind?' said one of the other directors hurriedly, in an attempt to ease Dunlop away from his ever more blood-thirsty schemes.

'Thank you,' said Alan. 'First things first. We need to get our concession back. We'll make the moral case forcefully, of course. The Shah's acting illegally and he knows it. On the other hand, we need to be realistic. He's the king and it's his country. He can do as he pleases. We'll have to pay more than we're paying now. A lot more. But we need the oil. It's as simple as that.'

There was general agreement. Even Dunlop's warlike muttering died down to little more than a background hum.

'You'll go to Tehran, I suppose?' asked one of the directors. 'How long do you think . . . ?'

But Alan was shaking his head. 'No. We'll send one of our best men.'

'But the negotiations? Shouldn't *you* handle them?'

Alan's thin smile reappeared. It wasn't warm inside the boardroom, but there was a thin glaze of sweat on his forehead, as though the pea-souper fog outside had crept in and settled.

'Hear me out. I said the first thing was to get the concession back, but we need to face facts. And the fact is that these countries are unstable. Persia has just proved it this year. Iraq may do the same next year. In my opinion, the long-term security of our business is at stake. Does anyone present disagree?'

Alan gazed round the room. A few of the directors shook their heads. Nobody spoke.

'Good.' Alan nodded. 'Then there's only one place to invest. A place of abundant oil, abundant freedom, known stability: America.'

Again he paused, looking for doubters. There wasn't so much as a ripple of hesitation. Alan smiled to himself. Tom wanted a fight, did he? Tom was keen for a scrap, was he? Well, Alan had no intention of disappointing his twin.

147

'Happy fortieth birthday . . . Jesus Christ!'

Bard, now in his late fifties, was still a strong man. But the suitcase that came thundering down onto Tom's desk was so heavy it virtually split the rolltop.

'You're gonna be lifting the next one, pal.'

Tom grinned. His birthday gift was hardly a surprise, but it was a damned nice one all the same. He released the catch on the suitcase and wrenched it open. Inside lay a half-dozen drill bits, each one battered and worn, and each one labelled: 'Gator Bay No. 1', 'Arthur Roland No. 2', and so on.

Tom's grin widened.

As the price of oil had settled back down, so Tom had begun to drill again. Bard's gift was a collection of the drill bits that had struck oil from the last eight months of Norgaard's drilling. They'd join the other bits that already decorated the walls of Tom's office. Tom's contentment was growing by the month.

And it was growing, even though one of the main outcomes of his actions in Persia had been to bring Alanto Oil right onto his own doorstep. Alanto had invested in a company named Blackwater Oil, based right here in Texas. In the past, the move would have sent Tom crazy. But not now. Tom was at peace. He knew he'd caused Alanto a problem. If Alanto took the obvious steps to fix it, then Tom was hardly in a position to object. If he'd been in Alan's shoes, he'd have done the exact same thing.

He got up and strolled to the window. Over the road, he could see a Blackwater service station selling gas. Even that sight didn't bother him now.

'Life's pretty good, eh, Lyman?' he said.

'Not bad. Could be worse. Yeah, I reckon.'

The two men stared out of the window. Out on the Blackwater forecourt, a white-shirted man was struggling to fix a big red sign in place by the roadside.

'Doing anything tonight?' asked Bard.

'No. Just going home.'

'Well, there's worse places, I guess.'

Tom nodded.

The guy out on the forecourt got his sign in place and stood back, sweating but happy. Tom's gaze suddenly sharpened.

'Is that . . . ?' he said. His voice was tense.

Bard came closer. He too stiffened. 'No! They couldn't . . .'

The sign hadn't been properly secured and it swung sluggishly in the hot, thin air. One of the flaps brought the sign into closer view.

'What in the name of shit . . . ?'

'Jesus Christ! Does that say . . . ?'

The sign flapped again and its message was unmistakable: huge red letters glaring on a white background. The sign said:

GAS
only
15c.!!

'Fifteen cents!' said Bard. 'Have they gone crazy? *Fifteen* cents?!'

For a moment Tom continued to stare. His knuckles were white and there was a look on his face that Bard had never seen before.

'Go check this out, willya?' said Tom.

That was all. He meant: go and find out if it's just this one garage, or the whole chain of them.

But he already knew the answer. It would be the whole damn lot of them. Alan had discovered his twin's identity and here was the proof. The Blackwater sign wasn't a coincidence, it wasn't a mistake. It was a fortieth birthday card addressed to Tom and signed by Alan.

And that was when Tom knew it. That the past wasn't over. That the past would never be over. And that whatever might have happened in the past was nothing, *nothing* compared with what was yet to come.

PART SEVEN

Shortage of petrol! It's enough to make one weep.

General Erwin Rommel, Commander of the
German Afrika Korps, during the retreat from
El Alamein, November 1942.

148

The thirties had started badly, but they were ending worse.

In China: war. In Russia: tyranny. In Germany: the seeds of disaster, still unripe but growing all the time.

Just one generation after the Great War, another war loomed. It was a hard time to be optimistic, and few people were.

It was summer 1939.

For oilmen, the thirties had been OK. Not great, but good enough. The glut of oil from the East Texan boom hadn't exactly dried up, but somehow the system had adapted. Auto makers still built cars. People still drove 'em. They still needed gas.

Profits had been tough to come by, but finding a profit had always been tough. For oilmen, the thirties had been not great, but OK.

But there were exceptions.

Two, in particular.

In Britain, Alanto Oil had stumbled from catastrophe to crisis. Bad luck sat over the company like a storm cloud. Alanto still hauled oil from the ground. It still explored, drilled, struck, pumped, piped, refined, shipped and marketed the valuable liquid. But all for nothing. The company had huge revenues and zero profits. There were literally years in which Mr and Mrs Havelock, the elderly couple who ran the one-roomed village grocery on Whitcombe High Street, were able to report bigger profits than Alanto Oil, the third biggest oil company in Europe.

The second exception was Norgaard.

In Tom Calloway, the company was blessed with one of the finest chief executives in the oil industry. When misfortune struck the company in one area of its operations, he flung the company hard in a different direction. He dodged, twisted, rolled and spun. To no avail. Bad luck pursued him like a swarm of bees. Profits disappeared. Losses spread. There were literally years in which Jim and Minnie Singer, the elderly couple who ran the hardware store on Kilgore Main Street, were able to report bigger profits than Norgaard Petroleum, the third biggest oil company in the American South.

The war between Alan and Tom had intensified and grown bitter. As kids they'd fought in play. As adults they fought for real. But though some things had changed, other things hadn't.

Never submit.

Never give up.

The old rules were still the same. Unless things changed, not one but both companies would be destroyed.

And, despite many losses, there was one in particular that had affected Tom to the bone.

One fine autumn day in 1936, there was a death in the family: a sad one. Pipsqueak, seventeen years old, and the loyalest little heart Tom had ever known, had died peacefully in her sleep, snoozing in the sun at Rebecca's feet. Tom had been inspecting one of his oilfields on the Gulf Coast when he heard the news, and he'd dropped everything to return straight home. He, Mitch and Rebecca had stood beneath a cottonwood tree and buried the little mongrel in its shade, with a roll of cooked bacon between her paws. When Tom shovelled the earth over the little white body, he turned his eyes so nobody could see them.

And so the thirties had passed away. They had begun badly and were ending worse.

149

Guy rubbed his hand over his face. He looked tired. And more than tired: he looked old.

'Drink?' he asked.

He didn't wait for an answer. He poured whisky like it was water and added water as though the stuff cost twenty guineas the sip.

'There'll be war soon,' he said bluntly. 'I suppose you know.'

'It seems possible.'

Guy shook his head, handing his brother a glass. 'Certain. It's certain. And d'you want to know if we're prepared for it?'

'I imagine you'll say not.'

'Not remotely. Nowhere close. Our navy is fine, but won't cope with submarines. Our army is ridiculous. Decent men and all that, but their equipment is a joke, a bad one. Our air force is splendid, but it needs ten times the number of aircraft. I'm talking only about defence, you understand. I'm not talking about taking the war to the enemy.'

'You seem despairing.'

Guy laughed. For the first time, Alan thought that his elder brother had lost his looks. Even when he'd put on weight in middle age, Guy had been able to carry it. He'd had a charm that deflected attention from his physical decline. But no longer. For the first time in his life, Guy looked older than his years, not younger.

'Despairing? Me? Hardly. I've no marriage. No money. Not much of a career, even. I've a lot less to lose than most. And I'll say this for the English: we fight best when our position is impossible.'

Alan paused, weighing up not just Guy's words, but the way he said them.

'Money,' he said. 'You said you had none. Did you mean –'

'Mean that I have none? Yes. Pretty much.' Guy jerked his chin upwards a little: a pale reflection of his old arrogance. 'What I had I spent, if you have to know. Wasted it, I suppose you would say. Dorothy had some money. It's why I married her, as I don't doubt you knew.' He shrugged, as though no longer able to shock himself. 'Her money's largely gone now, in any case.'

'I once asked you if you wanted me to –'

'Yes. Yes, please. I'd be grateful for whatever you can spare. I'm not very good at living within my means, I'm afraid.'

Alan nodded. Guy still had his official salary, of course, but an official salary was hardly likely to keep pace with Guy's expenses. 'If you let my banker know how much you'd like, I'll see that you get it.' He gave his brother a name and address, hoping the amount was not too large. Alan had an excellent salary, but in the past it had been dwarfed by the millions of pounds he'd received in dividends from his Alanto shareholding. Those days were gone. Alanto had thrown all its resources into its war with Norgaard, and exhausted itself in so doing. Alan's only consolation was that Norgaard was in precisely the same predicament. None of this did he mention, though, simply adding, 'Please don't think anything of it. And I see no need to mention the arrangement to Father or Mother, if you don't.'

'Thank you.'

Alan shrugged. 'We're family, Guy.'

'Family, eh?'

Guy spoke savagely, and Alan noticed that he had already drained his whisky glass and was standing up to get more. Looking around Guy's drawing room, Alan could see the creeping shabbiness that was a sign of his brother's bachelor status and shortage of money.

'The money,' said Guy. 'Thank you.'

'Please. I don't want –'

Guy rudely waved Alan down. 'I'm not going to go on thanking you, you needn't worry about that. As a matter of fact, there was one thing I thought I would do in exchange.'

'Oh?'

'I thought I would tell you that you're a bloody fool.'

Alan gaped in surprise. 'What?!'

'You're a fool. Since no one else seems to be telling you that, I thought I better had.'

'Any particular kind of fool?'

'Yes . . . Tom's alive, you said.'

Alan stiffened. 'Yes,' he said shortly. He had no idea what was coming, and for all his anger with Tom, he never liked it when Guy spoke of him.

'Do you know how to find him?'

Alan made a gesture with his hand. He meant he didn't want to say, but Guy interpreted it as Alan not knowing.

'Well, in any case. Don't you think you should tell Mother and Father? Tell them he's alive?'

Alan licked his lips. 'It would be hard to do that without . . .'

'Without telling them about why he ran? About his quarrel with me? You can tell them what you like. I can't see it matters now.'

Alan was entirely focused now. He had never heard his brother talk like this. He wasn't quite sure if he was comfortable with Guy's new truthfulness, but it was certainly a change.

'Why shouldn't it matter?' he said. 'For better or worse, Tom has chosen to leave us. There's no reason why –'

Again Guy interrupted.

'Oh, balderdash! Shall I tell you something?' He nodded forcefully, as though encouraging himself. 'Do you want to know why I hated Tom? And I did, by the way. I truly did.'

Alan nodded slowly. 'Yes. Yes, I would like to know.'

'You can't guess? No? I don't suppose you could.' Guy's lips worked silently for a moment or two, before finally releasing the words that lay inside. 'You and Tom . . . the pair of you . . . You were always so . . . I don't know . . . you were always so bloody *splendid*. I was seven years older than you. I was the eldest son and heir. I was meant to be someone the two of you could have looked up to. And instead . . . well, I don't think I was so rotten, as a matter of fact, but I wasn't like you. Either of you. Not splendid. I felt that then. I feel it now. I wish you weren't so bloody perfect. That's why it was hard taking money from you. You're such a damned saint.'

Alan didn't know what expression to wear. He was half sad, half smiling. 'Sorry.'

Guy shrugged. 'I don't care now. Not so much, anyway.' He waved his glass of whisky. 'I'm halfway drunk, in any case. And with a war coming . . . Well, you know, that's the one thing in my life I've been really good at. I was a damned good staff officer. One of the best. I'll be a lot of use in the War Office too. I know that.'

'I'm sure you will.'

'Tell Father and Mother. Tell them that Tom's alive. That you don't know where he is. They ought to know.'

Slowly, seriously, Alan shook his head. For more than six years he had fought Tom from Persia to Texas. He'd done it in anger. Now, perhaps, the anger had left, but the habit was there, and there wasn't enough of anything else to challenge it.

'No,' he said. 'They're old. They've made their peace. I've made mine. You . . .' He paused. Guy didn't precisely look like a man at peace. 'Well, you've got your whisky.'

'Yes, I've got my whisky.'

Alan stood up to go.

'Tell them,' said Guy. 'I shan't say it again.'

Alan shook his head. 'I won't. But thank you.'

It was 12 June 1939.

150

It's summer in Texas. The evening is pleasantly warm, not hot. The year is 1939.

Over in Europe, tensions are mounting. German newspapers are full of stories about Polish attacks on German farmhouses. The stories are lies, of course, and dangerous lies at that: lies that may yet lead to war. But out here in Texas on a lovely July night, Europe seems a million miles away.

In an effort to catch the evening breeze, Rebecca had had the table placed outdoors on the veranda, where the last of the sun was dying away across the level lawns and towering cottonwoods. A couple of round-backed armadillos were tussling over something in the grass. Bard was in the middle of a story.

'They were bringing pipes up, so one of the roughnecks had run up eighty foot to rack 'em as they came. But he musta lost a hold of the ladder or something, because the next thing I hear is a yell. Guy comes tumbling down from eighty feet up, hits a beam in the derrick, spins over and lands on the pump shed, new tin roof, nice and springy. He looks at me. I look at him. He says, "Gotta cigarette?" I only had my chew-tobacco, so I says, "No." He looks at me real sad, and says, "Well, don't just stand there, go get a smoke for this dumb, broken-assed son-of-a-bitch." Pardon me, Rebecca. Damn true, though, I swear it.'

Tom laughed because he believed it. Rebecca laughed because she didn't. Bard laughed out of embarrassment at using coarse language in front of his boss's sophisticated European wife – and despite the fact that Bard knew damn well how she'd made a living back in the days they were all working the oilfields of Wyoming.

'Lyman,' she said, breaking into the flow of oil talk, 'can you answer me something?'

'Why sure,' he said, wiping his mouth.

'How is it that my husband has got one of the best oil companies in the southern United States, and yet he hasn't made one bent nickel out of the thing for the last six years?'

'Aw, come on now, you need to ask your husband that.'

'I do, but he tells me nothing.'

Bard and Tom exchanged glances. Since that first year or two of whirlwind deal-making following Tom's oil strike, Rebecca had become ever less involved in the details of his business. For one thing, the accounting challenge was simply too vast now to be handled by her working at home. For another thing, the thrill had gone out of it. Professional accountants had taken over. Rebecca had other outlets for her energy now.

'You see, I'm running a foundation called the American-Jewish Resettlement Society,' she continued. 'So far we've brought seven thousand refugees across from Germany. We've found them houses, schools for their children, and jobs. The work we do is wonderful and Norgaard Petroleum is our biggest contributor. By far our biggest. The trouble is, there are still hundreds of thousands of Jews in Germany, not to mention millions more in Poland, Lithuania and in all the countries that Hitler threatens. These are Jews who need us, Jews who may yet die without us. The more we can get out, the more we can save. Tom would be happy to give us money, only Norgaard

580

doesn't have it. That's why I'm asking.' Rebecca controlled her voice closely, careful to keep her emotion out of it.

Bard glanced at Tom again, but Tom's face didn't tell him what to do. He was on his own.

'It's been tough times, I guess,' he said.

'Well now, that's what Tom says when I ask him. But it's not what Standard Oil says when it announces its results to stockholders. It's not what Union Oil says. It's not what Texaco says.'

'Yeah, it's kind of a more local thing.'

'Now that'd be a fine answer, except whenever you say it – you or Tom, that is – you never quite look at me straight. That's what makes me wonder.'

A moth flickered inside one of the glass candle-shades. Rebecca lifted the glass with her napkin and released the moth. She was wearing a sleek black evening dress imported from Paris. Bard thought she was one of the most beautiful women he had ever seen.

He looked challengingly at Tom. 'Maybe you ought to ask Tom again and have him look at you straight.'

Bard and Rebecca both stared at Tom. He tweaked his plate of meatballs and mashed potato closer to him and curled his arm round it in his old gesture of defensiveness. He felt ganged up on.

'Darling?' said Rebecca.

'Aw . . . We've been having a bit of a ruckus with one of our competitors. Outfit name of Blackwater.'

'And what would happen if you stopped your ruckus?'

Tom was silent.

'Lyman, what would happen if you stopped your ruckus?'

Rebecca looked straight at Bard. He couldn't hold her gaze, but he couldn't lie to her either. Hell, he was on her side in this, anyways. Looking fiercely down at his plate, he said, 'If we stopped the ruckus, then we'd begin to make a little money and the other fellows would begin to make a little money and we'd all make a little money.'

Rebecca smiled brilliantly. She dropped her napkin on the table.

'Well, now, how about we stop the ruckus?'

Rebecca was staring straight at Bard when she said this, but both men knew she was talking directly to Tom.

'It's not so simple,' he said. 'The other guys are in this too.'

'Lyman?' said Rebecca.

Lyman had a desperate urge to spit, but couldn't do so with Rebecca there. Instead, he scratched the back of his head furiously and reddened. He said, 'He's right. The other guys are in this too. But if we stopped – hell, Rebecca, they'd have to stop. They're a stock market outfit, see? Board of directors. Regular accounts. Management would have to stop. If they didn't they'd be out on their as– – out on their back-sides.'

Rebecca nodded. 'I see. That sounds fairly simple. Tomek?'

And Tom knew that Lyman was right. That Rebecca was right. He could choose. He could continue to punish Alanto. Or he could give up his ancient grudge. But he'd never cried surrender as a child. He was determined not to now. He sat motionless and silent.

Bard was about to say something, in an attempt to argue him round, but Rebecca held up a finger.

'Let him answer.'

It was Tom's choice. He'd have to make it for himself.

Tom sat and tried to find the ancient heart of his grudge: the images of prison camp that had caused his anger to burn strong and steady through two decades and more. He tried to call to mind his more recent causes for bitterness, the endless painful wounds his precious Norgaard had sustained in recent years.

But he failed.

Instead, an entirely unexpected image sprang to his mind, a memory he hadn't had for years. He remembered a cold spring in Hetterscheidt. He remembered a stomach jammed full of wind and emptiness. He remembered a guard shouting to him across the frozen yard. He remembered walking slowly over and the miraculous gift placed in his astounded hands: goose fat, jam, a bag of sugar. He remembered the moment as if it had been yesterday. And the guard had been Jewish. Silver-haired, elderly, and Jewish.

For almost two minutes, Tom tried to speak. If he had spoken, he didn't even know what he'd have said. There was a lump in his throat and the honest-to-God truth of it was that, just like that time twenty-two years before, he was once again close to tears.

Eventually Rebecca broke the silence. 'We're not saying you have to go all the way. Maybe just ease up a little.'

The silence continued, but Tom knew what he wanted to say. The past was the past. Anger and compassion faced each other and for the first time compassion stood the taller.

'Sure,' he said. 'Ease up a little. Why not?'

It was 28 July 1939.

151

Alan blinked himself awake. Jackson, the butler, was twitching back the curtains. Lottie, who always looked at her most peaceful and serene when sleeping, burrowed her face into her pillow and muttered something inaudible.

'Jackson?' said Alan in surprise.

'Sir?'

'Is Adderley not well?'

Adderley was Alan's valet and it was always he who woke Alan, not Jackson.

'He's perfectly well, sir . . . There's news today, I thought you would wish to have. I thought it better to bring it myself.'

'Yes?'

'Not good news, I'm afraid.'

Alan sat up. A sudden foreboding seized his heart. 'Just a moment.' Alan jumped out of bed and pulled on the dressing gown that Jackson held ready. 'We'll go next door.' They moved through to Alan's dressing room, where a cup of tea was already steaming on the bedside table along with a couple of slices of brown bread, cut very thin. Alan noted his servant's tactful forethought with approval. He sat down heavily on the bed. 'It's Hitler, isn't it?' he said.

'Yes, sir. In the small hours of this morning, German troops crossed into Poland. The news on the radio is still a little confused, but it appears to be a full-scale invasion. I believe the Poles have little chance of resistance.'

'None at all.'

'Should I prepare you a bath, sir?'

'To hell with baths, Jackson.'

'Yes, sir . . . If I may ask, do you believe that Chamberlain will feel obliged to declare war?'

Jackson looked directly at Alan, and Alan looked squarely back again. In that moment, both men knew that another war would bring about a permanent change in the positions of servant and master. Well, and if so, it would be no bad thing, thought Alan.

With a tiny smile, he replied, 'Declare war, Jackson? I should bloody well hope so.'

Jackson picked a speck of fluff from Alan's dressing table with a tiny frown. 'Yes, sir. And I should bloody well hope so too.'

Chamberlain hesitated one day, then acted.

Speaking on behalf of his country, he told Hitler to cease hostilities or face war. Hitler listened to the warning and ignored it. At midday on 3 September, for the second time in a quarter of a century, Great Britain declared war on Germany.

The effect on Alan was electric.

For those two days – from getting the news early on the morning of 1 September to the British declaration of war two days later – he hardly slept. He listened to the wireless whenever there was news, turning the dial down again as soon as the bulletin finished. He bought every edition of every paper. If he ate at all, he ate standing up, pacing around, hardly remembering to chew.

And why?

He could hardly say. Of course, the entire country, the entire world, wanted to know if war was coming. But Alan was all but certain that it was. So why? Why couldn't he eat or sleep? Why the restlessness? Why his addiction to news?

He had things to worry about, of course. His son, Tommy, was almost fifteen. If the war lasted three years or more, then, almost certainly, the youngster would be heading out to fight. Then there was the risk of bombing, the risk to Alanto, the terrible risk that England might lose. What then for Britain? What then for Alan and his family?

All this troubled him hugely, of course. But the real reason for his agitation was something deeper, something older, something connected with his own terrible experience of war. He couldn't have put into words precisely what he felt but, in any case, what was certain was this.

Upon hearing Chamberlain, in sombre tones, announce that Britain was at war again, Alan's agitation lifted at once. In a state of complete calm, complete certainty, he did three things.

The first was to enter the Alanto offices and issue instructions that nothing was to be done in any part of the company that might harm the strategic interests of any British ally or friend. What he meant was: end the conflict with Norgaard. Prices were to be raised. Competing installations were to be closed or moved. The conflict was to end overnight, utterly and for ever.

The second thing he did was to call on his father-in-law, Egham Dunlop, for the last fifteen years the Chairman of Alanto Oil. The meeting was a short one, but significant. Alan tendered his resignation. 'And in view of the international situation, Chairman, I must ask that my resignation be accepted with immediate effect.' Dunlop, not usually the warmest man in the world, grasped his son-in-law's hand, thanked him for everything, and allowed him to go.

And the final thing he did that day was to write a letter. It was three pages long and took four drafts. When finally satisfied, Alan summoned a clerk and gave instructions for the letter to be hand-delivered without delay. The address on the envelope read:

The Prime Minister,
10 Downing Street,
London SW1.

~

Alan was forty-six years old. Twenty-five years earlier, another European war had devastated his life; snatched the best friend he'd ever had or would ever have; had killed or wounded far, far too many of the men he'd served with. A second war seemed like the very worst nightmare of history, resurrected and magnified.

But there was a difference.

Unlike the Great War of Tom and Alan's youth, this one would be a war of tanks and planes, Jeeps and bombers, baggage trucks and armoured cars. It would be a fast war, a mobile war.

An oil war.

152

Fire burst on the horizon: red, yellow and brilliant titanium white. The air shuddered and crashed. Some of the explosions were so violent, it almost felt as though the ground itself was shaking.

Tom watched white-faced, white-lipped, as the air caught fire.

~

Strange how a man can settle.

Tom had first set foot in Texas in 1924. He'd been just thirty-one years old, but had already had enough experience to fill a lifetime twice that long. Since joining the British Army in 1914, he'd never been in the same place longer than a couple of years. He'd been with scores of women. He'd fought, been wounded, captured, and nearly starved. He'd never owned a home. He'd worked at so many jobs, he couldn't even count them.

And yet he'd settled. Arriving in Texas had felt like a homecoming. Even before the Nellie Holling oil strike, Tom had known that Texas would always be his home. Since then the feeling had grown. In addition to Norgaard House, his mansion on the outskirts of Houston, he'd bought himself a ten-thousand-acre cattle ranch, with fine mountain trails where he and Mitch could ride and shoot. Meantime, each trip out of state felt like a journey to another country. He and Lyman Bard privately divided their oil operations into 'Domestic' and 'International', meaning Texan and everything else.

But if even Louisiana and Florida felt foreign, then Washington DC felt like a whole new continent.

$$\sim$$

Another explosion.

Another brilliant flare-up against the night sky: red and green this time, with a centre of pink stars that hissed and moaned as they fell downwards to the Potomac.

'Isn't it wonderful?' said Rebecca, floating up alongside him in her long silver gown. 'I do adore fireworks.' Her lovely dark hair had been taken prisoner by fashion, and it had been cut short and tightly curled at the back, a style that didn't really do her justice. Her face shone. The ball had been thrown by the Association of American Jews as a way of thanking America for all it had done for the Jewish people. Now, in October 1939, the importance of saving Jewish refugees could hardly be more obvious. There were many people to thank, but chief amongst them was Rebecca, the undisputed queen of the ball.

Tom smiled crookedly. 'They're pretty, I guess. But I've had my fill of explosions for one lifetime.'

'Oh, Tomek, I am sorry. I should have thought.'

He shrugged. 'This time no one's trying to explode me.'

There was another loud bang, and the side of Rebecca's face was lit up in green and purple as the sparks fell glittering to the ground. The oil feud with Alan was over. Dead and buried. The price war had ended. At the gas station pump and the refinery door, rates were back to their old levels, or at least close to them. They had stopped interfering with each other's labour force or harming each other in any of the other ten thousand ways they'd invented over the years.

Rebecca looked seriously at her husband. He spoke so seldom about the past, she still knew nothing of his former life beyond war and prison camp. 'Do you want to come inside? I don't need to watch the rest of the show.'

He shook his head. 'I'm fine. It's finishing anyway.' He gestured over to a couple of men with expensive suits and professional smiles, who were headed their way. 'And I think there are a couple of senators who haven't yet got themselves photographed shaking your hand.'

Her face radiated smiles once again. She hadn't done what she'd done to get praised for it, but since the praise came free, she didn't mind collecting it. Tom bent and whispered in her ear, 'Not bad for a little Jewish girl from Lithuania.'

She squeezed his hand. 'Thank you, Tomek.'

She advanced on the two senators, who did indeed have a tame photographer in embarrassingly close attendance. Tom watched as his wife won two more hearts that evening. The fireworks blazed their last. He sipped champagne.

Then: 'Mr Calloway, I believe?'

There was a voice at his left elbow. Tom spun round. A tall silver-haired gentleman with something courtly in his manner was standing there.

'Yes, indeed, I –'

'May I introduce myself? My name is Cordell Hull, Secretary of State.'

'Mr Secretary.' Tom shook hands.

'Allow me to congratulate you and your wife. It's a fine thing the two of you have done.'

Tom had grown cynical enough of Washington politics that he virtually looked around for the camera, but there wasn't one. 'Thank you. It's all my wife's doing. I just loaned her the chequebook.'

'Well, the chequebook's important too.'

There was something sincere in Hull's manner and Tom accepted the praise with a smile. He *was* proud of himself. Thousands of Jews had had their lives saved by Rebecca's energy and Tom's generosity. If they could possibly manage it, they'd continue their charitable efforts right through the war in Europe. Wherever and whenever the Nazis threatened, he and Rebecca would aim to snatch their prey out from under their noses. Their achievement already had been colossal. It was nothing compared with what they still intended. Not bad for a gardener's boy from Hampshire.

'I introduced myself partly to congratulate you,' said Hull, 'but mostly because I wanted to ask you a favour.'

'Yes?'

Tom couldn't think for the life of him what favour Hull could possibly want. He remembered reading something of Hull's background. He'd been raised in a log cabin in the backwoods of Tennessee. He'd become a judge. He'd fought in the Spanish-American war. He'd become Congressman, Senator, now Secretary of State. What could Hull possibly want of Tom?

'You will be aware that we – the administration, the President, all of us – are deeply concerned about Japanese aggrandisement in the Pacific? The war on China, the build-up of armaments.'

'Uh.' Tom's answer was almost a grunt. He'd been through one war in his life. He wanted nothing to do with another.

'The situation is becoming exceptionally serious,' persisted Hull. 'We know that Japan wants to make itself economically independent of the United States, because it fears that excessive dependence might cripple it in case of war. The Japanese are concerned about a number of things, but most of all they're concerned about oil.'

'Why? Why the hell should there be a war? Who cares if they're independent?'

'Everything the Japanese are doing to reduce their dependence makes war more likely. The closest available source of oil is the the Dutch East Indies. If they attack that, they know the United States will declare war. The Pacific Ocean is our western frontier. It must remain free. It will remain free.'

591

'You're telling me the Japs want oil for fear of war, but if they get the oil they'll get a war too?'

'That's pretty much it.'

Tom felt the implacable logic tightening round him, as it had done a quarter of a century before. 'Mr Secretary, I don't know about any of this. I'm just a businessman.'

'Your business is oil –'

'Right. Just oil.'

'And oil *is* the business of war. There's no difference these days. You can't escape the facts.'

Tom shook his head. 'You may be right, Mr Secretary. If war comes, I'll play whatever role my country requires of me, but until then . . .'

'Your country needs you now, Mr Calloway.'

Tom shook his head.

'May I make my request even?'

It was impossible to deny Hull's gentlemanly persuasiveness. Tom nodded, already half defeated.

'We need a man, an oilman, of exceptional and penetrating thinking, to assist us with our deliberations. It's no use leaving this sort of thing to politicians and diplomats alone.'

'Ah!' Tom's exclamation was one of denial. He didn't want to hear this. He wanted to be back in Texas, among his beloved oil wells, away from the politics of a world he cared nothing for.

'Oil is at the centre of everything,' said Hull. 'We've embargoed aviaton fuel exports over a certain octane limit. They've responded by buying five times more fuel below that limit. To conserve oil stocks for their navy, they've banned their fishing fleet from using oil. We know they're buying up oil drilling equipment, which can only be because they plan to be in the Dutch East Indies before too long. The biggest policy debate in Washington at the moment is when to institute a total ban on all oil sales to Japan.'

Tom was shaking his head, but Hull persisted.

'Most of the bigger oil companies have Japanese and Asian

businesses, which might confuse their loyalties. Many of them have Japanese-born Americans in sensitive positions. They may have conflicts of interest. We're coming to you because you don't. We trust you, Calloway.'

'Heck, no, Hull. I appreciate the offer. It's a compliment, really, but no. I have to say no.'

'You'll think it over?'

Tom wanted to escape. He hated the sense of being encircled, by a logic and a situation that he wanted nothing to do with. He threw up his hands. 'I guess. If you really want, but I . . .'

'Would it make a difference if I invited you to meet with the President? He knows I'm speaking to you tonight. He was very enthusiastic about the idea.'

'Jesus, Hull, Jesus . . .'

'Of course, you'd need an office here in Washington. We'd pay for all costs associated with the move.'

'For God's sakes . . . Listen, please excuse me, I gotta go.'

Using a glimpse of Rebecca as a pretext, he ran.

He ran from Hull. He ran from war. He ran from a mad world he thought he'd escaped for ever.

153

The years passed; the terrible years of war.

Tom had failed, of course. However much he had wanted to avoid entanglement, his sense of duty, his deep-down nobility had triumphed, as Cordell Hull had somehow always known it would.

So Tom had served. For two long years in Washington, 1939 to 1941, he'd done everything he could to pull Japan back from the brink. But without success. The Japanese attack on Pearl Harbor had simply consolidated Tom's position as one of the most vital strategic elements in the American administration.

And Hull had been right. The business of oil *was* the business of war. From the very first, the Americans had understood that better than the Japanese. Take the attack on Pearl Harbor itself. The Japanese planes had hit the American airfields, they'd hit their battleships and cruisers. But they'd missed the one single target that had really mattered.

The oil.

Four and a half million barrels, lying in unarmoured storage tanks, exposed not simply to bombs, but even bullets. Without oil, the whole Pacific Fleet would have been so much junk. Without fuel, the American air bases might as well have been museums. Without oil, the Americans would have had to refuel Hawaii across half a hostile ocean in the teeth of Japanese submarine attack. And the Japanese hadn't hit the oil, for the simple reason that they'd never even tried.

From that day on, the oil war began to turn in the American favour. Having taken the Dutch East Indies – the source of the oil they so badly craved, the Japanese began drilling. They got lucky. They struck oil in such quantities that they possessed the richest oil field anywhere between California and the Middle East. But the strike was useless.

Finding oil was one thing. Getting it to Japan was another. And they couldn't do it. At Tom's strongly expressed insistence, American submarines and American planes concentrated their efforts on the oil tankers running north to the Home Islands. And one by one the tankers were sunk. So effective were the American submariners that the Japanese launched ships virtually certain that they'd be sunk before finding harbour.

The oil noose began to tighten.

The Japanese were brave, resourceful and determined. They never stopped trying to get their tankers through. They found a way to brew gasoline from pine tree roots. They did everything they could – and more. But it was no use. Their ships were squandered for lack of fuel, their air force crippled.

'Before long,' said Tom, only one-quarter joking, 'they'll have to fly their planes in one direction only.'

In London, Alan faced his own torrent of work. In his letter to Neville Chamberlain, he'd offered his services as 'a co-ordinator of the nation's war effort as it relates to oil. I am willing to serve in any capacity and on any terms whatsoever.' His offer had been immediately accepted. He'd been appointed head of the British Petroleum Board: the High Command of Britain's petroleum industry.

From the very first day in his post, Alan had been obsessional about one thing above all else: kerosene – aircraft fuel.

Alan made it a priority because he knew what all oilmen knew and most airmen knew, and pretty much nobody else cared enough to know.

Which was this.

In 1936, Shell Oil had discovered a way of making 100-octane fuel. The new substance was abominably expensive and didn't seem to have any obvious buyers. A lot of people would have considered the discovery worthless and done nothing about it. But not Shell. Convinced the product had a future, they built a plant in the United States. They were right to do it. It wasn't long before the Western air forces understood that the new fuel was dynamite. Compared with lower octane alternatives, the 100-octane offered up to thirty per cent more speed, more acceleration, more manoeuvrability.

And it was available only in the United States.

Alan fought to get that fuel to England. Cash was found for it. Tankers were filled with it. Destroyers were snatched from other duties to escort it over. When the Battle of Britain began to break over British skies, the RAF were flying a 100-octane war, the Luftwaffe was not.

The advantage was a narrow one.

It took the skill and commitment of brave men to press it home. But, whatever the reason, the statistics told a consistent tale. For every British plane lost in combat, the Germans lost two and, on some days, three. Tiny as the British Air Force was, it inflicted losses too great for the war planners in Berlin to bear. Nazi attention turned away from England. The projected invasion of Russia took priority.

The Battle of Britain had been won.

But every month brought new perils. In 1941, the German U-boat campaign threatened to strangle the shipping routes that gave Britain life. German submarines, hunting in wolfpacks, sunk the huge, heavy and slow-moving tankers with insolent ease. British naval supplies of oil were down to just two months. Stocks of motor oil were sufficient for just five weeks. The country was silently and invisibly drawing to the point of collapse. Alan did everything he could. Everyone did everything they could. Even so, the task seemed impossible.

Seemed, but wasn't.

Somehow, anyhow, the country survived.

Then, sometime late in 1941, things began to turn. It was Hitler's turn to become desperate.

The attack on Russia had been an oil disaster. Russian roads were so much worse than German ones, that the invading tanks had used fuel at double the expected rate. Although the Germans had captured vast amounts of Russian fuel, the booty was useless. Russian tanks ran off diesel. The German ones needed petrol.

Then winter had started.

It was appallingly cold. German tanks had never been designed for such work. They wouldn't start. They were literally frozen, just like the heavy artillery pieces that wouldn't fire. The Russians threw fresh troops into counterattack. For the first time since the start of the war, the German armies were halted and rolled back.

Hitler had two options and he tried them both.

He sent an army to attack the Russian oil fields of Baku, fighting desperately over the mountains of the Caucasus. The army never arrived. Hitler's successes had always relied on devastating speed and surprise, but speed needs petrol and the German supply lines were infinitely overstretched. The German armies battled forward, but they moved too slow. Trucks carrying petrol to the front ran out of petrol themselves. The Germans put oil cans on the backs of camels and drove them forwards. But it was far too little, far too late.

In the search for Russian oil, the Germans had run out of fuel.

The second option was North Africa. Through Libya. Through Egypt. Through Palestine and Transjordan to the abundant oil of Iraq and Persia. That was the theory and the theory was sound. In February 1941, just as the British had been on the point of driving the Italians out of North Africa, a German commander, General Erwin Rommel, had been sent to help. He succeeded brilliantly. With victory after victory, he drove the British back. By August 1942, he was within a few miles of Cairo. The British rulers burned secret papers in preparation for escape. In the winding bazaars, merchants had portraits of Hitler and Mussolini ready to plaster over their pictures of Churchill and George VI. But the tide of war was about to change.

Rommel urgently needed fuel, but the British had cracked the German codes. Though tankers were sent from Italy to supply him, the British knew when the ships were coming. When and where.

One by one, with devastating accuracy, the RAF and the Royal Navy sank them all.

Rommel pleaded for petrol. He flew to Germany to intercede directly with Hitler. His armies had to have fuel. Hitler listened. He was passionate about oil. He knew the history of every oil field. He could quote by heart how much fuel a plane needed, how much fuel a tank needed. He listened. He gave Rommel a field marshal's baton and a set of promises. The baton was useless. The promises came to nothing. There was no fuel.

Then, at El Alamein, Montgomery attacked. Rommel fell back. Often he saw opportunities to turn on his enemy and deliver devastating counterattacks, but attacks need fuel and Rommel had none. He retreated. And even the retreat used petrol that he couldn't afford.

In the search for Middle Eastern oil, the Germans had run out of fuel.

❧

War is a strange beast. With a single flick of its paw, it can destroy a man or be the making of him. It can find the worst in humans and magnify it, but it can also find the best and raise it to an intensity unthinkable in any other circumstance. The First World War had taken Tom and Alan and had all but destroyed them. It had smashed a friendship, left Tom half-crazy in prison camp, brought Alan to a state of near collapse. It had found that darkness and preyed upon it.

This second war, terrible as it was, was proving different from the start.

Tom in Washington and Alan in London were both keenly aware of the other's existence. Because of Tom's concentration on the Pacific war and because of Alan's all-absorbing focus on Europe and the home front, the two men had never been obliged to meet. And yet, each was enabled to look sideways at the other man's activities and did so with a kind of fascination.

Alan saw Tom's work and saw that it was extraordinary. Tom saw Alan's work and knew it couldn't be bettered. In a time of crisis for the whole of humanity history called upon all good men to do their utmost. Neither Alan nor Tom would let history down.

The two men kept their distance.

They were as far as ever from forgiveness, still less from reconciliation. And yet something else happened. The two men came to admire in late adulthood precisely those things that they had nourished together in their childhood and early manhood. They both knew that if the war ended and they went back to their respective companies, the oil feud of old would never be reborn. They would live and let live. As long as they could live apart, they would live happily. It was only if they had to meet that there'd be an explosion.

But war allows no time for introspection. On the Eastern Front, Stalin's armies were beginning, finally, to smash their German attackers. The great advance, from Moscow to Berlin, had begun. To any sober observer of the war, it was clear that Hitler would never now be victorious.

But that raised a pressing problem of its own. From the point of view of the Western Allies, it had become time to take the war into Europe. It would have been a calamity to free Europe of Hitler, only to turn it over to his cousin in dictatorship, Uncle Joe Stalin. Of course, a land invasion would be a massive undertaking. It would need fine generals. It would rely on brave soldiers, courageous airmen and dedicated sailors.

And oil.

It was going to take an awful lot of oil.

154

It had been back in April 1943 that the topic had first come up.

The air-raid sirens had begun their wailing more than five minutes before and the Whitehall that Alan hurried through was all but deserted. A military policeman on a bike shouted, 'Hurry up, sir. Look lively.' Alan ran down a side street, down a short flight of stone steps and came to a sandbagged wall and steel door. A sentry stood outside.

'Alan Montague, Petroleum Board,' said Alan, 'I'm here to –'

'Yes, sir. Right on in, if you would.'

'George Street', as the complex was invariably called, looked like nothing at all. It *was* nothing at all. In its former life it had been a depot for maintenance men and janitors. Not now. Not any more.

Alan hurried on through a smoke-filled corridor. The air throughout the underground suite stung with the prick of tobacco smoke. The smoke hung bluish-grey in the air, so that walking forwards was like swimming in an aquarium. Alan was reminded of a Flanders dugout he'd once shared with Tom . . .

His ruminations were interrupted. A gum-chewing American colonel, James Renwick, stood in front of him.

'You Montague?'

Alan admitted as much.

'Alan Montague? Got a brother in the War Office?'

'That's right. Guy.'

'Yeah. He's a good man you got there. We think a lot of him.' Renwick nodded, as if to confirm the point to himself. 'Say, I've got a call to make back to base. Is there a phone . . . ? In here, maybe?'

He swung open a door. The room was cleanly painted, but bare except for a phone, a desk, a lamp and a wooden armchair. If it looked like a converted broom cupboard, that should have come as no surprise. It was a converted broom cupboard. 'Can I use this?'

Alan laughed. 'If you want to reach your president, yes.'

'President *Roose*velt?'

'I believe that's the name of the man.'

The American looked at the claustrophobic little room in amazement. He pointed to the office next door. 'Does he . . . ? I mean, is this . . . ?'

Alan nodded. The American had opened his mouth to say something further, but a secretary in WREN uniform came to interrupt. 'He's ready for you now.'

Alan and Colonel Renwick were ushered into another cramped and unlovely room. There was a single bed made up in one corner, a big desk in another, a microphone, a water decanter, a box of cigars, a phone. Behind a cloud of cigar-smoke, sat Winston Churchill. He was smartly dressed and his face wore the mixture of tiredness, charm and pugnaciousness with which Alan had grown familiar. It was the face of the British people, a guarantee of victory.

'Montague! Renwick,' said Churchill, half-rising from his seat out of politeness, but only half because he was growing old and had better uses for his energy. 'You both know Brooke, of course.' General Brooke, the Chief of the Imperial General Staff, was present in full uniform, a small glass of water by his side. Brooke and Alan were reasonably well acquainted by now and Brooke clearly knew Renwick as well. The men greeted each other with a minimum of fuss.

'Now, Montague, you won't think us premature, I hope, but we have a matter of the profoundest importance for your consideration.'

Churchill began to speak, giving the floor to either Brooke or Renwick when it was necessary to clarify details. Alan listened in astonishment. Churchill was asking for the impossible – and yet in time of war it was often essential to do the impossible, and to do it before breakfast at that. What was more, this was no ordinary assignment, it was one on which the entire course of the war might yet turn.

'Well? What do you say? Can we do it?' Churchill asked the question as though needing an answer on the spot. As so often before, Alan felt the man's remorseless determination. The feeling was like a jolt of energy, a surge of will.

'Goodness gracious. Good Lord.'

Alan sat in thought. Churchill was right, of course. With America now in the war, the matter had become nothing less than critical. And yet the problem seemed all but insoluble . . .

'Well?' said Brooke.

'Will you need to get back to us on this?' said the American.

Alan looked up. He hadn't heard the others, only Churchill.

'Do it? Yes, sir, I dare say we can do it.'

'Excellent. And can you tell us how?'

Churchill was silent. The soldiers were silent. Alan felt the whole of England – the whole free world – waiting on his answer. He shook his head.

'No, sir, I'm afraid not. I've absolutely no idea.'

155

Now, in early 1944, that day had been weeks and months ago.

Since then, Alan had spent a vast part of his life answering Churchill's question. The rest of it he'd spent on other war-related matters and, in the few hours snatched from the all-consuming monster of work, with his family. Lottie had become dearer to him than ever. She was the ground on which he walked, the sun he looked to for support. His family was growing fast, and Alan was missing too much of it. Polly was turning into a beauty. Eliza was, at twenty-one, taking after her mother and doing heroic work in Lottie's hospital, which (to its founder's horror) was once again beginning to fill with wounded men, fresh from war. Young Tom was already enlisted as a lieutenant in one of the tank regiments, and Alan prayed daily and hourly for his continued safety.

But there had also been losses.

His father, for one, who had died peacefully in his sleep one night. His last words to Pamela had been, 'Shall I turn off the light now, dear? There we are. Good night.'

And Guy. He had been true to his word.

In his position in the War Office, he had devoted his energies to victory. He had still drunk far too much. His mood had often been black and pessimistic. But he'd flourished. He and his abilities had finally found the position and the time that suited them best. He had done well.

Had.

Because Guy had followed his father into the night. He had been returning from a visit to Russia, with what amounted to a shopping list of urgently required military hardware. Somewhere near Cairo, the plane had run into engine trouble and the pilot had crash-landed. The plane had begun to burn. At that stage, Guy could have rescued himself and followed the pilot and co-pilot through the cockpit. But he didn't. Instead, he had fought his way back into the burning fuselage and retrieved the package of Soviet documents that was so urgently needed in London. He tossed them out of the window, before making the leap himself.

He saved the documents and lost his life. Rushed to hospital with exceptionally severe burns, he died shortly after admission.

Alan had been saddened by the news – but also, in a funny way, pleased. Guy had no longer taken much pleasure in life. In some ways, Alan guessed, he had actually wanted to die. And in his death, finally, he had succeeded in doing something he'd wanted for so long. He had done a thing of which he could be entirely proud. He had died *splendid*.

156

It was 14 March 1944, a chilly day by Texas standards.

Tom was on one of his rare visits home – a trip only made possible by official business down in Dallas. They ate a big family supper together. Rebecca tried to make Tom sit down and eat, but in a way all any of them wanted to do was talk. Mitchell, who, at twenty, was already more than old enough to start learning about the oil business, had started work as a roustabout on a Norgaard well near Houston. The boy had fought to join up, of course, but oil work was war work – and Tom, whose aversion to war hadn't grown any less by becoming reacquainted with it, had out-and-out forbidden his son from donning a soldier's uniform.

Though Mitch had protested, he'd come to love the oil world. His conversation was all oil-talk, oil-gossip and oil-questions, which Tom, laughingly, struggled to answer. Eventually, the pace subsided. Mitch went to bed. The servants finished for the night. Tom and Rebecca sat alone in their immense drawing room, a bottle of brandy for him, a mug of cocoa for her and a log fire roaring in the fireplace.

They gazed at each other. Tom's long absence made their times together even more special, even more intense. Rebecca thought how she loved her husband more with each passing year.

'How are you, my love?' said Rebecca. 'Really, I mean. Really how are you?'

Tom nodded. 'OK. Overworked. Wishing I never had to go back to DC.'

'Something else,' she said. 'There's some kind of sadness in you. Something I haven't seen before.'

He shrugged. 'War, I guess. It's not meant to be fun.'

She shook her head. When she was on the hunt for emotional truth, she was never deflected by that kind of answer. 'When you were talking about the war with Germany, you became sad. Troubled. Something like that. All the time you've been busy with the Japanese situation, I've heard you get mad, or frustrated, even bored at times – but never sad.'

Tom threw logs on the fire, though the fire didn't need it. In the Texan climate, firewood was tinder dry and flames roared upwards in a blaze of heat and sparks.

'There's a possibility Roosevelt might want me to transfer across to Europe for a while. I'm not too keen on the idea. If it comes up again, I'll shoot it down. I'm not going across there, no matter who's asking.'

Rebecca laughed and leaned out to stroke his arm. Then, having missed his touch for so long, she couldn't let go of it once she had it. She hooked her chair forwards with her foot so she could sit holding his hand. 'It's because that would put you in the war alongside England, isn't it? I guess you'd be fighting alongside a lot of your oldest friends. The ones you won't ever talk about.'

Tom stiffened and his hand went dead to her touch.

'Ah, no!' she cried. 'I'm completely wrong! The opposite. The reason you left England. Whatever that was. If you went back, you'd have to face it again.' She scanned his face again, her eyes flashing at speed from mouth to eyes to body and back to the face again. 'The only time I've ever seen you like this was over that stupid affair with Blackwater Oil – your precious ruckus . . . What was the name of the British company involved? Alto Oil? Alamo Oil? *Alanto*. That's it. Alanto.'

Tom said nothing, but he could feel the presence of the past here in the room. Rebecca was invoking it and he was wordless in the face of it. Rebecca's cocoa cooled and grew a skin. She was deep in thought, trying to remember something.

'That name. Alanto. I've heard it recently.' She scoured her memory, as Tom sat in a trance beside her. 'It must be to do with the war. The British petrol people. The Petroleum Board. The head of that used to be boss of Alanto Oil, right?'

Tom nodded like a dummy.

'It's him, isn't it?' said Rebecca.

Tom hadn't changed his position since Rebecca first leaned out to stroke his arm. But his face had lost its colour. He sat stiffer than a board.

'Him? What d'you mean, him?'

His words rang false, even to him. Almost thirty years after the fatal rupture with Alan, Rebecca had ferreted out his dark secret. He'd been found out and he knew it.

'What's his name?' she said. Her voice had changed once again. She didn't need to go hunting for the truth now; the truth was lying there in front of her. Her voice was kind. Her hand was warm again on his arm.

'Montague,' said Tom woodenly. 'Alan Montague.'

'And? You knew each other?'

Tom nodded. His feelings were numb. He spoke the words as though drugged.

'You knew each other well? You were friends? Friends from childhood?'

'No, not friends. Never friends.'

'No? The truth, Tomek, the truth.'

'No, no, not friends.' Tom shook his head decisively. 'We were much, much more than friends.'

He swallowed once, then told her everything. He told her about their childhood, about their occasional quarrels, about the war, about that awful time he'd been in bed with Lisette when the bedroom door had crashed open to reveal Alan swaying with anger and outrage.

'You slept with his girl?'

Tom nodded. 'But that wasn't it. I mean, it was a low and mean thing to do, but we'd have got over it – leastways, I think we would. Only we never got as far as that.'

And Tom told her the rest of it. The suicide mission for which Alan had volunteered him. His unlikely survival. His time in prison. Escape and recapture. The letters that went unanswered. The death of his father. 'There was nothing left for me in England. I wanted to leave and never go back.' He shrugged. 'That's it. Everything. The rest of it you know.'

He spoke in a flat voice. His feelings were still hidden from him. Anger, love, bitterness, self-pity all swirled together in a thin cloud a few yards out of his reach. Rebecca nodded. The fire had burned down to a heap of embers, a waste of grey ash. Neither she nor Tom felt like moving to help it.

'The ruckus,' she said. 'You were trying to get Blackwater out of your back yard. No wonder you got mad about it.'

'It seemed all wrong to have Brits – any Brits – buying up pieces of Texas. It made it worse who it was.'

'I can see that.'

Tom shrugged. 'We fought as kids. We never gave up. Never. It was like that again. Only for real.'

She nodded. 'My poor love.'

'It doesn't matter, though,' said Tom. 'There's no reason for me to ever go out there.'

'Oh, Tomek!'

'What?'

'Truth, Tomek, truth.'

'What? I've told you everything. I swear I've –'

'Don't swear anything. I know you've told the truth. But here's another one for you. You will have to go to him. You will have to meet him.'

'No. Why? Why the hell should I? I *won't* see him. It's that simple'

'You will.'

'I will *not*. He tried to kill me. He tried to wreck my company.'

'You will do it because he's here with you now. You've been fighting this same old argument every day of your life. All those horrible years after Signal Hill, I knew you were fighting something. I never knew what. Now I do.' Rebecca frowned a little. The memory of those first few difficult years still caused her pain.

'I just wanted to strike some oil.'

'No.' Rebecca shook her head. The lights had been turned down low for the evening, and it was hard to read the message in her deep, dark eyes. 'You were fighting him. You fought him over Signal Hill. You fought him over all those stupid dry holes in Texas. You fought him over Blackwater Oil. You fight him still. You'll never rest until you meet him.'

'He's the last man on earth I want to meet.'

'Exactly. And that's why you must.'

157

Churchill's request of Alan had been simple. Not easy, but simple. It was this.

To fuel a land invasion of Europe.

To be ready within a year.

To eliminate the possibility of failure.

As a rough estimate the invasion forces would be equipped with approximately one hundred and fifty thousand vehicles. Those vehicles would need an astronomical amount of petrol – and the faster and more successful the invasion, the more demanding the fuel requirements would be. That fuel had to be brought from England and America to the beaches of France. It would have to be brought under conditions of constant attack.

There were only two ways of transporting oil. Either by pipeline or by tanker. But there were problems with either route. A pipeline was all very well, but it couldn't be built underwater and it couldn't be built in a matter of days. A tanker was all very fine, but few things crawled more slowly across the sea than an oil tanker – and few targets were easier for roaming Luftwaffe pilots to spot and destroy.

That was the problem. It was, beyond question, the toughest assignment in the history of military logistics.

And the fate of the free world depended on getting it right.

158

'Hey there!' Lyman Bard was elated to see the man who was still theoretically his boss come striding over the sun-bleached acres. 'Welcome to West Osiman Four. Three hundred barrels a day. More, if we can find a way to jack the pressure up.'

'This a discovery hole?'

'Discovery, pal?' Bard was shocked. In the old days, there was no way that Tom wouldn't know every last detail about the oil wells he owned. 'This is a step-out, remember. We hit oil with Number One. Two, Three and Four have all been step-outs, trying to gauge the size of the field.'

'Oh right, sure. I remember.'

Bard looked worried. 'Did you even recall that we had this field? Eight thousand acres under lease. Three wildcats came up dusters, East Osiman One through Three. The geology types were telling us to go to hell, but the exploration boys swore they could smell the juice, so we sunk another just to show 'em. Hit West Osiman One, our first producer.'

'Yeah, yeah, now you mention it.'

Tom sat down heavily on a field pipe.

Not for long.

'Ow! Hell!' Tom leaped up like a scalded cat, beating at his backside with his hands.

'Jeez, pal. I'm gonna take you away from Washington if you can't even recognise a steam pipe when you see it. That pipe's hotter'n a hog on spit roast.'

'Screw it.'

Tom kicked the pipe. He *had* been away too long. Though Tom excelled at his Washington work, he hated it. He hung out with soldiers and politicians, navy types and bureaucrats. They were good guys to a man, but they weren't oilers. They didn't know what it was to sink a new hole. They treated oil like it was just another munition of war, like tanks or bullets. They didn't know the stuff was holy. Tom looked properly at West Osiman Four for the first time. The derrick was unnaturally full of drill pipe.

'What the hell you got nesting there?' said Tom. 'That don't look like a rig, it looks like a housemarm's pantie drawer.'

Bard laughed. 'Boy, have you been gone too long! We're sinking fields more than ten thousand feet here. You need plenty of pipe to go down ten thousand.'

'Ten thousand! Sheez! What's that costing us?'

The two men sunk into oil-talk. For Tom it was like a warm bath, a glass of whisky. He never wanted to leave Texas again. He never wanted to be further than a short drive from an oilfield. Perhaps some day when the war was won but not yet over, he'd quit his Washington job and return to Norgaard. He could sink some wells, pump some oil, make some money . . . The two men chatted for half an hour; a blissful interlude in the midst of war.

After a while, Tom sighed.

'Is Mitch around?'

'Yeah, sure. He's a good lad, that boy.' Bard halted, bursting to tell Tom something, but holding himself back.

'What? What's that?'

'Nothing.'

'Sure it's something.'

'No, don't worry. I wasn't going to say nothing.'

'Lyman, will you please quit –'

613

'Hey, hey, OK. Only don't tell Rebecca. She'll pretty near kill me if she learns. Kill you too, at that.'

Tom nodded and Bard continued.

'We had a well blow out on us, pretty bad. We was fighting to control it, get it capped off. Your Mitch was like a lion. Balls of steel and worked his ass off too. Anyhow, we'd pretty much got the flow shut off, when some dunghead drops a load of well casing on the floor of the pumphouse. Sparks fly. Gas ignites. *Boom!* Your boy, Mitch, was out of there like some kinda fire beetle. Head on fire. Clothes on fire. Now, just as Mitch runs out, that guy Fishtail Shorthausen – you remember him, right? Called Fishtail on account of –'

'Lyman, you gonna spend time telling me how Fishtail Shorthausen got his name? You got my only boy with his head on fire there.'

'Uh, OK, sorry. Any case, Fishtail grabs a hold of him and jumps with him right into the water tank we got set up there. They stay under maybe a minute. Mitch ain't on fire any more, but he's pretty near drownded. He manages to punch his way outa Fishtail's grip and comes to the surface. We make him stay in that tank most of the night. Only way to keep him cold. His skin turned out fine, only his head got crisped down bald as a cue ball. Had to send him off to check out our gas stations in Florida for a few weeks, cause I knew I'd catch hell from Rebecca if she knew we'd tried to fry him.'

'He OK now?'

'Fine. Just as much hair as you or me, only his eyebrows don't seem to have come back too good. Question of time, I reckon. Any case, what the hell are eyebrows for, exactly?'

Tom nodded. Oilfields were dangerous places, but he'd never want to shelter Mitch – not that Mitch would let him, anyway.

'I oughta see him, really.'

Bard nodded, but he caught something in Tom's tone that wasn't right. 'You down here long, pal? You spend too long

614

in DC and you're going to start thinking DC. You heard they want motorists to cut down petrol usage? Like something out of Russia, ain't it?'

'There's a war on, in case you were forgetting.'

'And this is America, in case you were forgetting.' Bard spat. In America you should be able to fight a world war in Asia and Europe, win in both places, and still give motorists as much cheap gas as they wanted.

'I'm going to Europe,' said Tom.

It was true. Tom's role in the Pacific war was increasingly unnecessary. The oil war had been won so conclusively, that there wasn't much more for an oilman to do there. From an oil perspective, the real action was transferring to Europe. Tom was America's top oil strategist. It made every sense for Tom to go out there and liaise closely with the British Petroleum Board.

But that didn't mean he wanted to go. The Secretary of State had suggested it. Tom had refused. President Roosevelt had suggested it. Tom had refused. Then Roosevelt had called Tom into the Oval Office, told Tom he was damn well going to go if he, Roosevelt, had ordered him to go. And it was only then, deeply reluctant, but no longer able to say no, that Tom had agreed.

'You just going for a trip,' said Bard, 'or –'

'No. There's work to be done. Plenty of it.'

Bard stared hard at his boss. There could be only one reason for Tom going to Europe. The Americans were finally going to take the war to Hitler, and Tom was going to be the man holding the petrol pump.

'Sheez,' said Bard, 'you gonna have your work cut out there, no mistake. Oil business is hard enough, never mind Kraut-heads shooting at you.'

Tom nodded agreement. He couldn't say anything, but Bard was right. Never in the history of war had anything been attempted on the scale now envisaged, and in terms of supply logistics, by far the toughest part related to oil. The American

Quartermaster Corps reckoned each allied soldier would need to be supported by approximately seventy pounds of supplies and equipment. Fully half of that total was oil-related.

But as the moment drew nearer, Tom found it harder and harder to concentrate. *He was going to London to meet Alan.* He couldn't think about it. The very idea was like a plate of red-hot metal. If he allowed his mind to touch upon it, even for a second, he had to snatch his attention away with a mental shriek of pain. *Alan had tried to kill him, had tried to wreck his company, had tried every way he could to ruin his life.* Tom would have given all the money he had – his oil wells, even – to avoid meeting his twin again.

Bard was looking at his boss with concern. 'You OK, bud?'

Tom forced himself to grin. 'Yeah, guess they'll keep me busy.'

'So this is like a kind of goodbye visit, then?'

Tom nodded. 'Yeah.'

'Well, good luck, pal. I guess you have the honour of serving your country, and all.'

Tom nodded.

'I'll take you to Mitch.'

Tom nodded again. 'Yeah.' He hesitated.

Bard raised an eyebrow. 'Can I help you?'

'Yeah, look, do me a favour, would you?'

'Sure. Whatever.'

'Just don't tell him I sat on the goddamn steam pipe, willya?'

It was 18 May 1944.

159

Pipeline or tanker.

That was the choice. One alternative which couldn't be built. A second alternative which was a please-bomb-here invitation to the Luftwaffe. So what was to be done?

Alan did the only thing he could do. Working with his best engineers, he ordered the development of a brand-new technology, one never used anywhere in the world before. They hammered out the concept during an all-night conference that began with tea and cigarettes and ended with dawn tangling in the London trees and the air thick with tobacco smoke and optimism. They built scale models. The mathematicians ran computations, came up with the wrong answers, and worked their numbers again. Alan ordered prototypes and simulations and dummy runs, until he was sure he had something that could work. But the fact remained there was only one test that mattered, and it was coming up shortly.

The project had been kept top secret, of course – though, naturally enough, Tom Calloway had been kept in the loop. But it needed a codename and Alan had been the one to christen it. The name, once you thought about it for a moment, was obvious. There was only one thing it could be called: PLUTO.

The fate of the free world would hang on a thing called PLUTO.

160

The Boeing Clipper seaplane bobbed uncomfortably on its ungainly floats. The engines started up, the propellers beating the grey water into spray. The engine noise ascended into a high whine, the plane lurched, then took off, slewing a little in a vicious little sidewind. They gained height and the pilot took the plane round in a long arc, heading east. Beneath them, a dirty Atlantic surf creamed round the rocky Newfoundland coast, before it too passed behind them. They wouldn't see a coastline again until just a few minutes short of their destination.

The plane was unheated and it quickly grew freezing. There was a pile of American army-issue blankets at the back of the cabin, and Tom and the four other passengers helped themselves generously. Although it was theoretically a night flight, there wasn't much darkness this far north at this time of year. Tom attempted to sleep and failed. Instead, for the long thirteen-hour flight, he sat beneath a mound of blankets, half-deafened by the noise, sipped from a flask of coffee he'd brought with him and stared out of the window at the grey-blue world beneath.

He tried to think of other things. He tried thinking of Rebecca or Mitch or Lyman Bard or Norgaard Petroleum. He tried focusing on work. He thought about PLUTO and the huge test it was about to face. But it was hopeless.

For the first time since he embarked from Liverpool in 1919, he was returning to the country of his birth. To England. To Alan. He tried to wrestle his thoughts away, but couldn't. His heart was locked and inaccessible. His feelings were numb. He felt like the seascape passing under the wing: frozen, grey, desolate.

161

An odd-looking coaster with a salt-caked smoke-stack nosed her way towards them. The wind was at cross-purposes with the tide, and sharp little waves griddled the water. Alan looked at the boat long and hard through a pair of binoculars. She looked like nothing at all: a snub-nosed sea-tramp out of place amidst the jam of naval shipping. But though less than beautiful, she was the most important ship in port.

On the dockside with Alan – Sir Alan Montague now, following the death of his father and brother – there was a lieutenant colonel from the American staff. He had the spacious sun-filled manner of a born Westerner, but the slow intelligent eyes of a serious professional. The American looked at the coaster for a little, then said, 'So? Can we go see it now?'

'I beg your pardon?'

'Go see it. PLUTO.'

Though Alan was tired all the time these days, he couldn't help but laugh. Obviously no one had told the American what to expect. Alan pointed out across the water. 'There. PLUTO.'

'*What?* You're kidding, right?'

'No.'

'That little . . . boat?'

'Well, not the ship so much, it's what's on board her.'

The American took another look. The coaster had passed them now. It was clear that her hold had been adapted for some specific type of cargo, but the cargo space itself was empty.

'I'm not getting you,' said the American. 'There's nothing on board her.'

'Precisely. That's precisely the beauty of it.'

But Alan wasn't thinking about PLUTO. He was thinking about Tom. Tom was in England now. In little more than a day, they'd meet. He tried to wrestle his thoughts away, but couldn't. His heart was locked and inaccessible. His feelings were numb. He felt like the crowded seascape in front of him: wind-blown, grey, desolate.

162

The Clipper landed neatly on the windy waters at Stranraer, Scotland. The breeze outside the plane was salt and sharp, and Tom was half soaked by the time they made it from the plane to shore. An American GI had a car waiting.

'Welcome to Britain, sir. This your first time over?'

Tom didn't even answer that. The car whisked him to a railway station and left him there with his bags. It was all so familiar. The Victorian railway architecture. The big station clock. The tiny rituals of politeness, meticulously observed. The smell of hot tea coming from the station waiting room.

It was all so familiar – but also different. For a while Tom couldn't understand it, but then he could. It was to do with class. It wasn't as though everything had changed, far from it. But the country he'd returned to was no longer the one he'd left. With the entire country at war, who was the gentleman and who the working man? With the entire country governed by ration-book and sacrifice, who was the rich man and who was the poor?

For a while, Tom waited on the station platform over-whelmed equally by the new and the old. He waited a while, then couldn't stand it.

He left his bags and ran from the station. Opposite him, there stood the inevitable Station Hotel. He ran inside.

'I have a call to make to the United States. It's extremely urgent.'

He dropped papers on the desk, indicating his seniority. The girl on the desk glanced at them and took Tom to a horrible little booth, overheated, red plush, airless. There was a phone there and a tiny pad of paper. He called the operator and asked for a connection. For forty-four minutes, he waited. And waited. Time slid by and his train wouldn't wait. When there was just three minutes to go, he gave up. He had stood up to go, when the phone rang. He snatched at it.

'I have your line for you now,' said the operator.

Then a ringing tone.

Far away in Norgaard House a maid picked up the phone. Tom asked her to get Rebecca, to run, to fetch her as quick as possible. He could hear the girl's footsteps running across the wooden floor as she ran for her mistress. Tom looked at his watch. Two minutes. One and a half. Then more steps, and: 'Tom?'

'Becca, my God, I can't stand it here –'

'But you can only just have arrived. Why don't –'

'Can you join me? As soon as possible? My office can arrange transport.'

'Not very easily. I'm busy here. Perhaps when things at the Foundation quieten down in July.'

'Christ, I'd better not still be here in July. Can't you come over right away?'

There was a pause. The lines were unreliable, but this break wasn't to do with the lines. 'Is it being in England? Is it meeting Alan Montague?'

'I just need to see you.'

There was another pause, longer this time. 'No, dearest Tomek, you need to do this by yourself . . . Call me from London.'

'Please, Becca, I –'

'Call me from London, Tomek. Good luck.'

❧

It was 4 June 1944.

The following day, 5 June, Tom Calloway-Creeley would meet his one-time twin, Alan Montague, for the first time in nearly thirty years. And the day after that, in the very first hours of 6 June, an invasion fleet would begin the landings in Normandy, which would determine the fate of the war.

Tom sat in an empty first-class compartment and watched the countryside slide past. Time and distance were narrowing now. In a matter of hours, he and Alan would meet again. Tom had no idea what he would say, no idea what he would feel.

163

Dusk, 5 June 1944.

The big car rolled onwards. The trees moaned in the wind and the car's feeble lights turned little shadows into great ones. Alan was driving and Lottie sat beside him in the passenger seat. The American Petroleum Administration had its British office in a small village a few miles outside Windsor. They were driving there now: driving to meet Tom.

'How do you feel?' asked Lottie.

Alan shook his head. 'Great God! I have no idea at all.'

Lottie smiled. 'Well, do you feel more inclined to kill him or more inclined to embrace him?'

Alan shook his head again. 'No idea. Though I don't suppose I'll embrace him . . . not unless . . .'

Lottie's tone sharpened an inch or two. 'Not unless he apologises first? And do you just think it's possible he's saying the same?'

'I don't in all honesty care.'

Lottie didn't answer, just pursed her lips and looked crossly out of the window. She knew everything, of course. She knew about her husband's lunatic war against Tom. She had argued against it, then given up. Like Rebecca in Texas, she had urged the two men to meet, but without success.

Alan drove on in silence. A burst tyre earlier in the drive

had caused them to lose several hours, and the twilight drive had been slow and arduous. Alan was tense and drove too fast. A convoy of army trucks rumbled by, heading south. It was one of the few visible signs of the momentous events that would be taking place in Normandy at dawn tomorrow.

'There are a lot of trucks on the road,' said Lottie.

'There's a big operation being launched tomorrow,' said Alan, who had carefully avoided the topic before.

'The invasion?'

Alan nodded.

'Of France, I suppose?'

Alan nodded again. Lottie's question hadn't been foolish. The Allied plan had been shrouded in the very highest secrecy from the start. Only a few people in Britain knew. Alan had been one of them. Lottie had not.

She took a deep breath. 'Will it . . . ? I suppose it will . . . ?'

Alan snatched a glance sideways before looking back at the road. 'Be successful? Yes, probably. Might it go wrong? Yes, possibly. Either way, we're about to find out.'

He didn't mention PLUTO, but, of course, the thought was never far from his mind.

The conversation fell silent. Lottie decided to get some rest and curled up in the back under a travelling blanket.

Just before the outbreak of war, Alan had bought himself a wine-red Bentley. The car was a pleasure to drive and its huge motor purred evenly under the bonnet. The miles dropped away. But he found it hard to concentrate. A couple of times, he'd taken a bend badly. A couple of times, he'd snatched at the wheel and recovered in time. Each time he'd done so, he glanced in the mirror to see if he'd woken Lottie. Each time, he found her wide blue eyes open and turned on him. He murmured an apology for carelessness and let her sink back into sleep.

They drew closer to Windsor. He checked the directions and began to head down a steep slope into the little valley below.

Then it happened.

'Watch out!' Lottie screamed from the back.

There was a huge shape, reddish-grey in the headlights. Alan slammed on a brake and swerved. The shape was a deer that bounded away, startled, into the undergrowth.

'Careful,' said Lottie, 'careful!'

Alan, in his anxiety, was annoyed with her for making a meal of what was trivial. He stepped on the accelerator, guiding the big car back into the centre of the road. There was a strange sound, like a sort of metallic sigh. Just for a moment, then nothing.

Then something else appeared in the lamplight. A tyre, bounding black and silver down the steepening hill. It was their tyre. It bolted downhill, bounced high a couple of times, then vanished.

'Darling!'

Lottie's voice was high-pitched and desperately strained.

Alan tried touching the brakes, but as soon as he did so the big car threatened to dive out of control. He decided to take the hill as well as he could and lose speed naturally on the flat.

'Hold tight!' he said.

He flashed the car's headlights full on, so the road was brilliantly lit. The hill was dangerously steep. With clenched mouth, Alan watched as the gleaming tarmac rode up at him. He took one corner. Then another. The big car was leaping forwards faster and faster. He tried touching the brake again.

A mistake.

Control of the car was snatched out of his hands. There was a moment of terrifying freedom. In the sudden blare of headlights, a huge tree appeared, shining white. The tree and the car leaped towards each other.

There was a colossal smash.

164

Oddly enough to those who had known him earlier in his life, Tom had gained a reputation for coolness and calm among his Washington colleagues. Not tonight.

Every gust of wind that came through the trees sounded like the arrival of a car. Against all blackout regulations, Tom had had big lights put on in the drive. Five times Tom had checked that the telephone lines were working. He paced and paced. He was a frenzy of nerves.

By ten o'clock, it was solidly dark. Tom sent his aides and the British house staff back to their lodgings, off to bed. He was the only person left in the house: a former rectory that had been converted into offices. He would have given anything in the world to be away from England, away from Alan.

He went down into the kitchen, looking for something warm to drink. There was no coffee, only tea. The kitchen was supplied with an old-fashioned range, black kettles, and a tap that ran explosively or not at all. The whole place seemed exactly like the Whitcombe House of forty years earlier. Even the draughty whistle in the chimney struck the same notes. Tom half expected to turn and find Mrs White, the old cook, making pastries in a corner. He shook coal into the range, filled the kettle, found tea leaves. The big stove began to warm. The kettle slowly rose above room temperature.

Tom waited impatiently for the kettle, burned his finger on the range, longed for home. He wondered what Rebecca was doing right this moment. He wondered how Mitch was doing on the rigs. The kettle began to sing.

Tom reached to lift it from the stove, but, as he reached, all of a sudden, there was a bang at the door, the jiggle of a latch, a blast of cool air. A woman ran in, as though blown by the wind.

'Please . . . my husband . . . please help, there's been the most terrible accident . . . He's on the road back there . . . I saw your lights . . . Thank God you're up.'

Lottie had no idea whose house she had entered.

She had been asleep in the back of the car and had no idea where the crash had happened. But one thing was clear: by sheer good fortune, she had come to beg help from a man superbly equipped to give it. Despite Lottie's shocked and shaken state, the strong American quickly and accurately found out from her what had happened. Instantly, he was on the phone, giving orders, sending for doctors, cutting equipment, fire wardens, an ambulance.

'Thank you,' said Lottie. 'Thank you, thank you.'

He ignored her. Instead, he was bundling her into the Austin parked outside, forcing her to remember accurately where the accident had taken place. The Austin was old and small; but the American drove it like a racing machine. The drive had only lasted a minute or so, when the road turned. The Austin's headlamps illuminated the tree, the Bentley, and the skid-marks of disaster.

It was immediately apparent that the driver inside must surely be dead. The engine had shunted backwards into the front compartment of the car. All around, there was broken glass and twisted metal. Lottie, who was seeing the crash lit up for the first time, let out a gasp.

'Oh!' she cried. It was a wail more than a word.

As she spoke, there was a flicker of fire from inside the car engine. 'The engine!' cried Lottie. 'It's on fire! Get him out!'

The American hesitated.

Anybody would have done. The man inside was probably dead. The car was probably about to turn into an inferno. Lottie, desperate to help her husband, used the only card left to play.

'It's terribly important!' she cried. 'It's Alan Montague in there, from the Petroleum Board. You've got to –'

But even as she spoke, the flames inside the front of the car grew higher. The American's face was lit up in red, with sudden eerie flashes where paintwork from the bonnet flared up in green and purple. The American wore a look of horror, violently disturbed by something Lottie had said.

She turned to the car, about to beg for help again, but the sight closed her mouth. The flame was turning into a blaze. It would be insanity to enter the car now. Instinctively, Lottie drew away.

She glanced at the American, to see what he was doing. And she saw it. He was doing what anyone would do. He was running, fast. Not towards the car, but away from it.

All she could think was: *that man is leaving my husband to die.*

Tom ran.

Not towards the car, but away from it, knowing that Alan Montague was inside.

He ran *because* Alan was inside.

He ran to a little stream that trickled under the road some thirty yards down the hill. He tore off his coat and shirt and doused them in the water.

And then he ran again – *really* ran – ran like the wind uphill to the car. Using a fallen roadside log, he smashed away at the front of the bonnet, until it cannoned upwards, releasing a torrent of flame and burning air. Tom stood back as the rush of flame died back, then flung his sodden clothes on the engine. The flames sputtered but didn't die.

Tom saw the British woman – Alan's wife! – do as he had been doing, running down to the stream with her coat. Tom found a couple of blankets in the back of the Austin. He took the wet clothes from Mrs Montague and gave her the blankets. He approached the engine and arranged the sodden coat.

The flames were still dangerously active. There was plenty of petrol in the tank. Tom knew, and Lottie knew, that they were playing a game of chance with a loaded bomb. Tom gave Lottie quick two-word instructions that she obeyed instantly. They both worked until they had done as much as they could.

Tom piled sopping wet clothes over the engine. Here and there, little flares of scarlet reminded them that the game of chance was still being played out. They still didn't know if the man inside the car was alive or dead.

'Come away,' said Lottie.

Tom shook his head. His hand rested on the front wing of the Bentley, as though to claim the privilege of death if the car exploded.

'Come away,' said Lottie again, but when Tom shook his head a second time, she joined him and the two of them watched together. The flames flickered, surged, flickered again, then died.

'You know who I am?' he asked.

She shook her head. 'But whoever you are –'

'I'm Tom. Tom Calloway. I'm –'

'Ah!' She gaped open-mouthed at the news. 'Then, yes, I know who you are.'

They looked at each other and Tom grinned. For some reason, in the madness of the moment, the grin seemed perfectly natural, as though the two of them had just shared some colossal joke. They were both soaked, half-clothed, oil-stained and muddy. Lottie thought – how odd the things one thinks! – how handsome Calloway looked, nevertheless: his brilliant smile, his reckless daring.

Then Tom went to work on the car. He threw himself at it, wrenching away the tangled coachwork, brushing aside the shattered glass.

'Alan!' he shouted. 'Are you there? Alan! Alan!'

Lottie joined in: 'Alan? My love? Alan? Are you there?'

There was no answer. Lottie began to cry.

'Alan! Alan! It's me, it's Tom.'

Silence. Just the dripping of water from the sodden engine. And then a voice from inside the car, alive but weak.

'Bloody Americans. Always shouting.'

'Alan!'

'Tom!'

As Tom's eyes adjusted to the interior of the car, he could see a pale face crushed sideways against the steering wheel. It was a moment like no other in his life. All the hatred, all the bitterness, all the fury of their long rivalry was swallowed up and made meaningless. The only thing that mattered now was to make Alan safe.

'Don't die on me now, brother.'

'I wasn't planning to.'

Tom fought to get to Alan. Alan's legs were crushed by the engine casing. The rest of him appeared to be bloody and bruised but otherwise OK. But the legs were bleeding.

Bleeding heavily.

Every time Tom withdrew his hands from the wreckage they came out covered in blood. Lottie tore off her scarf and handed it to Tom, who used it as a tourniquet to tie over the one leg he could reach. Alan managed to get some of the cloth and jam it up against his other thigh in an effort to stanch the bleeding. The two men worked perfectly together, the way they had always done as kids.

Lottie watched them, Tom especially. It was strange to be meeting this man about whom she had heard so much. Strange and terrible to be meeting him under such circumstances. Finally they had done the best they could.

'There are people coming,' said Tom. 'We'll cut you out of there before long.'

'Yes . . . Is Lottie there?'

'Here.'

'Not too badly hurt?'

'Not a scratch.'

Lottie was at the other window of the car. The side door was smashed in, so that Lottie could reach across and put her hand to her husband's cheek. Alan caught her hand and held it.

'PLUTO?' he asked. 'Everything all right?'

Tom nodded. 'All set and ready to go.'

'Good.'

There was silence again. Lottie was crying and her hand communicated oceans to her husband. Alan wriggled in his seat, turning his face towards Tom. His mouth fought to form words.

Tom felt a sudden chill descend. He knew that the moment had finally approached: the moment when they would have to face the past. Tom bent his head.

'What was it? I knew everything else. But not that.' Alan's words were faint. He paused for breath after every sentence.

'What was what?' Tom's old suspicious anger returned. His head jerked backwards.

'What made you leave? We never knew.'

'You ask me that? You ask me that *now*?'

Alan's question had gone a good way towards shattering Tom's mood of reconciliation. It was an insult for Alan to pretend he didn't understand. He'd had his hand on Alan's shoulder but he withdrew it now, angry and ready to take offence.

Alan spoke again. 'For God's sake, the quarrel . . . we

always quarrelled. I was three-quarters gone. Shell-shock. You must have known.'

His voice was small. He sounded distant instead of just eighteen inches away. Tom could hear the drip of blood on the roadside grass. Tom's anger subsided. Alan was injured, maybe dying. What was the use of being angry with a dying man?

'It wasn't the quarrel,' he said. 'It was the mission that night. You tried to have me killed. You put my name forward. The machine guns, for heaven's sake! You knew it was lunacy, murderous lunacy. I couldn't forgive that.'

Tom ran on too long. Alan was shaking his head, trying to interrupt.

'Not me.'

'I *know* it was you.'

'Not me. Guy.'

Tom's head swam. He had played this encounter in his mind a thousand times over the years. He had never envisaged this response. Alan was either a vicious liar now, or else . . .

'A chap called Captain Morgan told me. Lieutenant Montague. I checked with him a dozen times. He was regular army, not the sort to confuse a major's uniform with a lieutenant's.'

Once again Tom had spoken too long.

'Tunic. He took my . . .' Alan's last word was inaudible.

'He was wearing your coat? But Guy was wounded. I know that because I . . . I . . .'

'Shot him.' Alan nodded to indicate he already knew.

'Well, how did he come to be sitting round with the brigadier? That wasn't like Guy.'

'Brig thought he was making bloody fuss . . . Told him to sit down, shut up.' Alan smiled feebly. It was so stupid. A lifetime apart because of one stupid case of mistaken identity.

'You . . . you didn't . . . Jesus Christ! So it wasn't you? I can't believe it.'

Tom spoke in a daze. The last thing he said wasn't even true: he *did* believe it. He had believed it already before Alan had finished explaining. What he found hard to believe was that all those years of anger had been for nothing. Tom didn't know whether to laugh or cry, except that he wanted to do both.

'Not your fault,' said Alan in a whisper.

Tom shook his head – uselessly, since Alan couldn't see him do it. 'It *was* my fault. I should have known, no matter how many Captain Morgans I'd run into.'

And he spoke the truth. For the past thirty years, he'd lived his life according to one gigantic error. And what made it worse was that he should have known. It was impossible that his brother could have tried to kill him. Impossible, no matter if two dozen Sandhurst captains had been there to witness it. For the first time, Tom saw Alan's love for what it was. Alan's love, and his own idiot pride.

'I'm sorry. God, I'm sorry!'

Alan made a little shrug of dismissal. 'Never mind. It's done with now.'

Tom put his hand to the bottom of the door, and found the blood still dripping. He did what he could to tighten the tourniquet.

'Do hold on, darling,' said Lottie. 'Tom here – your brother –' she stumbled over the unfamiliar word – 'has got half the village out fetching doctors and tackle to get you out of there. You'll be right in no time.'

Alan squeezed her hand. 'I've got you. All right now.'

Above them, the wind gusted strongly, humming loudly through the oak tree. Both Tom and Alan thought of the English Channel and the invasion fleet that had to cross it. Paratroopers and glider troops would already be in France now, snatching control of vital bridges from German hands, desperate to hold on for just long enough to meet the relieving armies. Even now, with Alan bleeding, possibly to death, both men thought of PLUTO.

'Came looking for you,' said Alan, after a pause. 'Then Guy told me about shooting . . . Shooting Guy . . . Didn't want to see man who did that . . . Bloody fool . . . Me, I mean. Should have come and found you anyway . . . but . . . but . . .'

'Why did I shoot Guy? My God! That's what stopped you from coming?'

Alan didn't answer, but the twin-communication was working at full strength now.

'Boy! Am I pleased I wasn't the only one to screw up. Guy never told you what happened?'

Alan shook his head a fraction of an inch. 'His version.'

Tom took a deep, juddering breath, raising his face to the sky so that the wind could blow over it, the same wind that was raising waves on the Channel . . .

'He was a good soldier, Guy,' he said. 'A first-rate staff officer. There should have been more like him. But as an infantryman? In the front line?'

There was a long pause. The two men stared at each other. Lottie caught herself wondering why Tom didn't just say whatever it was he had to say.

Then: 'Ah! I'm a bloody fool,' whispered Alan.

'What is it?' asked Lottie. 'What are you talking about?'

Tom looked across at her, but it was Alan who spoke.

'Heavy fighting . . . Lots of shooting, shells . . . Bloody awful.' Everything now made sense. He should have known it. 'Of course, he shot him. Only thing to do.'

'Please? I don't understand.'

It was Lottie again. Although she knew that Alan loved her utterly, she also saw that the bond between him and Tom was something unique, something extraordinary. She tried to catch up with their telepathic exchange.

'It was a day of heavy combat,' said Tom. 'The field telephones were shot to shreds and the battalion's runners had been mostly killed or wounded. Guy had been sent up to find out what was going on and to pass the information back to brigade staff . . . I don't believe he'd ever been in the front line before. Not on a day when there was real fighting.'

There was a tiny gesture of assent from Alan and Tom continued.

'He was terrified. He was a good staff officer, but as for physical courage . . . well, he never had any. Never. None at all. He was tearing down the line like a frightened rabbit. A British major in full flight from the enemy. I'd just come up the trench in the other direction. Just round the corner, there was a group of top brass including Colonel Jimmy, the brigadier, a few others. Colonel Jimmy was a soldier of the old school. He shot men for desertion as a matter of course. Guy was about to run right into him. Anyone could have seen Guy was running. He was out of his mind, virtually pissing himself . . . I yelled at Guy, trying to make him understand the situation. I pushed him. I probably hit him. I know I waved my gun in his face. It made no difference.'

'So you shot him?' said Lottie, in awe of the man on the other side of the car.

'There was nothing else to do. He couldn't very well be accused of desertion if he had a bullet hole in him. So I shot him. Maximum appearance for minimum effect. That was my intention anyway. I don't know how well I succeeded. That was that. I ran back up the line. I left Guy to make his own way back.'

'You *shot* him!'

Lottie's awe increased with every ripple of implication. Tom had coolly put himself into a situation where a court martial would have sentenced him to death by shooting squad, and all to protect a man he detested. Lottie didn't know which to admire more: his decisiveness, his courage or his selflessness. It was the remarkable action of a remarkable man.

'Bloody fool,' whispered Alan. 'I'm a bloody fool.'

And he too saw it. Saw that he should never once have doubted his brother. Of course, Tom was impulsive, quarrelsome, reckless and a thousand other things. But plunge

637

him into a moment of crisis, and his great-hearted side was always bigger than his petty one. Alan's failure to see that had condemned him to a dozen years of struggle and absence. He should have trusted himself. He should have trusted Tom. He sighed deeply.

'Make that a pair of fools,' said Tom. 'A pair of bloody fools.'

The wind gathered in the trees. There was a long silence. Down in the village, there were shouts and movements of lights.

'Why won't they come?' said Tom to himself.

He looked up to see Lottie looking down towards the lights as well. 'If we could only get him out . . .' she said.

Tom nodded. Perhaps the rescue party had the cutting equipment, but was waiting for an ambulance. If so, they were making a desperate error. Everything depended on stopping the bleeding. He looked across at Lottie, who was thinking the same thing: one of them should go down to the village to check what was going on.

'We ought to –'

'It'd be a good idea –'

They both spoke together, then stopped. Tom was about to speak again, but Lottie raised her hand.

'You stay,' she said. 'I'll go.'

Tom desperately wanted to stay, but he hesitated. This was Alan's wife, after all. 'No. You stay. I'll –'

'Stop it!' Lottie spoke so sharply that Tom actually jumped. 'Sorry,' she added, 'but I won't have it. I've had Alan to myself for twenty-two years. It's your turn now. I think you have some catching up to do.'

Tom swallowed and held her gaze.

'Thank you.'

She took the flashlight that Tom handed her and shot off into the night. The two brothers, reunited, were quiet for a long while.

Then, after a long pause, Alan spoke again. 'Guy.'

'Guy?' Tom queried, but Alan only nodded. Tom frowned

for a moment, then the old spark of understanding jumped between them, as it had so often done before. 'Guy,' said Tom. 'He's OK, is he? Not dead, surely?'

'Dead, yes. Died hero.'

'Guy died the hero, did he?' Tom couldn't help but smile. It was ironic in a way that of the three of them it should have been Guy who ended up being killed in action. He tried to find the place in his heart where the flame of his anger with Guy had been kept burning all these years, but it was gone. Tom felt he had no anger left; not towards Alan, not towards Guy, not towards Sir Adam, not towards anyone. 'Well, I'm pleased he found his courage in the end.'

'He wanted to mend things. Wanted me to tell Father you were alive.'

'Guy? Guy wanted you to?'

Alan nodded. 'I didn't, though. Silly sod. Too late now.'

'Too late? Uncle . . . is he?'

'He died. Very peaceful. Happy.'

'I'm so sorry.'

Alan tried to say something further, but his strength was ebbing away. Tom bent his head, closer and closer, until he heard.

'Whitcombe,' said Alan. 'Whitcombe. Look after it.'

And then Tom did hear. Or rather, he understood. With Sir Adam dead and Guy dead and Alan possibly dying, then Alan was asking him to take care of Whitcombe House, at least until the next generation, Alan's children, were old enough to take charge themselves. Nearly fifty-one years after Tom had struggled into the world, the motherless son of an English under-gardener, he was being entrusted with the care of one of the great country houses of Hampshire. He was suddenly and intensely moved. He shook his head.

'Lazy sod, you bloody well look after it.'

There was another pause. Tom spat silently. A light breeze fluttered in the trees. Tom put his hand to the bottom of the car. Blood was still dripping. Alan was still fading.

'Brother?'

'Yes?'

'I'm afraid we haven't got that tourniquet tight enough. You're still bleeding.'

There was a moment's silence. The two men looked at each other.

'I can, if you can,' said Alan.

'It's worth a try.'

Alan nodded. 'Just pull. Don't stop whatever. I trust you.'

'OK, buddy, hold tight.'

He put his arms under Alan's shoulders and began to heave. Alan's leg was crushed and trapped by the Bentley's massive engine. Tom pulled hard. Even in the moonlight, he could see his brother's face white with pain.

'Pull. Just pull,' said Alan in a croak.

For ten seconds, Tom pulled, harder and harder. Alan made no sound. The agony must have been indescribable. Tom stopped to adjust his grip, when something changed. Something inside the car had twisted, something had come free. Alan turned his head.

'We've done it,' he said. 'I think we've done it.'

Tom pulled again and with sudden, astonishing ease, he lifted Alan through the shattered window and out onto the grass.

They stared at each other, brilliant with joy.

Tom tore his shirt into strips and fastened a tourniquet so tight that the bleeding stopped. Alan's wound was no longer lethal. Already, it seemed, Alan was stronger, better.

They lay next to each other under the stars, just as they had done as babies, just as they had done as boys, just as they had done as young men and soldiers. And they laughed. For no reason, they laughed. Throwing their heads back into the tangle of buttercups and dandelions on the bank behind them, they laughed and laughed and laughed.

'Goddamn Bentley,' said Tom. 'Your fault for buying English.'

'Not the Bentley. The tree. Damned stupid place to put a tree. Careless.'

'You may as well rest. We've got all the time in the world now.'

Alan lay back on the grass. 'Yes. Leg hurts like hell, by the way.' He grinned once more, and closed his eyes. Tom laid his hand tenderly on his brother's forehead.

The great chains of the past had lost their hold now. All the years of war, of anger, of mourning, of searching, of fighting – all of it was meaningless now. Down below, from the village, there was a surge of motors. Cars and people began to swarm up the hill.

'Brother?' said Tom.

'Yes?'

'We're fools, we two. A pair of bloody fools.'

Alan nodded. 'Yes. But we struck oil, didn't we? We're fools who struck oil.'

And as they lay on the grass, listening to the wind and the sound of the cars racing up the hill towards them, down on the south coast an invasion fleet was setting sail.

The ships contained the troops that would liberate first France, then Germany from Hitler's grasp. Everything good in the world depended on their success.

And at a distance behind the main fleet, waiting until the beaches were cleared of mines, an ugly-looking coaster would steam south to Normandy. The coaster was an unremarkable little vessel, but her hold had been adapted for a special sort of cargo: more than a hundred thousand yards of coiled black three-inch pipe. From the back of the ship, the pipe ran out silently into the water and disappeared. This was PLUTO, the Pipe-Line Under The Ocean, the world's first ever undersea pipeline and nothing short of a technological master-stroke. In a few hours' time a pumping station would begin to beat, the pipe would begin to stiffen, and on a sandy beach in

Northern France, a couple of soldiers would manage to soak themselves as the first liquid came tumbling out.

This was the oil that would fuel the invasion.

This was the oil that would win the war.

HISTORICAL NOTE

When history and fiction collide, it's usually history which comes off worse. This book would be the same, except that its subject is oil and, where oil is concerned, fiction may alter history, but is hardly likely to better it.

Time and again, the most improbable facts contained in this book are literally true.

Aside from some minor jiggling of dates, I've taken care to be true to history. My description of the oil boom on Signal Hill is drawn from eyewitness accounts. My description of the oil strike in East Texas is so carefully based on fact that it could have been cribbed from the drilling log of Ed Laster, the driller who actually brought the well home.

In Signal Hill, the flow of oil really was as sudden and prolific as described. Barbershops did sprout oil wells. The dead buried in churchyards really did become goldmines for the living. In East Texas, things were, if possible, even crazier. Within months of the first oil strike, local towns had increased in size ten or even fifty times over. Derricks were built so close together that their legs interlaced. The flood of oil was so strong – and the collapse of order so total – that martial law had to be declared and enforced at gunpoint.

In Persia, the account of Anglo-Persian's beginnings is likewise close to the truth, except that the concession was never divided between two companies. Alan's experience in the Zagros would have been all too familiar to the pioneers of Persian oil, the only exception being that Alan had a quick and easy time of it by comparison.

Nor is it just the events and settings of the book that are drawn from fact. A number of the minor characters are genuine historical characters (Knox D'Arcy, Sir Charles Greenaway and Cordell Hull, to name a few). Much of the incidental detail is taken straight from actual events. The early Persian pioneers really did use watermelons to cool their trucks. There really was a rigger who dropped eighty foot from a derrick then bummed a cigarette. Even Tom's scam for making money in Wyoming is based on truth.

But most important of all, there are two major characters in the book loosely based on real individuals. The first of those is Titch Harrelson, who draws inspiration from Columbus Joiner. Like Harrelson, Joiner was a dreamer and a fraudster, an oilman and a conman. Having made the most important strike in American history, he found himself threatened with the courtroom. Like Harrelson, Joiner had vastly oversold his leases – some of them eleven times over. This hadn't mattered when the leases were worthless, but mattered a lot as soon as oil was struck. Joiner was lucky to escape jail. He ended his life, wild-catting to the last, never striking oil again, virtually penniless.

Likewise, the George Reynolds of *The Sons of Adam* owes a debt to the real-life George Reynolds who was Knox D'Arcy's man in Persia from 1901 to the 1908 strike and beyond. The real-life George Reynolds showed an extraordinary drive and tenacity of purpose, without which no oil strike would ever have been made. It says something about the man's ability to get things done that he first struck oil in the Middle East in 1904, with his first major well yielding in 1908. By comparison, the first strike in Iraq didn't come until 1927, the first strike in the Gulf not coming until 1932 in Bahrain. My George Reynolds was blessed by a good relationship with his boss, not to mention a good parcel of stock in Alanto Oil. The real-life George Reynolds had no such pleasure – though one hopes he would have been pleased to know that Anglo-Persian would grow into a company (later renamed British Petroleum) worth as much as two hundred billion dollars by the century's end.

But my debt to history goes deeper still. In a way, the story of oil *is* the story of the twentieth century.

In the Great War, oil already signalled its importance. The British Army started the war with virtually no motorised equipment. By the end of the war, the Western allies had two hundred thousand vehicles in action. They had built aeroplanes by the tens of thousands. They had launched and won the first tank battles in history. Lord Curzon was hardly exaggerating when he declared that 'the Allied cause had floated to victory upon a wave of oil'.

In the two inter-war decades, oil continued to grow in importance. By the time of the Second World War, oil was, beyond doubt, the most important commodity in the world. The German failure to reach oil in either North Africa or the Caucasus, the Japanese failure to strike the oil at Pearl Harbor, the British ability to use 100-octane fuels in the Battle of Britain were all matters of the utmost strategic importance. As for PLUTO, the Pipe-Line Under The Ocean, it's a staggering fact that the world's first undersea pipeline should have been laid within hours of the largest-ever seaborne invasion. While there were some early teething problems, the technology eventually delivered more than a million gallons of fuel per day to the Allied forces in Europe – and conferred a strategic advantage that the oil-poor German forces were never able to overcome.

Finally, one cannot write about the two world wars without being conscious of an enormous debt to the men who fought them. This book has attempted to walk a fine line between entertainment on the one hand and respect for what actually occurred on the other. It is to be hoped that the balance is right. From George Reynolds to the infantrymen of the Somme, from Knox D'Arcy to the pilots of the Battle of Britain, from Columbus 'Dad' Joiner in East Texas to the mounted tribesmen of the Persian oilfields, this book is intended to honour them all.